THURSDAY'S CHILD

ELEANOR - PART 1

SHANA J CARR

DEDICATION

For my mum, Joan Mason, whose discerning wit and sharp intellect I could only hope to emulate; for her special sense of humour that none of us could have done without; for her patience and understanding that I have diligently tried to apply to the raising of my own children, and for instilling in me her love of the written word....Love always x

.

CHAPTER ONE

1917

Nettie cursed silently to herself and not for the first time that morning as a spot of ash from the box iron leaked out on Mr McKinney's shirt collar. Why had she ever got rid of the detachable set that her mother had given her? At least it had been a cleaner way of pressing clothes – none of this incessant leakage and smudging to wear her nerves down.

Nettie was tired. Her legs ached, and with her stomach being so big now, it weighed heavily upon her, putting a strain on her back. The baby had been due last week, and Nettie was growing steadily more impatient with every passing day. She wasn't even sure if Harry had received her news about the baby. The few letters she'd received from him had contained nothing about it at all; in fact, nothing in any of them had held any reference to any of the things she'd mentioned in hers. Nothing about Ted's first tooth or Lizzie's school concert or his mother's visits... *Or anything!* she thought.

She wondered now if he'd received her letters at all...

She went to wipe the ash off as gently as possible but only succeeded in leaving a line of black from top to bottom on the crisp white cotton. She cursed again, though still only to herself. Nettie wasn't in the habit of swearing out loud, even though she was alone in the small kitchen. It was something her mother had always frowned at, always telling her it was something a lady simply didn't do. Men on the other hand were able to curse and swear as much as was necessary it seemed, though never, *ever* in front of the gentler sex.

Nettie sighed. It seemed to her that men were able to do almost anything they chose and rarely suffered any lasting consequences for it. She wondered what would happen if *she* stayed out to all hours down at the local hotel, swilling back beer at a precious tuppence a glass!

She stifled a giggle as she conjured up a picture of herself the way she'd witnessed Harry so many times in the past, when after closing time and finally bidding his friends goodbye, he'd made his way home by stumbling down the main street in his drunken stupor, singing some bawdy song loudly and off-key. What would any of her fine, upstanding neighbours say if she were to do that instead of Harry? she wondered. Heaven forbid! What would they say indeed!

Still, Nettie reasoned that she would be happy to see Harry home doing just that, instead of across the other side of the world having to contend with God only knows what kind of conditions. As a woman, her only duty was to remain home with the family, a not-so-easy task in these times, with the added worry of her husband's well-being to weigh her down all the more. Nettie felt she had long since summoned all the extra strength possible to see her through these past few months, and if more were yet to be required, she fretted, for she was sure her reserve had run dry. Though her steadfast resolve had failed her at times when she pictured the hell that

Harry must be living through, oddly enough it was that very thought that also succeeded in pulling her back from the brink of her own despair.

Nettie missed the companionship of her own parents, especially her mother. They'd always had a way of breaking down a situation into a list of priorities and decisively dealing with them one at a time. In so doing, a situation could be dealt with considerably easier. *First things first, Nettie! One must first deal with the things one is able, in order to best endure the things that one can't.*

Nettie had tried to do just that at times, but all too often, her worries about Harry and her circumstances at home would come raining in on her, till all she could do was let herself be carried away by an overwhelming flood of despair or depression. She had never missed her parents so terribly as she did now. They'd never seen Teddy, and Lizzie had barely been twelve months old the last time they'd seen her. She wondered what their first reaction had been on learning she was expecting yet another. The letters she received from her mother were regular enough, and though they brought news of their life in Queensland and her brother Frank, it was not quite the same as having her mother's comforting shoulder to cry upon, or being able to rely on her father's unyielding dependability.

Frank had joined the navy around the same time Harry had left, and though she feared for her brother's safety, she couldn't help but think her parents' worry must be tenfold. Nettie felt blessed that her children were nowhere near an age to be thinking of going to war, or even to be deeply or lastingly affected by its outcome, and thought that the burden of a son away fighting or even a daughter – for there were women nursing on the firing lines she'd heard – must be utterly unbearable.

Nettie had prayed for both husband and brother. But with the constant, almost daily influx of returning soldiers, some of them now disabled or horribly disfigured, she secretly feared that any good fortune granted her might not be sufficient to guard them both.

Her thoughts wandered back the way they so often did to the last time she'd seen Harry and the words they'd said to each other. The scene with him in his brand-new army uniform, duffel bag slung across his back, his face reflecting both the anticipation of where he was headed and the distress he'd felt at leaving his family, had been stamped upon her memory. It was a scene she'd replayed many times in her mind over the eight and a half months he'd been gone.

She'd stood on the platform holding Teddy, Lizzie by her side, his mother a little apart from them, and had joked with him in an effort to hide her tears.

'You can't fool me, Harold Grayson… you're only going because they've put a six o'clock closing on the pub!'

She'd tried to laugh, and in an effort to hide his own emotions, he'd joked back. 'Well, what else is there to stay here for now, Mrs Grayson?'

He'd placed an arm about her and the baby then and had given her such a long, heartfelt kiss and clasped her to him so hard, it still brought tears to her eyes to remember it. After hugging Lizzie and his mother and making them both promise to look after her, he'd boarded the train at the last minute, he and Charlie both waving madly through the window. T

The last words she'd heard had come from Charlie. 'I'll make sure he stays out o' trouble, Net, you'll see… don't worry about a thing!'

Hillary Grayson, after a long moment of watching the tracks in the distance, the train long out of sight, had finally turned to look at Nettie. She'd sniffed once, in that indignant way she had, as though to punctuate anything she said or did. And then with her face somehow devoid of emotion, she'd turned and moved off without a backward glance.

Nettie sighed. Harry's mother was a hard one to figure out. Oh, she was certainly clear as to Hillary's opinions regarding her – after all, she'd made that plain enough since the day they'd met. But in the face of such loneliness, with her son overseas, and Nettie, and especially his children, being the closest link she had to the only thing she'd ever held dear, Nettie thought Hillary might finally have tried to bridge the gap.

It seems the Grayson stubbornness – or pride – or whatever it was, mused Nettie, would remain firmly in place.

She shook her head and sighed again.

As for Charlie, she hoped and prayed that he would be able to keep his promise to her and look after her Harry.

At twenty-two years old, Charles Bradford, or Charlie to all but Hillary, was still unmarried and was considered, unofficially of course, the 'catch' of Lower North Adelaide – well, at least amongst everyone she and Harry knew. Charlie and Harry had been lifelong friends, going to the same school, living in the same neighbourhood and had signed up together, but Nettie suspected Charlie had only signed on when he found out Harry had been talked into it.

Charlie lived with his Aunt Aggie, a woman who was considered by all who knew her to be a kind, friendly woman who always helped out at the local jumble sales or cake stalls. It was a familiar sight to pass Aggie heavily engrossed in conversation with a neighbour about upcoming fundraisers and the like, especially of late with most of the men overseas. She was what most people liked to call 'doing her bit'. And Agatha Bradford did it well.

She and Hillary were friends. Not best friends, as Nettie felt sure Hillary wouldn't let anybody get that close, though she begrudgingly acknowledged her opinion on the matter might be a little unfair. In any case, Hillary and Aggie, though friendly and polite to one another, weren't the sort of friends that lived in each other's pockets, and Nettie had wondered in the past if their sons hadn't been the best of friends, whether Aggie and Hillary would have bothered being quite so amicable to one another.

Harry had always been the type that could be talked into most things. And Charlie, bless his soul, had managed to bail her husband out of more than one sticky situation in the past. To sign up to this war had been another of Harry's spur of the moment decisions that she hoped would not turn out to be his last.

She was at least being provided with a few extra shillings due to her husband being away in the service, but this was small compensation for the absence of husband and father. Harry was a good man, and a kind man, but a hopeless dreamer, and unfortunately this type of nature did not contribute well to making him a good provider for his family. Nettie had lost count of the jobs he'd started and then lost or given away, always telling her there would be something else better around the corner. Occasionally, he would stay long enough in one of these jobs to get his first pay packet, sometimes even two. And at these times, she'd been able to at least pay the butcher or grocer or whoever else had been growing impatient, waiting for their money. And now with her weekly ironing for Mrs McKinney and the money paid to her for Harry's time away, she'd managed somehow to keep their heads above water.

Another bit of ash leaked out of the iron and Nettie shook her head, telling herself she should be keeping her mind focused on the job at hand rather than letting it wander off onto things that did her no good to think about. If she'd been paying more attention to what she was doing, the tedious chore of pressing Mr McKinney's shirts would be done by now. The few shillings she received for just a few hours' ironing for Mrs McKinney was nothing to be sneezed at, but this morning Nettie felt as though she'd earned every penny!

Her thoughts were abruptly cut off as five-year-old Lizzie came running into the kitchen. 'Mum! I want to go to the shop – can I please? Please? Ruby said she'd take me! Please!'

Nettie sighed. She had barely a shilling left in her purse, and she hadn't bought tea yet. 'Shh, Lizzie, you'll wake your brother!'

Ruby came in behind Lizzie, her own daughter Kathy in tow as she pinned the familiar brown, wide-brimmed hat she always wore atop her pulled-back blonde hair. Nettie had never seen her in any other hat and had worked out long ago that it must be the only one Ruby owned, and though totally unsuitable for June weather, Nettie understood, difficult as these times were.

'I said she could come with us. Hope you don't mind.' Her expression was apologetic. 'I've got to go down and pay old Bixby the money I owe him or he's threatening to send his creditors.' Ruby pulled a face, her pretty features now reflecting her irritation.

Ruby Jenson lived next door. The petite and attractive young woman had been Nettie's godsend since Harry had been away, Ruby's own husband, Lenny, having left to fight with the Australian Light Horse the year before, leaving Ruby alone to raise their only daughter in his absence. Little Kathy was the same age as Lizzie and they were inseparable. Despite Ruby's usual cheerful conversation and her optimistic outlook on most things, Nettie knew underneath she was just as fearful for her husband's safety as any of the wives left behind to shoulder the responsibilities in these worrisome times.

It was strange. They all carried on a kind of façade of going about their business of raising the family and caring for the home as though their husbands and loved ones weren't facing mortal danger on a daily basis. Whether it was for the benefit of everyone else or themselves, Nettie wasn't sure. It was as if their husbands had merely taken a position in the country or some such thing, and sometime soon, they would just come walking back through the door. In spite of the daily news of war and its casualties, none of them chose to dwell on the very real possibility of their own husband being injured or killed. Nettie thought that was for the best. After all, one could not possibly go on—

She shook the thoughts from her mind. Putting on one of her brightest smiles, she turned to Ruby.

'Never mind about Mr Bixby, Rube, Lenny will sort him out when he comes home.' Nettie reached for her purse and fished around for a halfpenny, which she handed to Lizzie. 'Be careful what you spend it on, sweetie. No sticky toffee. I can't afford a dentist on top of everything else.'

Nettie pulled a dry face at Ruby and then they both laughed. It was a common reaction with both women, their financial circumstances being what they were – after all, what else was there to do except fall back on their sense of humour.

Lizzie and Kathy were out the door in a flash, followed closely by Ruby, and Nettie turned her attention back to her ironing.

She'd no sooner filled the iron again when she heard the bang of the front screen door followed by a sniff behind her, and Nettie rolled her eyes. She knew that sniff, and who else would let herself into her house and creep up behind her like a cat getting ready to pounce?

Nettie turned to see a flustered Hillary Grayson, her coat slightly askew on her shoulders, her pinched face indignant as ever as she patted a gloved hand across the back her head, smoothing any imaginary misplaced strands of hair back under an expensive-looking felt hat.

'Well! That daughter of yours is getting more unruly by the day, Henrietta! By the time my son comes home, Elizabeth will have positively run wild! She nearly knocked me over just now on your pathway!'

Nettie flinched. The use of her full name always grated on her, or perhaps it was just the way her mother-in-law said it, as though she was talking to an errant maid in her employ. She sighed inwardly and went to reply but wasn't able to utter a word as Hillary went on.

'And that Ruby Jenson! Do you think it's good for the child to be consorting with the likes of… well, I mean, with that sort of person?' Hillary sniffed again and looked down her nose at her daughter-in-law, a gesture that never ceased to amaze Nettie considering the older woman was much the same height as her.

'Little Kathy has been good company for Lizzie, and Ruby a good friend to me,' Nettie answered quietly, secretly relishing the opportunity to use the short from of her daughter's name.

Another sniff was Hillary's only reply before her gaze scanned the room, stopping momentarily on the pile of ironing at Nettie's side, and then locked on her daughter-in-law's extended girth before looking away.

'Do you think it a wise thing to be having another when it's been hard enough to provide for the two you already have?' Hillary tried to smile before going on. 'You know, Margaret McKinney is a good friend of mine. If you like, I can ask her to take her ironing elsewhere… at least until after your confinement. After all, Henrietta, it can't be good for the baby.'

Nettie stared back at her incredulously. Was she serious? Get rid of the only income Nettie was able to make on her own while in her condition? Did Hillary think Nettie did ironing for the fun of it?

She managed a tight smile. 'No, thank you, Hillary. I don't mind, really I don't, and in actual fact, I feel it's worse for the baby to be sitting around doing nothing… so I keep myself busy.'

Hillary sniffed again. 'Well, have it your own way. I thought I might stop by to visit my grandchildren, but as Edward is nowhere to be seen and Elizabeth fairly knocked me over as I passed her at the gate, I suppose I must be on my way.'

Nettie ignored the comment about Lizzie and mentally thanked God for keeping her two-year-old son asleep. Hillary always succeeded in making him cry, proof to Nettie that children sensed things about people before they were even old enough to know anything about them.

'Teddy is taking his morning sleep… what a shame.' Nettie didn't smile, nor could she hide the sarcasm from her voice, though it appeared to go unnoticed by the older woman.

'And have you heard from Harold?' Hillary scanned the kitchen as she spoke, her distaste at the surroundings in which she found herself undisguised, though Nettie knew that inwardly, Hillary was poised anxiously for any news of her son. She never knew what to say to her about Harry. What could she say in any case? Tell her about the endearments of his letters or how he missed her and the kids?

'Yes, but not for a month or so now. He's… all right. He's missing home and everyone here.' If Hillary wanted to include herself in the 'everyone' that would be entirely up to her. Didn't she get any letters from him? Nettie could bring herself to ask.

Hillary's face softened momentarily at her daughter-in-law's words, but just as quickly her expression changed back, leaving Nettie to wonder if perhaps she'd imagined it.

Hillary sniffed. 'You and the children must come visit for tea one afternoon, Henrietta.' It was a standard invitation that Hillary gave every time Nettie saw her, and one that had never been acted upon. Neither woman had ever gone that step further to narrow down a particular time or afternoon.

'The children would love it.'

And as usual, both women felt they'd done their duty to the other. One had invited and one had accepted.

Nettie could hear the excited chatter of Lizzie and Kathy through the window as they neared the gate and hoped they would pass right by to go into Ruby's instead, but it was not to be. The front door slammed.

'Mum, look what I got!' Lizzie bounded into the kitchen holding up a small bag of lollies but stopped short when she saw her grandmother standing there.

Nettie groaned inwardly. Like Teddy, Lizzie was unable to hide her feelings the way adults could, this fact made abundantly clear by the way Lizzie stood regarding Hillary in much the same way one would a complete stranger.

Ruby and Kathy stood in the doorway, the little girl in awe of the finely garbed lady standing in Lizzie's kitchen, her wide eyes darting from her friend to the lady and back again.

Ruby spoke first. 'Hello, Mrs Grayson. How are you today?'

Hillary looked Ruby up and down, her expression conveying to all present that the cheap floral house dress and equally cheap hat and worn shoes that Ruby stood in had not gone unnoticed.

'I'm fine thank you, Mrs Jenson.' As an afterthought, she added politely, 'Have you heard from your husband at all?'

Ruby folded her arms and leant on the door frame with a *you're no better than me* look on her face, and answered just as politely, 'Yes, a letter came last week.' She didn't go into anything that might have been in the letter. As far as Ruby was concerned, her life had nothing to do with this dried-up old witch.

Hillary raised her eyebrows ever so slightly. 'Well... I'd best be getting on then. She nodded at everyone in turn, starting with Nettie. 'Good day, Henrietta, Elizabeth... Mrs Jenson.' Kathy was overlooked.

Nettie walked her to the front door. 'Goodbye, Hillary.'

She'd no sooner shut the door behind her when Ruby's sound of relief filled the passageway behind her.

'Phew-ee! That woman must have ice running through her veins! How do you put up with her? I'm always wishing Lenny's parents were close by during these times, but if they're anything like her, then I'm glad they're both in Sydney!'

Nettie breezed past Ruby and shrugged. 'I don't know why I put up with her really.' In a quieter voice, so the young ones didn't hear, she added, 'I suppose with Harry being over there and if anything... well... were to happen, then I'd feel kind of sorry for her... being on her own, I mean. Harry's all she's got.'

Ruby rolled her eyes. 'Don't look now, kiddo, but if

anything happened to Harry, that old battleaxe isn't the only one who's going to be left on her own. What about you and the kids?' Ruby nodded in the direction of Nettie's stomach, before adding, 'And with another one on the way!'

Ruby didn't realize it, but her words triggered the painful realization for Nettie that Harry might not actually come back. Of course, this same realization had made itself known to her before, but the often dreaded and heartbreaking glimpse of a future alone with the kids and without her beloved Harry was something Nettie had always managed to keep firmly at a safe and bearable distance. Her eyes now filled with tears.

Ruby rushed to her side and put an arm about her shoulders. 'Oh, Nettie, I'm so sorry! Don't mind me – I'm always running off at the mouth without thinking…'

Lizzie came running out into the hallway with an excited Kathy hard on her heels, and Nettie turned her back to them as she quickly wiped her eyes with the back of her hand.

'We going to see the swans, Ruby? You said if we were good, we could go and feed the swans… Can we still?'

Ruby looked a little lost as to what to say ° she hadn't got around to asking Nettie yet.

Nettie managed to make her voice sound reprimanding. 'Lizzie, I've told you before it's Mrs Jenson or Auntie Ruby to you… and what's all this about swans?'

'Sorry, Nettie, I told the girls I'd take them down to the Torrens if they behaved down the street, but if you'd rather I didn't…'

Kathy cut her mother off. 'But, Mummy, you promised!'

Lizzie chimed in. 'Please?' She hung on her mother's apron.

Nettie just laughed and shook her head. 'It's up to you,

Ruby. I don't know where you get all your energy from, I honestly don't.'

'That's easy! I don't think I'd be so ready to frolic around with these two either if I were in the same condition as you.'

Nettie laughed and nodded. 'I suppose so. What us women put ourselves through!'

The girls bolted out through the front door, and Ruby said in a quieter voice, 'I'm sorry about before… and don't worry – we're all dealing with our own demons.'

Nettie nodded. 'I know you are. Don't worry about it, Rube. Harry will be back… and Lenny too – you'll see.'

Nettie wasn't to dwell on it any further as a healthy wail sounded from behind her bedroom door. She raised her eyebrows to Ruby. 'Seems his lordship wants to get up.'

Ruby nodded and laughed. 'I'll see you later then.'

The rattle of the heavy guns sounded all around as shells whizzed by overhead. Harry felt like he couldn't breathe properly, as though the fear had taken hold of his insides, constricting his airflow and preventing him from taking in air normally, as though each time he inhaled it was a conscious effort. His clothes clung to him, soaked in perspiration that now began trickling down the back of his neck, his wide-brimmed helmet firmly in place upon his head. His adrenalin ran so high it threatened to push him over the flimsy edge of his barely controlled emotions into full panic as the sounds of battle raged around him.

He squashed himself up against the boards of the trench and leant his forehead against his rifle, his helmet being pushed back as he clenched his eyes shut, the cool metal of his rifle's barrel the only thing amid all the carnage to help clear his mind, keep him sane. He closed his eyes and prayed, not for the first time in the preceding months, that he would come out of this hell alive. He was not alone.

The men from his battalion, Australians like him, were down in the trench too, some also pressed up against the side and squeezed tight alongside him while others crouched low, all with their own thoughts, their own fears.

Charlie made his way down the tightly packed line and squeezed himself in next to Harry, who spared him no longer than a brief look, though in that brief look, Charlie read the fearful panic in his best friend's eyes and it filled him with a feeling of dread. Charlie was not without his own fears, but he opted to keep them firmly hidden as he sought to put a show of bravado he didn't feel into his voice.

'Not long now, mate.' Charlie nodded encouragingly as Harry turned to look at him fully.

Harry's voice was shaky, his features twisting slightly as though he were on the verge of breaking down, his eyes darting from Charlie to outside the trench and back again.

'What are we doin' here, Charlie? What made us come here? Some smart-arsed joker in the pub, that's what started all this! Tellin' us we owed it to our country… makin' us feel like cowards if we didn't come… bet 'e didn't even sign on himself! Nettie was right… bloody fools… both of us! Gettin' ourselves into this bloody war 'stead of stayin' home with my fam'ly… that would've been the right thing to do! Well, I'm not…'

'Pull yourself together, man!' One of the other soldiers leant over, his head ducking as another round of shells whizzed overhead to explode nearby. 'We're all in this together, like it or not… We're here now, ain't we?'

Charlie pulled Harry down, both of them now with their backs against the side as he leant closer to Harry. More shells lit up the dark expanse of an early morning sky above them, and the sound of heavy guns could still be heard not far away.

'He's right, mate. Ya gotta keep it together... just a while longer... war can't last forever.' Even to Charlie's ears, his words sounded hollow, but he clapped a hand on Harry's shoulder just the same, and as he went to get up, a volley of gunfire tore along the top of the trench, ground churning up above their heads as dirt now mixed with blood sprayed out across the trench to cover the men below. The man who had leant across only moments before now fell forward, a gaping hole in the side of his face.

The sight of the dead man sprawled out in front of him snapped the last of Harry's control and he crumpled to the ground, his helmet falling to the dirt at his feet as he covered his head with his hands and rocked himself in an effort to expel the image of it from his mind.

Charlie reached up and rubbed a trembling hand across the back of his own neck, wondering what to do. The last thing he wanted was for Harry to lose it... not now... not with all this going on and him feeling like it wouldn't take much for him to go the same way...

The war raged all around them. The heavy guns and field artillery had fired thousands of shells upon the enemy, while allies in the air had dropped their bombs down upon the German base supplies and aerodromes. The attack had begun days ago, a barrage of fire from air and ground to take the Messines Ridge, a long hill only 300 feet in height that sat as a barrier to the Allied advance between Ypres and Armentières.

The Allies' placement of 500 tons of high explosives at several strategic points along the hill were ready to go as the British concentrated their batteries along the nine-mile front at the foot of the ridge.

In the early hours of the morning there was a deathly silence, and a kind of eeriness fell over the men in the trenches.

Harry looked up, his voice now quiet... calm. 'I'm not gonna make it, Charlie,' he said simply.

'Don't talk rot, mate... ya think I'm gonna let anything happen to you? Nettie'd skin me alive!' Charlie tried to smile, hoping the thought of Harry's wife would snap his friend out of it.

'No, mate, I'm tellin' ya, I'm calm now, I'm all right... and I know I'm not going home.' Harry's voice was almost a whisper in the surrounding stillness, his eyes showing no fear now, nothing of his earlier panic. He stared at Charlie and slowly shook his head, as though he were merely informing him of some inevitable certainty.

Charlie could do nothing for a few seconds but stare back, fully aware that his friend believed every word.

He tried to push it away. 'Bullshit! Ya hear me, Harry? That's bullshit! Brits have got it corked up out there. You'll be all right... we'll both be all right!'

Anything Harry might have said was cut off as a deep rumbling seemed to penetrate the very ground on which they stood, followed almost immediately by a thunderous and ear-splitting sound of such magnitude that it could be heard through France, over Belgium and even as far away as England. The Allies' explosives had ripped through the hill one by one as towering flames pierced the night sky, sending earth and debris hurtling out to rain down upon both sides of the mighty conflict.

Almost immediately the men started to move, yelling at each other as they did. 'Now! Now! Now!' They hurled themselves over the side of the trench.

There was the shrill sound of a whistle. 'Go! Come on,

lads… let's go!' They were up and running, some being struck down by enemy bullets before they even had a chance to raise their rifle. Charlie grabbed Harry's helmet and plonked it down on his head as he half dragged, half pushed his friend up and over the side, pulling him to his feet amid the screams of wounded men as more bullets churned the ground at their feet… and they began to run.

Harry ran close behind Charlie, a silly thought occurring to him that it was much the same as when they were kids, running through his backyard playing shoot-out games with makeshift rifles fashioned out of wood. His thoughts skidded to a halt as he saw Charlie falter… then fall.

'Charlie!' Harry then felt a searing pain as a bullet tore deep into his side, followed by another in his upper thigh, as still another shattered his kneecap…

The battle raged on while the sun rose in the sky as the British, Australians and now the Irish fought on valiantly and fearlessly for control over the Messines Ridge…

Harry awoke with a start to find himself within the medical tent. Stretchers bearing the wounded lay alongside him and, with great effort, he lifted his head to see still more out through the front on the ground outside. His body was numb… medication of sorts? He closed his eyes once more only to open them again in what he thought had only been a second or two, but he couldn't be sure. The serious but sympathetic face of an army medic now peered down at him. Harry tried to talk… tried to ask about Charlie, but his voice wouldn't work. The medic shook his head… Harry wondered why.

'How long, Doc?' a familiar voice said from off to the

side somewhere. Harry tried to turn his head to see... he knew that voice.

'Charlie?' He found his voice at last, but it sounded strange, not like his at all, almost as though he'd borrowed it from somebody else.

'Harry?' Charlie came instantly to his side. Harry noticed the bandaged arm and Charlie lifted it slightly, wincing as he did, but then smiled.

'Close shave, mate, but I'll be right as rain in no time.'

Charlie's face then became grave. He'd already been told that Harry might not make it. He didn't want to look down at his friend's body, didn't want to see the damage. He'd been watching Harry for the past hour or more and he'd already born witness to the torn and bleeding wound that now lay tightly bound beneath the bandage stretched tight across his middle, its purpose to stem the flow of blood beneath its many layers, though patches of bright red were already making their way through. His leg was a different matter: the shattered knee would be Harry's ticket home, the wound to his thigh superficial by comparison, but Charlie hoped that the bullet wound through the left side of his stomach would not lay claim to him first.

He tried to put on a brave face and swallowed hard.

Harry lay quiet, feeling somehow strange. He looked towards the front of the tent, his eyebrows coming together in puzzlement as he did, his breathing shallow.

'Hey, Charlie, some kind of flares or somethin'? What's goin' on?'

Charlie looked at him in confusion. 'What was that, mate?'

'Mist... kinda hazy... look... it's comin' in fast...' Harry's head fell back down, his eyelids fluttering closed then opening again as he now looked to the side of him.

Charlie was lost for words and looked around, wondering what Harry was on about. All he saw was the hustle and bustle of medical personnel as they went about their duties among the various wounded.

Harry watched the purple mist through half-closed eyes as it swirled in through the tent, curling around the wounded, going unnoticed by the medics as they went about their business. Someone seemed to be walking out of the haze… coming towards him… coming *for* him maybe? Harry felt suddenly peaceful, as if everything was going to be all right. He closed his eyes.

'Harry! Harry!' Charlie became frantic. 'Medic! Get over here… now!'

A man came rushing over, his clothes splattered in blood, the red cross armband the only sign that put him apart from the wounded as he immediately checked all of Harry's vital signs. He let out a sigh of relief. 'It's okay, mate; your friend's sleeping. If he lasts the next few hours, it's quite possible he'll pull through.'

Charlie couldn't believe it. 'You sure? He's not…'

'No, his body's shut down, but he's still with us. Better let him rest as much as possible… and you'd be best getting a bit of rest yourself.'

Charlie bent over Harry, unwilling to leave him alone just yet, not sure if he was being told the truth or not. 'Harry?'

'For God's sake, man, let the poor bastard sleep!' The medic pulled on Charlie's good arm, trying to lead him away. Reluctantly, Charlie did as he was told.

Harry looked on… he saw Nettie… and a baby. Little Teddy? But no, the baby was suddenly now a small child… a girl… not his Lizzie.

Harry was spiralling back then… to where? He saw himself, his life… Charlie, Nettie as she was when he first met her, a frothy young thing, her hair in pink ribbons… that auburn hair. But it wasn't Nettie at all…

A voice spoke to him. 'It's not your time, Harry… not yet… Better you get on with it.'

Harry slept.

Nettie awoke in the early hours of the morning in pain. Her body was bathed in perspiration although the night was cool, suggesting to her that her labour had started while she'd slept. She peered through the darkness at Teddy's cot, trying to make out if he'd stirred at all, but all seemed quiet.

Not wanting to wake him, she slipped as silently as she could from the covers and fumbled for her dressing gown in the dark. It was easier if she got up and walked about.

Peering at the clock on her side dresser, she was thankful to see the time read ten to five. It meant it would be getting light outside soon and she hadn't wanted to go next door and wake Ruby until morning if she could possibly help it. Her pains were close, but not that close yet – hopefully she could hang on.

Nettie felt another contraction grip her and she turned quickly, stubbing her toe on the leg of the bed as she went. Teddy stirred and she gritted her teeth to stop from crying out.

Tears sprang instantly to her eyes as she rubbed her toe with the bottom of her other foot. It was impossible for her to bend over in her condition and rub it otherwise.

The pain subsided, from her contractions as well as her foot, and Nettie wiped her eyes with the sleeve of her dressing gown. She sat alone in the darkened room listening to Teddy's soft, even breathing and assessed her predicament.

She was alone, her husband was fighting across the other

side of the world for reasons that were still a little unclear to her, she had very little money and two children whom she struggled to keep fed and clothed... and still another who was about to make its way into their lives. Yet Nettie felt suddenly nonplussed... and for reasons unknown to her, she began to giggle.

But her misplaced humour was suddenly cut off as another pain took hold, and before she could stop herself, she cursed out loud between clenched teeth... 'A lady be damned! Jesus Christ!'

By noon of the next day, Nettie rested in her bed as Ruby fussed about her, fluffing her pillows and straightening her blankets, the new baby girl sleeping peacefully in the wooden crib at her side. The crib had been Lizzie's, and then Teddy's and now it belonged to... Eleanor.

'I still don't know why you didn't wake me when it all started. You know I wouldn't have minded one bit. A woman ought not to be alone during such a time!'

Nettie had been listening to Ruby's scolding all morning.

'Oh, Rube, I know you wouldn't have minded, but you had your own household to attend to, and I was all right... really I was!'

Ruby side-glanced her, her tone slightly mocking as she replied, 'Oh yes, I could see that right off when I came in!'

Lizzie had come into her mother's bedroom the morning before to find Nettie on the floor, sagging against the foot of the bed, her body racked by the full onslaught of labour while Teddy jumped up and down in his cot, surprisingly not yet crying for his breakfast. The little girl had run next door to

Ruby, who had rushed over and, taken one look at Nettie and immediately sent for Betty Cohen, the midwife.

By the time Betty had arrived, Ruby had Nettie back up on the bed, all children in the kitchen eating breakfast and was making Nettie's bedroom ready for the coming event.

Nettie was suitably contrite now. 'Thank you, Ruby. I don't know what I would have done without you… and thank you for seeing to Lizzie and Teddy.'

Ruby was embarrassed. 'Oh bosh to that! It gives me something to do – besides you'd have done the same for me.' Ruby sought to change the subject; she felt uncomfortable under Nettie's appreciative gaze. 'You know, you really do have an appallingly low stock of linen for such an event. I had to scrounge the household for something to use!'

It was Nettie's turn to be embarrassed. 'Oh dear,' was all she could say.

Ruby had an air of devilment about her as she went on. 'We'd used everything from sheet to washcloth to clean up, and then at the last minute, I remembered Mr McKinney's nicely pressed shirts in the kitchen, so—'

'You didn't!' Nettie's head lifted upright off the pillow, her eyes wide in shock, her face horror-stricken. 'Oh, Ruby, tell me you didn't use Mr McKinney's shirts to… to…'

'Well, not exactly, but we had to wrap poor little Eleanor in something! After all, how many shirts does a man need? Surely he won't miss just one!'

Nettie let her head drop back upon the pillow with a groan. 'Obviously you don't know *Mrs* McKinney very well,' she said quietly.'

Ruby came to stand at the side of Nettie's bed, a grin spread wide across her face. Nettie stared up at her and couldn't help but grin right back until both women were laughing so hard, Nettie had to hold her stomach for fear she might do damage to herself.

Nettie's thoughts sobered then as she thought of Harry's mother. 'I suppose someone ought to let Hillary know… it's the dutiful thing to do.'

Ruby, still smiling, nodded back at her. 'I'll send word.'

Eleanor stirred and Ruby bent to pick her up, her eyes softening as they took in the tiny features, and to the baby she said quietly, 'Personally, I think one of Mr McKinney's shirts went to where it did the most use, don't you?'

A yawn was her only response.

Ruby lay the baby down next to Nettie, who was now so tired, it was all she could do to cradle her in the crook of her arm. She gazed down at the tiny addition to her family.

'Well now, I wonder what your father is going to say when he learns of you… Eleanor.'

And so once again she'd been sent… and so he must follow. And during this time of 'infancy' as so named, she would remain one with him until her age demanded that earthly limitations be placed upon her. And then once more he would watch… and wait… until later in her time, when he would reawaken her to his presence…

It was nearly two months later when Nettie received the news of Harry's injuries. Just three weeks after her 'laying in' period from the birth of Eleanor, a letter from an address in London, England had arrived on her doorstep, the untidy scrawl on the front of the envelope undeniably belonging to her husband.

My dearest Nettie,

Seems I'll be coming home sooner than expected. I'm in a hospital in London. Took a bad one in the side, knocked me around a bit but I'm all right. These Brits are a bit crusty but they're not a bad lot really once you get to know them. Told the army chaplain not to write – sooner write to you myself. Took one in the leg too, going to be a bit stiff I think but I'm whole, that's the main thing. Some chaps here aren't so lucky.

I'm being sent home when I'm well enough to travel, though not sure when that will be. Looking forward to seeing you; miss you and the kids terribly. Tell Mum will you, love? Bet that son of ours is already walking by now; can't wait to see him. Charlie got hurt in the arm but he's all right too. He's been sent somewhere else. Can't mention it here. Have to go now – terribly short on paper here. Will send you a message by telegraph when I arrive back in Australia. Can't wait to see you, Nettie – miss you and kids so much.

Your loving husband, Harry

Nettie hadn't dared breathe throughout the reading of the letter. Now she held it to her pounding heart and closed her eyes as she let out a deep sigh of relief. She read it once more to make absolutely sure he was all right. On reading it a third time, she was able to smile… and then laugh out loud. She jumped up and hugged the letter to her chest, yelling as she did so.

'Lizzie! Lizzie! Your father's coming home!'

Two-year-old Teddy toddled out into the kitchen to stare

warily up at the unusual spectacle of his mother shrieking and dancing around in front of the wood stove. Nettie spied him and bent down, swooping him up into her arms.

'Oh, Teddy, my precious darling boy! Your daddy is coming home!'

Nettie remembered then that Lizzie was at Ruby's and, with a puzzled Teddy in her arms, quickly ran next door to break the news. Eleanor slept on soundly in her crib, as unaware of the astounding news that had just unfolded as she was of the ongoing war that would tragically and irreversibly shape the world into which she'd been born.

Four months later, Nettie, with an excited Lizzie at her side, a bored and restless Teddy in the pushchair before her and an anxious Hillary, stood upon the platform at Adelaide train station in the midday heat, awaiting the return of husband, father and son respectively. Christmas was only days away. On receiving the news of Harry's arrival, Nettie had gone down to the butcher and ordered a full leg of mutton for the occasion. Then, as an added treat, she'd ventured into Mr Bixby's store and bought a quarter pound of dates, a cup each of raisins and sultanas along with a half bag of custard powder to make a steamed pudding for dessert. Hang the expense! They were going to be a family again, and she wanted this Christmas to be especially memorable.

The crowd around them had grown considerably in the last half hour or so. Harry wasn't the only returning soldier with an impatient family waiting on the platform.

Ruby had graciously offered to lighten Nettie's load by staying behind to mind Eleanor. A good thing too, thought Nettie. This meeting with Harry would be overwhelming as it was without the added surprise of the latest addition to their family.

Hillary's eyes strayed nervously from the track in the distance to the small family beside her, a handkerchief held up to her lips in anticipation of that first view of her son, a son who'd been absent for a year and a half, a son who now returned to her... maimed. When she'd first heard the news of his injuries, she'd taken to her bed for a week. Nettie had informed her that he would be well, but what would she know? As far as Hillary was concerned, no one knew her Harold as well as she. No one had prayed for his safe return as much as she. Well, her prayers had been answered. Harold had returned all right, and now her dear boy might be a cripple! And all because of this abominable war! How she'd missed him!

'I see it!' Lizzie pulled on Nettie's dress. 'There it is, look!'

Nettie screwed her eyes up to peer into the distance, as did several other onlookers. Her heart began to pound as Teddy began to cry. Hillary became agitated, alternately sniffing and dabbing at her lips with her handkerchief.

Minutes later, the train pulled up alongside them, its brakes giving a long-drawn-out screech in protest as steam poured out along the platform, causing many to stand back momentarily.

Nettie began to move quickly down the length of the platform, her eyes scanning the people alighting from its doors, a frown creasing her forehead as she struggled to maneuver the pushchair through the excited crowd.

'Come on, Lizzie, mind you stay close... Do you see him yet?'

And then... there he was!

All of them stopped as Harry hung on to the rail and

swung down from the top step, his stiffened leg preventing him from using the middle step as he planted his good leg squarely upon the platform, a walking stick under his arm.

'Oh my dear sweet son!' Hillary, unable to mask her shock at the sight of what she believed to be a terrible infirmity, covered her mouth with her handkerchief.

Nettie only saw Harry... home... at last! And safe! She called out, trying to make herself heard over the hustle and bustle of the crowd.

'Harry! Harry! Over here!'

But Lizzie was able to get through the crush and reach him first before she came to a sudden halt. Her father had been gone for a year and a half, a long time out of her young life, and she was suddenly shy.

Harry laughed. 'Hey, princess!' He swooped her up and held her to him. 'You must have grown a full two inches! Have you been looking after your mother like I told you?'

Harry stopped laughing, the smile frozen upon his face as he spied Nettie coming towards him. He simply stood staring with Lizzie upon his hip. In his time away, he'd seen the lush green of England and the grand buildings of London; he'd seen the picturesque villages and countryside of France as well as the vast beauty of the ocean between, but never had he seen anything so beautiful as the sight before him now... his Nettie.

She stood about six feet away, her face partially covered by the broad-rimmed sun hat she wore, exposing little of the long auburn hair tied back underneath. Her light cotton dress with its puffed shoulders and long sleeves was tied at the waist and ran the full length of her body, as was fashionably decent. Her brown eyes brimmed with tears as her lips formed his name, though no sound was heard. To Harry, there wasn't a woman alive who could hold a candle to her.

He let Lizzie slide down from his hip and made to move towards her, but before he could reach her, Hillary rushed forward to throw her arms about him, sobbing uncontrollably as she said his name over and over again. Harry was taken aback. He tried comforting her, patting her back as she wept into his shoulder. Never had he seen his mother put on such a show of emotion, not even when his father died!

'Hey, Mum, what's all this? Is this any way to behave? You see I'm just fine… leg like a board but all in one piece just the same, see?' Harry held her from him and smacked down on his leg to show her he was as sturdy as ever, but Hillary refused to look at it as she quickly composed herself and stepped back.

It was then that Nettie stepped forward. 'Hello, Harry… welcome home,' she said in a shaky voice. It was all she could think of to say. In an instant, Harry's mother was forgotten, as was the milling crowd, as he leant forward quickly and held her tightly to him.

'My God, Net, it's good to see you,' he whispered in her ear. 'I thought for a while there that I wouldn't make it back… do you understand what I mean?' He leant back and looked at her. Nettie nodded and hugged him once more.

Over his shoulder she noticed another family waiting at the door of the next carriage, though there were no smiles… no joy. Mickey Phipps, a boy she used to go to school with, and who used to tease her relentlessly in the schoolyard, was lifted down from the train, his legs missing below the knees. His parents stood close by – his father's face grim, his mother clutching the arm of Mickey's wife, Alice, both women struggling to hold back tears as little Lucy, Mickey's three-year-old daughter, hid behind her mother's skirts. Mickey was placed in a wheelchair, his features rigidly set as he looked neither left nor right. The family followed silently behind as he was wheeled off.

Nettie felt her stomach lurch at the sight of them and thought how easily it might have been Harry in that chair instead of poor Mickey, and she closed her eyes and hugged her husband tighter still.

Teddy's cry of protest at being forgotten penetrated the tender scene, and Harry laughingly bent down and swooped him up in his arms. While Lizzie's memory of her father was dim, Teddy's memory of him was practically non-existent and he sat rigidly upright, his eyes fixed warily on the tall man that held him close. Curiosity got the better of him however, and he proceeded to poke one of his small fingers into the smiling mouth before him in an effort to feel Harry's teeth.

This made Harry laugh all the more and even Hillary gave some semblance of a smile, the corners of her mouth twitching slightly upward before she could stop herself.

Later that afternoon, Harry, reclining in what had always been 'his' armchair in the drawing room, his stiffened leg stretched out in front of him, gazed at his newest daughter as she lay upon a blanket spread out on the rug in the center of the room. It was the hottest part of the day and Nettie had stripped the baby down to her nappy, her small naked back showing the imprint of patterns from the blanket as she rolled first one way and then the other. Harry, his shirt sleeves rolled up to his elbows, watched on in fascination at what he thought to be nothing short of a miracle. Perhaps because he'd had no knowledge of her coming, or because he wasn't present for Nettie's pregnancy, little Eleanor seemed to have appeared from nowhere. Of course, he knew she hadn't come from nowhere; after all, he'd definitely had a hand in it. He smiled. But it was strange. There was... something... he remembered, wasn't there? Something from that terrible day when he'd been injured, and he'd thought… no… he'd been shown… hadn't he? Odd really, now he came to think on it…

Harry had been struck dumb when Nettie had led him into their bedroom and shown him Eleanor asleep in the crib. He'd been surprised at first to find Ruby there and had tipped his hat towards her before she'd discreetly stepped outside. Nettie had simply stood smiling at him. When he'd realized why, his good leg had seemed to fail him and he'd plonked himself down upon the side of the bed, his mouth gaping as he looked on in awe.

Harry decided that as soon as he was able, he was going to seek work and look after them the way they should have been looked after. There would be no more shirking his responsibilities, no more drinking his money away and Nettie would no longer have to do that McKinney woman's ironing. If there was one thing the war had taught him, it was the value of home and family, and he made a silent promise to himself and Nettie that he would never let them down again.

CHAPTER TWO

J ust six months later, Harry stumbled down the road towards home in a drunken stupor, his progress all the more cumbersome due to his leg. In the preceding months, he'd obtained and lost four positions. His first had been with Mawson's Wood & Kindling, which he'd kept for a little over six weeks until Mawson's son had returned from the war and subsequently replaced Harry. Still undaunted, Harry had then taken up a position as a machinist at the paper mill, but this job lasted just over a week due to Harry convincing himself he was not an 'indoor' man. Regardless of this, his next two jobs were indoors as well – one at a furniture manufacturing establishment and the next at a tannery. But Harry failed to turn up on too frequent an occasion – due mainly to his drinking the night before – and there had been no other recourse than for him to be fired from both. Now, however, he felt in high spirits, for he'd just received an offer of a job from Louie Crompton. Louie was the overseer of the stockyards up at the slaughter sheds and Harry's job would be to unload the sheep and cattle as they came in, water them down and ready them for slaughter, as well as clean the stockyards as they emptied. The job was less than clean, but Harry didn't mind getting his hands dirty at all – he knew some of the chaps from down at the yards and he considered them his type of people. He couldn't wait to tell Nettie about this latest development… at three pounds, nine shillings and sixpence a week too!

Now, if only he could find his way home…

Nettie heard the sound of her husband's tread on the gravel pathway outside and pursed her lips. There was no mistaking the drag of his leg on the stones, always more prominent when he'd been drinking. She sighed and went to the stove to check on his tea. The wood had burnt down long ago, but his plate was still warm.

Nettie cleared a space for him at the small table in the kitchen. No point in setting the table out in the drawing room for a husband who was more than likely in no state to notice where he ate in any case, she reasoned.

Harry stumbled in the door as Nettie placed a plate of beef stew upon the table, a tea towel protecting her hands from the heat of the plate. Free of the stew, she threw the tea towel over her shoulder and stood with her arms crossed in front of her, glaring at him.

Harry looked suitably sheepish as he slid off his hat and placed it on the table next to his plate before sitting down. But then on remembering his news, he turned and gave her a cagey smile, his eyebrows arching upward as though he was in possession of a big secret.

To Nettie, the idiotic look upon her husband's face merely

reflected the alcohol-sodden brain behind it. She rolled her eyes in irritation.

'Harold Grayson, I have absolutely no idea what you've got to smile about. Your children have been in bed this past hour!' Nettie's point was that he was later than usual. As a rule, he usually made it home before their bedtime, and with the six o'clock closing these days, she'd expected him home at a more respectable hour. Where else had he been?

Snatching up his hat from the table, Nettie made a show of stomping firmly out into the hallway to place it on the stand just outside the door.

Harry ignored her mood and declared loudly, 'Nettie, my dearest wife, I have fine news!' But then, on noticing the stew in front of him, he proceeded to dig his fork in. Nettie now stood tapping her foot in frustration.

'Am I to guess this fine news? Or are you going to share it with me?'

Harry, his cheeks bulging with food, looked at his wife with a twinkle in his eyes and nodded. Then, swallowing, he went to wipe his mouth with his sleeve.

'Harry, don't you dare! Here!' She practically threw the tea towel at him. 'Use this!'

Harry wiped his mouth and, scraping his chair back, pulled Nettie down upon his lap. 'Nettie, your husband has obtained empl—'

'Harry, please! You smell like a brewery!'

Nettie got up immediately, her nose wrinkling in disgust. Harry opened his eyes wide in surprise.

'But I've been with none other than Louie Crompton!' He looked at her, waiting for the name to register, but Nettie's expression didn't change.

The name did in fact ring a bell somewhere in her mind, but he would have to be a little more forthcoming!

At least her question about where her husband had been since closing time had been more or less answered. Obviously, he'd been keeping company with this Crompton fellow.

Harry decided to enlighten his wife. 'Louie Crompton is the overseer at the stockyards and he has offered *me* a job!' Pleased with himself, he waited for her reaction

But all Nettie could do was throw up her hands in vexation. 'Oh, Harry… if I had a shilling for every time you've walked in that door the worse for drink and informed me of another job, we'd have enough money to pay the butcher, the grocer and even old Bixby as well!'

Harry looked at her, his face softening at the way she became flushed when she was angry. But Nettie had become accustomed to his ways long ago, as well as those puppy-dog looks he gave her.

'And don't be thinking you can soft talk me around, Harold Grayson!' She turned abruptly and went back to the stove. Bending over, she took the iron from the cupboard and proceeded to fill it up before the embers grew too cold.

Harry came up behind her and placed his arms about her waist. 'No need to do any of that now, is there, love?'

Nettie moved quickly out of his embrace. 'Mrs McKinney wants her ironing back in the morning.'

Harry swung her around, frowning. 'You're not *still* doing ironing for that woman, are you?'

Nettie looked up at him and bit her lip, her manner becoming suddenly hesitant as she replied. 'Harry… I've been doing ironing for Mrs McKinney, Mrs Trimble, as well as… as Mrs Kluntz!' She said the last name defiantly.

Harry's eyes widened; his features set in disbelief. 'Kluntz? But that woman is German!'

Nettie pressed her lips together tightly. 'I'll have you

know that Mr and Mrs Kluntz lost their only son overseas fighting for king and country... *our* king and country!'

Harry's face changed to one of conflicting emotions, but still he protested. 'But to do *ironing* for this woman? I mean, for *any* of these women?'

Nettie's tone softened. 'Oh, Harry, what do you think puts food on our table most of the time? And where do you suppose the children get their clothes? Harry... the children are growing, in case you haven't noticed.'

Harry's face fell. Though his drinking tonight had been slightly heavier than usual, and his brain more fuddled because of it, what she was saying had successfully penetrated it enough to make him feel ashamed. Suddenly, he squared his shoulders. 'Look, Net, I've got a job, a good job... down at the stockyards – three pounds, nine and six a week. I start tomorrow, but to see us through until my first pay, I'll go and see Mum...'

'No!' Nettie cut him off and turned her back on him. 'I don't want charity. And least of all from your mother!' She turned back to him, her expression pleading. 'I think it's wonderful that you have a job, and we'll get through some way until your first pay... we've been doing it so far, haven't we? Just... well, just try to stick it out this time, Harry, that's all I ask.' Nettie thought a moment and then added quietly, 'And I promise that if you keep this job... then I won't do another scrap of ironing apart from the clothes on our own backs.'

Harry looked at her a long moment, and then he smiled, his voice quiet as he said, 'All right, Net... all right.'

Over the following few months, Harry did keep his job, and, true to her word, Nettie no longer took in ironing. No more did she have to book things on credit either. It was with great relief that she was able to finally pay in full the accounts owing to the butcher and grocer, as well as the milliners. Even Mr Bixby took to smiling when she entered his store, so valued a customer had she become.

Harry had taken to his job quite amiably, the tasks he was responsible for in the stockyards enabling him to make decisions as well as giving him freedom of movement, so he wasn't confined to one spot like at the paper mill or the furniture manufacturers. Indeed, Louie Crompton was very pleased with Harry's efforts, which in turn fed Harry's self-worth and gave him a sense of long-sought stability. His newfound self-esteem, however, did not stop Harry's regular jaunts to the pub. He still drank too much and too often, but at least he was home at a decent hour and up of a morning to go to work.

Nettie was at least thankful that Harry did not turn mean when he drank. She'd heard tell of women who cowered in their kitchens at the sound of their men coming up the path after a bout of drinking – so jovial and entertaining only a short time before at the bar with their friends yet, on stepping over the threshold of their own homes, suddenly turning short-tempered and unpredictable. Harry would simply be Harry… perhaps more amorous, and at times a little sillier… but just Harry all the same.

Despite his drinking, life had definitely become easier for the Grayson family. With Harry's steady income, Nettie no longer worried about things like new shoes for the children, or endlessly darned socks that had long seen their day. No longer did she have to worry about the lack of ingredients in her cupboard to make a cake for an approaching birthday, and what's more, she even had money enough to buy candles to place on top! Things were comfortable and worry-free, at least as much as they could be amid the ever present and daily war news. Even the unavoidable visits from Hillary failed to irritate Nettie as much as they once had, and on two or three occasions, she'd actually found herself participating in affable conversation with the woman!

Lizzie was now six years old and Teddy now three as Eleanor approached her first birthday. To the other members of the household, Eleanor was a quiet child, seemingly satisfied to just sit and observe or crawl about the house, prattling away in her baby gibberish to no one in particular. She slept soundly all night, ate well and hardly ever grizzled over anything.

One Sunday afternoon, Harry, stretched out in his usual chair, watched Eleanor as she sat quietly inspecting the patterns in the rug on the drawing-room floor and remarked to Nettie, 'You know, Net, if that child could speak, I bet she could tell us what her life's plans are even now!'

Nettie, her expression one of concentration as she sat mending a hole in his trousers, looked up and raised an eyebrow at him. 'My guess is that if she could speak, she'd tell her father that his head was stuffed full of ridiculous nonsense.'

Harry looked affronted at her comment before breaking out into a wide grin. Nettie chuckled to herself and went back to her mending.

He smiled at her, guiding her small fingers around the outline of rose petals within the tightly woven pile... She was unaware that he was seen by no one but her. And though it was not a conscious thought that could form in her young mind, she automatically looked on him as being as much a

part of her life as the others in her small world. It amused him that she perceived him merely as a man with pretty eyes. She was too young to realize that no one else spoke to him or acknowledged his presence. Nor was her young mind able to stretch ahead to a time soon when he would suddenly disappear. To a child of her age, he was simply... here.

She'd already grown accustomed to the comforting smell of her mother and the warm affection of her father – as it should be – and as time went on, he would fade from her memory as he reluctantly 'stepped back' from her mind... and the protective cocoon of her family would be all she would remember.

Peace was at hand. Rumours of it were circulating everywhere and people yearned for confirmation that the war had finally come to an end. It had been four long years of worry, heartache and tragedy that had been felt right across the nation. There was hardly a family that hadn't endured the grief and suffering of a lost or injured loved one or friend. Returned soldiers, so many of them now disabled, could be seen in the streets of Adelaide, a scene that weighed heavy on the hearts of many.

Over the past few years, women and children on the home front had done their share for the war effort as well. Women had held stalls and social events to raise money, while children had been organized by their schools to perform their 'rightful duties to our brave men in uniform'. Those who'd been proficient with knitting needles had been put to knitting socks, while others had gathered anything from bones, bottles or even the sheep's wool stuck in fences to help raise money for the war effort. Parcels of blankets, pots and utensils had been sent to the Red Cross, and the littler ones had made Christmas cards in the hope of bringing some measure of comfort to the homesick and weary soldiers.

Though both Nettie and Ruby had never actually participated in these money-raising concerns in the past, they had on many occasion donated old toys or clothes and, at their more affluent times, a cake or pudding to sell.

Although the plight of many stared Nettie in the face every day in the streets, for her, a major part of the war had already ended with the return of her own husband. Were it not for worrying about Frank, Charlie or Ruby's husband Lenny, Nettie would have been determined to find a way of blotting out the news. She hated the war and what it had done to so many people she knew. And like everyone else, she wished for it all to be over. Nettie had had enough! But then when she looked at Ruby, she would recall how barely a year ago, she would sit and pray and worry for the safety of Harry, just the way Ruby still did for Lenny, and thinking on her own good fortune, guilt would wash over her.

On 12 November 1918, the Governor Sir Henry Galway read the proclamation of the Armistice at Parliament House, and Adelaide revelled in its long-awaited celebration of the end of the war. Peace had finally arrived, but it had been hard-won, and the toll on Australia and its population had been horrendous. As a result, the Australian way of life would never be quite the same again.

A little way into January of the following year, Lenny finally returned home to Ruby. In the preceding months, he'd been cared for in an army hospital in France suffering from a nervous breakdown... 'Shell shock they called it,' said Ruby. Nettie accompanied Ruby and Kathy on the tram down to the station to meet him, and though Nettie felt a little uncomfortable with this idea, believing that Lenny's first meeting should be just with his family, Ruby had pleaded with her to come. Lenny had been gone for over three years. Most of the men in his company had fallen at Gallipoli, and Ruby had felt somewhat nervous and unsure of how things would be.

When Lenny stepped onto the platform, Ruby unconsciously placed a hand over her mouth at the sight of him, a gesture that did not go unnoticed by her husband. Lenny resembled nothing of the largely built man with the kindly face that Nettie remembered, and realizing Ruby must think the same, she nudged Ruby discreetly in the back, propelling her forward.

Kathy remained with Nettie, a frightened look upon her face, the tall thin man in front of her nothing like the man she had conjured up from her dim memory.

Lenny had lost so much weight that he didn't look like Lenny at all and there was a kind of tired strain around his eyes. But then he smiled, his voice quiet. 'Hello, love.'

And Ruby burst into tears, her old brown hat falling to the ground behind her as she threw herself into his arms. Lenny shut his eyes tight as he crushed her to him, and Nettie had to look away lest she be caught up in the emotion of it herself and weep too.

When Lenny saw Kathy, he shook his head, unable to believe she could grow so much in the time he'd been gone. His laughter was infectious as he swung her up in the air to hold her above him, and Nettie couldn't help but notice the look of pure adoration upon Ruby's face as she leant comfortably against her husband.

The tram ride home was oddly amusing to Nettie. While Ruby had pleaded with Nettie to accompany her to the station, on the way home, the small family settled happily on the seat in front of her wasn't even aware of her presence. But of course Nettie understood.

The weeks turned into months, and still there was no sign of Charlie, though Harry was not overly worried. He'd heard through Charlie's aunt Aggie, that he was alive and well and staying with a family in Western Australia, presumably working as a station hand on a property situated only a few hundred miles from Perth. What confused Harry was the fact that Charlie hadn't been in touch. He wondered why he'd not received a letter or even a telegram, even if it was just to inform him that Charlie was back in Australia.

He knew Charlie to be a friendly soul who fit in easily with most people, and Harry thought that perhaps he'd got in with some people over in Western Australia who had offered him work and had simply decided to stay there for a while. It still didn't explain why his best mate hadn't been in touch with him though. On discussing it with Nettie one day, he said, 'I think I'll pay that aunt Aggie of his a visit and find out what's going on.'

But when Harry returned home, he'd been no more the wiser, and Nettie could see he was a bit hurt by Charlie's lack of contact.

He shrugged as he walked into the kitchen. 'All she would say is that he's doing well and she doesn't know when he might be returning.'

Nettie was at a loss as to what to say, but secretly she wondered if there was anything wrong with Charlie that he had perhaps not told his aunt about.

She supposed time would tell.

The next few weeks went on relatively normally. Lizzie was to perform in a school play dressed as a snowflake and went about the house in continuous rehearsal, until Nettie, driven to the brink of madness by her daughter's constant fluttering of hands and moving her arms in a floating motion, finally put a stop to it. Teddy was nearly four years old now and seemed hell-bent on destroying anything he came into contact with, especially if it belonged to Lizzie. Quite often, Nettie would catch him in the nick of time as he wandered out with Lizzie's doll-house furniture, intent on watching it drop down the outside toilet. And Nettie had lost count of the times she'd sat hurriedly stitching an arm or leg back on Lizzie's doll before she arrived home from school. At times, she would be at her wits' end with Teddy and would end up complaining to Harry. Harry, only too willing to try to appease his wife, would threaten the boy with a sound smack if he didn't learn to leave things alone, while at the same time barely suppressing a smirk at his young son's exploits. Nettie would end up scolding her husband instead.

Eleanor was now walking, her newfound freedom opening up her small world, and on discovering she no longer had to confine her adventures to the house, she would toddle out through the back door, sometimes making it through the wire fence adjoining Ruby's backyard. And on discovering Lenny down the back at his grapevine or in his vegetable garden, she would chatter a while with him in her baby talk, to which Lenny, having no idea what she was saying, would nod and oblige with 'Oh I see' or 'Oh yes' to his curly-headed, pint-sized visitor. Other times, she would wander right through Ruby's back door and, moments later, Ruby would escort her back to a surprised and mortified Nettie, who'd had no idea that her youngest child had even left the house.

Nettie had finally received the long-awaited letter from her parents informing her that Frank had come home safe and sound, and she was overjoyed. He'd been retained aboard his ship, which had been in quarantine due to the dreaded influenza that had been sweeping through many parts of Australia.

It was thought that the infection had been brought in by the returning troops, a deadly strain in which people were suddenly besieged with aches and pains in the legs and arms, or sudden dizziness, followed by a raging fever. Three days was often all it took to prove fatal, and while a lot survived, there were many who did not. Places of work shut their doors instantly on discovery of one of their staff falling ill, and all were detained inside until it was deemed safe to return to the outside population again, as was the case with Frank. The petty officer aboard his ship had dropped to the floor just two days out from port. Two others had fallen ill within the week, and many more followed over the next month. Frank himself was struck down with the infection, but as fate would have it, he was one of the lucky ones. His ship remained in dock, none allowed on or off until authorities were sure the influenza had run its course.

Nettie's mother had explained that she hadn't wanted to write until she'd been sure that Frank had been cleared. Now that he was, Nettie was over the moon that her brother was home – it was like life was finally coming back to some kind of rightful order.

Frank was home and well, Charlie had come back too, though not so far as Adelaide yet, and Ruby and Lenny were presumably doing a lot better now that he'd obtained a position at Woodroofe's bottling plant at Norwood. Ruby had paraded with hands on hips around Nettie's kitchen one day showing off her brand-new hat!

'What do you think, Net? Like it? Got it for a steal at Bixby's for only three and six!'

Nettie had been literally struck dumb by the monstrosity that sat atop Ruby's head. The wide straw brim with its overlarge arrangement of flowers and plumes was quite possibly the ugliest thing Nettie had ever seen, but not wanting to offend her best friend, she had only been able to muster a doubtful smile. Ruby, on seeing the look on Nettie's face, had then erupted into laughter and tossed the offensive item across the room to land on Nettie's meat locker. But then she'd abruptly stopped as she plonked herself down at the small kitchen table, groaning as she rested her head upon her hands.

'Oh Lord, Net, what am I to do? Lenny bought it for me.' She glanced up at Nettie, who still hadn't said a thing. 'Well, you didn't really think *I* would have bought such an object do you? I mean, who would be seen out around town in that godawful thing?'

Nettie's shoulders began to shake then with suppressed laughter. 'Well, I suppose you could always say it was taken away by a strong gust of wind down at the Torrens… couldn't you?'

Nettie then picked up the hat and held it up, her face now openly reflecting her dislike. Both women started to giggle until Harry walked in and, catching sight of the hat, remarked, 'New hat, Net? Quite nice.'

Both women erupted into laughter, Harry shaking his head as he left the room, thinking that women had to be the silliest creatures that God ever saw fit to put upon the earth.

It was Hillary's birthday and they'd all been invited to take tea with her that afternoon. She lived in one of the large spacious homes in North Adelaide on the main street facing St Peter's Cathedral. It had been her home for the past twenty-five years, the first fifteen of which she'd shared with her husband George, until his death in 1910 of an undisclosed illness which she would not discuss. Not long into their courting days, Nettie had asked Harry the reason for his father's death and Harry had informed her it was his heart, leaving Nettie wondering why Hillary would feel it should be undisclosed. There was certainly no dishonour or indignity in dying from a heart attack! But it was just one more peculiarity in a long line of many where Hillary was concerned.

It was a Saturday afternoon as the family made their way down King William Street towards Hillary's home. Being fine outside, Harry decided that it might be nicer to walk the half-hour distance instead of catching the tram. Nettie had dressed all the children in their finest: Lizzie was decked out in matching yellow dress and hat, Teddy in his corduroy shorts and braces, with bow tie and hat, and Eleanor in a pink dress and sun bonnet. But what started out as a nice leisurely stroll ended with Harry carrying Teddy piggyback while taking it in turns with Nettie to push Eleanor and a weary Lizzie perched on the front of the pushchair. Harry was limping as well, more so from his good leg taking much of his weight, which prompted Nettie to ask why he'd insisted on walking when they all would have been better off catching the tram.

Rosemary, or Rosie as she was more affectionately known, Hillary's housekeeper of more than thirty years, met them at the front steps. Over the years, Rosie had become a kind of companion to Hillary, and with George's death, the two women had become closer still. Rosemary appeared to be around the same age as Hillary. She was a kindly woman and understood Hillary like no other, having become accustomed to her employer's moods and eccentricities over the years, and while Hillary could be downright infuriating at times, Rosie couldn't help but hold a soft spot for her crotchety benefactor – as well as feeling fortunate to have had security all these years in very comfortable surroundings.

The weary family stood at the foot of the stairs looking up at her, but Harry's tired smile didn't hide the devilment in his eyes as he greeted her. 'Hello, Rosie old girl.'

Rosie fought to maintain her composure and nearly smiled back at him... nearly. She covered it quickly with a reprimand. 'Don't you "old girl" me, Harold Grayson! And what do you think you're doing dragging your poor wife and kiddies about on a warm day like this? Come inside this instant and sit yourselves down in the cool while I get you all some refreshments.'

Harry burst out laughing and Rosie's frown deepened, but then the sternness fell away from her face the second her eyes fell on Nettie and the children, and her mouth widened into a warm smile. 'Hello, Henrietta.' Nettie didn't have time to answer as Rosie began clucking over the young ones, especially Eleanor. 'Oh look at this little dear... oh my goodness how she's grown!'

Nettie could do nothing but smile, and feeling as though she might faint on the spot if she didn't sit down soon, she looked over pleadingly at Harry, who caught her meaning and instantly began herding them all inside.

They were all ushered into the parlour and Nettie stood blinking as her eyes tried to adjust to the dimness of the room after being outside in the sunshine. Hillary's parlour, like the rest of the house, was overdone. An assortment of paintings, photographs and tapestries covered the wall and barely a foot of floor space could be seen between the various chairs, side tables and dressers, all littered with brocaded or woollen overthrows. The mantle shelf above the hearth was covered with a heavy velvet antimacassar with golden threaded tassels hanging low at the sides, while the shelf at the top was cluttered with statues and assorted knick-knacks – as was every other available surface in the room – and Nettie couldn't help thinking that if Hillary were to hold a jumble sale, she would make a small fortune from this room alone! With all of them now standing in the centre of the floor, the room became almost stifling.

Nettie heard a distinctive sniff from the corner and looked up to see Hillary sitting in the overstuffed chair, studying them all intently. *Like a queen bee*, thought Nettie and groaned inwardly. It was going to be *that* sort of afternoon.

Harry leant over and kissed his mother's cheek. 'Hello, Mum.'

Hillary tilted her cheek towards him, her expression one of obliging fondness.

Nettie rolled her eyes and then took a deep breath before greeting her. 'Hello, Hillary.'

The elderly face changed to one of dutiful politeness. 'Good afternoon, Henrietta.' Her eyes then quickly glanced over the flushed cheeks of her grandchildren and she looked back at Nettie. 'Goodness me. Why didn't you catch a tram down? I thought it would have been obvious that their skin is much too fair to be exposed to the sun for such a length of time.'

Nettie's mind raced in an effort to say something. 'Well…'

But Hillary went on. 'And Harold's leg shouldn't be subjected to so much walking either. Harold dear, you really must think of yourself now and then.'

Nettie glared back at her mother-in-law and bit her lip in anger, her mind still racing. 'What did the old battleaxe think? That she'd her family at gunpoint and forced them all to walk?'

Out loud she addressed Harry, the sarcasm evident in her

tone. 'Yes, Harold dear, shame on me for forcing you to walk so far. Whatever was I thinking?' Nettie's eyes momentarily blazed as she stared pointedly at her husband and then back at Hillary.

The sarcasm found its mark, and the hurt look on the older woman's face made Nettie feel instantly ashamed. She looked away, and Harry cleared his throat. It was an awkward moment.

Lizzie chose to stand well back; she knew her mother had somehow said the wrong thing, but just what, she wasn't sure. Teddy took his sister's lead and stood behind her, sucking his thumb and waiting for a smile or a word from either of his parents to let him know everything was all right again. Eleanor, totally unaware of any friction in the room, proceeded to pull her frock up over her head until her mother pulled it back down again. She settled for chewing on the hem instead.

The uncomfortable silence that hung in the air was suddenly and mercifully interrupted as Rosie entered carrying a tray laden with pitcher and glasses.

'Here you are – a nice glass of lemonade should do the trick.' Rosie set the tray down and proceeded to fill the glasses. She suddenly spied Eleanor, who had now pulled her bonnet from her head and was crushing it between her small fists.

'And what about this precious little thing, Nettie? Will she be drinking this too?' Rosie bent over and smiled at Eleanor, who now seemed more interested in studying her grandmother than she was in responding to the kindly woman only inches away from her face.

Rosie shrugged and went on chattering away. 'Goodness, it's been a long time since Harold was that age. They'll all be grown in no time, Nettie, mark my words!' Rosie's soft laughter filled the room as she handed out glasses of lemonade, and gradually everyone started to relax.

Even Hillary seemed detached from the previous friction, her attention now taken up with her youngest granddaughter, who stood gazing curiously back at her. Then Eleanor toddled over to the elderly woman, who hadn't moved since they'd all come in, and leant across her grandmother's knees as she reached up to touch her face. Hillary was taken aback by this sudden show of informality, though she made no move to still her granddaughter's small fingers pushing experimentally against the side of her cheek.

'Hey there, mustn't prod Grandma like that, Eleanor.' Harry reached for his small daughter, but Hillary stopped him.

'Leave her be, Harold. Little Eleanor is simply becoming acquainted with her grandmother... aren't you, dear?' Hillary bestowed a rare smile upon Eleanor, which in turn made Eleanor giggle as the small audience surrounding them in the room looked on in astonishment.

It set the scene for the remainder of the afternoon. As the modest spread of birthday fare was served, Hillary insisted that Eleanor be seated next to her, offering her sweet cakes, pastries and cold meats. Both Nettie and Harry couldn't ever remember an afternoon at his mother's home being quite so relaxing – or, for that matter, almost enjoyable.

That afternoon was the start of an ongoing easiness between Hillary and Eleanor. And although Nettie was pleased that her mother-in-law could be halfway normal around her youngest child, it irked her somewhat that her other two children were not treated the same. To Nettie, all her children were as precious as each other, and when she voiced this to Harry, he only pleaded with her to be thankful his mother was actually taking part in their family as a grandmother should, even if it was only with one of her grandchildren.

'As long as all of them know that we love them equally, Net, what harm can it do?'

Nettie wasn't so sure, but she decided that as long as Lizzie and Teddy didn't seem to worry, then neither would she… at least for the present time.

A few months later, Harry stood at the bar with Louie Crompton. It was Friday, and with no work the following day, Saturday work having been cancelled for a few weeks now, they were tired but relaxed. In a short space of time, their conversation had moved from the weather, the steady increase of beer prices and onto the people they knew and their present post-war circumstances. The day's events in the stockyards had followed and by their fourth or fifth beer, they were both considering the reasons behind the falling off of stock being delivered to the abattoirs of late. By the seventh or eighth beer, both men had become persistent in making the other listen to their own well-thought-out and profound opinions on the matter, each of them fully believing they knew the 'real' reasons, as though suddenly they were privy to things that no one else knew.

'You know what I reckon it is, Louie?' Harry didn't wait for him to answer. 'I think it's those bloody farmers, that's what I think it is – always wantin' more, all the time! And now they figure with the war over, they can make their money in hiking up the prices of beef for us poor bastards at home!'

Louie signaled for another round and turned back to Harry. 'Don't be daft, man! You don't know what you're talkin' about. *Everything* is going up – beef, mutton… you name it! Why the wife was only saying the other day about how much bread had gone up…'

Harry nodded knowingly. 'What did I tell you? Bloody farmers again… price of grain… flour… whatever… Even the dairies are getting in for their extra quid. Mark my words!'

Louie shook his head, the action proving too much for his drink-sodden brain as he wobbled momentarily on his stool. 'No, it's the government, that's who's behind it. The new tax on everything is killin' us! And what's more, it forces everybody to put their prices up in the first place. That's what the crux of the matter is!'

Jerry McClellan, the publican, placed two beers down in front of the two men, and as he caught the tail end of their conversation, he couldn't help but shake his head. It was a topic he'd heard discussed time and again at his bar, and one that had no easy answers. For his part, he knew that the war had drained Australia of much of its productive workforce and materials, the breweries included, and as a result, he'd had to pay more for his orders, consequently forcing him to up his prices.

His features turned grim as he shook his head again. Whether it was the government, the farmers or the effects of the whole bloody war for that matter, it was the average blokes – like these two – who were left to shoulder the burden… be it on the battlefield or now back on the home front. And Jerry also knew that with the return of many men from the war, all of whom were looking for work, it was going to get worse before it got better. He moved off, wiping the bar as he went.

Harry and Louie were still deep in their debate when a hand clapped down hard on Harry's shoulder from behind. 'You never would listen to anybody else, would you, mate?'

The sudden interruption startled Harry – so much so that the effects of the last two beers were instantly wiped from his brain as he turned, ready to brace himself against whoever he must have offended. But then his mouth opened in surprise as he stared disbelievingly. 'Charlie!'

Charlie grinned back at him as he reached for Harry's hand and proceeded to shake it vigorously. Neither wanted to let go, each slapping the other on the back and grabbing the other's arm. It was the closest they could come without actually hugging each other, a gesture that would have been totally unacceptable to their upbringing, not to mention their present surroundings.

'Jesus, Charlie, when did ya get back?'

'Couple of days ago... I—'

Harry cut him off. 'Louie, this is Charlie, the best mate a bloke ever had.'

Louie shook Charlie's hand as they nodded to one another. 'I remember you, Charlie... thought maybe you didn't make it back. Glad to see you did.'

Charlie went a little quiet but it was unnoticed by Louie and Harry.

'Jerry! Another beer for a returned soldier!' Harry yelled out to the publican, who by now was down the end of the bar.

Charlie paled slightly at Harry's words, his voice quiet as he leant towards him. 'Cut it out will ya, Harry... war's over.'

Harry, not to be silenced on the matter, turned to him. 'I'll say it is, Charlie m'boy, and here you are... and here I am too, thanks to you!'

Harry leant towards Louie. 'You know if it wasn't for this bloke, I would have lost it for sure over there! But he kept me together... yep, that he did!' Harry had been poking his finger down on the bar counter as he spoke, and now he slapped Charlie's shoulder. If Charlie was quiet, neither man noticed. Jerry placed three more beers on the bar.

'Good to see you back, Charlie.' Jerry leant across and shook Charlie's hand. 'Last drinks, you blokes – nearly closing time. This one's on me.' He nodded to Charlie and said again, 'Really good to see you back,' before moving off.

Charlie called out after him. 'Thanks, Jerry.'

Louie piped up. 'Pity ya didn't come in earlier, mate – we could have had a few more to celebrate your homecoming.' He downed half his beer in one swallow. As did Harry.

Charlie picked up his glass but could only sip at it. Harry noticed.

'Hey, what's this? Lost your taste, mate?' Harry smiled and then suddenly frowned. 'And what's this about you being back for a couple of days? Why didn't ya come round and see me before now? And how come you didn't let me know where you were? I had to get the news from your aunt Aggie that you were okay.' Harry suddenly remembered all the unanswered questions he'd been carrying around with him for months and he now looked at Charlie for explanations.

Charlie laughed, but his mind was racing. He sought to change the subject. 'Well, I came round to see you tonight, but Nettie said you were here, and I'm afraid all the explaining will have to wait until tomorrow on account of Nettie sending me down here with strict orders to get you home.'

The ploy worked. Harry, now reminded of his family waiting at home, said to Charlie, 'Hey, did you know we had another one? A girl, Eleanor, and you wouldn't believe it, but my mother happens to think she's the best thing since Armistice!'

Charlie laughed again. 'Yeah, Aunt Aggie told me. Congratulations, mate.'

Louie finished the last of his beer and stood up to leave. 'Well, I'm off home. Good to see you, Charlie; we'll catch up for a beer sometime... See you Monday, Harry, and don't be too long in getting home to that wife of yours.' He laughed and walked off.

Things were quiet between the two men as Charlie steered Harry down the street ten minutes later, and then Harry held back and stopped, his eyes focusing on his friend.

'Okay, Charlie, so what happened? I'm a bit the worse for the drink, but I know you well enough to see you're not quite your old self... so tell me what happened.'

Charlie didn't look at him but stood staring down the street, his voice quiet as he answered. 'The war happened, Harry... simple.' He shrugged and turned to his friend. 'Look, let's get you home and I'll come round tomorrow. We'll talk then, okay, mate?'

Harry stared back at him for a long moment. He blinked, the action slow, his eyes showing all the telltale signs of his recent drinking session. Suddenly, they widened.

'I told you about Eleanor, didn't I?'

Charlie smiled and nodded. 'Yeah, you did... it's great.'

'No, I mean... that day... at the ridge. I knew then, well, kind of... I mean, I didn't know, Nettie hadn't said, but I saw, only I didn't know then it was her...' Harry knew he wasn't making any sense and he ran a hand through his hair.

Charlie frowned. 'The ridge? What... you mean...' Charlie gestured towards Harry's leg.

'Yeah, the day I got this. I'm tellin' ya, Charlie, I was in the tent and I thought it was gas or flares or somethin' like that and I had a kind of dream... I heard a voice...' Harry became suddenly embarrassed but went on. 'And there she was. Mate, I swear I didn't even know Net was expectin'! And then when I came home... she was there, like a gift

55

from… well, I mean, out of nowhere – you know what I'm saying?'

Charlie stared at him and slowly he nodded. 'Yeah, well it was a bad day all round. I remember you saying some stuff. You were pretty much out of things and nothing was normal… for any of us, if you get my meaning.' Charlie didn't know what else to say, nor could he explain the sudden shiver running around the back of his neck, making his hairs stand on end. He mentally shook the feeling off.

'Come on, Harry, bet your tea's gone stone motherless cold by now – better get a move on.'

Harry made to walk on but stumbled slightly, his leg now unwilling to work properly. Charlie grabbed his arm and hooked it over the back of his shoulders as he steadied Harry with an arm about his waist. Then he laughed. 'Guess some things never change, eh?'

Harry laughed but then thought of Nettie, the smile dying on his face. 'You know I'll have to blame this all on you, don't you?'

Charlie gave him a dry look. 'Like I said, some things never change.'

With one supporting the other, they made their way awkwardly down the street towards home, the sound of laughter echoing in their wake.

Charlie didn't visit the next day, nor did he come the day after that, so as the week wore on, Harry decided to visit Charlie at his aunt's to find out what was going on. He was going to get to the bottom of this once and for all. This wasn't like Charlie at all – at least not the Charlie that Harry had always known in the past. And so it was that on the following Saturday afternoon, Harry and Charlie wandered about his aunt's back garden, their conversation low, easy and about nothing in particular. It was Charlie who brought it up first.

'You know, Harry, when we first went over there, I wasn't entirely sure why we were going. Oh, I remember all the bluster about "freedom for our country" and "the right to our way of life". Just how our way of life would be threatened I don't know, and what's more, I expect the bloody politicians didn't know either! But you know what? All I really thought at the time was about going over there and showing them all what us Australians were made of… or coming home a hero, for Christ's sake!' Charlie shook his head and sat down on one of the wicker chairs on the back veranda. Harry followed suit and sat looking at his friend in silence. Charlie went on.

'You know how it was. Men were being mown down… blown to bits on both sides – men like us, Harry. And I got to thinking. Germans, British, Turks, Irish, you name it… all sons or fathers… just like us. And did they know what they were fighting about? In the beginning I didn't know and didn't care, but it gets to you, Harry, you know what I mean? After a while, there's just you and them, and the rest of the world and the reasons you're there don't exist anymore.'

Charlie fell silent. Harry wasn't sure what to say. He knew what the war was like – he'd been there and it was exactly like Charlie had said. He'd seen and experienced first-hand what war could do to a man, and by God, he could still remember what it had been like to step down off that train and see Nettie and the kids, and to be able to finally distance himself, if only physically, from the far-away horror of it all. For there were still nights when he woke up in a sweat, his mind trapped back on the battlefield and every nerve in his body screaming out in fear. He would wrap himself around Nettie until the feeling left him and gradually some kind of normality would return.

Strange, thought Harry, how these things weren't talked about much.

'You stayed away so long, Charlie.' It was more a question than a statement.

Charlie leant back in his chair and gave a slight shrug. 'I wasn't ready to come home to any flag-waving or adulation. I didn't feel much like a hero, couldn't bear the thought of men patting me on the back or shaking my hand, buying me beers, simply because I was in a uniform. I mean, what was it really for? Was it for all the men I helped kill over there? Was it for putting myself through hell and returning home with all my limbs intact? And what about those blokes who *don't* have limbs intact? Do you see them celebrating their return?'

Charlie shook his head and let out a deep breath. 'I knew as soon as I got off the ship in Perth that I wouldn't be able to face things just yet. And then as luck would have it, I was sitting at the local bar one afternoon, still trying to shake off my sea legs, when I met a teamster and we got talking. He told me of a station he rode out to each week with supplies and that they needed someone to work the shearing sheds. I jumped at the chance! I needed to get out into the country, soak up the land, forget about things – or at least try to. I didn't write to anyone for a while. Finally, I wrote to Aunt Aggie; I knew she'd be worried. But I couldn't write to you, Harry, especially you, because you were over there with me, and you most of all knew what it was like. I didn't want to be reminded… not yet. I kind of lost touch with everything. Wasn't good for anything either – not conversation or company. Even lost the taste for a beer!' Charlie laughed at that last comment. Harry smiled along with him and nodded.

'You know, mate, if I didn't have Nettie and the kids to come home to, I might have done the same thing. Come to think of it, if it wasn't for Nettie and the kids, I think I would have gone around the twist. Over there it was so clear-cut, regardless of what we were fighting for – it was either you live or you die… that simple. Back here, it's not so simple. Over there, we didn't have to listen to our conscience; there was no right and wrong, just survival. But back here, it starts creeping in… I mean nobody – not you, not me, not anyone – can do what we had to do, I mean over there… live through what we had to live through, and then come home and slip right back into their old lives without it messing them about in some way.'

Harry raised his eyebrows and leant forward, his elbows on his knees, his hands clasped in front of him. 'Whatever the reason we were there, Charlie, the fact is, we *were* there, and we were so bloody lucky to come home in one piece and now… well, now I suppose we all have to deal with it in one way or another.'

Charlie was staring down at the ground as Harry spoke, but after a while, he looked up, his face thoughtful. 'So… what do you say we have a beer, mate… and we start dealing with it?'

Harry's face spread slowly into a smile.

Nettie stood watching Frank play the piano, his unruly mass of red hair flopping over his brow, his face set in concentration as his hands seemed to glide effortlessly over the keys.

She couldn't believe it. Frank! Here in her drawing room at last!

When his letter had come some weeks back informing them of his impending visit, Nettie had been over the moon. And then yesterday, when he'd actually stood on her doorstep in front of her, Nettie had thrown her arms about him and burst into tears. He'd come to stay for a few days, and Nettie had put him up in Teddy's bedroom, with Teddy being shifted back in with her and Harry. It was a bit of a tight squeeze, what with Eleanor there as well, but Nettie had been only too happy to do it. Her brother had finally come to visit, and everything was wonderful.

The piano had hardly been used since her parents had left – 'a present for the children' her mother had said. Unfortunately, neither Lizzie nor Teddy had shown much interest. In fact, if it weren't for the few times Charlie had sat down to play, they wouldn't have been familiar with the instrument at all.

They, along with Kathy, sat at the centre of the rug, oblivious to the goings-on about them as they played their various games. Eleanor, on the other hand, now three years old, stood by Frank's side, mesmerized by the sound that came out of it. To her, the huge box had had no other function in the past than being a good thing to hide behind, but Nettie now wondered if her youngest would turn out to be more musical than her siblings.

It had been a lovely afternoon. Lenny, Ruby and Kathy had come over, along with Charlie and his latest lady love, Vera, though Harry had given Nettie the impression that from Charlie's point of view, 'love' had very little to do with it. Still, thought Nettie, Vera seemed like a nice girl, and it was about time that Charlie established himself with a wife and family, given how unsettled he'd been since the war. Then again, she reasoned, Charlie hadn't been very settled *before* the war.

They'd all had a glass of sherry, a drink that made Nettie screw up her face when she sipped it, but she felt she should put on a show of being sociable despite her distaste. Ruby on the other hand, threw hers back like an old salt, as did the men, each of their faces peering into the bottom of the glass when they'd finished, evidently finding it wanting and much preferring a 'real' drink. Vera sipped hers like a lady should, giving Nettie no hint as to whether the taste was to her liking or not.

Frank was now joined at the piano by Charlie, both of them going over old tunes and working out how to play a duet while Harry stood deep in conversation with Lenny and Vera across the other side of the drawing room.

Ruby joined Nettie on the other side of the piano. 'It's been a delightful afternoon, Nettie – pity it has to end soon. I'll have to get Kathy home for tea.'

Nettie sighed, though she was happy. 'Yes, I suppose I'll have to whip something up for this lot soon myself.

'When does Frank leave?'

'Too soon I'm afraid, at the end of the week. I'll miss him when he leaves.'

'Yes.' The quiet way in which Ruby answered caused Nettie to side-glance her friend and she suddenly noticed how Ruby was looking at her brother. It dawned on her that she'd seen Ruby looking at him like that before and she wondered if Frank had noticed too. *Oh dear*.

At that moment, Frank looked up and caught them both watching him, and he smiled. 'Hey, Net, how does that song go that Mum and you used to play together on the piano?'

Nettie shrugged. 'Oh Lord, Frank, I was only a girl! I can't remember that long ago.'

The small group at the piano laughed as Frank picked Eleanor up and placed her on his lap, his attention now taken up with guiding her small hands across the keys. Nettie looked back at Ruby, who now glanced over at her husband, and Nettie wondered if it was to see if Lenny had noticed his wife's attention being taken up elsewhere. Nettie hoped not. As for Frank, Nettie was relieved to see he hadn't noticed anything, and she breathed a sigh of relief. She thought the world of Ruby, and if circumstances had been different, she might have tried a bit of matchmaking herself. But Ruby was married, to Lenny no less – the kindest and gentlest man Nettie had ever had the good fortune to know – and she didn't want anyone getting hurt, especially little Kathy. It simply wouldn't do.

Nettie bit her lip and leant towards Ruby. 'You know Frank is getting married when he returns to Queensland. I haven't met her, but both Mum and Dad say she's lovely.'

Ruby turned to Nettie, her eyes wide, her mouth hanging open. 'Really, Nettie? Oh that's wonderful news! We should give him a proper send-off before he goes, a sort of pre-wedding bash!' Ruby laughed then, leaving Nettie wondering if she'd imagined the whole thing. She made up her mind to talk to Ruby at the earliest convenience.

'I heard that, Net! I hadn't quite made up my mind to tell anyone yet!' Frank pretended annoyance at his sister's words but couldn't help smiling.

'Too late, brother dear! Now, will you make the announcement to everyone, or shall I?'

'What announcement?' Harry called out across the room.

Frank looked a little embarrassed as he stood up, taking his time to settle Eleanor on the seat next to Charlie. He cleared his throat. 'Well, the banns haven't been set yet, but—'

Everyone in the room began cheering before he could finish and Frank started to laugh. He held up his hands to silence them, and they obliged. 'Well, all going well, I'm going to be married in a few months to a wonderful lady by the name of Susan Hartwell.'

Everyone in the room suddenly surrounded Frank, whose face was turning nearly as red as his hair. The men took turns shaking his hand and congratulating him, while Vera reached up and kissed him on the cheek before stepping back to look dreamily at Charlie. Both Ruby and Nettie caught the look and exchanged glances at each other, both suppressing a knowing smile. Ruby then stepped forward and gave Frank a brief hug.

'I'm sure you'll both be very happy… and you must bring her down to meet all of us one day too!'

Frank nodded. 'Thanks, Rube. I'll do that.'

Nettie was sure now that she must have imagined the whole thing. Silly goose.

It was the perfect ending to a lovely day, and when everyone had said their goodbyes, Nettie realized how tired she was. But first there were things to be done, like cleaning up and cooking tea, and getting the kids ready for bed.

By the time she slipped between the sheets that night, she was exhausted and fell asleep almost immediately, alongside her already sleeping husband.

Eleanor lay awake in her cot. The house was silent as she stared up into the darkness, looking for the familiar presence, but it wasn't there. And in her young mind, she wasn't able to perceive who or what she was looking for and an awareness of sorts began to dawn on her that she was alone. It made her sad, fretful and suddenly insecure, and for the first time in a long time, Eleanor began to cry.

Nettie, awoken from a deep sleep by the unusual sound, rushed to her cot and picked her up. She stood there holding her close, talking to her quietly, soothingly, while patting her lightly on the back… as dark violet eyes watched on.

The next day was baking day. Ruby had come over that morning after breakfast and together they'd made puddings, cakes, beefsteak pies and a kind of fruit slice from a recipe that Lenny's mother had recently sent over. Ruby and Nettie quite often got together on baking day. It cut the job in half having two of them in the kitchen, and with Ruby having only Lenny and Kathy to bake for, it made good sense for the two women to pool their resources and then split the end product, with a bit more left for Nettie given that she had a couple of extra mouths to feed.

Harry and Lenny were both at work, and Frank had gone down the street to 'stretch the legs and browse a bit', he'd said. Lizzie, Teddy and Kathy were playing out in the backyard, while Eleanor sat on the high stool at the bench. Nettie had given her an offcut of pastry with strict instructions not to eat it, as it would give her indigestion. Eleanor now sat flattening it out and then rolling it up again upon the wooden surface, until it resembled nothing more than a grubby piece of rubber. She sang as she worked, her soft, high-pitched voice ringing out in some silly tune that had apparently sprung from her own youthful imagination. The women worked around her, scraping flour from the sideboard and stacking bowls, trays and utensils ready for washing as they talked.

'How's Lenny going at his job, Rube?' The kitchen was hot from the stove and Nettie went to open the window while Ruby filled the kettle.

'Oh, okay I suppose… he doesn't say much about it really.'

Nettie turned to her in surprise. 'He doesn't? Harry talks about his job so much, I practically know the life story of everyone he works with!' Nettie started to giggle but stopped when she saw the thoughtful look on Ruby's face. She reached up for the cups, the thought occurring to her that this wasn't the first time of late that Ruby had been non-committal where Lenny was concerned. She wondered if she should pursue it.

'You know it was good to see him the other day, what with Frank here and all… I hardly clap my eyes on him at all these days.' Nettie placed the cups on the small table and went to fetch the teapot while Ruby wiped the bench around Eleanor, her back conspicuously turned so Nettie couldn't see her face.

'No, none of us do.' Ruby's voice was quiet and a little muffled as she ran her cloth needlessly over the same spots on the bench. Nettie frowned and plonked the teapot down on the table so she could stand with her hands on her hips. 'Okay, Ruby Jenson, are you going to tell me what's been going on?'

Ruby's hand stilled and slowly she turned to Nettie, her eyes noticeably glassy, her expression strained. Nettie took one look at her and reached for Eleanor.

'Sweetie, we have to clean up now. Why don't you go and find Stella? I think she may be under your cot.'

Nettie smiled at her youngest daughter and, trying to keep things light, said airily, 'She calls her doll Stella, though where she got the name from is anybody's guess.'

Ruby tried to smile. 'Hillary perhaps?'

Eleanor, now suddenly bored with the pastry at the mention of her doll, ran from the room calling out its name, as though it would be perfectly natural for Stella, on hearing herself being summoned, to come running out to meet her.

Nettie now gave her undivided attention to her friend.

Ruby simply stared at Nettie as though willing her to understand, but Nettie didn't want to make any assumptions. The kettle was boiling and she went over to take it off the stove.

'Come and sit down. We'll have a cup of tea… and we'll try out one of these cakes.'

Nettie reached for the tray on the side bench.

'I think Lenny is seeing someone else.'

Nettie didn't say anything for a moment as she calmly scooped some tea leaves into the pot and then poured the water in, before sitting down and looking at Ruby. 'Are you sure?'

Ruby shrugged, her eyes downcast. 'He doesn't talk about his work at all, not like he used to… and while he's home, he spends all his time inventing things to do or places to go, like he doesn't want to spend any time with me and Kathy. And when he goes out, he's gone for the longest time, even when he says he's just stepping out for tobacco or going to see if some seeds for the garden have come in yet. Seeds! What seeds is he talking about, Nettie? It's just some trumped-up excuse to leave…' Ruby threw her hands up to cover her face and just as quickly took them away again as she took a deep breath, blinking rapidly. Nettie was stunned.

'Have you spoken to him about it? I mean, perhaps it's all a misunderstanding.'

But Ruby was shaking her head as she spoke. 'I can't. And I don't think I want to know… not if it's another woman… I couldn't bear it, Nettie, do you understand?'

Nettie nodded. 'What about… well… um…'

Ruby's raised her eyebrows and finished for her. 'He doesn't come near me.'

Nettie sat dumbfounded. Words failed her as her mind scrambled for something to say.

Ruby continued, her voice now a little guilty. 'You know, the other day, when Frank was here, I wondered what it would be like to actually do… that… with a man other than Lenny.'

Nettie's eyes widened, memories of her own perceptions that day coming back to her, and she suddenly understood. 'And you thought about Frank?'

Ruby gave a slight nod. 'He was so friendly and easy-going, and Lenny had been so distant that I... thought... just for a moment... Of course I don't think I could actually go through with it... and for that matter, Frank wouldn't have in any case. You don't think badly of me, do you?'

Nettie was quick to reassure her. 'Of course not! How could I?'

Ruby smiled at her, a little more relaxed now that she'd put things out in the open. Nettie set about pouring tea into the cups before her. 'Rube, Lenny is a good man, and he loves you, I'm sure. I think, regardless of what he might say, you have to at least talk to him; it may be something completely different, or perhaps you're building it up into more than it is.'

Ruby thought a moment and nodded. 'I guess I can't go on like this, can I?

Nettie shook her head. 'It can't be good for you... or Kathy for that matter. You need to find out what's going on.'

Ruby looked at Nettie for a moment, her expression thoughtful, and then suddenly she leant across and grabbed a cake from the tray. 'Oh bosh to it all!' In one quick movement, she bit off half the cake, her eyes widening in disbelief at what she'd just done, her cheeks bulging as she tried to chew. Nettie's mouth hung open as she watched her and then she burst out laughing.

'Taste okay?'

Ruby nearly choked as she laughed too, her words coming out distorted as she tried to answer with her mouth full. 'Shoulda iced 'em firs'!'

They laughed so loud the children came running in from

outside, as did Eleanor from the bedroom, their eyes wide and curious as to what the commotion was all about. Seconds later, Frank entered the kitchen, his hat dangling from his hand as he, too, watched the small group and wondered if the two women had been secretly tucking into the sherry while he'd been gone.

CHAPTER THREE

A week later, Lenny wandered aimlessly down the main street, his noticeable size and stature marking his meandering progress through the usual hustle and bustle of everyday activities. He'd been dismissed from work early, an increasingly worrisome occurrence over the last few weeks, due to shortages beyond the company's control… or so he'd been informed. Ruby had no idea of his recent falling-off in hours, though just why Lenny had kept his wife ignorant of this fact, he couldn't say. Still, whether he would choose to tell her or not would be taken out of his hands soon enough when it became apparent that his wages were down. But the impending lack of money wasn't the only thing that was causing him disquiet. It was his own growing anxiety and restlessness over the preceding months that really had him worried.

When he'd first come home from France, he'd felt finally that there had been an end to it. To be back among his family and friends was the one thing he'd been sure he'd needed – that just the simple normality of his roots would give him back his sense of security and well-being. But nothing had been quite the same. Oh, he loved Ruby all right, and the thought of anything happening to her or Kathy was a hell ten times worse than anything he'd had to experience overseas. But something was lacking, something he couldn't quite explain.

They'd told him he might experience periods of anxiety, and he'd had his share of those, indeed he had. At times, he'd found himself so overwhelmed by it that his mind would slip momentarily into a kind of paranoia, until all he'd been able to do was leave the house, go walking, anywhere and for as long as it took, for the feeling to leave him. It was something he couldn't talk about, not with anyone – not even Ruby. He knew she was aware that all wasn't right with him but talking about it seemed to weaken his ability to push it away, and he was convinced that to bring it out in the open like that would surely push him into some kind of breakdown. He'd been told it would take time to adjust, find his feet again, but he hadn't counted on it taking this long.

He'd been home nearly two years now. No one else around him seemed to be feeling the same way. Harry was the same Harry he'd always been, nothing wrong there, and Charlie, though he'd apparently got off to a shaky start on arriving back in Australia, was now going about his life the way he'd always done.

Lenny stopped to look through the window of a café. Peering through the glass at the various scones and pastries on display, he felt his stomach growl and contemplated a cup of tea and something to eat – then dismissed the idea and walked on. He sidestepped a man on a bicycle and promptly bumped into a woman, causing her to drop her shopping case, its contents spilling out onto the road. After retrieving her goods and with much apology, he tipped his hat and decided to cross the road, his idea being to take himself out of harm's way for a spell and sit awhile in the park opposite, perhaps fill his pipe and smoke a bit.

As he stepped off the side path, the offensive noise of a motor car passing close by caused him to look up, while at the same time, a baker in his horse-drawn cart going about his daily rounds stalled as the horse reared, its ears slanted back in fear at the sudden noise Lenny stopped momentarily to watch the spectacle, his attention taken away from the main thoroughfare in which he now stood. A bell sounded off to his right, and too late Lenny looked around to see the advancing tram almost upon him. He heard someone yell. 'Look out there!'

The last thing he remembered was the pain shooting across the back of his head…

Vera sat at Nettie's kitchen table. She'd been a regular visitor since that afternoon they'd all crowded around the piano as Frank had played. Already, Nettie was missing her brother, and she now longed for his next visit, hopefully with his new wife in tow. As for Vera, Nettie could well imagine why the pretty brunette spent so much time at their home, Charlie being such a close friend of Harry's.

It was apparent to all that she had her sights set on the elusive young man and Nettie sighed. It wasn't the first time some young filly had set her cap for Charlie, though Nettie thought it might be the last as she hadn't ever met a girl as single-minded as Vera. Her cunning and trickery in getting him alone even for just a moment was to be applauded, and Nettie smiled to herself. Both she and Ruby had made bets as to how long it would take Charlie to come around.

And what about Charlie's views on the matter? Her

questions to Harry on the subject were met with glib replies and non-committals, as was the way with men on such matters… especially where their friends were concerned. Indeed, thought Nettie, Charlie was probably heralded as the last surviving bachelor among his peers, a status not easily relinquished, or so it would seem.

'You know, we could take a walk along the Torrens, Nettie. You never seem to get out enough in my book, and I'm sure the children would relish the outing.' Vera looked hopeful and Nettie smiled secretively.

'That's right. And you never know who we might meet either! Why, Charlie was saying just the other day how he liked to accompany his aunt Aggie for a stroll along the banks, and I suppose if we did the same, then we might be fortunate enough to see them there!'

Vera blushed and looked away. Nettie giggled. 'Oh, Vera, you don't have to pretend with me. It's plain to everyone how you feel about him.'

Vera looked horrified, her eyes opening wide. 'Everyone?'

The smile left Nettie's face instantly as she realized her slip-up. She hadn't meant to embarrass Vera and she immediately set about rectifying the situation.

'Well, no, not everyone exactly… just me and Ruby really, and then only because, well, we're women and… we see these things a little more plainly than the men do, I'm sure… and… well, you really don't have to worry, Vera. I mean… well, neither Charlie or Harry has said anything to me…'

Oh dear, thought Nettie. She seemed to be digging herself in deeper here. She threw up her hands in frustration. 'Oh for goodness' sake, Vera, you're a fine catch, and if Charlie hasn't realized that by now, why then he's a fool and he doesn't deserve you at all!'

Nettie now stood staring at Vera boldly, her hands on her hips and an expression of *so there, I've said it* upon her face.

Vera was quiet and then she sighed. 'I wish someone would convince him of that fact.'

Nettie gave a slight nod and raised her eyebrows. 'Ah well, that's always the hard part.' Then she began to chuckle softly. 'Mind you, it can also be the fun part too, if I remember correctly!'

Vera cagily side-glanced Nettie, a small smile playing about her mouth. 'I suppose I'll have to wait and see, won't I?'

The conversation was abruptly ended as Eleanor came running into the kitchen, an angry Teddy close on her heels. Teddy had been kept home from school that morning after complaining of a stomachache, but his behaviour over the day had Nettie wondering if he'd invented his ailment just to play hooky.

'Mum, she's got my soldiers and she won't give 'em back! Make her give 'em back to me!'

Nettie sighed, her expression apologetic as she glanced over at Vera, who in turn could only manage a tight smile.

Vera regarded the two children in front of her as nothing more than a bothersome disturbance. She'd made up her mind that when Charlie finally realized his feelings for her and made her his wife, she would have to make it perfectly clear to him that children were not in the picture. After all, they could be so upsetting to one's social calendar… just look at poor Nettie! She was never out and about, was she? Everywhere she went, she had her entire brood at her side! *Not for me,* thought Vera.

Nettie chased her youngest daughter around the table,

finally heading her off when Eleanor cornered herself between the wood stove and the kitchen bench, her apron rolled upward, her small fingers clutching the edge of it possessively as she held her ill-gotten stash of Teddy's soldiers away from her mother.

'Come on, Eleanor, give them back. They're Teddy's – you know they are.' Nettie squatted down in front of her daughter, her expression beseeching but her tone authoritative.

Eleanor knew she would have to give them back but then looked over her mother's shoulder at her brother and saw him smirking in satisfaction. She suddenly changed her mind and pulled her apron towards herself, grasping it tighter.

It was then that Vera decided to take her leave. 'Well, it seems you have your hands full, Nettie. Perhaps we'll take a walk down the Torrens another day.' Vera smoothed the back of her hair down with a gloved hand and walked daintily out of the kitchen to retrieve her hat.

Nettie peered up at her from her position by the stove, and in the second it took to look away, Eleanor darted out from her corner and bolted off around the counter and out through the door. Teddy started to yell once more as he made a dash for his sister, startling Vera and causing her to swing round, her hand at her throat, her eyes wide in sudden fright. Nettie pursed her lips in annoyance and thought she'd better offload her uneasy visitor first. She would deal with her wayward children in a moment.

But as she saw Vera to the door, it occurred to Nettie that she wasn't entirely sure that she favoured the dark-haired beauty after all. *Lacking in substance, Nettie!* her mother would say.

· · ·

Nettie found Teddy and Eleanor sitting on the mat in her bedroom, their previous hostilities seemingly forgotten as Eleanor doled out brightly coloured French cavaliers from the stash in her apron, one for Teddy and then one for her and so on. Teddy looked up as his mother entered and grinned at her.

'I'm going to be Napoleon, Mum!'

Nettie smiled indulgently. 'Are you, dear?' She looked at Eleanor. 'And who are you going to be, sweetie?'

Eleanor didn't look up. She seemed captivated by the soldier in her hand, her finger running over the smooth surface of the tin figure, her eyes unblinking as her young mind tried to grasp something just out of reach.

She could hear the cheering of the crowd… see them… a sea of faces, cruel, laughing… Some other place; she didn't know it… A woman crying, scared and crying… It was a feeling rather than a memory. She didn't understand… then a tall man… nice man… he made everything all right again… Trying to hold the thoughts flashing by… only fragments…

'Eleanor?'

Nettie's voice startled Eleanor and she looked up sharply before looking about her as though suddenly remembering where she was. 'I wanna be Napollan too!'

Teddy rolled his eyes. 'You can't be Napoleon, silly – there can only be one and I'm him!'

Eleanor frowned at her brother and then, without warning, threw the soldier at him, hitting him in the face. Teddy, his hand over his cheek, began to yell, while Nettie closed her eyes and sighed, silently praying for tolerance.

She didn't see Harry come up behind her. 'What's all this then?'

Nettie swung around, surprised at his voice and grateful too that now he was home, he could sort these two out for her. 'You're home early.'

Teddy was still wailing in the background, and Harry walked swiftly over to pick him up.

He turned to Nettie, his face serious as he ruffled his young son's mop of fair hair. Teddy immediately stopped crying and slid down out of his father's grasp to sit down once more with his sister, hoping to renew his game, even though she was only a girl.

Nettie was looking at her husband's grim face. 'What's the matter? What's happened? Is it work?'

Harry steered her out the door by the elbow and spoke close to her, his voice quiet.

'Net, there's been an accident with Lenny.'

Nettie's hand instantly came up to cover her mouth.

'Some sort of tram accident. He's in hospital… they say he might not wake up.'

'A tram accident?' Nettie's heart was racing, expecting the worst. 'Is he going to be all right?' Suddenly she remembered Ruby. 'Oh, Harry, where's Ruby? Does she know?'

Harry nodded. 'She's down there with him now. I was thinking it might be better if you go down there and sit with her awhile, leave the kids here with me.'

Nettie went to hurry off but then turned back. 'Watch for Lizzie, won't you? She should be home from school soon.'

Harry nodded while waving at her to hurry her along. He turned back to his other two. 'So, Ted… why are you home from school today?'

Teddy was suddenly still. He looked up guiltily to find his father looking back down at him, his eyebrows raised, an indulgent yet all-knowing smirk upon his face.

Ruby sat alongside Lenny at the hospital, her hands wrapped firmly around his large one, her eyes red-rimmed and fretful as she stared fixedly at his profile, willing him to wake up. Nettie had been and gone some two hours before; she'd stayed for a while with Ruby and then had finally suggested she take Kathy home with her. Ruby was thankful for that at least; she didn't know what she would have done without Nettie.

Why wouldn't he wake up! She leant over further, her expression pleading. 'Lenny… please, Lenny, you have to wake up… please!'

The doctor had not been forthcoming. He'd merely informed her that due to Lenny's head injury, it was impossible to tell how long he would remain in this state; nor could he tell her how Lenny would be if and when he did finally wake up. He appealed to her to be patient; however patience was not one of Ruby's strong points.

And so now she sat anxiously waiting for any signs of consciousness and eagerly watching the nurses as they came to check Lenny's vital signs every hour, hoping they could shed some more light on his situation. But they barely acknowledged her. *Bunch of starched white prigs, the lot of them!* thought Ruby. *That's what they are.*

Just then, as if to prove her wrong, a nurse appeared by Ruby's side. 'Can I get you anything, Mrs Jenson? A cup of tea perhaps?'

'Oh… no, thank you… I'll be fine.' Ruby decided to smile at the nurse.

'Your husband may not wake up all night, you know. Are you sure?'

Ruby shook her head. 'No, thank you… I'm fine. Are you positive he'll be asleep all night?'

The nurse tried to explain. 'It's hard to tell with head

injuries. He could wake up soon or he could wake up tomorrow or… We can't be sure really. He's taken a bit of a knock so perhaps it wouldn't be a good idea to count on anything too soon.'

Ruby's shoulders slumped. 'Perhaps I will have that cup of tea after all.'

The nurse went to walk away and, as an afterthought, Ruby called after her, 'Thank you.'

Lenny didn't wake up that night or all the next day, but finally in the early hours of the next morning, he opened his eyes. It was dark and he didn't know where he was. He tried to remember what happened.

As he moved his head to look about him, a wave of pain shot across the back of his head, causing him to groan loudly.

'Lenny?'

Lenny knew that voice and turned towards it, the action causing another wave of pain.

'Rube?' His voice was a mere whisper, his mouth so parched and his throat so raw and gritty, he felt sure it must be lined with sand.

Ruby's form now hovered over him. He could just make out her face in the dim light. Why was it so dark? She swam in and out of focus as his vision blurred.

'Lenny? Are you awake?'

His vision cleared momentarily at the sound of her voice. 'What happened?'

'Oh, I'm so glad you're awake! You were knocked over by a tram.'

He frowned, and then groaned once more, even that small movement causing him pain. 'How come I can't see properly? Something happened to my eyes?'

It dawned on Ruby then that he wasn't aware of the time of day. She giggled in relief.

'It's still night time, the lamps have been turned low… everyone in the hospital is still asleep.'

Lenny tried to peer through the darkness. 'Hospital?'

By the afternoon of the next day, Lenny was more alert. It still hurt a great deal for him to move his head too much, and the lump at the back was what Lenny had described as the 'size of a small country', but he was getting better.

Nettie came in to visit him and brought Kathy along with her. The little girl proceeded to climb up on the bed and hug her father, until the nurse came in and put a stop to it, telling them all that they must 'observe hospital regulations'.

Harry called in after work but didn't stay long. He felt awkward and uncomfortable in hospital surroundings, much preferring to have a beer with Lenny down the pub when he was better.

After the first couple of days, Ruby started going home of a night and coming back to see him while Kathy was at school. And towards the end of the week, Charlie came, accompanied by a clinging Vera, who seemed more interested in hanging off Charlie's arm than visiting Lenny. Nettie happened to be present at the time, and as she observed Vera's fawning – and as much as she knew it was none of her affair – she couldn't stop herself from thinking that her opinion of the girl had slipped down another notch.

But the bad news came the following week. Lenny was due to go home the next day, pending the doctor's visit, when his boss, Arthur Tremworth, came in to see him. Lenny had been let go from his job, a cruel blow at such a time, but one that was unavoidable.

A sheepish Arthur stood at the side of his bed with hat in hands and apologized.

'With all the ex-servicemen that are out there looking for work and your position remaining vacant for so long… I'm sorry, Lenny, I tried to beg off as long as I could, but in the end, they couldn't be swayed. I'm afraid it became a question of priorities.'

He'd apologized again and then left. Lenny was stunned by the news; Ruby was fit to be tied. 'What are we supposed to do now? How can they just drop people as though there were suddenly no mouths to feed at home or no bills to pay?'

Lenny tried calming her down. 'Shh, love, don't worry. I'm sure I'll get another job… It's not the end of the world. I'll be up in no time and all will be well again – you'll see.'

Ruby felt ashamed at her sudden outburst. 'I'm sorry, Lenny. It's enough for the present time that you're going to be all right.' Her voice became stern. 'What would I have done without you? You could have been killed!'

Lenny smiled. That was more like the Ruby he knew.

A few weeks later, Lenny, now home and fit again, trod the streets every day looking for work. But the story was the same everywhere: too many people and not enough work, and until factories and other places of business were able to revert to normal productivity, away from their previous function of meeting war-time requirements, things would remain the same.

To make matters worse, what available products had soared in price, and with such a broad employment list to pick from, employers did not feel the need to bring wages into line with the increases and new taxes, causing further grief on already burdened households.

On the home front, however, things had been working out well for Lenny and Ruby. The recent tram accident had seemed to bring things into perspective for Lenny a lot more, and he'd spoken at length to Ruby about the anxieties and apprehensions he'd been carrying about with him. No longer did he feel the need to get away as he had before and talking to Ruby ended up being the best kind of therapy he could have hoped for by far.

Ruby, on discovering his past attitudes had nothing to do with another woman, told herself what a fool she'd been for not asking her husband in the first place what the problem was, but the Jenson household was now a happy one. Getting poorer... but happy just the same.

Harry's job had remained secure, but with prices going through the roof, things were a little tighter than they had been, though he and Nettie were by no means struggling yet. Nettie had simply cut back on the unnecessary things, like more expensive cuts of meat or buying an unneeded dress for Lizzie or Eleanor, simply because she liked the colour. Teddy learned to play with the toys he had instead of Nettie always adding more to a set of soldiers or farm animals, though Nettie noticed that Harry's spending at the local bar hadn't seemed to diminish at all and was slightly put out that not all in the family were sacrificing.

She helped Ruby out as much as she could without it appearing like charity, though every time she did, Nettie could see the conflicting emotions upon her friend's face. Ruby's pride forbade her from taking handouts, while at the same time, the much-needed food or spare shillings that Nettie sent her way were invaluable to the comfort of her family, and so she was forced to set aside her wounded pride and tell herself that these times called for practicality and common sense. Ruby's face would flame red in embarrassment as she thanked Nettie time and again, but as always, Nettie would simply wave her thanks away while telling her, 'Don't give it another thought, Rube – you'd do the same for me.'

≈

Charlie sat at the bar, a beer at one elbow, his hat set down beside the other as his fingers unconsciously stacked and restacked his small change upon the highly polished wooden surface in front of him. He sat gazing at the wall behind the bar with its various paintings, mirrors and advertisements of 'best beers' and 'ladies' wines'. Charlie reckoned he could describe every curve and colour in the paintings, as well as every flaw or crack in the plastered cornicing above without ever having to lay eyes on it again.

He looked about him occasionally at the changing clientele and watched Jerry go about his business. He was so adept at handling his patrons, seemingly giving his undivided attention to them with his friendly banter and his setting out of drinks upon the bar, yet his eyes never missed a thing in other parts of the room. Charlie thought Jerry was undoubtedly in his element, almost certainly doing the thing he was both best at and liked doing.

It prompted Charlie to assess his own situation, something he'd done quite often over the last few months. And like before, his thoughts brought him to the idea of going west again. Having got used to working in a different environment than the city, he craved now the open spaces and a less complex lifestyle than the one he had. The family near Perth had told him he would be welcome back whenever he chose, and though shearing could be back-breaking work, it gave him more satisfaction than anything he could think of doing in the city.

He would come into his own when Aunt Aggie died. A trust fund had been set up for him by his father, though the thought of his beloved aunt not being around anymore was something Charlie didn't want to think about. But he had a sneaking suspicion that Vera had thought of it – after all, it was common knowledge among those who knew him so there was no reason she wouldn't be privy to it as well.

It had occurred to Charlie that he'd become a bit of a wandering soul since the war, the hustle and bustle of city life only making him feel hemmed in and 'itchy' to get moving. He also knew that if he stayed in Adelaide, Vera would have him walking down an aisle before he'd even made up his mind to do so, and while she'd been good company, if a little smothering at times, he was not one to settle himself down to a life of domestic stability. To Charlie, the matrimonial state would be anything but stable for him, and he knew he would want out in no time.

Already his mind wandered back to the peaceful evenings he'd spent walking around the outskirts of the station in Western Australia, the only sound in the surrounding stillness coming from a late crow in the distance or an occasional bleat of protest from the sheep as he waded through their woolly huddle, all set against the backdrop of a breathtaking sunset of orange and reds on an uncluttered horizon. Charlie had had his fill of busy streets and bustling crowds. He could envision a life with Vera, all set out with house payments and a six-day working week, an obligatory requirement until his money came in, with his weekends spent digging the garden or fixing the fence and his grand reward to be seen out in society on a Saturday night at some well-planned and tedious affair. To Charlie, that was a life not worth living.

His father's trust fund was worth several thousand pounds and such an amount would be well over what a man needed to buy himself property or a business, or some nice townhouse in the hobnob part of Adelaide. This could all be bought complete with a sound reputation and an instant circle of respectable friends. And of course, a man of that standing would be welcomed anywhere and in any home with a wife by his side; the right wife, of course – one of beauty, good taste and style. Vera would no doubt fill that role flawlessly, he thought, and frowned. Thinking on it now, Charlie would much prefer the six-day working week and a garden to dig than the sham of an existence he envisioned if Vera were to get her claws into him.

At least now, the friends he had were real friends who took an honest approach and led an honest life and who measured his friendship by himself alone and not what he had in his bank account. *Yep*, thought Charlie, *time to move on*.

Lenny's problem of gaining employment was to be short-lived, for one evening as he and Ruby sat contemplating their finances, Arthur Tremworth appeared at the door. He was delighted to be able to offer Lenny his old job back… that is, if Lenny still wanted it. It seemed business was slowly starting to pick up again, and Arthur thought it was only fair to offer work to those who had recently been retrenched, rather than get new people in. Besides, Arthur liked Lenny and his wife. The visit to their home was not the required thing to do, but Arthur wanted to inform Lenny himself, in case the big man didn't find out in time. He informed the much-relieved couple that Lenny's hours would not be as much as before, but things were picking up.

That night, both Lenny and Ruby slept soundly.

The post-war industry quickly went back to normal over the next couple of years, bringing with it an equally quick increase in employment opportunities. Australia's industry then hit its peak as it hurriedly tried to fill a backlog of consumer demands for products that had previously been in short supply. Most worked a forty-eight-hour week, and with the changing of government, many of the workforce, both men and women, became unionized, enabling them to demand better working conditions.

Harry and Nettie bought their first car, a Ford Model T. It had been Harry's dream to own a car for quite a while, and though it cost around two hundred pounds – much more money than Nettie had managed to put away – Harry had arranged hire purchase with the bank, something Nettie had no experience with and, therefore, very little trust in. But Harry had finally brought his wife round to his way of thinking with proposed trips to the country and by reminding her that she wouldn't have to rely on public transport all the time.

'Frank and Susan have been driving about in their own car for months now, Net! And Mum has had some sort of motor car or other for years now… even though she doesn't drive it herself… though I hear Rosie has been getting quite familiar behind the wheel.'

Harry laughed at the idea of dear old Rosie driving about in a car, but then it didn't surprise him really, for Rosie had always been willing to try anything once. His mother, on the other hand, would think it far too undignified to be seen driving one's self about. She'd remarked to him before that it was a job for servants or chauffeurs – that is, if one was fortunate enough to have a chauffeur in one's employ.

'Yes, I know, Harry, but Hillary can afford such luxuries, and Frank and Susan can too, at least for the moment – after all, they haven't a family to feed yet. Are you sure we haven't bitten off more than we can chew?'

Harry pulled her into his arms and kissed the top of her

head. 'It's definitely the wave of the future, and we must keep up with the times, if only for the children's sake.'

Nettie leaned back to look up at his face, her eyes wide. 'Harry Grayson, don't you dare treat me like some idiot who's only just come down in the last hail. We both know you're the one who wants the car, so don't go handing me this twaddle about any future waves or whatever, and as for our children's sake? Well, they can keep up with the times in their way and on their own money too!'

Harry threw back his head and laughed loudly, hugging her all the more. A smile tugged at Nettie's mouth until she, too, was laughing along with him.

The family's first ride in the shiny black car was a momentous occasion. Lenny, Ruby and even Hillary stood on the roadside to watch, her face set in dignified curiosity, alternating between the familiar sniff as she looked up the street and back again and waving encouragingly at an awestruck Eleanor, wedged in between her parents on the front seat. Lizzie sat erect and important, hoping some of her friends would be out and about to see her parading down the main street, while Teddy sat eying his father's maneuvering of the complicated vehicle and secretly envisioning himself at the wheel.

It was the first of many family outings, and true to his word, Harry took them out for a ride in the country, though he would only venture as far as half a tank would take them, as petrol was nearly double the price once out of the city limits.

Charlie, after talking about going west for some time, finally did. As was his nature, he simply up and left one day with little warning and no fanfare, leaving a distraught Vera to wonder where she'd gone wrong. He'd managed a flying visit to Harry and Nettie the night before to inform them of his intentions, and then, with a promise to write, he was gone.

Although Vera wasn't one of Nettie's favourite people, she couldn't help feeling sorry for the crestfallen beauty and said as much to Harry. Harry looked at her with a hint of a smile upon his face.

'You weren't so bothered about Vera's feelings when she was trying to become Mrs Bradford. Now Charlie leaves, Vera's upset and you're saying, "Oh the poor thing!"' Harry tried to mimic Nettie's voice.

Nettie was not amused. 'If you must know, I don't like to see anyone upset – that is, if it's genuine – but in any case, I stand by my opinion that I don't think she would have made a good wife for Charlie!'

Harry knew what his wife meant; after all, he'd secretly thought the same thing.

Nettie went on. 'Well, in any case, it looks like Charlie hasn't been influenced much at all by Vera… otherwise he wouldn't be leaving, would he?'

Harry shrugged. 'I suppose you're right.' He knew exactly what Charlie thought of Vera. Charlie had informed him of everything there was to know about that particular union – their intimacies, as well as Charlie's doubts and Vera's preoccupation with her and Charlie's future plans. He'd decided it wasn't something he would discuss with Nettie.

When Hillary heard of Charlie's departure, she was a little disappointed; she'd always had a soft spot for Agatha Bradford's nephew and grudgingly admitted to herself that he was a good influence on her son as well. Like many people, she'd thought Vera was a good match for Charlie, a girl that would help put him in what she thought of as his proper place in society, but on getting to know more about her, she'd decided the girl was a little too vain for her liking, even a little shallow… which would definitely *not* suit Charlie. A pity, as they would have made a handsome pair.

Her remarks on this to Harry one day simply made him groan. 'Mum, don't you see? Charlie doesn't worry about such things as "society"' and appearances. He only wants to do what makes him happy and right now… he's happy!'

Hillary had only sniffed in reply.

Her visits in the last couple of years had become more frequent, due mainly to her affection for her youngest granddaughter, a situation that Nettie still fretted about as being a little unhealthy for her other two children.

Hillary would greet Lizzie and Teddy in the way she always had, so to them she seemed unapproachable and a little condescending, which made them uncomfortable around her. Lizzie, especially, was starting to act in much the same way towards her grandmother, another concern of Nettie's – one that had yet to be dealt with.

As for Eleanor, she had no such feelings where Hillary was concerned. When her grandmother came to visit, she would run and hug her with no thought to any lack of propriety or pretence of decorum, and astoundingly to all present, Hillary would just as warmly return her greeting.

Just why Hillary had taken to her youngest daughter so easily and quickly, Nettie could not fathom. As a mother, she could well see her youngest child's attributes, but what of her other two?

Eleanor was now at school, and she didn't like it. She saw most of the teachers as crotchety and overbearing, more interested in their set of unwavering rules than in any worthwhile education. Of course, this wasn't entirely true, but to the five-year-old Eleanor, they were darkly clad tyrants with wizened and often pinched features who seemed to stare imperiously down at her, so if she saw any of them coming towards her, it was enough to intimidate her to the point of violent trembling. She often longed to be home beside her mother, where the game of school she'd played with her doll, Stella – where she was the teacher and Stella the pupil – was far and away more pleasant than the real thing, but her constant pleas to Nettie had been met first with sympathy and understanding, then optimistic encouragement and finally stern reprimand.

Both Lizzie and Teddy were in sixth and third grade respectively, and the times Eleanor spied them in the schoolyard, they appeared to be coping much better than she was. Eleanor would stand watching her siblings at play, just the mere familiarity of them lending her at least some measure of comfort. Occasionally, Teddy would spy his younger sister and come skipping up to her, his friends crowding around in curiosity, but Eleanor would only hang her head shyly and scrape the ground in front of her with her shoe until Teddy, his attention taken up with yet another game in the offing, would bolt right off again.

Like Eleanor, there was one girl at school who also didn't join in with the others. She was one of the younger children in Lizzie's mixed class of third and fourth graders but still three years older than Eleanor. Her name was Lucy Phipps.

Eleanor and Lucy had noticed each other on many an occasion during the lunch period and took to smiling at each other shyly, and though Lucy was well into her eighth year – perhaps owing to a kind of unusual astuteness that seemed to surround Eleanor – it didn't seem to bother her that Eleanor was considerably younger. Before long they had taken to searching for each other when the lunch bell sounded.

Lucy was timid and not like the others, which suited Eleanor just fine. 'Her father is a cripple,' it was whispered, and, 'My mother said he has no legs at all… Can you imagine anything so dreadful? It must be awful!', while someone else was heard saying, 'I heard Lucy's mother ran away because she couldn't stand to look at him!'

These cruel taunts were true in part. Lucy lived with her father, whose legs had been lost below the knees in the war. They lived at the home of her father's parents, and though her mother, Alice, had indeed left, it was perhaps not for the reasons of her husband's infirmity, but more because of what that infirmity had done to him. Mickey Phipps was no longer the man he used to be. He had turned quickly from the outgoing, friendly and devil-may-care person he'd once been into an embittered and haunted soul whose only outlet was to be found at the bottom of a whiskey bottle.

His tormented spirit was considerably worsened by his wife's absence. Most days he would lock himself away in the downstairs parlour, peering out from behind the lace curtains at a world he saw as having no place for him anymore, a small table equipped with bottle and glass at his side, while cursing the day he ever went to war. Mickey was barely civil to his parents, who now held only a glimmer of hope for their son's salvation, and as for his daughter… Mickey tried to forget he had one.

None of this mattered to Eleanor. She'd found a friend in Lucy, and whatever the other children said about her did nothing to sway her newfound friendship with the quiet, though sometimes sad, older girl.

Lizzie found their friendship odd and said as much to Nettie. 'All my friends are talking about it, Mum! How Eleanor and Lucy are friends, and you know what? She's eight years old! Why doesn't she find someone else her own age instead of my sister!' Lizzie then stared accusingly at

Eleanor, who, for some reason that escaped her, thought she was going to be in trouble.

Nettie had heard her own stories about the troubled Phipps household and though her heart went out to them, she wasn't entirely sure if it was a good idea for her daughter, who was at such an impressionable age, to be influenced in any way by things she didn't understand... though in just what way, Nettie wasn't sure. She looked thoughtfully at Eleanor and realized that it could have so easily been her father instead of Mickey living the remainder of his life in a wheelchair, and she imagined what it must be like to live with such dire consequences.

Her voice was quiet as she spoke. 'Why don't you bring young Lucy over to play on the weekend, sweetie? I'd like to meet her.'

Lizzie's groan sounded behind her. 'You don't really mean that, Mum? What would I say to her?'

Nettie gave a half-smile to her eldest daughter. 'Well, I suppose you don't really have to worry about that, do you, dear? After all, Lucy is Eleanor's friend, not yours.'

'But she's only a grade below me! I don't know what to say to her, and she'll think I don't like her!'

Nettie's raised eyebrow was the only reply she needed to give. Lizzie stormed out of the room in a huff.

Nettie turned back to Eleanor. 'She may prove to be a little old for you, dear, but we'll see, all right?'

Eleanor wasn't entirely sure what all the fuss was about, but she nodded and grinned back at her mother. She was going to have a friend over on the weekend! Nothing could spoil that!

But when Saturday morning came and the eagerly awaited knock on the front door finally came, a breathless Eleanor ran to the door to be met only by a young boy holding an envelope towards her.

'This be the Grayson place?' The boy wiped his nose with the back of his sleeve as he waited for Eleanor to acknowledge his question.

Nettie had come to the door behind Eleanor and answered for her. 'Yes, it is. Can I help you?'

Eleanor stood staring at the boy, her eyes wide and curious.

Now in the presence of an adult, the boy stood suddenly erect and slid a dirty chequered cap from his head. 'I got a note here for you... ran all the way down two streets to bring it.'

Nettie nodded. 'Just a moment.' She left Eleanor still gaping at the boy, who now proceeded to stare right back at her.

Nettie reappeared and handed him tuppence.

'Thanks, missus.' And with that he was off, but not before slyly darting his tongue out at the strange little girl still staring at him.

Nettie ushered Eleanor inside and opened the envelope. She frowned as she read it.

'Seems Lucy can't stop by today after all, dear. This note is from her grandmother. She says that Lucy has too much to do at home on weekends and won't be able to come.'

Eleanor was instantly crestfallen but then looked up at her mother hopefully. 'Next weekend then?'

Nettie let out a sigh. 'I think she means not on any weekend.'

Eleanor couldn't understand what Lucy could possibly have to do that would take up all of Saturday *and* Sunday. Nettie understood Eleanor's puzzlement and sought to explain.

'I suppose, without a mother about the home, Lucy has to help her grandmother out a good deal, and I suppose that during the week, while Lucy is at school, there isn't time for all the things that she needs to… well…' Nettie shrugged and smiled down at her daughter.

'I think it's the best thing for everybody anyway! Now perhaps you'll make friends with someone who doesn't give everyone the willies!'

Nettie hadn't noticed Lizzie standing in the doorway of the kitchen, her arms folded in front of her. She turned to reprimand her oldest daughter, but it was too late.

Eleanor's eyes blazed and before Nettie could stop her, she flew down the hallway and knocked her sister to the floor.

'She doesn't give anyone the willies! She doesn't! Take it back! You take it back now!' Eleanor sat astride Lizzie with her hands caught up in her sister's hair and pulled as Lizzie screamed for her to stop.

Nettie grabbed Eleanor's apron strings at the back and yanked her off the howling Lizzie.

'Enough, Eleanor! Get to your room!'

Eleanor struggled free from her mother's grasp and fled to her room crying.

Nettie looked down at Lizzie, who was holding her head, sure that most of her hair had been pulled out at the roots. 'And you get to yours!'

Lizzie stopped crying instantly.

'But she started it! It's not my fault!'

Nettie's temper was beginning to get the best of her now as she yanked her oldest daughter to her feet. 'You're just as much to blame… now get to your room! And don't come out until I say so!'

Like Eleanor, Lizzie fled to her room crying as Nettie took a few deep breaths in an effort to calm down. She spied the envelope on the floor and swooped it up in anger. Looking about for the note, she found the crumpled bit of paper by the front door and snatched it up also, and ripping both to shreds, she stomped out to the kitchen, opened the wood-stove door, threw the pieces in and slammed the door as loudly as she could while muttering under her breath about motherhood surely being God's perverse sense of humour.

An hour later, Eleanor, still in her room, played quietly with Stella after confiding in the doll that she would never *ever* forgive Lizzie, and she would refuse to come out for lunch, even if her mother pleaded with her.

But after spying another dress among her doll's clothes that she hadn't tried on Stella in some time, her determination to stand firm had soon left her and she now sat humming a monotonous tune while setting up her tea set on the floor in front of her.

On remembering the earlier fight in the hallway, she had now changed her mind and confided to Stella that she would probably be all right with Mum... and that she would have to see about Lizzie. Besides, she was getting hungry.

Her stomach began to growl, and as she started to pack away her tea set, she suddenly felt the hairs on the back of her neck stand on end. Eleanor dropped a cup and turned her head sharply, expecting or rather hoping to see her mother or Lizzie in the doorway, but there was no one. She glanced about the room again, a strange but somehow comforting feeling coursing through her body.

'What?' Her voice was a whisper, the word springing from her mouth before she was even aware she'd uttered a sound.

It seemed to break some sort of spell and she now stood up. Everything seemed normal again, but to Eleanor it was as though it was the second time today that someone had changed their mind about coming to visit her.

Eleanor jumped as Nettie stuck her head around the door. 'You can come out now and have some lunch. Lizzie is already at the table, but I don't want any more arguments, understand?'

Eleanor gave another quick glance about the room and then nodded to her mother before quickly following her out through the door.

It was too soon… he knew it. But he needed to make contact no matter how slight… she was as yet too young to comprehend, though he sensed in her an openness of mind… an acceptance of things though they'd yet to be laid before her. Perhaps this would serve… and perhaps this would not.

He moved effortlessly through her possessions, creating no breeze, stirring nothing… He lingered momentarily by her pillowcase, the sweetness of her scent filtering through the very space that held his force. He drew in close to her cherished doll… its stitched-on features registering nothing at his presence. Soon she would be aware… soon she would know him once again… And as he left, a fallen teacup rattled on its side…

Over the next few years, Eleanor warmed to her lessons at school, especially in history, with her teacher, Miss Ringwald, declaring her 'an absolute marvel' to her scholarly peers. Eleanor's ease with the subject had been duly noted as a result of her forthright opinions in class, as well as the accurate and well-presented work she'd handed in.

'Most gratifying, Eleanor – most gratifying indeed!' Eleanor had come to learn that Miss Ringwald's most favoured word was 'gratifying' and that the stout and cheerful teacher would apply it to almost anything that pleased her. 'I think it would be most gratifying to us, class, if we were to sit outside this afternoon and take our lesson.' Or 'Mr Dix has informed me that he would find it very gratifying if you could all refrain from so much noise of a morning on entering your classroom.'

Most of the students liked to refer to her as Miss Ringworm in place of her proper name, with one student earning himself a good whacking with Mr Dix's cane one afternoon after accidentally addressing her as such to her face.

As for Eleanor's history lessons, her keenness to explore the world of bygone years was as much a mystery to her as her ability to take it all in and retain it. For some reason, it was as though she was able to visibly grasp the events of centuries long past as clearly as the events of her own present. And the purpose of this – for it did seem to her there was a purpose – was yet to be made known to her.

Lucy Phipps was never to visit the Grayson household. This didn't stop her friendship with the younger Eleanor from blossoming, although it was kept to the schoolyard and an occasional get-together down by the Torrens or the main street, whenever Lucy was able to get out of the house.

Although Lucy was only a year younger than Lizzie, her closeted upbringing and home circumstances had not afforded her the normal habits and views of growing up that other girls her age had. Thus she was more at ease with the younger Eleanor, their friendship being much less complicated and affording her all the simplicities of youth that she craved and had been unable to obtain under her own roof.

Lizzie, however, was now approaching her fifteenth year and had confided in Eleanor that she'd had her first kiss down by the Torrens with Bobby Pinkle. As her 'shocking' news registered on her younger sister's face, Lizzie had given a satisfied smile and gone on to relate all the events leading up to it and what immediately followed. Eleanor had watched with wide eyes, awestruck, as Lizzie primped herself in front of the mirror, her final declaration to Eleanor being that 'I couldn't possibly marry Bobby though – after all, who would want to be known as Elizabeth Pinkle!'

Teddy, now twelve and not wanting to be called Teddy anymore but Ted, at least around his friends, was hell-bent on tearing around the neighbourhood on his bicycle, so fast and reckless that there'd been more than one knock on Nettie's front door from various neighbours complaining about their garden or her son's dangerous riding. When a constable knocked on the door one day and informed them that their son had nearly caused an accident on King William Street, it was the last straw. Ted was confined to the house for a fortnight, and when finally he was allowed to venture out again, he was made to promise his parents that if they heard just one more word about him riding too fast or so far away, then his bicycle would be confiscated all together.

Harry's hard work at the abattoirs had been rewarded in the last year with a promotion to supervisor. The job did not entail much more than his previous position had, only now he was responsible for the men below him and chasing up overdue or short deliveries of stock.

Unfortunately, Harry's leg had begun to give him hell over the preceding months, and on visiting the local doctor, he'd been told he was suffering from gout and that he would have to cut back on his drinking. Harry's idea of cutting back was not going down the pub as often, but when he did, he drank just as much as he'd done previously – sometimes more – telling himself that he'd not had a drink for a day or two and so, therefore, he was entitled.

Nettie shook her head at this behaviour and secretly told herself that her husband would have to learn the hard way. And when the doctor was called to the house due to Harry being unable to walk, he gave strict instructions that under no circumstances could Harry have a drink for at least a month. Harry, driven to distraction through his longing for the taste of beer but not wanting to experience such pain again, finally made an honest attempt at cutting back.

Hillary's visits to the modest household were no easier to bear than they'd ever been. However, the dutiful politeness from her daughter-in-law, as well as the aloofness from Lizzie and the disregard from Ted, did not seem to faze her, for it was made plain to all that the true purpose of her visits was seeing her son and youngest granddaughter.

Nettie would tolerate an afternoon of her mother-in-law's thinly veiled disapproval, her incessant sniffing and her 'well-intended' but often uncalled-for advice on everything from housework to the raising of her children, and just when she thought she could take no more, Hillary would suddenly be off, leaving Nettie in a bad mood for the rest of the day. Nettie told herself that one day she would tell Hillary just what she thought of her insufferable opinions and interfering ways, and that any advice she had to offer could go straight to the Devil!

Charlie had made several trips back to Adelaide in his time away, and these visits were always cause for much celebration, though the last time he had been called back suddenly under unhappy circumstances. His aunt Aggie had died suddenly from a stroke, and Charlie, not having been with her the last few years, felt suddenly flooded with guilt and remorse. Her funeral was a quiet affair with a small gathering, among them Hillary, Rosie, Charlie, Harry, Nettie, Lenny, Ruby and the maid, Clarice, who'd been her daily for the last twenty years. Clarice, of slim stature and maturing years, stood a little back from the rest of the gathering, quietly mourning the loss of her employer and friend of the last two decades, mopping the tears from her face with an already sodden handkerchief.

Agatha Bradford, who had never married and who had carried the name Bradford since the day she'd been born, was laid to rest alongside her brother, Kenneth, Charlie's father, and her sister-in-law Josephine, Charlie's mother.

As Charlie had stood by his family's plot, he'd been swamped with a feeling of sad nostalgia, though for what he hadn't been sure; he could not remember his mother and barely remembered his father. All Charlie knew was that beneath the soil before him lay the people who'd given birth to him and who'd known him best. Without them, and for the first time in his life, he felt so terribly alone.

He'd spotted Clarice behind him and his heart had gone out to her. His aunt's maid had been a godsend over the years, and Charlie had always been glad that there had been someone at home to keep his aunt company, especially in the years he hadn't been there. He'd edged back to stand next to her and, noticing Clarice's poor excuse for a handkerchief, reached into his pocket and pulled out a clean and folded one of his own and handed it to her. Clarice had grasped it quickly as though it was some sort of lifeline, her quick smile through her tears conveying her gratitude.

With the passing of Aunt Aggie, Charlie had then come into his fortune, though the legal red tape was to take a few more weeks. The will had also stated that there was to be an annuity set up for Clarice, which Charlie had been thankful for.

Charlie had been happy to go back to his shearing until all this had taken place, but he was required to settle his affairs in person, which required him to remain in Adelaide a bit longer. Besides, there was his aunt's house to clear out, a job that Charlie had been reluctant to undertake, though Nettie and Ruby had obliged.

It was on this occasion that Vera came knocking on Aggie's front door.

'Vera! My goodness, it's been a long time!' Nettie was genuinely surprised.

Ruby didn't seem surprised at all. 'Hello, Vera,' was all she could muster. Vera smiled back at them both and Nettie wondered why she'd never noticed before how Vera's smiles didn't quite seem to reach her eyes.

'Hello, Nettie, Ruby. I heard about Charlie's aunt – thought I'd stop by and give him my condolences.'

Ruby's face was deadpan. 'Pity you missed the funeral then.' Her sarcasm was evident.

Nettie nudged Ruby in the side and spoke quickly. 'He's not here. The house needed to be cleared out, but it didn't sit well on him to be here, so Ruby and I offered... But come in... please.'

Ruby stood back for Vera to enter, but Vera declined. 'No, but thank you all the same. I'd best be on my way... um... I have a car waiting. But I'd like to catch up with you soon...' Vera eyed Ruby, who was looking back at her with disdain. 'If it's not inconvenient that is.'

'Of course not... love to see you... whenever you can make it.' Nettie smiled as they said their goodbyes and then shut the door behind her before turning on Ruby.

'Ruby! How could you!'

'Oh bosh! Why didn't she come to the funeral if she was so concerned? Seems to me she was only interested in Charlie and his newly acquired inheritance. Why else would she come here when she thinks no one else would be here… giving her a clear run to play her silly games, I bet!'

But Nettie was starting to giggle. Ruby joined in and stuck her nose in the air melodramatically. 'I have a car waiting!'

With that, Nettie burst into loud laughter.

'You know, she *could* have been genuine.'

'Bosh to that too. That woman has been seen out at the opera and other grand affairs on at least half a dozen different occasions and each time on the arm of a different man! Seems to me she's still shopping.'

'Really?' Nettie was shocked, and then her eyes narrowed. 'I think I'm envious, Rube!'

It was Ruby's turn to be shocked. 'Henrietta Grayson! You have nothing to be envious about at all! And what would your husband say to all this?'

Nettie smiled and held up her hand. 'No, Harry means the world to me… for all his boozy ways and clumsy approaches. I mean… well, don't you ever remember what it was like to be… well… out there? I mean single?'

Ruby started chuckling. 'Clumsy approaches, Net?'

Nettie shrugged. 'Never mind about that, Ruby Jenson… you know what I mean in any case!'

'All right, all right – I know what you mean. But yes, I do remember what it was like to be "out there" as you put it, and I also thank my lucky stars I'm not anymore.'

Nettie nodded and gazed off into space. 'I wonder what it's going to be like when the kids take up with someone… I mean, how will you feel when Kathy comes home with her first real beau?'

Ruby sat down on one of the packing crates. 'I just hope he's right for her – that's all I want.'

Nettie sighed. 'I have an idea that Lizzie will bring home several "real" beaus. I have this awful feeling that both Harry and I will be tearing our hair out with that one. As for Eleanor, who knows… she's a tricky one.'

Ruby nodded. 'I'll agree with you there.'

Nettie laughed then. 'And as for Teddy…' At the mention of his name, they both threw their hands up in exasperation.

CHAPTER FOUR

'I don't know how you manage to take it all in, Eleanor, I really don't!' Lucy sat up and threw her study book down upon the grass, looked down towards the water's edge and sighed. 'Can't we go down to the swans instead?'

Eleanor and Lucy had been stretched out upon the banks of the Torrens for the past hour or more, their shoes and socks lying discarded at their side, taking pleasure in the feel of the fresh grass between their toes. Eleanor was attempting to help Lucy with her social-studies lesson, a task that was becoming increasingly difficult due to her friend's concentration being constantly distracted by their surroundings. Eleanor had to admit, it was a beautiful spring day, and rarely did Lucy get to enjoy a Saturday morning to do as she pleased, even though it was under the proviso of learning for her Intermediate exams. Lucy's usual Saturday mornings consisted of doing the laundry or pot scrubbing or some other such thing from a long list of chores that old lady Phipps saw fit to hand down to her only granddaughter.

Eleanor closed her social-studies book with a thud and sat

up. She moved over to lean against the tree and sighed, her hand coming up to shield her eyes from the sun as she looked out across the water.

'The swans have been scared away in any case. It's all those silly boats… look.' Eleanor pointed to a spot on the bend of the river where brightly coloured rowboats were making their way across from the other side. As the boats drew closer, the girls could hear the splashing of the oars as they broke water, along with the squeals of laughter and animated conversion going back and forth between the rowboats' occupants. Eleanor was dismayed to see that one of them was Lizzie. If she'd been alone on the bank, it wouldn't matter, but Lucy's presence almost always brought a snide remark from her sister.

'Perhaps if we walk down further towards the reeds, we'll find some swans there.' Eleanor looked hopefully towards her friend, but Lucy had already seen Lizzie and now turned away shyly to stare at her shoes nearby, her face red from embarrassment.

Lucy gave not a whit for what Lizzie Grayson would say to her. She was more aware of the scene in which she found herself, the difference in ages between her and her friend a constant reminder to people of her unusual circumstances, that she didn't engage in any of the normal activities that girls of her age did… that she was different. Eleanor had been her one true friend, and though their age difference had always been apparent to her, she had never minded, for Lucy looked on the auburn-haired girl with the intelligent face as the sister she'd never had.

Her mother had left when she was very young; any contact had been through her grandmother, who, Lucy felt, had raised her granddaughter out of a sense of duty rather than any maternal feelings. She had been fed, clothed and taught to abide the social morals and strict rules befitting a young girl, though never allowed to exercise the inquisitiveness of her youth – nor had she ever been able to voice her curiosities to any member of her household. She had always been told firmly 'that sort of thing shouldn't concern you' or 'you should be thinking about more important things'.

The day her menses had begun, her grandmother had hustled her from the room to sit her down in the drawing-room and give her a long-drawn-out lecture on the proper conduct to be expected from a young woman, now that she was of 'marriageable age'. The true origin of her monthly flow had not been explained to her at all, and if it weren't for Mrs Bingham, she would not have known to this day. Mrs Bingham lived next door and was one of the kindest women that Lucy knew – perhaps the only woman with whom she'd had much contact beyond family and teachers. The well-rounded but robust Mrs Bingham had birthed five of her own and had taken it upon herself to draw Lucy under her wing at any given opportunity. *No need to tell your grandmother about our little talks, dear. We don't want to upset her, do we?'*

Lucy had liked that idea.

As for her grandfather, he kept to himself, moving about the house in an important manner but never really having much to say, at least not to her. And as for her father, Lucy could go three or four days sometimes without ever laying eyes on him. He was unreachable, an unknown entity that occupied the downstairs parlour most of the time and was given to fits of melancholy. Lucy had learnt at a very young age not to bother him. As a result of this, and as she'd grown older, he'd ceased to hold much consequence amongst the many things that daily life crowded into her mind.

Such was Lucy's life.

'Well, good afternoon, little sister!' Lionel Holt yelled out to Eleanor, his podgy frame struggling to remain upright, as he stood in the centre of the little boat, trying to bow low and grace her with a dramatic sweep of his hat. Lizzie sat by his side and gripped the sides of the boat as it started to sway.

'For goodness' sake, Lionel, sit down! You're tipping the boat!'

Lionel had always been a show pony – anything for a laugh and at anyone else's expense. Eleanor was instantly on her guard. Lucy refused to look at them.

In another boat, Lionel's twin brother, Lance, called out to him. 'Don't be an idiot! You'll dump the both of you!'

Lance was slightly thinner than his brother and slightly more sensible. Kathy partnered him in his boat, her eyes widening in horror as she looked on at Lionel's antics.

There were four more of Lizzie's friends between the other two boats, but Eleanor didn't know them. In one there was a red-headed boy who looked like he'd had too much sun – or perhaps that was just his colouring; Eleanor couldn't be sure – and a girl of similar colouring, though not so red-faced due to her hat... his sister perhaps? She sat there looking demure, almost awkward.

In the other boat sat two dark-haired boys, one with his mouth opened unflatteringly wide in laughter and the other broody, his attentions seemingly taken up with Lizzie's plight.

The broody one frowned and called out to Lionel. 'For God's sake, man, sit down!'

Lionel tried to sit down again, but his ridiculous gestures had begun to make the boat rock and he lost his footing, coming down hard on his rump and causing the boat to tip to one side. It came back down again with a hard thump, spraying water up into the air to rain down upon Lizzie. This made the dark-haired wide-mouthed boy laugh all the more. Lizzie was not impressed; her hat was now dripping wet.

'This is not my idea of a pleasant morning, Lionel Holt! I don't know why I ever said I'd see you today!' She snatched the hat from her head and began shaking it. Turning around to the boats behind, she called out. 'Benjamin, I want to go back with you!'

'Oh come on, Lizzie, I was only larking about! I promise I'll be good on the way back.' But Lionel's expression belied his promise as he pulled a face at the others, causing his brother Lance to stifle a chuckle behind his hand.

Eleanor realized that the broody, dark-haired boy must be Benjamin, as he now reached out to grasp Lizzie's boat and pull himself alongside.

The two girls on the bank had been all but forgotten. They sat watching the scene in front of them, a quick smile thrown back and forth between them now and then as they looked on. As Lizzie settled herself in the boat next to Benjamin, she chanced to look up and catch them. She was instantly angered.

'You think it's funny do you, Lucy Phipps?'

Lucy turned instantly away again, her face a flaming red at being suddenly singled out.

'Well I think it's rather funny, don't you, Perce?' Lionel's podgy face spread out in a grin. Eleanor realized that Perce must be the mouthy one, who now erupted into yet another bout of laughter.

'Oh shut up, Lionel! You too, *Percival!* Lizzie emphasized his name in a mocking tone. She turned back to Eleanor now, ignoring Lucy completely. 'And you'd better not stay down here too long either, or Mum will have something to say about it!'

Eleanor merely frowned back at her sister. 'Like what?'

'Oh come on, Lizzie! We have to get back!' It was Kathy. 'We're wasting time!'

One by one, they started pulling away in their boats, a disgruntled Lizzie sitting huffily with her arms folded in front of her as she glared at Lucy.

As they drifted further away, Eleanor and Lucy looked at one another.

'Well, that wasn't too bad, was it?'

Lucy shrugged. Eleanor started to giggle.

'You know what my father calls the Holt twins?'

Lucy started to smile and shook her head. Eleanor leant forward. 'He said they should be called the two *dolts*… not Holts!'

She fell back on the grass, her giggling contagious as Lucy started to laugh as well. Their laughter was in full swing as they began relating the incident over to each other with an extra squeal of laughter at Lizzie's expense as they recalled her sodden hat.

An hour later it was time to leave. Social studies had taken a back seat to the morning's events, and Lucy was now suddenly fretful of her exams again. Both girls wiped stray bits of grass from the bottom of their feet as best they could before donning their shoes and socks once more. Lucy stood up, frowning.

'I don't know how I'm going to get through this exam… I should have been more mindful of my studies this morning instead of letting my thoughts get carried away with swans and things.'

They were strolling up the hill away from the river.

'Just sit up a bit longer tonight and read it through until it sticks in your brain,' was Eleanor's remedy. But Lucy merely gave her friend a doleful glance.

'In my house?' Lucy was suddenly glum. 'My grandmother always insists that I study by daylight; she says I waste the lamp by staying up at night.'

Eleanor wasn't sure what to say. 'Oh,' was all she could manage. They walked on in silence for a while until Lucy sighed loudly.

'You know, it did look like a bit of fun… rowing on the river I mean. What do you think?'

Eleanor shook her head. 'Not for me. I'm scared of water. I'd be too scared of falling in, and then what would I do?'

'You could always learn to swim first. I could teach you if you'd like… I learnt how to swim last summer,' she finished up importantly.

Eleanor's face was doubtful, 'I don't know, the idea of being in deep water scares me to death.' She then turned to her friend. 'Your grandmother let you go bathing?

'Yes, remember? It was with the school and one of the few things my grandmother let me do outside the school grounds. We went down to the swimming baths every day for two weeks.' Lucy laughed. 'She wasn't going to let me until Miss Prichard sent a letter home explaining how swimming was an essential part of our gymnastics and that it counted in my yearly marks. You should have heard her complain about having to buy me a costume… you should have *seen* the costume!'

Eleanor laughed as well. 'Perhaps you could get Miss Prichard to send a letter home telling your grandmother that you have to go boating on the Torrens.'

Lucy giggled in response. 'Ha! She complained enough when I went swimming; imagine what she'd say… Eleanor? What is it? What's wrong?'

They'd come to the top of Lucy's street and something had made Eleanor stop dead in her tracks. She now stood rooted to the spot, swallowing hard, a prickly feeling running up and down her back. She grabbed hold of Lucy's arm and started pulling her back and shaking her head.

'Eleanor? You're scaring me. What's wrong? Are you sick?' Lucy was frowning, her expression concerned as she too began to feel apprehensive.

'Come away, Lucy… Don't go down there – you don't have to. Come home with me… now! Please!'

'What? For goodness' sake, Eleanor…'

But Eleanor began to cry. 'Please, Lucy…' She could feel her heart thumping against her chest… a warning… someone warning her… telling her to try and remain calm… *'Calm your fears, Eleanor… she must go…'*

Eleanor looked about her, searching… but there was no one there. She looked up at Lucy, but Lucy was peering down the street, her eyebrows wrinkled together, and nervously biting her bottom lip. Lucy began to move forward slowly and Eleanor, still blinking back her tears, could do nothing but follow, a feeling of inevitable doom settling low in her stomach.

As the girls drew closer, they saw the crowd and they suddenly stopped, now not more than twenty yards away. Outside Lucy's house, people were milling around. Even from a distance, the girls could see their agitation. Among them was old Mr Hill from across the street, Mrs Bingham… others, people they didn't know, all talking animatedly amongst themselves and peering in through Lucy's front door… and then the girls saw Lucy's grandmother rushing out the door and into Mrs Bingham's arms, the rest huddling around her. Eleanor sneaked a look at Lucy, the older girl standing stony-faced, peering on.

Then Lucy took a deep breath, linked her arm through Eleanor's and said quietly, 'Come on. You have to stay with me.' Eleanor's reluctant nod went unnoticed.

The girls drew closer still, but before anyone in the crowd saw them, Lucy quickly pulled Eleanor into the small lane that ran near her house. Eleanor looked up hopefully. 'Do you want to go to my house now?'

Lucy shook her head. 'No… please come with me. We can go around through the back from here.' Lucy looked at Eleanor and grabbed her by the shoulders, her expression pleading. 'I don't want to go in alone. I need you to come with me… will you?'

Again, Eleanor nodded, her eyes wide, her thoughts in turmoil. She thought it would have been better if they'd gone to her house, or at least if the people out front had seen them approach. That way, she would have felt safer. There were others there who knew what was going on… knew what to do. What Lucy had asked her to do filled her with dread, yet she had little idea why. She knew something terrible had happened but, beyond that, Eleanor was too fearful to contemplate what.

They stepped through a wire fence that ran down the side of a grapevine and managed to pull themselves through the tangled undergrowth, giving no heed to the sharp twigs and branches scratching their legs. Lucy then led Eleanor alongside a shed and peeked around the corner. Turning back to Eleanor, she held her finger to her lips – a sign to keep quiet – and proceeded to slip through the fruit trees, pulling the younger girl behind her as she went. Eleanor stumbled over fallen peaches and apricots lying on the ground, idly thinking that surely old lady Phipps didn't let these go to waste.

She slammed into the back of Lucy who had suddenly stopped.

'Over there.' Lucy pointed to her back door.

Eleanor shook her head. 'Are you sure you want to go in? Wouldn't it be better if you went to see your grandmother?' But Lucy grabbed Eleanor's hand and ran up to the back of the house.

Slipping through the back door, they both suddenly stilled. Eleanor took in her surroundings; she'd never been inside Lucy's house before, having never been allowed past the front door. They now stood in a kind of lobby. There were rubber boots on the floor in front of them, an old dresser that looked like it was used more for storage now and a rope strung up to the rafters as an inside line of sorts where old Mr Phipps' coat had been slung over, presumably to air. Opposite them was a door leading off to what Eleanor could see was a small laundry and another screen door leading off to the right of Lucy.

Her perusal of Lucy's house was suddenly interrupted as different voices started talking in the front of the house. Lucy straightened up against the wall and, bringing her hand up to cover her face, she began to cry. Eleanor was at a loss at what to do for her friend.

Lucy stopped and took a deep breath, then opened the screen door as she hung on to Eleanor's arm for dear life. They now stood inside a huge kitchen, but still out of sight from the hallway that led to the front door. The voices were clearer now. The milling crowd at the front door could be heard, as well as the sound of unfamiliar footsteps, some quick, others slower as they made their way backward and forward across the polished hallway floor, the squeaking hinge on the front screen door marking the many times it was opened and closed.

'How long does it take the police to get here? And where's the ambulance?' It was a man's voice.

Lucy's sharp intake of breath made Eleanor turn and look at her.

'I suppose it's not an emergency is it, just a matter of transport really… Where's the old man?' It was another man's voice.

'Upstairs, won't come down,' the first one said. 'Margaret's beside herself. Can't say I blame her, finding him like that.'

'I remember Mickey, you know – served with him in France for a time.'

Lucy was silent, her eyes unblinking and fixed on some point in front of her. Eleanor placed her arm about her waist. 'Come on, Lucy. Let's go… please. You don't want to be here.'

But Lucy shook her off and made to walk out through the kitchen door. Eleanor pulled on her arm, whispering loudly. 'No… Lucy… no!'

The voices faded off as they moved further away. Lucy walked slowly out into the hallway. She knew where she had to go, though she didn't want to. She needed proof of what the voices were saying, needed to see for herself, at the same time terrified of what she might find.

Eleanor hung out of the kitchen door behind Lucy in one last-ditch effort to make her friend stop. 'Lucy!' she whispered as loud as she dared. But Lucy kept walking.

It took a full two seconds for Eleanor to decide what she should do, and then without giving it another thought, she crept down the side of the hallway after her friend.

Eleanor heard the sound of an ambulance pulling up outside. She could hear the ominous clanging of its bell, and from where she now stood, she could see the crowd outside huddling around the back doors of the vehicle, all stretching their necks in an effort to get a first-hand look… at anything.

'Lucy?' Eleanor entered the doorway where Lucy had disappeared and almost fell down the small step she hadn't known was there. As she righted herself, she noticed the room was dark, and looking over at the window, she saw that the drapes were closed.

As her eyes became accustomed to the dark, Eleanor peered around the opened door looking for Lucy and immediately felt again the same prickly feeling shooting up the middle of her back. She shivered. With a shaky voice, she called out to Lucy. There was no answer. She took another step forward and looking down, her eyes widening as she stood transfixed at the scene before her.

On the carpet in front of her was an overturned side table, its tablecloth fanned out across the floor and partly covering what appeared to be a shattered liquor bottle and upturned ashtray nearby. Looking up and across the room, Eleanor's mouth dropped open. Near the top of the wall, it was as though someone had purposely thrown a bucket of red paint at it. Some had even splashed up further onto the ceiling above to hang down in long, congealing drips of darkening red. Eleanor remembered when her uncle Charlie had knocked the paint tin over on the small garden table on their back veranda. It had made the same sort of drips. *But that was green*, she told herself.

Thin rivulets of the red paint had escaped from the main splatter to run down over the rose-patterned wallpaper and Eleanor followed their trail downward. It was then that she noticed the wheelchair lying on its side, its wicker backrest partially hiding the blanket on the floor behind it, the tartan pattern made almost unrecognizable by the same red paint. Without warning, Eleanor's eyes fell upon the hand protruding from beneath it, so still that she'd almost dismissed it as just another inanimate object.

As it suddenly dawned on her young mind what had happened, her heartbeat instantly quickened, her breath caught in her throat and her thoughts suddenly screamed out from within her brain, the words sounding over and over inside her head… telling her what she suddenly realized she'd known all along.

It isn't paint… it isn't paint…

Eleanor tried to speak but couldn't find her voice. It was then that she became aware of Lucy sitting on a side stool in the corner and staring down, looking so calm with her hands clasped on her lap that she could easily have been contemplating her social-studies lesson instead of the tragedy before her… save for the tears running unchecked down her face. Eleanor made to hurry over to her but tripped on the ashtray and fell down hard upon the floor, her face landing only inches away from the lifeless hand. She couldn't take her eyes off it; nor did she hear the front door squeak or the footsteps behind her.

'What in the blazes are you doing here, girl!' She felt strong hands lift her off the floor and still she didn't take her eyes off the hand. Dimly, she became aware of Lucy screaming…

Eleanor stood in a garden filled with flowers… all kinds of flowers… a brilliant array of yellows, reds, mauves and other colours she couldn't put a name to. They grew along the ground around her feet… up the sides of rocks and around trees, bouquets of vibrant colours in every direction…

She looked about her and wondered what she was doing

here, why she'd been brought here, and with that flow of her thoughts she suddenly realized she'd been waiting.

'Eleanor.'

She swung round. Her eyes widened.

He stood amid the foliage about ten feet away from her, tall and broad, with shoulder-length black hair... and those eyes... those eyes that held a colour all of their own, a strange shade of violet that no mere flower could match...

'It's you!'

'Yes.'

'I know you.'

He smiled. At least she thought he smiled... now she wasn't sure.

'Yes, you know me.'

She stared at him, an odd feeling coursing through her. A kind of understanding... a dawning... something emerging to the surface of her awareness, like a long-buried memory. Eleanor's mouth curved slowly into a smile.

'Parquin?'

Eleanor's eyes slowly opened and then instantly closed to shut out the sun streaming in through her bedroom window. She frowned, screwing her eyes up against the offending light. What had she been dreaming about? She couldn't remember now. She knew there'd been flowers... lots of flowers... and someone...

Eleanor sat bolt upright. 'Lucy!' Her voice rang out in the quiet room. Where was everyone? She swung her legs over the side of the bed but the action made her feel woozy. Leaning on the bed, she got up, testing her legs. What was the matter with her?

Horrible pictures sprang up in her mind. Lucy crying... the wall with... blood – she was able to call it by its proper name now – and that hand... Lucy's father... Oh, how could he?

Eleanor fell back on the bed again, her hand coming up to cover her mouth as she held back a sob.

The direction of the sun coming through her window told her it was late afternoon, but what afternoon? Eleanor felt as though she'd been asleep for a very long time. Those awful events seemed like a lifetime ago.

She remembered lying there, the ambulance orderly picking her off the floor and ushering her quickly out of the room. She had been taken to the drawing room and made to wait, her whole body quaking at what she knew to be in the room across the hall. Lucy had also been taken out, though to where Eleanor hadn't known.

A little while later, her father had arrived and she'd thrown herself into his arms and he'd picked her up, something he hadn't done since she'd been about six or seven years old, when he used to pick her up on arriving home from work and she would wrap her arms around his neck.

But it had been different at Lucy's house – no light-heartedness but for the safety and comfort of her father's arms as he'd carried her through the crowd surrounding the front gate, and she'd hid her face against his shoulder, not wanting to look at anyone.

When they'd arrived home, her mother had met them at the front door, a fretful look upon her face. Minutes later, the doctor had arrived and given her a little pill, and as her mother had undressed her and tucked her into bed, her mind had mercifully already begun to close down.

Eleanor now thought about Lucy and made up her mind that she had to see her. With determination, she rose again and walked shakily to her bedroom door. Opening it, she could now hear the raised voices of her parents in the kitchen. They appeared to be arguing, and Eleanor strained to listen.

'I don't care if they're good friends, Net! No daughter of mine had any business being in that house!' Her father seemed adamant.

'But they would have had no idea, Harry. Something like that doesn't exactly get advertised first, does it?' Her mother's voice was a little quieter, reasoning.

'Advertised? Who could have missed what was going on? That morbid lot of stickybeaks hanging around the front door! The ambulance for Christ's sake!'

'No need to swear.' Her mother's voice went up a notch.

Eleanor was surprised to hear the older and more refined voice of her grandmother.

'If you don't mind, I would like to go and see my granddaughter. This isn't getting either of you anywhere!

There was a pause before her father said quietly, 'She's asleep, Mum. The doctor's given her a sedative.'

'What on earth for? She'll only remember everything all over again when she wakes up… Was the girl hysterical?' Her grandmother's voice held a trace of urgency.

Eleanor didn't see her father shake his head.

'I agree with Hillary. When Eleanor comes to, she'll only be upset all over again, and she'll have to contend with it sooner or later – better to come to terms with it as soon as possible.'

If the whole situation hadn't been so much of a tragedy, Eleanor might have lingered more on the surprise of hearing her mother agree with her grandmother for once.

'She's barely twelve years old! Who knows what this may do to her, and while she's asleep, neither of you can talk to her in any case! At least leave her be for now… let her sleep.'

Her father seemed to have won out on this occasion for

their voices quietened somewhat, and with that, Eleanor thought she'd better go back to bed, especially since her head was beginning to spin. As much as she wanted to see her friend, it was obvious to her that she'd have to wait. She crept back into her bedroom and quietly closed the door.

Harry was pacing the kitchen floor. He'd been turning the soil over in the garden that morning, his appearance now dishevelled, a shadow of whiskers covering his chin. 'Where's Lizzie and Ted? Do they know what's happened?'

'Lizzie was to meet one of the Holt boys this morning, so she and Kathy left early. There were a few of them meeting at the Torrens to go boating.'

'Holt boys? Which one?' Hillary sat in her usual upright position in one of the kitchen chairs, a habit she'd been taught as a girl, and one she'd always adhered to. *Good for your carriage*, she'd always been told.

Harry gave a slight snort of irritation at his daughter's choice of escort. 'Does it matter? One is as much of an idiot as the other in my book – hard to tell the difference between them.'

Hillary sniffed at his remark.

Nettie had begun mincing vegetables for the pasties she planned to make for their evening meal, her attention taken up with keeping her fingers out of the screw in the middle as it ground the vegetables to pulp. She now stopped mid-turn to look at her husband. 'It could be worse. Better an idiot than a boy with other things on his mind.'

Harry nearly laughed outright. 'My dear wife, believe me, at their age, *all* boys have *other* things on their minds! Idiots or not!'

Nettie turned back to her mincing, a worried frown upon her face and slightly put out by her husband's patronizing tone.

'Please, Harold, must you be so vulgar?' Hillary sniffed, her expression indignant.

Harry shrugged and threw his hands up, rolling his eyes. The two women in his company had no idea what the opposite sex were really like.

Hillary moved on quickly. 'And what about Edward?'

'He's down with Mr Crowley, in his shed… can't seem to drag him away from those dirty engines and things these days… comes home with grease from top to toe! I've had to boil his clothes to get it all out!'

Hillary nodded as Nettie spoke, and Harry rolled his eyes again. Hearing the procedures of the laundry did little to settle the topsy-turvy thoughts about Mickey Phipps running through his mind.

Nettie went on. 'Hopefully he would have still been tinkering down there and was far removed from this morning's events.'

Hillary nodded again. There was pause in conversation before she turned to her son, her voice low. 'Harold, what would make a man do such a thing?'

Harry sighed. 'Don't really know, Mum. I know that… well, *everyone* knew how Mickey was since the war, and then his wife leaving him… I suppose none of us know what would have been going through his head, day after day, barely talking to anybody—'

'So different from the Mickey I used to know in school…' Nettie cut in.

'Should have gone to see him. A visit every now and then might have done him the world of good, who knows?' Harry looked thoughtful, a hint of guilt flashing across his unshaven features.

Nettie frowned as she wiped her hands on the tea towel, the pan of minced vegetables now leaning on a slant to help drain off their excess liquid. 'It's not your fault, Harry.'

'Indeed it is not!' Hillary chimed in.

Nettie carried on. 'That man barely acknowledged his own daughter! And rarely his parents, or so I'm told. If his own family couldn't get close to him, well then, whether you'd called on him or not wouldn't have made a scrap of difference!'

Hillary sniffed. 'Exactly!'

Harry shook his head, more to himself. 'So, a man comes home from war minus his legs, his wife leaves him, he doesn't know how to act around his parents or his daughter and everyone uses this as an excuse not to go and bother him, and then the man ends up blowing his brains out! What I want to know then is whose bloody fault is it?'

'Harold, you're being unreasonable!' His mother sniffed and looked away.

'It's not like that.' Nettie's voice was quiet as she spoke. It was obvious to her that her husband felt somehow responsible for Mickey Phipps' suicide, which to her was ridiculous. But she kept her head. 'None of us wanted to see the poor man end up the way he did, but to take on any guilt or responsibility for his actions is no more helping him now than it would have done then.' Nettie kept her eyes on her husband, but he wouldn't look at her, his attentions now seemingly taken up with staring out of the kitchen window.

Hillary remained quiet save for a familiar sniff or two.

Nettie walked up to Harry and placed her hand on his shoulder. 'I'm sure many of us are wondering if there was anything we could have done, but to dwell on it now is pointless – it won't serve anybody.'

Harry turned to look at her, an awkward smile playing around the corners of his mouth. He went to say something but anything he might have said was cut off as the front door banged and Ted came running in, breathless, his face flushed with excitement.

'Did you hear? Everyone's talking about it! Old man Phipps went and topped himself!'

All three occupants of the kitchen spoke out at once.

'Shh! We know, Edward! Keep your voice down – your sister has had a time of it already!'

'Not so loud – Eleanor is sleeping!'

'Ted, we've already heard about poor Mickey. How did you find out?'

Ted looked at all three, something close to bewilderment spreading across his features, his fair hair flopping across his face as he swallowed hard. 'Then you don't know! I don't mean Lucy Phipps' father; I mean her *grandfather!* Old man Phipps! Shot himself up in his bedroom about an hour ago. You should see the front of their house, Dad! He must have done it by the window. There's broken glass down on the road and lots of blood on the outside window ledge, lots of people there!'

Hillary held a hand to her mouth. 'Oh my God! Gaylord… *shot* himself you say?'

Harry and Nettie stared at one another. 'The old man?' they said in unison.

Ted blinked twice and turned to his grandmother, a quizzical look upon his face. 'His name was Gaylord?'

'That will do, Ted. Best you stay indoors for the rest of the day.' Nettie could hardly believe this latest bit of news and sat down in the chair opposite Hillary, her hand on the older woman's arm.

'Aw, but, Mum, everyone's down there… and I want to see Eleanor too. Is it true she was in the house this morning the whole time? I reckon I might go back down and—'

'Do as your mother tells you, Ted! I'll have no son of mine sticking his nose in like the rest of those morbid gossip hounds!' Harry had spoken, his word final, and Ted slumped into one of the chairs in the kitchen, obviously put out.

Harry ran a hand through his hair as he started to pace the kitchen floor once more.

Hillary stood up, her hand at her breast, her breathing uneven. It was plain to all that she was distraught. 'I can't believe it! Poor Margaret! What that poor woman must be suffering!' She looked down at her grandson. 'And the daughter? Where is she?'

Ted sat up straight again, his excitement now increased at the prospect of being able to talk about it once more. 'The doctor packed Lucy off to the hospital… under sedation they say. They're sending for her mother, I heard Mrs Bingham say.'

Hillary looked at Harry and Nettie. 'Mrs Bingham?' The name was unfamiliar to her.

'The lady next door,' Nettie obliged.

Hillary turned back to Ted. 'And Margaret? Where is she?'

'Dunno.' Ted caught the warning look from his mother. 'I mean… I don't know, Grandma.'

Hillary turned to her son. 'Harold, I think I need to go home and rest awhile. The events of the day have been a little unsettling to say the least. Would you mind taking me home?'

'It may be the best idea, Mum. I'll drive you.'

Hillary turned back to Nettie, who was trying to force her

thoughts back to the pasty making. 'I'll come by tomorrow and see Eleanor.'

Nettie nodded and rose from the chair. To her it most definitely would be better if Hillary went home so her family could get back to some sort of normality. She felt it was what they all needed right now.

Not long before tea that night, the aroma of baked pasties filling the kitchen, Lizzie finally came home. She had no idea of the day's events, having gone boating and then on to a drive in the country for a picnic.

'Smells good, Mum! My goodness, what a day we've all had! A snake nearly bit Lionel until Benjamin knocked him out of the way at the last minute – I'm telling you, it was the most frightening thing! And then his stupid brother went and — Have you met Lance? Well, Lance got himself tangled in a barbed-wire fence, ripped his trousers nearly to shreds in the process. I told him to go around through the gate like everyone else but would he? Oh no, not Lance the idiot! Percival bet him he couldn't jump it and...'

Lizzie rambled on for the next few minutes. Nettie could do nothing more than nod every now and then as she sliced into the pasties and set about serving them. Every so often she would look at her oldest daughter with a pretended mask of interest set on her face.

'... and I told Kathy not to eat so much – you know how strawberries don't agree with her – but...'

Nettie looked over at her another time. '... of course you know how I hate to be rude, so I tried to bring his sister into the conversation, but she just sat there, Mum, looking gooey-eyed at Benjamin, and it's not my fault if...'

By the time Harry and Ted sat down for tea, Lizzie had finally finished her prattling and, as yet not noticing that

Eleanor was nowhere to be seen, merely looked over at Nettie. 'So… what's been going on around here today?'

Alice Phipps sat on a chair at the side of her bed. A tray of poached eggs and toast, barely touched, lay on the small nightstand on the other side of the bed. Alice hadn't been able to bring herself to go back to the house where it had all happened, preferring to take a hotel room in the city, and anyway, it was closer to Lucy, her daughter her only priority now.

She was racked by guilt… for her husband and for her father-in-law, but most of all she felt guilty for her daughter. She'd left it too long. If only she'd come back months ago, Lucy would have been spared these tragic events. Of course, she'd had no idea it would come to this. Alice knew Lucy's upbringing had been anything but normal, but what could she have done?

When she'd decided to leave Mickey, Alice had thought it was for the best. She'd had no money, nowhere to go, and until she got herself set up somewhere, she had decided that her daughter would be better cared for and safer with Mickey's parents, normal upbringing or not. Alice thought she would make up for all the years she'd been absent from Lucy's life, sending for her just as soon as she was able. She'd decided that Melbourne would be the best place to go. It was a bigger city so it would be easier for her to obtain a position somewhere, as well as being far removed from Adelaide.

But things had not gone as smoothly as she'd planned. It hadn't been easy for her to get a job after the war – she'd barely made enough to scrape by herself and she'd nearly gone back to Mickey. But strength of purpose had prevailed and finally she'd acquired a position in the haberdashery section of one of the big city stores. The wages weren't much, but they were enough for her to rent a small two-roomed cottage on the outskirts of Melbourne. And then little by little, she'd saved enough for a bigger place that was closer to the city, but things had still been tight and to bring Lucy over there then would have meant two mouths to feed and two people to buy clothes for, and then there would have been school expenses to contend with…

Alice hadn't been able to see her way clear until just this past year when she'd been made floor supervisor, but by then Lucy was nearly finished school in Adelaide and to tear her away would have been too unsettling and rather pointless.

Oh how Alice now wished she had.

And then when she'd got off the train in Adelaide, there had been that pushy reporter sticking his notebook in her face and asking her all kinds of impertinent questions that he had no business asking her. They were personal things… private things.

Did her husband's suicide have anything to do with their separation? Did she know of any friction between her husband and her father-in-law? Ridiculous questions. She'd been estranged from Mickey for nearly seven years, so what would she know? And if she had been privy to any inside knowledge of any kind, Alice was certain she wouldn't have shared it with anyone else!

He wasn't to be the last nosey reporter. One had come knocking on her door at the hotel and Alice had had to call the desk to have him thrown out, and then two more had accosted her at the funeral. Had these people no decency?

Alice thought about the funeral. Strange, she thought, how many of Mickey's friends had come out to witness his final farewell, some having donned their old uniforms… as a mark of respect? Or was it just one more excuse to pull their uniforms out of mothballs as a way of rewarding themselves with one more final hurrah down the local pub later?

Alice knew she was bitter about the war and that her present thoughts were cynical at best. But for the five years following Mickey's return, she couldn't remember any of those men knocking on their front door. And apart from the occasional question as to his health or well-being down the street, none had even bothered to pass on any well wishes or greetings to him. It was no wonder Mickey had retreated inside of himself.

Alice's face fell. She hadn't stayed by his side either, and thinking on it now, had she stayed, would Mickey have eventually come out of his shell and therefore still be alive today? It was a question that had always haunted her and now probably always would. For deep down, Alice felt she was to blame. Regardless of any previous friends he may have had who didn't come to visit, and regardless of how he would lock himself away in his own world, refusing to see anyone, not even his daughter, Alice felt that the final blow must have been her leaving him. It shouldn't have mattered that he'd cut her and Lucy off. If she'd been any sort of a loving wife, she would have stayed on and at least kept trying – if not for their sake then for Lucy's.

Alice felt her insides turn over from the guilt and the shame that now ate away at them. She sat now, her eyes unblinking and staring into space. A single tear escaped to run down the side of her cheek as she remembered a tall, robust man who swaggered about, brimming with confidence, and who had the ability to make others laugh and an easy way of talking that made people feel comfortable.

Her mouth suddenly curved up in a tremulous smile at her

memories, but it was gone just as quickly and she hung her head. 'I'm so sorry, Mickey,' she whispered.

Eleanor sat opposite Lucy on the next hospital bed in the ward. Lucy was dressed and ready to go, and she sat quietly, her hands clasped in her lap, a small suitcase on the floor by her side, waiting for Mrs Bingham to come and collect her and put her on the nine o'clock train. She was to meet up with her mother at the last stop out of Adelaide. Alice Phipps had drawn an unwelcome amount of public speculation when she'd arrived the week before to see her daughter and attend the funeral of her estranged husband and father-in-law, so as a way of avoiding any more stress than was necessary, she had arranged to meet Lucy elsewhere, rather than come into Adelaide again.

Lucy had been confined to the hospital for privacy rather than any medical reason. The doctor had declared she was ready to leave just two days after that terrible day, but Lucy, with nowhere to go, and with gossip and public curiosity hard on her heels, was advised to stay a while longer. She couldn't go back to her house. No one was there now and, in any case, Lucy felt she could never set foot inside that front door ever again. As far as everyone knew, her grandmother had gone to Sydney to be with relatives, though in actual fact, Margaret was merely taking sanctuary with friends of her husband's a few streets away. There she would recover, and in time, when all the publicity had died down, she would close the family home and move on. Lucy had not seen her since that fateful day, however the absence of her grandmother did not seem to cause her grief.

'I should have listened to you, Eleanor. I should have gone home with you.'

Eleanor smiled. 'It wouldn't have changed anything. It wouldn't have stopped what happened.'

'No, but I wouldn't have been witness to it... and nor would have you.'

Eleanor reached over and gave her friend's hand a squeeze. In truth, Eleanor most certainly could have done without the horrible pictures that still managed to creep into her mind at times, but she couldn't have let her friend go in alone. She didn't do anything to help Lucy, but at least Lucy knew there was someone else who had witnessed everything she had, for whatever small comfort it would give.

'Will you write?' Eleanor asked.

Lucy shook her head. 'Best not I think, but I'll come back and visit you someday if that's all right.'

It wouldn't do for Eleanor to be getting mail from 'the Phipps girl', Lucy thought. Better to let it go. That way, if anyone asked Eleanor about her, her friend could honestly say she didn't know instead of feeling put upon for gossip. She explained this to Eleanor, and Eleanor only nodded, not quite understanding. Lucy smiled. It was times like this that the difference in their ages was made apparent.

'Eleanor, I need to tell you something.' Lucy cleared her throat and went on. 'You've been my one true friend ever since I was eight years old. When everyone else ignored me, you never did, and I just wanted you to know how much that meant to me. If I'd ever had a sister, I would have wanted her to be just like you.' Lucy finished and went bright red with embarrassment.

Eleanor began to blink back tears, and then for some reason unknown to them both, they started to laugh. For the next hour or more, they spoke of the times they'd had and the funny things they'd done and then all too soon, Mrs Bingham arrived at the ward, a nurse following close behind.

'Are you ready, dear?' The kindly woman smiled, first at Lucy and then at Eleanor.

Lucy nodded and rose to go as Mrs Bingham picked up the small suitcase and made to leave. Lucy started to follow her but stopped. She ran back to Eleanor and hugged her tightly, and then without another word, turned and disappeared through the door.

Eleanor went on with her life. She went back to school, to her history books, and to her solitary lifestyle as it had been before. But slowly, and over time, she began to acquire new friends. At first, she'd been the source of much rumour. She would hear conversations fade off as she passed groups of her peers in the schoolyard, and even the teachers had treated her with kid gloves, watching over her, studying her to look for any signs of maladjusted behaviour. But there were none. Truth be told, Eleanor seemed more adjusted to her surroundings and children her age than she ever had been in the past.

A girl named Marjorie Cummings befriended her. Marjorie was one of those girls who existed on the social 'outer'. She was not passed over entirely by the others, but nor was she made fun of. She didn't bear any of the physical mishaps that would instantly banish her from the in crowd, like obesity or awkwardness; nor did she have anyone in her family to be 'discussed' or ridiculed.

Marjorie wasn't overly pretty but had what people would call a nice, evenly featured face. She had an unruly shock of black hair that made her skin look pale by comparison, and though tall for her age, and still a bit gangly, it was clear to the more experienced eye that she would become more statuesque as she matured. Her father owned a hardware store in Adelaide, so she was spared the embarrassment of being poor. And while it was in her power to acquire a more popular group of friends, she was more interested in people who didn't have their heads full of nonsense. Eleanor had looked quiet, reserved and, more importantly, she'd looked intelligent. And so one afternoon, Marjorie had simply walked up to the quiet auburn-haired girl with the intelligent face and introduced herself.

They'd become firm friends, and with Eleanor no longer going about the schoolyard on her own, the gossip had stopped. Eleanor would, from time to time, think about that terrible day of the double suicides, and then she would wonder about Lucy and where she was and how she was fairing, but the blessing of youth was that it tended to let many episodes slip back into the past where they rightfully belonged. Her recollections surrounding that fateful day had already begun to fade into a kind of hazy memory, and though her fondness for Lucy had remained strong, the horror of that day had begun to soften around the edges in her mind. Sometimes, Eleanor was astonished to think she'd ever been part of such a terrible ordeal.

Unlike Lucy, Marjorie was allowed to visit Eleanor's house on weekends and the two girls took to these weekends with relish, whether it was going down to the Torrens to listen to the spruikers on the banks, catching an afternoon flick at the Regent on Rundle Street when money and parents permitted, or staying home and trying their hand at a bit of dressmaking.

The only oddity in Eleanor's life, if indeed she would call it that, existed in her dreams. She knew him as Parquin, and though she'd only recently been acquainted with him, his existence somehow wasn't entirely new to her. He'd always been there – she knew that now; had felt him with her. He was the feeling that crept up her back as a warning when things were about to happen, like that day with Lucy's father, and other times when she'd become lost in her daydreams, she now knew that she was not merely dreaming of other places... she'd been *remembering* them.

Parquin seemed to wait for her in her dreams, and absurd as that notion was each morning on waking, even to her fanciful young mind, he was becoming just as real to her as her conscious life. She'd found herself impatient at times to fall asleep so she could speak with him again. Of course, on those nights, sleep would elude her, and she would toss and turn in her bed while scolding herself for being so much of a ninny.

It was apparent to her now that her affinity for history or social studies was based more on her actual first-hand knowledge of historical events, rather than the simple idea that she was a good pupil, and as time went on, Eleanor found a kind of whimsical nostalgia would settle over her during those lessons.

Parquin had accompanied her on many tours of her past lives – 'expeditions' she liked to call them, which he'd found amusing. Eleanor liked those times best, when Parquin became amused, but it didn't happen very often, his intentions more focused on showing her where she'd been, what she'd done... and who she really was.

The romantic in her loved visiting what she had nicknamed 'their' time. Parquin had been of the earth then, a man to whom she'd been married, and though she'd found it difficult to absorb this as fact, it had thrilled her young, impractical heart all the same. But he'd been firm on one thing in particular, and that was that she not abandon the responsibilities of her present life or see it as secondary to her past.

'Your path has been fraught with both sorrow and joy, Eleanor… and so too will your present course run. Take heed that you decipher one from the other, for though I can show you your past, it is you who must live your present.'

Eleanor always sensed a kind of sadness in Parquin when he spoke in this way and that there were things he kept to himself, for reasons unknown to her. But then she thought that it was only his way and that perhaps she would come to learn those ways a little better in time.

CHAPTER FIVE

Eleanor stood frozen, every nerve in her body screaming out in fear. She must have chided herself a dozen times in the past few weeks and at least a dozen more only that morning. But it was no use: she couldn't do it.

'Eleanor Grayson! You'll never learn to swim if you don't at least step into the water!' Miss Prichard's voice rang out over the splashing water and laughter of the girls already frolicking about in the pool. A few turned to stare up at her and giggled between themselves at 'scaredy-cat Grayson' standing rigid as a statue on the edge of the steps.

Eleanor's heart lurched at the sight of Miss Prichard shaking her head and striding purposefully towards her around the outer edge. What she going to do? Was she going to push her in?

'It's all right, Eleanor, don't worry. I'll help you. It'll be all right – really.' Marjorie had seen her friend's anxiety and had hurried over to her side. Eleanor turned frightened eyes towards her, and Marjorie stepped back out of the way as Miss Prichard reached the two girls. Grabbing hold of Eleanor, she started to lead her into the water, but Eleanor resisted, her whole body straining against the teacher's grip on her upper arm, her eyes wide, her breath suddenly strangled in her throat.

'No, I don't want to… I-I mean, I feel sick. That's it, yes… it's my time of the month!'

Miss Prichard wasn't fooled. She stopped and stared hard at Eleanor, a look of irritation on her face, and then as if suddenly deciding what to do, she turned to Marjorie. 'Marjorie Cummings, I want you to stay with Eleanor for a while.' The teacher gave a sigh of frustration, barely able to conceal her impatience. 'Perhaps then if you *sit* on the side of the pool for a while – get used to it that way, Eleanor – perhaps then you'll see that there is nothing to fear!'

Marjorie came forward quickly and guided Eleanor down to sit on the edge so they could dangle their feet in the water. Eleanor calmed down almost immediately. It was then she felt the humiliation sink in. She felt sure every girl in her class thought her to be a first-rate idiot! She wondered what Marjorie thought of her immature display of panic, but her friend only gave her a reassuring smile.

Miss Prichard went back to the lesson at hand. 'Quiet down, girls! Now some of you already know how to swim, but over the next two weeks, we will be learning the correct movements and way of breathing as you move through the water.'

Eleanor and Marjorie sat over in the corner of the pool, feigning interest in everything the teacher was saying, though neither of them had their mind on the stern and full-figured Miss Prichard at all. Eleanor's thoughts were taken up by the ease with which the other girls waded through the water, some with their bodies lying stretched out on the surface, and she marvelled at their confidence to float about with their feet off the bottom.

Marjorie's thoughts, however, were most decidedly on the lifeguard standing high up on a small platform, his gaze ever watchful on the many people swimming and splashing about below him. Marjorie's eyes darted slyly upward time and again, her fascination rising more each time she caught a glimpse of his muscular legs and handsome profile. She elbowed Eleanor and nodded in his direction. Eleanor glanced up just in time for him to look down and catch her looking, and he smiled, causing her face to burn with embarrassment.

'Eleanor Grayson! If you are not to participate in today's instruction, you can at least pay attention to what is being said!'

Miss Prichard's reprimand made the other girls look over at her, and Eleanor felt her face flame even more. She didn't dare look up to the lifeguard again… though it didn't stop Marjorie.

Eleanor concentrated in kicking her feet through the water. She didn't mind the water lapping over her feet at all; she thought it actually felt quite nice. Being this close to the water had never frightened her; it was only when she was expected to immerse herself in it that it terrified her.

She and Marjorie sat that way for some time before Marjorie finally slipped off the edge and into the waist-deep water. Eleanor ran a quick, envious eye over Marjorie's swimming costume, noticing how well it looked on her – very different to her own ill-fitting garment. Marjorie had filled out a little in the past couple of years, most of her gangliness having disappeared as she'd reached her early teens, her long legs now shapely, her waist slim and her bustline well formed.

Eleanor's lack of attributes seemed more apparent alongside those of her friend's. She peered down at her own bustline, or lack of, the thick material sagging and wrinkled across her chest with nothing there to fill it out. Her body was 'up and down like a drink of water' as Lizzie would say. 'A bit of a late starter, dear, don't worry,' her mother kept telling her.

Miss Prichard's attention was now taken up with guiding one of the girls through the water while teaching her the proper strokes.

'Try standing up in the water, Eleanor. You don't have to try and swim; it's only up to my waist… look!' Marjorie jumped up and down to prove her point as a way of trying to coax her friend into the water. Eleanor eyed the whole thing with apprehension, but then scolded herself yet again for her cowardice and, after a long moment, she gathered her courage, took a deep breath and slipped into the water also, instantly bracing herself against the cooler temperature.

'You see? That wasn't so bad, was it?'

Eleanor shivered, her teeth clattering together, though it was more through her uneasiness than any chilliness she might be feeling. The other girls began swimming about in circles, their legs kicking, occasionally knocking against Eleanor's.

'Hey, watch it!' said Marjorie. Just then, one of the girls swam up close and Eleanor went to move out of the way, her foot slipping on the bottom, causing her to stumble backward. In a flash she was below the surface. Her distress was instant, the sensation of water covering her eyes, nose and mouth terrifying as she tried desperately to right herself once more. But each time she tried to stand, her foot slipped on the smooth bottom, and Eleanor was gripped by instant panic, thinking she was most certainly about to drown.

Hands reached for her beneath the surface, but in her alarm she fought them off, fingers slipping over her arms and shoulders as they tried to take hold. Her lungs felt as though they would surely burst, her senses locked out from the world above. Her mind hazed over... dimmed... everything starting to go dark. She seemed to drift...

'Elexia, go! He's found you! Swim! Go now and I will find you... go!'

The words circled in her brain, taking her away... taking her back.

She was sobbing... he was kissing her... Parquin was kissing her? But there was danger... much danger... 'Parquin!'

Eleanor felt a mouth over hers, blowing... no, breathing. Her mind became confused, her chest felt heavy... so heavy... The mouth disappeared and then someone was leaning on her. She felt she was choking. She started to cough, and strong arms hauled her over onto her side as water spewed forth from her mouth and out through her nose, making it burn. She coughed some more, striving to breathe. Gradually and painfully, her lungs began to take in air, and she opened her eyes to see... whom? Parquin? No... not Parquin, but the lifeguard she'd been caught staring at. He had a worried look upon his face and then he smiled in relief. 'I think she's going to be all right now, miss.'

'Eleanor?' She recognized Marjorie's voice but she couldn't see her amongst the sea of faces that crowded around.

'Thank heavens! We better get her home, I think... Can she stand?'

Eleanor tried to move but her limbs were a dead weight – she had no more control over her body than a rag doll.

'I don't think she's up to it yet. Better let her lie here a while longer. I'll sit her up in a minute, and then we better have her moved into the sickbay, let someone take a look at her.'

Eleanor remembered all at once what had happened, and she was suddenly mortified at the spectacle she must have made of herself. She became conscious of her position on the side of the pool, her head now resting in the lifeguard's lap, and being in this position, she was able to look freely upon his face, a thought springing to mind that she'd never *ever* been this close to a member of the opposite sex before, beyond her family of course. The thought both thrilled her and made her nervous.

Close up, he was quite handsome in a rugged kind of way, and she now realized why Marjorie had kept ogling him. Eleanor was so close she was able to watch as droplets of water ran down his face and changed direction as they hit the faint regrowth of whiskers around the edge of his jawline. She almost smiled at the ridiculous little striped regulation cap stretched across the top of his head and strapped below his chin, partially covering his hair... brown hair as far as she could make out.

His face was turned away from her at present and so Eleanor took the opportunity to continue her inspection. She noticed the width of his shoulders and chest, appropriately covered by his tunic – also regulation – and she was instantly reminded of his maleness and how close he was. The thought made her feel strange in her stomach and she began to cough, causing him to look down at her again, his face a mask of concern... *But only concern*, thought Eleanor. She struggled to sit up and, looking down at her own body, she noticed her swimming costume had sagged ridiculously low across her chest, showing more of herself than was decent. Eleanor, her face flaming, couldn't help wishing that she'd drowned after all.

∼

'I don't care how much it means to her marks! You know Eleanor has always been scared of the water! And I don't think "facing her fears" or "getting back in the saddle" like that overblown teacher of hers says is going to make one bloody scrap of difference!'

Harry stood inside their bedroom door throwing his hands about in mounting anger as Nettie, her back to him, searched through the stack of spare blankets in the cupboard. Now with a blue and white knitted overthrow under her arm she turned on her husband.

'Harry, there's no need to swear! I'm with you on this matter. I'm just passing on what Miss Prichard told me, that's all!'

She breezed past him and out through the door, making her way to Eleanor's room. Harry followed her until they were just outside Eleanor's bedroom door, but he stopped her before she entered and turned her round to face him.

'Net, she could have drowned at those bloody baths today!'

Harry noticed his wife's frown at his choice of words again and he held his hands up by way of apology before she could say anything. He went on, his voice quieter as he leant in close. 'I am not going to let my daughter risk body and soul for some school lesson, just because some dried-up old spinster said she might fail in that subject.'

Nettie smothered a grin at her husband's reference to Miss Prichard. 'I wouldn't be quite so uncharitable, dear, but just the same, I will write a letter to the school informing them that Eleanor is to be excused from gymnastics for the next two weeks.'

Harry seemed content with that remark and nodded to himself. Nettie crept silently into Eleanor's room and added the overthrow to the blankets already covering her soundly sleeping daughter. Harry strained his neck in an effort to make out if Eleanor was all right, his look going from her to Nettie. His wife nodded at him in assurance as she crept just as quietly out of the room again.

'She's all right, Harry. Come on, I'll make us some lunch. You have to get back to work – they'll be wondering where you are.' Nettie pulled on his arm, motioning for him go with her.

Nettie had already made up her mind to go down to the school the following day. No mere letter would suffice for what she had to say to that Miss Prichard! When Marjorie had told her how the teacher had tried to pull her youngest into the water, Nettie was fit to be tied! Though it was something she dared not tell Harry for fear of what he might do with that bit of information under his belt. He was already angry as it was! She imagined him storming down to the school, ranting and swearing at whoever dared to stand in his way. It wouldn't surprise her if he were to upend a desk or two in his blind rage to get to that Miss Prichard! *That would definitely never do, even if that overstuffed prig had it coming!* thought Nettie. And then she stifled a giggle at her own uncharitable thoughts.

'Where are we going?'

Parquin said nothing. He always appeared to have his thoughts centred on something else, though oddly enough, Eleanor knew that she was his prime reason for visiting her dreams.

'My throat and chest hurt.'

Parquin seemed to find this amusing, his violet eyes

growing brighter, more vibrant with humour. Eleanor didn't see the humour.

Eleanor rolled over in her sleep, swallowing uncomfortably.

'You must learn to leave it behind, Eleanor. You have no need of your physical restraints. Come.'

Eleanor went, or was she being pulled? She was never sure. Nevertheless, her whole being seemed somehow lighter now, more... uninhibited.

She seemed to be drifting through a mist towards something, though she wasn't moving. It was almost like being everywhere at once, but that was impossible. It was as though she was part of everything while existing in nothingness at the same time. She only ever experienced this 'parallel' state while in the presence of Parquin.

The familiar golden mist that surrounded her began to swirl about her now, almost as though Parquin himself was circling her as well...

Suddenly, she was standing inside some sort of roughly made dwelling. She knew this place; had seen it before... hadn't she? She turned looking for Parquin but he'd gone.

'Parquin?' But he was nowhere to be seen.

Eleanor looked about her at the interior of the shack. There was a table and chairs made from wood, and a hearth set into a stoned chimney. A bed of sorts sat in the corner, with a crude kind of material strung across its base. Down one side was perhaps the biggest cabinet she'd ever seen, its surface and shelves filled with all kinds of jars and crockery.

Eleanor heard noises in the distance: children laughing... a man's deep baritone voice. The sounds came closer. She stood stock-still, wondering... hoping... expecting to see... whom? She remembered... something... someone. She felt herself being pulled away... though strangely she didn't want to go...

Suddenly she was no longer part of the scene but was looking down on it, Parquin now back at her side. He moved around her, through her. She felt his force, beckoning her to understand... She looked down. She saw a man, a black man... and two young children. The man called out... 'Hey, Evie, where ya at? Ya menfolk be hungry!'

Eleanor watched as a woman came to the door of the shack. She was laughing... Eleanor looked on in bewilderment. Evie? That black woman was Evie?

She turned to Parquin. 'That's me! That's me, isn't it? I don't understand...'

Parquin did. To show Eleanor as she'd been in a different time meant showing her a different likeness... even a different 'race', though Parquin thought the word to be ill-used and of no consequence.

'Skin colour carries no more importance than the changing colours of a dawn... 'tis the same forces at work... and it will always be so.'

'You talk in riddles!'

Eleanor felt his laughter all around.

'And stop mocking me!' This time, Eleanor did not like his amusement.

Eleanor coughed in her sleep, her eyebrows furrowing into a deep frown, her mind held spellbound by her dreams.

She felt a cool hand upon her forehead, instantly wiping the sleep from her brain, and along with it went her dreams, the black man, Evie... and Parquin.

'Eleanor? How are you feeling, dear?' Nettie bent over her, worry evident on her face.

Eleanor opened her eyes, becoming instantly aware of the soreness in her chest and throat all over again. She made a mental note to ask Parquin to keep her 'physical restraints' with him in future. Her mind still lingered very much on Evie and the man… her man?

She frowned, from the discomfort of her chest and throat as well as all the unanswered questions swimming around in her mind.

'You were coughing so much, I thought I'd better wake you. Perhaps it might be better if you sat up for a bit.' Nettie placed a bottle of eucalyptus on the side table and helped Eleanor into a sitting position just as Lizzie breezed in the door.

'How are you feeling, Eleanor? You always seem to be getting yourself into some scrape or other, don't you?' Lizzie didn't wait for an answer; instead she made her way over to the small mirror mounted on the side wall and began preening her hair and turning her face this way and that while running a critical eye over her appearance. Of all the conversations Eleanor had had over the years with her sister, she noted that a good portion of them had been while Lizzie had been looking into a mirror.

Lizzie had left school last year and was now employed at the big and impressive John Martins department store on Rundle Street in the city. Lizzie worked behind the soaps, perfumes and toiletries counter, which for someone like her was a job made in heaven. Every week she would add yet another item to her already crowded dressing table, its surface beginning to resemble a booth from a toiletry or perfume shop itself.

On witnessing one of his daughter's spending sprees, Harry was to remark a little mockingly one afternoon to Nettie, 'I'm so glad all that schooling paid off… Lizzie can now work at making herself into more of an impulsive, self-indulged female than she was before!'

Harry was in fact happy to see his daughter with a job. He'd previously had visions of her marrying the first Holt boy or some other irresponsible good-for-nothing as soon as she'd left school. He'd been happy to be wrong.

Lizzie scrutinized her appearance. Her blonde hair, made blonder with a good dose of peroxide, was fashionably cut in the new bob. Lizzie thought that if it was good enough for the likes of Janet Gaynor and Jean Harlow, then it was definitely good enough for her!

She tried to push the finger waves back in at the side, but it was no use: her hair was too straight for them to remain in all day. Not like Eleanor's. Her sister had the good fortune of wavy hair, too long for her liking, but if she would only get it cut, she would appear older… and more modern.

She peered at Eleanor's reflection in the mirror… she really did look young sitting there, their mother fussing around her, plumping up her pillows and covering her up with blankets. Why, she looked like a girl of ten, or possibly eleven. It was hard to believe she was thirteen years old. She went back to the primping of her hair.

Nettie reached for the brush on the dresser. 'We might try to free some of those tangles from your hair, dear… perhaps if I plait it.'

'You really should have it cut, Eleanor; nobody goes about with that length of hair anymore!' Lizzie threw the words over her shoulder.

Nettie frowned. 'Your sister has beautiful hair, and I don't know why you cut yours, to tell you the truth… you end up spending more time on it now than you ever did when it was long.'

'Oh, Mum, it was hopelessly old-fashioned!' Lizzie was

leaning up close to the mirror now and scanning her skin for any blemishes. Lizzie had flawless skin, which was something that Eleanor always wished she'd had. To Eleanor, her own face always seemed blotchy and never completely free of pimples, though her mother was always telling her they would clear up... but when?

'I don't want to get it cut... well, not yet anyway.' The words made Eleanor cough.

Lizzie smiled slyly at her own reflection, knowing her next words would cause some curiosity. 'Are you sure? What if Mark preferred it shorter?'

Nettie straightened up immediately. 'Who in heaven's name is Mark?'

Eleanor looked curiously at her sister also waiting for her answer.

'Why, none other than the utterly gorgeous man who pulled you out of the water today.'

'I don't want to hear you talking like that, Lizzie, do you hear? And don't let your father hear you talking like that either!'

Lizzie finally took her eyes off her own reflection long enough to frown at her mother. 'But, Mum, I didn't say anything so terrible. I'm merely letting Eleanor know the name of the person who saved her!'

Lizzie's voice rose suddenly in her excitement. 'Everyone is talking about it, you know... how she nearly drowned... in only three feet of water no less! And how he skirted down as quick as you like and hauled her out...'

'*That* was Mark?' Eleanor cut her off. 'The Mark you always go on about? Mark... oh I can't remember... What's his name? It's something long.'

'That's enough! The both of you!' Nettie went back to her

ministrations, her hands now working roughly over Eleanor's hair and making her wince.

'Worthington-Cooke – his name is Mark Worthington-Cooke!' Lizzie stood up straighter, as if just stating his name out loud was something to be proud of.

'Lord, what a mouthful! You ought to call him WC for short!' The words were out before Nettie could help herself, and she quickly turned her back on the girls and started fussing about the top of the dresser in an attempt to hide the sudden giggle that seemed to have erupted from nowhere. But it was no use. Her shoulders started to shake with restrained laughter at such a name and she turned back, red-faced and holding a hand over her mouth.

Both Eleanor and Lizzie started to laugh at the sight of her, until Nettie, her finger up to her lips and shaking her head, began flapping her hands downward by way of trying to keep them both quiet. It was Eleanor's coughing that instantly sobered Nettie.

'That will be enough now,' she said with finality, her face still pink due to her exertions.

There was a knock on the door and Ted entered, his face set in his usual animated cheeriness as he beamed at everyone present. 'How are ya, Ellie? Heard you got yourself in a bit of a pickle today! It's all over the school!'

Ted was the only one who called Eleanor by that name, and quite possibly the only one whom she would abide doing so. She knew her mother didn't like it all that much, but she also knew that she wouldn't object to it… which might possibly have had something to do with how strongly her grandmother objected to it.

'If it weren't for Mark Worthington-Cooke, it may have been more than just a pickle!' Lizzie seemed hell-bent on pushing his name into the conversation whenever she could.

Nettie gave an exaggerated groan, conveying to all present that she clearly found the whole subject of the boy *and* his name decidedly tiresome.

'Cookie? It was Cookie who pulled you out? Heard he's an all-round athletic type – lucky for you he was there then, El.'

'You call him Cookie?' Eleanor felt somehow disappointed; the name didn't suit her idea of a hero.

'Mum calls him WC, don't you, Mum?' Lizzie stifled a grin.

Nettie sniffed, instantly reminding herself of Hillary.

'WC?' Ted's face screwed up in puzzlement and then, as it dawned on him what his sister meant, he started to laugh. 'WC! Oh I get it, Mum…'

Nettie rolled her eyes.

'Hey, Mum, that's not bad… water closet, right?'

Nettie threw her hands up in exasperation. 'Oh for goodness' sake, Ted! It sounds worse when *you* say it!'

Ted shrugged, his fair hair flopping over his eyes as he absently swept it away from his forehead.

'And you need a haircut too! I think you better go down to the barber's this afternoon. When your father gets home from work, I'll get him to take you.'

'Aw, but, Mum, I told Mr Crowley I'd be down after school! Why can't I go on Saturday instead?'

'Because it will save me boiling your clothes to get them clean for a change, and it will keep your father out of the pub for a night!' Nettie nodded in a firm *so that's that*!

Eleanor started coughing again and Nettie reached for the bottle of eucalyptus. 'Now off with the both of you. I have to rub some of this on Eleanor.'

Lizzie and a disgruntled Ted left the room, and Nettie set about hoisting Eleanor's cotton nightshift up over her shoulders and rubbing the strong-smelling elixir across her back, her hands moving vigorously in wide circles and making Eleanor sway from side to side.

Eleanor's chest still hurt slightly, and it still pained her to swallow. She thought about Parquin again and how he'd talked about her 'physical restraints.' Her thoughts rolled on to the dream and the shack… Evie… and…

'Gans!'

Eleanor sat bolt upright, her eyes widening as her mind now opened to a flood of memories, unaware she'd uttered his name out loud.

'Sorry, dear, what did you say? Am I rubbing too hard?' Nettie stopped and yanked Eleanor's nightie down over her back again. 'Best you rest a bit more I think, and then…'

But Eleanor wasn't listening. One scene after another was reeling through her mind like one of the silent flicks that still played occasionally down at the old picture house. She saw rows of shacks like the one she'd visited… and a big house, all polished wood and beautiful rugs, fine china… a huge kitchen… and Evie. There was a river with a track that ran down to it and alongside. And there was the same black man… Gans – she knew his name now – dressed in a uniform… and a baby. Evie's baby, *her* baby! But there'd been two children in her dream… hadn't there?

'Now is not the time, Eleanor. Go back.'

Eleanor frowned. What? Something was happening… someone shaking her.

'Parquin?' She blinked… became dimly aware… Her mother's voice slipped into her thoughts, becoming louder now.

'Eleanor! What's the matter? What is it?' Nettie was shaking her daughter frantically.

Eleanor turned, noticing her mother's frightened face. She looked about her in bewilderment. What had just happened?

'Eleanor? What's going on? Are you all right? I think I better send for the doctor…'

'No, Mum, I'm all right – really I am.' Her mother's words had jolted her back to normal clarity of mind once again and Eleanor now tried to reassure her with a smile, though her breathing was still a little uneven.

Nettie forced her daughter to lie down and covered her securely with the blankets. Leaning close, her voice was quiet, though tinged with urgency. 'I don't know what just happened, but you frightened me – you really did. I couldn't get through to you at all… Are you sure the accident today didn't… I mean, do you feel… faint at all?'

Eleanor thought the best thing to do was reassure her mother in a way she could understand and accept. 'A little, Mum. I suppose it has been a long day, hasn't it?'

In actual fact, Eleanor did feel suddenly tired, her experience having left her thoroughly worn out. And her temples had started to throb slightly. Perhaps sleep was just what she needed.

Nettie seemed satisfied with her daughter's answer. She stroked her forehead and rose from her bedside, then leant over to kiss her cheek, but Eleanor was already fast asleep. Nettie frowned down at her. She decided that she would have to watch her closely, look for any signs of something amiss… though just what, she wasn't sure.

'Damn that Miss Prichard!' Nettie whispered.

No sooner had the woman left than a faint golden mist floated softly down and settled around the girl in her bed. It circled

her form; moved through her… healing her… easing her discomfort. He would let her sleep, dream free…

'What are we to do? What may become of us? The one thing that may end it is the one thing I cannot show you… must never show you… though our release, be it simple, is not permitted.'

The sleeping girl did not hear his pleas. He had sent his words out into a vast and mystical void, like a whisper that reverberated through an immense hallway of time and space, and though there was no reply, he knew that someone… somewhere… was listening.

Eleanor was kept home from school for the remainder of the week, and in the second week had attended only the lessons that did not require her to go swimming. Nettie had gone down to the school and voiced her complaints personally to Mr Dix, the headmaster.

'Yes, I most certainly do understand what is required of the students,' he'd said, and, 'No, I don't think Miss Prichard has the right to manhandle your daughter into a situation she clearly wasn't comfortable with!'

After much apology, much discussion and a firm guarantee that it would never happen again – as well as Mr Dix's word that Miss Prichard would be spoken to – Nettie had been satisfied, leaving his office with her head held high.

When Hillary heard her favourite granddaughter had nearly drowned, she'd rushed down to be by her side with an air about her that said, 'Your Grandmother is here now, dear; everything will be all right.' She'd immediately sent word down to her own doctor to visit Eleanor. 'Not that the clinic attendants at the baths don't do a good job, Henrietta, but Dr

Crane is an excellent doctor and will do a thorough examination of her.'

Dr Crane had nothing more to report than the clinic attendants. Hillary then sent poor Rosie out for some chocolate and lemonade, 'to ease her throat'. Within days, Eleanor's skin began to break out all over and for Nettie that was the last straw. She had decided enough was enough and wasted no more time before complaining to Harry about his mother's interference.

Harry was then left with the dilemma of having to tell his mother not to interfere. *How does a son tell his mother not to interfere with her grandchildren without hurting her feelings?* he asked himself. Though better him than Nettie. Harry most certainly didn't want to test the mettle of these two women; he would have a colossal battle of wills on his hands given they could both be as stubborn as one another.

As it turned out, he didn't have to do anything. Eleanor got better and went back to school and Hillary's visits stopped... at least for a time.

'Think yourself lucky, Ruby Jenson! At least your mother-in-law is clear away in another state!' Nettie had to voice her displeasure with Hillary to somebody, and Ruby was the perfect ally, having borne witness to Hillary's interference in the past.

'Don't let it upset you so. The main thing is that Eleanor is all right.' Ruby was on her knees in her front garden, pulling out weeds around her geraniums. They were one of the few flowers Ruby was able to grow, confessing to Nettie that everything else she'd planted in the past had always died on her.

It was quite warm out for a spring day. Ruby pulled off her gloves and the straw hat from her head and mopped her brow with her handkerchief. Reaching a hand up to Nettie, she said, 'Help an old lady up will you, Net?'

'My goodness, Rube, you're not old! You're not even forty yet!' Nettie held a hand out in any case and helped her friend to stand.

'Perhaps it's motherhood that does it, who knows!' Ruby wiped her sweaty hands down the front of her apron before slipping it up and over her head, wisps of blonde hair escaping from her bun as she did. 'I've had enough for today. Fancy a cup of tea?'

Nettie nodded and followed her friend indoors.

It was considerably cooler inside Ruby's house.

Nettie watched as Ruby, not bothering to hang her hat on the hook just inside the door, threw both the hat and her garden gloves with a despondent *thud* onto the hallway table. Nettie peered down at them and raised one eyebrow at her friend's telltale sign that all was perhaps not right in the Jenson household. She marched on into the kitchen behind Ruby and sat down.

'Do I detect a bit of discontent in the air? Hmm?' Nettie asked a little overdramatically and then gave her friend a half-smile, but Ruby merely placed the kettle on the grid and reached for the teapot.

Nettie frowned. 'Seriously, Rube, is there anything wrong?'

Ruby sighed, sat down opposite her and shrugged. 'No, not really I suppose, just…' Ruby shrugged again.

'For goodness' sake, whatever is the matter? You know you can tell me!' Nettie leant closer now, but Ruby rose again and made her way over to the cabinet. Then, reaching for the cups and saucers, she suddenly turned. 'Do you ever worry about Lizzie… well, perhaps getting herself into a bit of trouble? You know what I mean.'

'Lizzie?' Nettie eyes widened. 'Why? Tell me, what have you heard!'

Ruby shook her head and held up her hands. 'No, no, nothing about Lizzie. It's Kathy I'm concerned about.' She sat down again in the other chair. 'Kathy isn't like Lizzie… I mean, Kathy can be easily led, perhaps into something that she'll regret and might… no, *will* ruin her. She used to be so open about her social activities, used to tell me everything – where she was going, where she'd been, what they'd all done – and, more importantly, who she was with. But now, she seems to not want to talk about things at all. She's at that age, Nettie – well, you know what I mean… that age where suddenly we know more than our parents, or think we do. And if she puts her trust in the wrong person…' Ruby shook her head.

Nettie understood. She could remember her and Harry getting down to some 'serious' dealings when she'd had no business taking such a chance… but thank God he'd been the right one. She sought to alleviate her friend's concern.

'Perhaps you worry too much, Rube. Perhaps it's just a mother's lot to worry about such things… especially for our daughters. But then this is the twentieth century too. It's not like it was in our mothers' time… I mean, surely a girl can hold her head up in this day and age and not have to carry around some mark of shame or disgrace the rest of her days.'

Though Nettie's face held a trace of skepticism at her own words, she blundered on. 'What about Lenny? Is he worried too? What does he think?'

'He thinks I'm overreacting, that she's not a schoolgirl anymore and that it's natural for her not to spout off about all her social doings like she did when she was younger. He reminded me of what I was like at that age and asked if I told my mother everything.'

Ruby gave a genuine smile for the first time that morning. 'Oh bosh! Imagine telling my mother everything I got up to at that age. Lord, Net, she would've kept me under lock and key!'

Nettie laughed outright. 'I know what you mean! Goodness, looking back on things now, I was lucky to come through unscathed!'

The smile left Ruby's face. 'I suppose I feel a little shelved though too… like I've been left behind suddenly. Lenny has his job and his friends, Kathy has moved on to whatever she's doing and I'm doing exactly the same thing I was doing twenty years ago and *will* probably be doing in another twenty. I suddenly feel outmoded and unnecessary. And it didn't seem to take all that long to get here either.'

Nettie nodded, understanding full well what Ruby was saying. 'Yes, in the blink of an eye, your children are grown, you balk at the newest fashions the way your mother used to and suddenly you're noticing the first signs of middle age creeping undeniably across your face each time you look in the mirror.'

Ruby laughed. 'Don't forget the waistline!' She stood up and smoothed her dress across her stomach, indicating her thickening middle. Nettie, not to be outdone, stood up also and gathered her own dress at the side to show off her figure.

'That's not a bulge! And you with three children to speak of as well!' Ruby started to laugh. Nettie also.

'At least you can still wear a belt around your middle without looking like an overstuffed pin cushion!' Nettie replied.

Both women threw back their heads and laughed raucously. It set the scene for the remainder of the morning, their conversation moving from rapidly increasing figures to the blessing of youth, the newest pattern of materials out and their prices, the 'must-try' recipe for an upside-down cake that Ruby had happened to stumble across and onto the likes and dislikes of every member of their families and how hard it was to please them all at once.

This comfortable domestic scene was interrupted when Nettie spied Hillary entering through her gate out of Ruby's kitchen window.

'Just what I need. Whatever does she want? The kids are at school and Harry is at work.'

Ruby started clearing the table of cups and saucers as Nettie bid her friend a fond goodbye.

'Hillary! How are you today?' Nettie called, once she was outside.

Hillary swung round at the sound of Nettie's voice behind her, her gloved hand poised and ready to knock a second time on the front door.

'I'm fine, Henrietta, and you?' Hillary didn't wait for Nettie to answer but went on, her hands now clasped in front of her as she waited for her daughter-in-law to approach. 'I see you've been visiting with Mrs Jenson.'

Why does she make it sound like she's caught me out doing something shameful?

'Yes, I have.' Nettie felt the older woman's eyes on her and regretted not having taken the time to put her hair up properly this morning. But then, what of it? She hadn't planned on going anywhere, and if she'd felt comfortable enough in front of Ruby, who meant more to her than her own mother-in-law, then Hillary would simply have to put up with her appearance!

Nettie opened the door and indicated that Hillary should

enter before her. She settled herself in Nettie's kitchen, and Nettie asked if she would like a cup of tea.

'No, thank you. I'll get right to the point. It's Eleanor.'

'Eleanor? What about Eleanor? She's at school just now.'

'Yes, I'm aware of that. That's why it was a good time to come and see you.'

Nettie frowned, her hand absently coming up to smooth a few auburn hairs back into place, but to no avail. She fidgeted with her dress, smoothing it down and pulling it into place, momentarily remembering her and Ruby's conversation about thickening waistlines. Nettie was nervous, and she didn't know why.

'Sit down, Henrietta… please.'

Nettie sat.

'When Eleanor was visiting me last Sunday afternoon, she had… well, it is what I would call an "episode" for want of a better way of explaining it. And it's not the first time.'

'An episode?' Nettie glared at her mother-in-law while making a mental note to herself that she would have to try and persuade Eleanor away from the usual weekly visits to her grandmother. Hillary cleared her throat.

'Have you noticed anything… well… different with Eleanor since her accident?'

Nettie blinked. 'You mean what happened down at the baths?'

Hillary sniffed impatiently. 'Yes, yes, the swimming incident. Well, have you?'

Nettie remembered the afternoon in Eleanor's bedroom, but since then she'd noticed nothing of importance. Eleanor was a bit of a bookworm and a dreamer, but she did all the things a girl of her age was apt to do. She went out with her friend Marjorie, to the movies, for walks, shopping and the like. Apart from her fear of water, which Nettie had no idea why or where her daughter had acquired, there was nothing else she thought strange.

'No, Hillary, I haven't. Would you mind telling me what all this is about?'

Hillary settled herself deeper into the chair and cleared her throat once more. 'I'd decided it was time to go through my attic. I hadn't even bothered to go up there in about two years – the stairs were steep you understand, and one can't get about like one used to…'

It was now Nettie's turn to get impatient. Hillary glanced over at her and went on.

'In any case, Eleanor informed me that she would be thrilled to help me… I suppose so she could look at the old fashions, books, toys… that sort of thing. You know how she likes anything from bygone years. Goodness me, there were things left up there from my husband's grandfather's time… an old uniform, his diaries and his grandmother's gowns… but I must get to the point, mustn't I? We opened up an old chest, and in it, among other things like old photographs and the like, were a stack of my husband's old history books. He attended the prestigious Derby College, you know; he rather fancied becoming a teacher.' Hillary paused long enough to let this sink in.

Nettie couldn't have cared less if old George had been a celebrated Master or if Hillary had told her that his portrait had hung in the halls of Cambridge! But she kept a straight face.

'Yes, well… when Eleanor picked up the books, she started leafing through them, you see… Old battle stratagems, maps of France and Europe and such – things my George learnt in his school years; things I would never have any use for. Nor George as it would seem: those old books have been up there since before he died and nary a one did I see him with… at any time. But Eleanor seemed fascinated with them. And then it happened!'

It was all Nettie could do not to lean over and strangle the old witch! 'What? What happened?'

'Well, she seemed to come over all peculiar and there was such an odd look in her eyes. It made no difference what I said or did… she didn't appear to even acknowledge me! And that's only the half of it, Henrietta!'

Nettie took a deep breath and tried to remain patient. 'What else?'

'Eleanor was talking in French!'

'French?' Nettie thought that quite possibly the old woman's mind was finally beginning to crumble. 'You know the language, do you?'

'Well no, but… well, I certainly know French when I hear it! One doesn't have to speak French in order to identify the language!' Hillary leant back in her chair and sniffed, waiting for her daughter-in-law to take in what she'd just said.

Nettie didn't know what to make of it. 'You mentioned this wasn't the first time?'

'Oh, the other times are insignificant by comparison, and I dare say I would not have given them another thought had it not been for last Sunday. Eleanor has, from time to time, gone off into what I'd always thought to be a silly daydream or some such thing, but now I'm not so certain.' Hillary's face became worried. 'You don't think her mind was affected by the swimming accident, do you? I've since learnt that being underwater for any length of time has been known to alter the function of the brain…'

Nettie had been staring into space while thinking hard on what Hillary had told her, but her mother-in-law's last words made her snap her head round to look at her. 'Alter the function of the brain? Eleanor is a bright, intelligent girl,

Hillary – there's nothing wrong with any function of her brain!'

Hillary sniffed in response.

There was silence between the two women for a time, and then Hillary spoke again. 'So what's to be done?'

Nettie raised her eyebrows. 'Nothing.'

'Nothing? Nothing at all?' Hillary looked at Nettie in astonishment.

'Not a thing. If I'd witnessed my daughter's "condition" as you apparently have, then I agree, I would most certainly look into it, and not that I disbelieve you, but I must see some solid proof myself before I feel the need for anything to be done. You must see my point on this, surely!'

'Indeed I do not! How much more proof do you need than my word?'

'Hillary, it has nothing to do with your word! I trust that you've witnessed… something, but as I am Eleanor's mother, I need to see something for myself, don't you see? What would you have me do? Send her off for all sorts of tests on the strength of just one account? I will watch her closely, and I will also be discussing this with Harry when he gets home, which is something I would do in any event.'

Hillary sniffed. As much as she felt slighted by Nettie's response, Hillary had to admit that her daughter-in-law had a point. For wouldn't she react the same way if anyone had come to her and said the same things about Harold? There was nothing for it, she thought grimly; she would have to concede to Nettie's course of action on the matter.

Hillary rose from the chair and readied herself to leave by doing her usual amount of unnecessary preening – patting her hair back up into place when none had fallen down or putting her hat right when it was still perched upon her head the way it had originally been placed. Nettie watched her go through her customary routine, waiting patiently for the last action. This was to pull up her gloves, smoothing first the back of one hand and then the other, which of course was just as needless an action as the rest of her touch-ups. And now with herself properly primped and straightened, she went to leave but suddenly stopped and looked at Nettie.

'I won't pretend that I am anything but dissatisfied, Henrietta! You and I have been at odds on many an issue, and this one is clearly no different. But…' Here Hillary let out a long breath before going on. 'I must content myself with the fact that we both have Eleanor's best interests in mind and that you will talk to Harold on the matter, I suppose then that I must force myself to wait and see.'

Hillary sniffed and nodded as a way of ending her visit, leaving a somewhat bewildered Nettie standing in the middle of her kitchen.

'And then she said that she would content herself with the fact that we both care for Eleanor… or something… and that she was happy I was going to talk to you, and that she would force herself to wait and see!

Harry rolled his eyes. Nettie had been ranting for the past hour or more, since he'd come home from work, walking close behind him wherever he went, leaning over his shoulder and complaining to him about his mother's visit. He'd heard the whole conversation practically from beginning to end and was now thinking he should have gone for a beer first instead of telling Louie he'd be down later. Work had finished early, being a Friday, and thank goodness Eleanor and Ted weren't home from school yet and Lizzie was still in the city.

Nettie hadn't let up, even as he'd stripped off his shirt and filled the basin. She'd absently taken his dirty shirt from him and then, when he'd washed his face and hands, she'd held out a towel to him, still going on about this afternoon.

Suddenly all was quiet, the silence causing Harry to turn and look at her. Nettie was standing there staring at him and tapping her foot.

'Well? What do you think?'

Harry frowned in confusion. 'What do I think? About what? About my mother's visit and what she was saying? About Eleanor and whatever it was that happened? About my father's horde of bits and pieces up in the attic?'

Harry smiled then, his eyes taking on a faraway look. 'You know, come to think of it… I used to go up to that attic and play when I was a kid… all sorts of stuff up there… Lord, Net, haven't been up there in years…'

'Harry! I want to talk about Eleanor!'

Harry gave a melodramatic sigh of relief. 'Phew! For a while there, I wasn't sure just *what* wanted to talk about.'

Nettie pursed her lips. 'All right, I admit to going a little over the top about Hillary, but she made me so angry – made me feel like I was on some sort of probation – with my own daughter no less! But I'm ashamed to say that my top priority should have been Eleanor… Well, it is. Now what do you think?'

They were in their bedroom, Harry now tucking a clean shirt into his trousers, his braces hanging loose at his sides. He turned sideways on in the mirror, sucking in his stomach and letting it out again. Then he turned to Nettie and smiled.

'There's nothing wrong with Eleanor. I admit, there is something a little different about her, but certainly nothing abnormal. As for this talking French thing…' Harry shrugged. 'I think what you told Mum about watching her close is probably the only thing you can do at this stage.'

Nettie nodded. 'There's something else, Harry. Eleanor displayed something similar to what Hillary said on the day of her swimming accident.'

Harry was brushing down his jacket but now gave her his full attention. 'What happened and why didn't you tell me?'

It was Nettie's turn to shrug. 'I put it down to some sort of "aftershock" or something… she'd nearly drowned for goodness' sake!' Nettie went on to explain Eleanor's episode that day. Harry was thoughtful, his memory of another day a long time ago suddenly pushing itself into his mind.

'Did you know that the day I was shot… I dreamt of her?' Harry felt suddenly embarrassed.

'Dreamt of her? What do you mean?' Nettie eyed her husband curiously. An unwelcome picture of Harry on some battlefield, shot and bleeding, flashed momentarily to mind, but she pushed it away. Harry's voice was so quiet, Nettie had to strain to listen.

'I woke up in the medical tent not sure if I was going to live or die. Lots of men lay bleeding… dying around me… Charlie was there. You know Charlie – wouldn't leave my side.' Harry smiled at the memory of his friend, then swallowed and cleared his throat.

'There was this… gas… or mist or something… It seemed to be floating in through the tent opening towards me… You ask Charlie; I thought it was the gas bombs or something. Only thing is… Charlie couldn't see it.'

Harry glanced quickly over at Nettie before going on. 'I fell asleep or… you know, went out of it. I'd lost a lot of blood… and I heard this voice telling me to 'get on with it' and that 'it wasn't my time'… and then I saw a girl with dark red hair… thought it was you, as a girl I mean, like you were when I met you. But then… oh I don't know, somehow I knew that it wasn't you. I don't know, Net, I can remember a lot of it, but it's hard to tell it… and it was so long ago that nowadays it's more like a feeling. Anyway, it turned out that it was almost the same time as you were having Eleanor… though I had no idea until I'd arrived home.'

Harry shrugged, embarrassed and feeling at his most vulnerable. He turned to look at Nettie, but her face was unreadable.

Nettie didn't know what to make of what Harry had just told her. 'So, you're saying… What are you saying?'

Harry almost laughed. 'I'm merely saying that there's something different about Eleanor. I've known it from the day she was born, but that's not to say that there's anything wrong with her.'

Nettie started to pace the bedroom floor, her hands fidgeting with each other. 'I'll keep an eye on her, Harry, just to make sure.'

Remembering Hillary, her anger surfaced once again. 'But I'm not going to send her to visit one of those psycho-thingamabobs… whatever they're called! Eleanor has had enough to contend with in her short life, what with that horrible day of those suicides and Lucy Phipps and… Well, I just don't want people to start gossiping about her like… well, the way they do about that old Mrs Timmons who never answers her door to anyone and who won't even come out of her house to check her letterbox until it's dark!'

Harry threw back his head and laughed. And then looking over at her, he was suddenly reminded of the young girl he'd fallen in love with, the years melting away in his mind and his stomach doing those strange flip-flops as though he were no more than a lad of seventeen again.

Reaching for her, he threw her across the bed, and then dived down beside her, his hands roving all over her body as he kissed her hungrily on the mouth, his senses aroused, his mind anticipating the feel of her bare skin against his while reminding himself he was no longer seventeen… and glad of it!

'Harry! The children will be home in a minute!' Nettie tried to fight him off, but only half-heartedly.

Harry was barely listening, one hand tugging at her bun, trying to unravel her hair from the knot at the back of her head, while the other pulled at the strings of her apron. 'Why do you women have to wear so many confounded clothes?'

Nettie laughed, a deliciously wicked feeling now coursing through her body.

The front door banged. 'Mum?' It was Ted.

Both Harry and Nettie jumped up, Harry nearly stumbling over his trousers, which had now fallen around his knees, as Nettie struggled to fix her hair, tie her apron and straighten the coverlet on the bed, all at the same time.

'I'm coming… be there in a minute!'

Nettie went to hurry out the door but Harry yanked her back inside the room, his arms encircling her as he leant close to her ear. 'I have to meet the boys for a few, but we'll continue this later, Mrs Grayson.' He let her go, the meaning of his words evident in his eyes as he stared down at her.

Nettie stood back and eyed him up and down, a meaningful look on her face, her eyes widening ever so slightly as they skimmed over that part of him below his waist. 'Not if you have too many, Mr Grayson.' Then, with a theatrical lift of her chin, she walked calmly out through the door.

Harry could do no more than grin and shake his head.

CHAPTER SIX

In 1930, Australia was on an economic decline due to the collapse of America's stock markets the year before. The crash of New York's Wall Street left thousands of Americans financially ruined as share prices took a sudden plunge, causing many to go bankrupt and even some, in the face of such despair, to commit suicide. Employment took a downward turn as industrial production slowed dramatically and international lending ground to a halt.

Australia's livelihood relied on overseas loans and the sale of her primary products. The value of exports fell by nearly half and share prices began to fall, so as in America, shops began to close, farms were abandoned, and rents and debts remained unpaid as unemployment steadily increased.

Australia found itself at the beginning of another depression. Those who had already suffered the hardships of depression in the 1890s braced themselves for a similar ordeal.

Many had learnt through those experiences that their money was not safe within a bank, no matter how 'airtight' it appeared, and that to spend wisely and frugally would be the only way of enduring the troubled course ahead.

By 1932, unemployment rose to a staggering thirty per cent, and those lucky enough to keep their jobs were forced to take a cut in hours and wages, while many men left the cities trying to find work in the country to feed their families back home.

Dole camps sprung up along North Terrace, in parks and along the Torrens, where, quite often, whole families that had been evicted through non-payment of rent would erect tents or makeshift homes made out of hessian, tin and other bits of scrap material that could be used for a roof or flooring. Knocking at the back door of houses for a meal or asking for handouts in the streets became a common occurrence though it was illegal. In any case, many who were barely a few shillings away from being on the streets themselves turned them away, some even erecting signs at their back door reading 'SORRY, NO HANDOUTS'. Others left boxes of old clothes and worn shoes, sometimes even a jar or two of preserved fruit or tinned food in a bid to stop door-knockers asking for anything else the family was unable to give.

Harry and Nettie were among the more fortunate. Harry had held his job, though he'd taken a cut in wages and sometimes he only worked a half day, or not at all. Nettie had stretched the family budget as much as she could. Some weeks were better than others, and in these weeks, Nettie was able to catch up on a few bills before the next lot came in, enabling them to keep one step ahead of the creditors, though she knew others were not so fortunate. Lizzie's job had been cut back to just a few hours a week and her pay was miserable. Gone were the days of buying a different perfume or lipstick every week. Lizzie now worked just to put clothes on her back, with an afternoon out at the pictures if money permitted and then only if one of her friends were able to afford it as well. She found no fun in going to the pictures alone. She still had her group of cronies she went about with, though their outings were spent walking down by the Torrens and poking fun at the spruikers or visiting each other in their homes – things that needed no money.

Ted had left school the year before, and with so many out of work, his employment prospects for the near future looked bleak. Occasionally, Mr Crowley would send him on an errand or get him to sweep up, earning him a penny or two, but Mr Crowley himself was feeling the pinch and so these occasions were rare. Though Ted, his pockets empty, still seemed perfectly content just to tinker away on an engine, and Nettie still complained about his greasy clothes and his blackened hands when he sat down to tea.

Eleanor was in her last year of school, and though her marks were extremely good and her teachers pleaded with her to go on with her studies, perhaps even becoming a teacher of history herself one day, Eleanor wasn't particularly enthusiastic. Hillary had even offered to pay for her tuition, but Eleanor wanted to go her own way, much preferring to sit back and let life take her where it may.

When pressed by a frustrated Hillary as to her reasons, Eleanor had none. She felt only that her life had been predetermined in some way, and though she knew that it was up to her to do the best she could with her life, she felt positive that going on with more studies was not for her.

She sometimes feared that her long acquaintance with Parquin had swayed her outlook on life, causing her to view its outcome a little apathetically at times. She'd had his lectures on this of course…

'*'Tis your road and no other's, Eleanor. To what end will depend on you and you alone.*'

But Eleanor had come to view her past lives as a never-ending series of stories, much the same as those ongoing detective novels that could be bought for a penny down at Bixby's. Every month, each new story revolved around the same heroine, surrounded by new people and different circumstances. But unlike the heroine, Eleanor could not even use her past experiences to help her through her present one. Her past lives were exactly that… the past.

Eleanor had asked Parquin recently what point there was in putting so much effort into a life that she would later view as just another memory and would neither influence nor matter to the present.

Parquin's cryptic answer had puzzled the fifteen-year-old Eleanor.

'You must look to yourself for answers. To limit your thoughts to only one direction will merely limit your expectations. To expand your mind is to widen your possibilities… I say that your past can *help your present, and when you come to understand this, you may then come to realize how your present can help your past…'*

These words had given Eleanor much to think on over the next few days. Her usual, or rather unusual, outlook on life and its complexities meant she'd always thought she knew, more so than others, the real story, so to speak. But it was beginning to dawn on Eleanor that she was in fact a novice when it came to the workings of life and the mysteries behind it. The frequent visits from Parquin and her many privileged looks into the past had always been for reasons that escaped her, and her constant questions to Parquin about it and 'why' had always been met with non-committal or cryptic answers.

Parquin's advice to her in looking to herself for answers was all very well, thought Eleanor, but how on earth was she able to do such a thing when she knew nothing more than what he had shown her? Eleanor knew there was something else he wasn't showing her, something behind it… a 'bigger' picture that lay waiting, just out of reach, for her to discover… perhaps in time…

Currently, Hillary sat knitting while eying her granddaughter curiously over the rims of her spectacles. She'd noticed Eleanor had been preoccupied all afternoon; the usual wide-eyed and informative banter that Hillary had come to expect during previous visits was conspicuously missing today, and she wondered if she should broach the subject of whatever was causing the concern reflected on the intelligent and usually serene countenance of her beloved granddaughter.

Hillary had asked Eleanor up to her own home once a week to help out with the dusting and polishing and the like. It was Hillary's way of being able to give her a shilling or two without it appearing like a handout. It lightened the burden on Rosie too, who in the past few months seemed to have been going through stretches of feeling 'off'. This was Rosie's way of explaining it, which didn't sit right with Hillary at all. Rosie was also getting on in years and was finding it difficult to keep the house up to the standard she always had, and so for her Eleanor's visits were a blessing. It also meant Hillary got to spend some time with her granddaughter alone.

Hillary had witnessed no more 'episodes' like that day in the attic, and even on the few occasions they'd ventured up there since, nothing had happened to cause her any undue worry. She now wondered if she'd imagined the whole thing.

Her granddaughter was different, to be sure, but Hillary liked to think that Eleanor was simply not addle-brained like a lot of girls her age, and that she had no time for frolicking about like that sister of hers. Hillary was fond of Elizabeth but found her a little too flighty for her own good, like a butterfly that goes from flower to flower. She would no sooner attach herself to one beau before flitting off to land on another. Eleanor, on the other hand, seemed to approach life a little more quietly, almost as though she were standing a bit aside from it, viewing it as one would a passing parade, to be looked at in wonder but not with the intention of taking part. Hillary had often been surprised by a kind of world-weariness that seemed to envelope Eleanor, which she thought also to be ridiculous; after all, the girl was only fifteen years old.

And Edward... well, Hillary gave him a bit more leeway. After all, he was a boy and boys were much more apt to run about wild. *Poor unsuspecting fools*, thought Hillary. *Forever chasing their tails until some girl catches it for them and pins them down.*

Eleanor sat in the opposite chair of the parlour, her own knitting all but forgotten as her hands kept pausing mid stitch while she gazed off into space.

Eleanor looked up just then and caught her grandmother's gaze, her face reddening under the older woman's intense scrutiny. Hillary decided to cut right through any preamble and address the situation.

'All right, young lady – out with it.'

'Out with what, Grandma?' Eleanor was not good at keeping secrets.

'You've been sitting there for the past hour knitting, and I don't think you've finished more than three rows. At this rate, your father will have to wait until next winter for his jumper!'

Eleanor's face reddened once again. 'I know I'm a bit slow, but I'm getting better, really I am.' Eleanor may not be able to keep secrets, but she was very adept at sidestepping them.

'It has nothing to do with your knitting expertise, Eleanor, and you know it, though with this depression on and clothes so ridiculously overpriced, your father could do with another jumper in his bureau, and the sooner the better.'

Hillary thought perhaps it was a boy that was disturbing her thoughts. Eleanor had filled out over the last couple of years, still a little underdeveloped, but getting there. Her deep auburn hair was now cut shorter to sit just below her shoulders, making her appear older than her fifteen years, and her face had all but cleared. She wore the straighter, more body-hugging dresses of the day, the hemline reaching mid-calf, which Hillary thought to be a little too short, though she supposed someone as young as Eleanor could get away with it. Hillary pondered her granddaughter's appearance and thought, yes, quite possibly it *was* a boy. She changed tactics.

'So who have you seen lately... anyone of interest?'

Eleanor's eyes flew open and she stared at her grandmother. What could she say? *Oh, most certainly, Grandma! I see a man every night! He takes me on these wonderful adventures back to before you were born, when I was a lady of the French court, and when I was a daughter of pilgrims living in the Carolinas, not to mention when I was a black slave serving her master in Louisiana!*

Eleanor smiled. 'No one of interest, Grandma.'

Hillary remained unconvinced but decided not to push the subject. 'Well, I dare say you will turn some boy's head soon enough – that is if these abominable times will allow us to get on with any sort of normal living.' Hillary sniffed.

Eleanor merely smiled at her. 'Yes, perhaps.' She readied herself to go. 'I must be getting back. Grandma. Will you tell Rosie I'm sorry I missed her?'

Hillary nodded, her expression turning worried now as she again thought on Rosie. Things didn't look good for her dearest friend. She'd been looking ill for a number of weeks now, and her usual energetic cheerfulness had been most decidedly on the decline.

At present, Rosie was taking a nap and had not roused all afternoon, even through Eleanor's cleaning of the upstairs parlour opposite her bedroom. Hillary frowned. They were both getting old!

She shook her mind free of such morbid thoughts and turned her attention back to her granddaughter, who was now pulling on her coat.

Hillary nodded to the hat stand. 'Take my scarf over there and wrap it around your shoulders… it's coming in cold.'

Eleanor reached for the royal blue woolen scarf her grandmother always wore. She draped it over her shoulders, throwing one end over the back. 'What will you wear?'

Hillary waved her away. 'I have plenty more.'

Eleanor pulled her one and only cloche hat down hard over her head, bundled her knitting bag under her arm and leant over to kiss her grandmother on the cheek. 'I'll see you next week, Grandma?'

Hillary sniffed and nodded. 'Next week, Eleanor… and I want to see at least one side of your father's jumper finished too!'

Hillary flashed a rare smile as Eleanor left.

It was much colder than Eleanor had anticipated as she made her way down the marble steps of her grandmother's house. She had decided to walk home rather than catch the tram. It would save money. Her father used to come and pick her up when it was time to leave, but the last few months, he'd been unable to afford the petrol.

Remembering her mother's constant warnings about keeping her money hidden, Eleanor patted her hip, making sure the small purse she carried was still safely tucked away in the inside pocket of her coat. Then, wrapping her grandmother's scarf more firmly about her, and hugging her knitting bag in front of her, Eleanor walked quickly in the direction of home, hoping her exertions would soon warm her up.

As she turned the corner, a misty rain started to fall, and Eleanor took shelter under the overhanging branches of a birch tree. It seemed to have come over dark suddenly, though Eleanor had guessed it to be only about four o'clock. She peered into the distance and noticed the horizon had become hazy and undefined, a sure sign of an approaching downfall, and it made her shiver. The tram she was to have caught clanged by on the dampened rails, its passengers looking warm and dry within, and Eleanor wished now that she'd taken it. She felt utterly miserable.

And then suddenly a feeling of cold unease seemed to creep up her back like a snake uncoiling from around her spine and Eleanor's senses pricked up. She knew the warning now; had felt it before. It was Parquin…

'Spare a penny, can ya, love?'

Eleanor whirled round to see a man standing behind her, half hidden by the tree trunk. The coldness up her back became more intense as he stared at her, and she hugged her knitting bag closer, taking a step back. He was dressed in a heavy coat, an old felt hat pulled down low over his head, dirty and wet from the rain. His eyes peered out at her from underneath, his face unshaven, and what little she could see of the shirt at his neck was dirty and threadbare.

Eleanor knew there were many people living on the brink of poverty, so bad were the times they lived in. It was the main topic of conversation around the table every night between her mother and father, and her heart would always go out to them, but this man scared her…

The man eyed her curiously, looking her up and down, then looked across the road and behind him before turning back to her, his eyes taking on a different light as he started smiling. Eleanor noticed the stained and rotten teeth and felt instantly repulsed.

'All alone, are ya, love? Bit of a thing like you shouldn't be out in this… What ya got there?' He reached for Eleanor's knitting bag and she abruptly moved back, but the man made a grab for it, trying to pull it free from her grasp.

'Don't! It's mine! Leave me alone!'

The rain then started to come down a little heavier as the man grabbed her arm and twisted it back, causing her to drop her knitting bag, its contents spilling out onto the wet grass at her feet. The sight of her father's partly knitted jumper now lying in the mud was her undoing and she began to cry. No longer under the shelter of the birch, her clothes quickly became soaked through, her tears mingling with the rain as she watched on helplessly at the man bent over and pawed through her things with his filthy hands. He pushed the knitting aside and threw the spare needles out of the way as though he was looking for something.

'Where is it, girlie? Well-turned-out thing like you must have a bit of coin put away somewhere.'

He straightened up to face her but as he did, Eleanor saw a flash of something whiz by her as a body seemed to come out of nowhere, charging into the man and knocking him to the ground. It startled Eleanor, and she stood fixed to the spot, too scared to utter a sound.

It was now pouring with rain and hard to see. All thoughts of the cold and rain seeping into her clothes went unnoticed as she tried to make out what was going on at the base of the tree. She could see two men scuffling, their bodies locked and struggling against one another as both tried to stop their shoes from slipping on the wet grass. It appeared to Eleanor that the man who'd tried to rob her was coming off second best... She hoped so!

There was a dull thud and the man fell backward. Almost instantly he scrambled to his feet, water and mud churning up in his effort to stand.

'Bastard!' With that he turned tail and ran. The other man now stood there, breathing heavily and slightly bent over, leaning with one hand on the tree. The rain began to ease off.

Eleanor suddenly became conscious of the chill in her body and her legs gave way beneath her. She fainted.

She opened her eyes to see a young man bending over her, his face worried. She'd seen that face before, and in exactly the same way it was now, with water streaming down it.

'Eleanor? Are you all right?'

She blinked. *He knows my name!*

'Yes... I think so.'

The rain had died down to a mist once more. Eleanor felt numb, not entirely sure if it was from the cold or her recent experience.

And then it dawned on her. 'Mark Worthington-Cooke!' She practically shouted his name at him and he raised his eyebrows. *And such nice eyes too*, thought Eleanor.

Then she realized where they were and what had just happened. He was cradling her head in his lap. *History repeats*, she thought. Looking down, she could see that his coat was covered in mud and that she must look a fright.

'I'm sorry.' Eleanor couldn't help it and she started to cry, feeling suddenly overwhelmed.

Mark frowned. 'Are you hurt?'

Apart from the embarrassment of looking like something the cat dragged in, the fact she was now chilled to the bone and had just been accosted by a terrible and repulsive man, she was feeling no pain whatsoever, but the words wouldn't come. She merely shook her head.

'Can you stand?' Mark slid his arm under hers and hoisted her up into a sitting position.

'Has he gone? Truly?' Eleanor sniffed and looked about her and then up at Mark. He smiled broadly for the first time, his mouth stretching generously over white even teeth, a smile that reached up into his deep blue eyes, which to Eleanor, seemed to twinkle at her.

Oh my, she thought, blinking and gazing up at him, utterly fascinated and wishing for the first time in her life that she was prettier. He helped her to her feet and gathered up the sodden knitting and her bag, holding it out to her.

'I think I better see you home.'

'But didn't he say anything else, Eleanor?'

Lizzie sat perched on the edge of her chair in the drawing room, leaning across on folded arms, the look on her face excited one moment, dreamy the next. Eleanor sat in the chair opposite, her legs tucked up under her on the overstuffed brocaded armchair usually reserved for her father, a steaming cup of tea clasped between her hands.

Her father paced the floor before her, his expression going from anger at the attack on his daughter to relief that she was home safe and sound. His eyes kept darting to Nettie, watching as she fussed and fretted over Eleanor, her own eyes darting back to her husband with a look that said, *Not now – we'll speak of it later*.

Ted sat over in the corner, his legs crossed, his head buried in the newspaper. Now that the main event concerning his sister was over, and she was safe at home, he was able to turn his attentions back to the account he was reading of Norman Smith's latest drive down Ninety Mile Beach in New Zealand, where he was attempting to break Malcolm Campbell's record of 254 mph.

'Don Harkness designed this one too.' Ted said to anyone who was interested. 'It's got a twelve-cylinder Napier in it.' He didn't look up, his words only serving to interrupt Lizzie's attempts to find out more about Eleanor's exchange with Mark. Lizzie rolled her eyes.

'Who cares about some silly engine?' Lizzie snapped at her brother and turned her attentions back to Eleanor, all trace of irritation instantly erased.

Ted yanked the newspaper down and stared at her, obviously put out by his sister's shallow disregard for something he thought was of the utmost importance.

Lizzie smiled, still staring at Eleanor. 'Well, I think it's just perfect!'

Eleanor was dressed in a flannelette nightgown, after having had a hot bath. Her mother had insisted that she sit in front of the fire to keep warm, even though the wood still burnt in the kitchen stove, the general rule of the house being that no more than one fire was to be lit at one time, as wood was hard come by. Her mother had also come out with her dressing gown and wrapped it around Eleanor's shoulders, even though Eleanor's own dressing gown was serviceable enough. Her mother's mauve candlewick robe draped around her shoulders signified to all present the importance of Eleanor's brush with calamity.

'Imagine Mark coming out of nowhere like that! I can't imagine anything more romantic, can you?'

Eleanor didn't have a chance to answer as her mother cut in.

'For goodness' sake, Lizzie! Give it a rest!'

Nettie stoked the fire, turning her face away from the onslaught of heat radiating out from the hearth. Harry came over and took the poker from her, indicating with a nod to her that he'd do it instead.

Lizzie had been in Eleanor's face since the moment she'd come home, her thoughts seemingly centered more on Mark's rescue than what he'd rescued her sister from.

Eleanor felt tired and thoroughly worn out now that it was over and happy to be back in the warmth and comfort of her own home amongst her family. And if she allowed herself to think on it, Eleanor was also a little dreamy of mind at the thought of being rescued in such a fashion by Mark Worthington-Cooke, but she dared not voice these feelings out loud, least of all to her sister. Lizzie went on.

'You should have asked him in, Eleanor! I'm sure Mum and Dad would have liked to have thanked him properly!'

Eleanor didn't have a chance to answer as Ted cut in from his position in the corner.

'That way, Lizzie could have thanked him too, I bet!' He gave a quiet snicker, arousing Lizzie's ire. Seeing it, he went further. 'Just think, Lizzie, all this time you've been running around with those idiot Holt twins when all you had to do was walk down some lonely street and get set upon by some "desperate" and some knight in shining armour might have come out and rescued you too!' Ted smirked, and Lizzie's face flamed in anger, fuelling his teasing. 'It might even have been Benjamin Kerns that came to your rescue!'

It was an understanding amongst those who knew Lizzie that her affections had long been with Benjamin Kerns. After showing her some degree of interest in the beginning, his affections now appeared to have cooled.

Lizzie stood up. Her anger was now at boiling point. She

looked around for something to throw at her brother but was interrupted by Harry.

'Be quiet the both of you!' he thundered.

Their father's word was law. Ted hid behind his newspaper once more as Lizzie, still red-faced, sat back down again, her eyes directed now towards the fire.

Nettie couldn't help but smile to herself, an action that was noticed by her husband, and he quickly turned away lest his children see the smile now forming on his own face.

Eleanor couldn't help but think to herself that while she might be back in the warmth and safety of her home, its comfort was another matter. Then her thoughts turned to Parquin and the special kind of comfort he always gave her that managed to make her feel all was right with the world again...

That evening, Harry and Nettie lay side by side in their bed, Harry chuckling softly to himself.

'You have to admit, Net, that crack Ted made about the Kerns boy hit the nail fairly well on the head... don't you think?'

Nettie lay smiling into the darkness. 'Even so, it's unfair of him to go teasing her like that. Ted doesn't feel like that about a girl yet; he doesn't realize how it hurts her. He thinks she's simply vain and shallow a lot of the time, when in fact she's not. Lizzie cares a great deal for this Benjamin fellow, and I think she's doing the best she can in not letting it get to her.'

Nettie had spoken about Ted, but her words were also aimed at her husband, suspecting he shared some of his son's views. She went on.

'She gives the outside appearance of not really caring for anybody, but believe me, she does.'

There was a pause in their conversation and then Harry broke the silence.

'Then why doesn't she just settle down a bit and see if this boy is serious about her... see what develops?'

Nettie nearly laughed out loud. 'Oh, Harry. For goodness' sake! If I had sat back and waited for you to come to me, would you have? You wouldn't have even known I was alive! I had to make myself known, let you see me out and about and hopefully bring about the chance of meeting you. Granted, my ways were a little, shall we say, more sedated than Lizzie's... but that was then, and this is now.' She sighed. 'Things have changed since we were out and about.'

Harry turned to her, the motion rocking the bed slightly. 'Well, I'm glad some things haven't changed, love.' He pulled her close and nuzzled her neck. Nettie started to giggle, and then she stopped and gave him a slight push.

'Not so fast! I want you to go and see that Mark and thank him properly for what he did for Eleanor.' Nettie was turned to face him, though he couldn't see her.

Harry sighed and rolled onto his back, placing one hand behind his head. 'You think so? He didn't seem to want to come in this afternoon; he just let Eleanor go at the gate. Perhaps he thought he'd done all that he could and wanted to be on his way.'

Nettie wouldn't let it go. 'And perhaps it was because Eleanor didn't invite him inside, like Lizzie said... No, we'd better do the right thing... promise?'

She rolled over towards him, her hand coming out to snake across Harry's stomach before making its way further down. Harry groaned and then chuckled softly, his voice now husky. 'Whatever you say, Mrs Grayson...

The next few days were uneventful by comparison. Eleanor went back to school the next day having no lasting effects of her attack. Hillary called round for a visit as soon as she heard and spouted off her warnings about 'the destitute men and women in our streets that were not to be trifled with'. Ruby and Kathy came round from next door, Ruby's visit valuable to Nettie in that they sat over a pot of tea discussing the world and what it was coming to while Kathy gleaned all that she could from Lizzie about Mark Worthington-Cooke and his part in the fiasco. Meanwhile, Eleanor's real comfort had been from her best friend, Marjorie, and for the first time, she was able to vent her own thoughts and feelings on Mark and what had happened without fear of it being misconstrued.

'Gosh, Eleanor. I know it must have been terribly frightening, but for Mark to come out of the blue like that is like something out of a movie!'

Eleanor blushed. 'Yes, something like that.' Both girls fell about laughing.

As for Mark Worthington-Cooke, Harry did the dutiful thing and called on him to formally thank him for his efforts and bravery. Mark was a little discomfited by Harry's praises but took the hand offered and shook it warmly. His parents, however, having no idea of their son's exploits, were both proud and dismayed that their son had done such an astounding thing. His father invited Harry in for a glass of port, which Harry politely declined, much preferring to get down the pub and have a beer with people he was more comfortable with. At least with them, he wouldn't have to put on any airs and graces. The Worthington-Cookes were his mother's type of people, and though Harry could hold his own with them, polite though they were, they weren't his cup of tea.

The winter was finally over. It had been a long, hard battle for most, and though the onset of spring did not alleviate the ever present anxieties surrounding money or lack of employment, the warmer weather was at least easier to bear for those living without a roof over their heads. Many more now took to the road in a hope that there would be a better chance to gain employment in the country. Even those ignorant of the workings of farmland or stations were lured by rumours of 'spring planting' or 'shearing'.

Charlie still worked on Mell Pell Station in Western Australia. His status on the property had now climbed to that of part-owner, having used a good portion of his inheritance to keep it running throughout the last two years. This, along with the fact that he was still unmarried and still the same likeable character he'd always been, made him a much sought-after partner at woolshed dances and afternoon gatherings of the local farm owners, even though he was now in his late thirties. Women seemed to flock to him, and not just women his age. Charlie had had to ward off the advances of some of the daughters of neighbouring properties, their inexperienced flirting and almost pitiful manoeuvres to get him alone only serving to make him back off even more. Charlie much preferred to seek his entertainment with women further afield, away from gossiping tongues and speculation. He wanted no ties or responsibilities, the women he attached himself to making no demands on him other than showing them a good time. After all, Charlie told himself, he was only human, and a man has his needs.

The letters he'd had from Harry and Nettie back home – for Charlie still considered Adelaide his home – brought him all the news of the Depression and its influence on the many families and friends in his old stomping ground. Charlie had been happy to find out that the country's present circumstances hadn't put too much of a strain on his best friend's family… at least not yet.

He figured that after the lambing season and before shearing began, he might take a trip east to visit them. He had a sudden longing to walk down the streets of North Adelaide, perhaps have a beer or two in the bar with Harry and even get to sit at Nettie's table once again, sharing their meal and their company and having a good laugh like the days of old.

Charlie had heard all about their growing family too and knew that even though he was aware of their ages now, he would have to prepare himself for just how grown up they'd become.

'Look, Eleanor! There he is!'

Marjorie leant closer to her friend just as Mark Worthington-Cooke came out through the café door a few feet away. Eleanor felt instantly embarrassed by her friend's animated gestures and whispering side-glances – they merely served to make her observations obvious instead of well-guarded.

Eleanor's face flamed when she realized Mark had heard Marjorie's ill-hidden comments as well. He seemed to falter in his step before coming up to them, his hand tipping his hat in greeting, and Eleanor wondered if he'd felt cornered into acknowledging them.

'Good afternoon, Eleanor, Marjorie… Cummings, isn't

it?' He smiled briefly at Marjorie before turning back to Eleanor, missing her dark-haired friend's answering nod.

'Hello.' It was all Eleanor could muster, her eyes turning towards the shop window nearby. It happened to be a tailor's, so she now feigned interest in a pinstriped suit in the window, as though the latest men's fashions were her one and only purpose of being out today. At the same moment, she caught her reflection in the glass and couldn't help wishing she'd worn her lime-green suit with the flowers on it. It suited her hair and colouring much better than the rose-coloured frock she now wore.

She immediately pulled herself up on her thoughts, telling herself it made no difference whatsoever as to how she was dressed.

'Hello, Mark.' Marjorie, on the other hand, suddenly took on all the pomp and preening of a prized peacock. Eleanor looked sideways at her friend and frowned. What was Marjorie doing?

'I'd meant to stop by and see how you were after… well, the last time we met, but I'm sorry I didn't. Seems like you had no lasting effects in any case… you're looking quite well.' Mark appeared to get a little uncomfortable and Eleanor wondered why.

'Oh yes, well… thank you… I mean, if you hadn't come along when you did… well…' Eleanor shrugged, not sure what to say next.

Marjorie cut in, gushing loudly. 'I think it was just wonderful that you were there, Mark. Eleanor was so happy you were there too… weren't you, Eleanor?' Marjorie linked arms with her friend and stared at her with a silly smile on her face, which made Eleanor stare back at her in puzzlement.

What on earth is the matter with her?

Mark cleared his throat, embarrassed. 'Well, thank you.'

He changed the subject quickly. 'Off to somewhere in particular? Or are you both just out for a walk?'

Eleanor made to answer, but Marjorie cut in again. 'We're off to the pictures. It's called *Red Dust* with Clark Gable; everyone is raving about it… Do you like going to the pictures?'

Marjorie's face was all smiles. Eleanor noticed how her skin glowed and her black hair shone in the sunlight and felt most decidedly at a disadvantage.

'Yes, sometimes… when I get the chance, that is.' Mark shot a look at Eleanor and smiled, but it was all she could do just to meet his eye. He looked thoughtful for all of a second. 'Well, I'd better not keep you then… have a nice afternoon.'

'You too, Mark. Nice to see you again.' Marjorie was practically swooning.

'Yes, goodbye then.' Eleanor merely smiled. Mark tipped his hat to both, but before turning away, he gave a sly wink to Eleanor.

He winked at me! Didn't he?

'Isn't he the handsomest man you've ever seen in your life, Eleanor?'

'Yes, quite nice I suppose.' *It was a wink, wasn't it?*

'You suppose? Don't tell me you haven't thought about him at least once or twice over the last few months!'

Eleanor was quite convinced that Marjorie viewed the chance meeting with Mark as the highlight of her day. She laughed at Marjorie now. 'Of course I have! But… well… he would be no more interested in me than… than… Well, he's older than Lizzie for goodness' sake!'

The girls made to cross the street, their original destination now filtering back into their minds.

'What's that got to do with anything? Besides, he's only about two years older in any case!' Marjorie gave Eleanor a friendly nudge. 'I think I would like an older man!' she declared.

Eleanor rolled her eyes heavenward. 'I'm beginning to think you'd like them older, younger, shorter, taller or any way they come, Marjorie!' They both laughed as they made their way to the ticket box.

'Two please.' Marjorie addressed the ticket lady.

Eleanor's smile left her face and she glanced back towards the way Mark had gone. *Probably had something in his eye.*

'You shouted the last time! It has to be my turn now, mate!' Harry went to move Charlie's money down the bar counter and away from him, but Charlie stopped him.

'Don't let it worry you. How often do I get to shout my friends? Besides, I don't have to worry about a family to support in these times, and things are looking up for me... You can shout me next time I'm in town.'

Harry saw the wisdom of his friend's words but it didn't sit right with him. Lenny, however, had other ideas, his big burly hand covering the money on the bar and sliding it back up to Charlie. 'Sounds like a good idea to me, mate... and one day when I've got some money, I'll shout you... as well as buy some of my pride back!'

All three men let out a loud guffaw, causing many to look their way, and Jerry McClellan sidled up along the other side of the counter. 'Another three?' He took their empty glasses anyway.

'Keep 'em coming, Jerry... thanks.' Charlie nodded towards the money on the bar and winked at the barman.

Charlie had arrived in town five days ago, his first call

Harry and Nettie's place. Their delight at seeing him had washed over him like a comforting balm, suddenly making him realize how much he'd missed his home. He was staying upstairs in one of the rooms at Jerry's but so far had rarely spent any time there other than to sleep and wash up. Mealtimes were spent round at Harry's and Nettie's. Of course, times being what they were, he'd had to compensate them the best way he could without it looking too much like a handout. He knew having another mouth to feed was rather a hefty expense, so he'd brought 'gifts' every day from the butcher or the grocer. As gifts, they were more acceptable.

Yesterday, he'd set up a barbeque at the back of Harry's house, and Lenny, Ruby and Kathy had come over as well. It had felt like Christmas, though it was only October.

Nettie had worried that others less fortunate on their street would find out about it, and Charlie could see she felt guilty about having an array of food on display when there were many who were still destitute and living without a roof over their heads.

Harry had reminded her that it was all right to count their blessings when they could.

To say Charlie had been surprised at how grown-up the kids were would be an understatement. Lizzie had grown into a beautiful young lady, though he secretly thought her ambitions amounted to no more than going out each Saturday night. But then he remembered how he'd been at that age and thought that he was perhaps being a bit harsh.

Ted was a likeable young lad, polite, inquisitive and seemingly untouched by the surrounding problems of the world he lived in, but Eleanor had been the most surprising of all. The last time Charlie had seen her, she'd been no more than a young child. She hadn't grown into a particularly pretty girl, but she was attractive enough. To Charlie, though, most of her appeal lay in her mystery. She gave the appearance of being intelligent and worldly, yet at the same time possessed an innocent shyness that made one want to keep her wrapped up in a cocoon of safety, away from the world and its ugliness.

Charlie had observed her moving about amongst her family in her quiet way, her face a little guarded at times, as though she was privy to something that no one else knew. But he put that down to his own imagination and then berated himself for taking far too much interest in his best friend's daughter... and *youngest* daughter at that, he reminded himself. It wouldn't do for anyone to notice his curiosity – it may be taken the wrong way.

After reflecting on it for a time, Charlie told himself that she was probably just like all the other girls her age, with impractical dreams and wistful imaginings, concerned mainly with the usual ideas of getting married and having a whole brood of children one day.

'I hear your old flame has got herself hooked up with some nob at Nailsworth.' Lenny's words caught Charlie mid-swallow and all he could do was raise his eyebrows in surprise before planting his glass down on the bar and quickly wiping the froth from his mouth.

'Vera, you mean? I thought she married one of the Bailey brothers, the older one... what was his name?' Charlie turned his question to Harry. Harry obliged.

'Yeah, Les Bailey. Didn't take though... don't know why. She's now married to Gilbert Haines – got married just recently apparently. Don't really know the bloke other than he's got a bit of money.' Harry shrugged. 'Don't really see anything of her anymore... just in passing down the street, you know what I mean.'

Lenny leant over towards Charlie. 'Maybe this one won't

take either once she learns you're in town, eh, Charlie?' He winked at Harry who in turn nudged Charlie.

Charlie laughed. 'Knock it off, you blokes! I've got no interest in Vera, and I reckon she only saw the inheritance up ahead where I was concerned anyway… Kids at all?'

Lenny shook his head.

'Nope,' Harry said.

Charlie raised his beer. 'Well… here's to Vera! May she find everything she's looking for… and may her husband find the means to give it to her!' He took a long swallow as the other two laughed.

Sometime later, the door of the bar opened and in walked Mark Worthington-Cooke with one of his friends. He and Harry spotted each other at the same moment and both nodded in greeting. The two younger men took a place down the other end of the bar.

'Who's that? Friend of Lizzie's? Ted's?' Charlie asked.

'Wish it *was* a friend of Lizzie's. Like to see her in the company of that boy instead of those other idiots she surrounds herself with.' Harry gave a wry look.

'To hear Kathy tell it, he's *Eleanor's* knight in shining armour!' Lenny rolled his eyes, his next words aimed at Charlie. 'Saved her from a bit of a nasty scrape a few months back… two in fact – there was that other thing at the baths.'

Lenny's brief scrap of information had Charlie looking to Harry for an explanation. Charlie knew about the swimming incident – Harry had written him about it – but he hadn't heard about anything else.

Harry signaled Jerry to bring another round and turned back to Lenny. 'Knight in shining armour? That's a new one on me! Does Eleanor see him in that light?' Harry then shook his head dismissively. 'She's too young anyway.'

Charlie was trying to follow the conversation, still waiting to be filled in on the whole story.

Lenny went on. 'And when you and Nettie met, you were how old?'

'That's different, we—'

'Ha! Typical words of any father!' Lenny cut him off.

Charlie had had enough. 'For Christ's sake! Are either of you two going to tell me what happened?'

Both Lenny and Harry looked at him now. Then Harry cleared his throat and went on to give Charlie a brief rundown on everything that had happened, as he knew it.

'You let Eleanor walk home alone in these times?' Charlie was frowning.

'Of course not! She took it upon herself to walk instead of catching the tram like she was supposed to… something she now knows *not* to do, thank Christ!'

Lenny wiped his mouth with the back of his hand and set his glass back down on the bar. 'Lucky for Eleanor young Mark was also walking that day.' Lenny began filling his pipe.

'Yep, lucky for her… lucky for us…' Harry took a long swallow.

Charlie peered over at the good-looking young man at the end of the bar, noting the well-formed physique and the full head of deep brown hair that would show no trace of grey for several more years, and just for a moment, his thoughts turned wistful… and if he was honest with himself, perhaps a little envious too.

That night, with Lenny away home to Ruby, Charlie sat at the table along with Harry, Nettie, Ted and Eleanor. Lizzie, to everyone's surprise, had been asked out finally by Benjamin Kerns. He'd called early, his intention being to take Lizzie out for something to eat first.

'Where were they going for tea?' Harry spooned another portion of cottage pie onto his plate, along with another helping of cabbage and carrots. He thought on more beans as well, but then changed his mind.

'He mentioned that little café on the corner – you know the one.' Nettie offered Charlie some more pie.

Charlie held up his hand. 'No thanks, Net. It was really nice, but I've had enough, really.'

'I thought that café closed down.' Harry's words were aimed at Nettie but then he looked over at Charlie. 'Want a beer to wash it down?'

Eleanor rose from the table. 'I'll get you one, Uncle Charlie.'

Ted, who'd been busy eating his tea, now piped up. 'I think they nearly did close down. It was really quiet there for a while – used to pass the window and not one person would be sitting at any of the tables, but then they started putting out those specials like all the hotels... you know, three-course meal for eight pence or whatever... and of course now they take dole tickets as well.'

'Eight pence! I suppose that's not too bad.' Nettie noticed Eleanor was taking a long time. She yelled out to her. 'You'll find a bottle down in the meat safe, Eleanor! I couldn't fit it in the chest!'

Charlie rose. 'I'll go and help her.'

Eleanor was kneeling down on the floor, searching the bottom shelf of the meat safe. She could hear the muffled conversation from the dining room.

'Want me to get it?'

Charlie's voice startled her, causing her to raise her head abruptly and bang it on the open door of the safe. She instantly cradled her head in her hand, feeling like a prized ninny.

'Are you all right?' Charlie chuckled, instantly belying any heartfelt concern for her head. Eleanor rubbed her scalp and was not amused.

'Here, let me.' Charlie leant over and grasped Eleanor beneath the arms, hoisting her up, her upturned elbow knocking him on the chin and causing her to laugh before she could stop herself. He now rubbed his chin. 'I suppose I deserved that for laughing at you.'

Eleanor looked up at him, amusement still playing around her eyes though her scalp was sore. Charlie looked down at her and for a split second was stunned by the flawless skin and the eyes that now peered at him… innocent, trusting… Such an intelligent face… lovely hair… *young…*

Charlie spun away abruptly. 'You run along into the dining room and I'll get the bottle.' He tried to shrug off his turbulent thoughts with a lightness he didn't feel. 'Knowing Nettie, she was probably trying to hide it from your father.'

Eleanor laughed in response, sensing she should make light of the situation too, though she didn't know why. Nor did she know why her heart was suddenly beating faster…

'Best you get back, Eleanor…'

Eleanor looked sharply at Charlie. 'What…' But she already knew that it wasn't Charlie who'd uttered the words she'd just heard.

'I said, your mother was probably trying to hide the bottle from your father.' He looked at Eleanor, his eyebrows now raised at the strange look upon her face.

Eleanor looked about her, confusion in her eyes. She tried calming her wild thoughts. *'Parquin?'*

No answer.

There was a knock at the door, effectively interrupting her uneasy thoughts. Her mother yelled out from the dining room, 'Can you get that, Eleanor?'

Eleanor took a deep breath and went to the door and opened it.

'Hello, Eleanor. I was just passing and thought I'd stop in and see how you were going… hope I haven't come at a bad time or anything.'

Eleanor couldn't believe it. Mark Worthington-Cooke was calling on her!

'Hello, Mark… no, that's all right. Won't you come in?' Eleanor remembered her manners at the last minute, opening the door wide for him to enter. Mark stepped inside but stood next to her, not sure where to go from there.

Eleanor led the way into the dining room, the table's occupants – including Charlie, who had now resumed his seat – were all straining their necks in an effort to see whom she was bringing into their midst.

'Mark! Haven't seen you in quite a while, and then twice in one day!' Harry filled Nettie in on how he'd seen Mark at the pub earlier.

Nettie looked at Mark with new eyes. *Another drinker*, she thought, though outwardly she smiled. 'Sit down, won't you? Would you like a cup of tea?'

'Or a glass of beer?' Harry chimed in.

'A cup of tea would be nice, thank you, Mrs Grayson.'

He was instantly redeemed in Nettie's mind.

Eleanor set about introducing Mark to all present, and Mark shook hands with Harry, though they'd already met, and then Ted, who informed everyone that he too had seen Mark 'out and about', and then Charlie, who shook the young man's hand warmly and flashed a quick wink at Eleanor, who blushed and then hurried out to the kitchen to get another teacup.

The conversation moved from Mark's family, who were in the building trade – though like everyone else, his parents were feeling the pinch – through to Harry's work, Ted's interest in owning his own business one day like Mr Crowley and on to Charlie's part ownership of a station in Western Australia and the fact he was on a temporary visit.

After a while, Charlie yawned and excused himself, saying it was time for him to get back to the hotel or Jerry would go to bed and not let him in. Everyone laughed and he rose to leave, thanking Nettie for another fine meal. Eleanor saw him to the door.

He turned and smiled at her. 'Well then, Eleanor, I suppose I'll see you next time.' He went to walk away, but before he could, Eleanor reached up and kissed him lightly on the cheek, her impulsiveness surprising herself as well as Charlie, who smiled down at her before placing his hat on his head and leaving through the front door.

But there was no smile on Charlie's face as he made his way down the path and out through the gate. His thoughts had suddenly become disordered, his gut registering that something had just happened, but he wasn't sure what.

Eleanor watched him leave, unaware of his turbulent thoughts. She liked Uncle Charlie, even though she knew he wasn't really her uncle. But tonight, there had been something else, hadn't there? She remembered Lizzie telling her when they'd been younger how she'd had a crush on him for a time. Eleanor had been hard-pressed to remember him, but now she understood what her sister had meant.

Her thoughts turned just as quickly back to Mark and the fact he was in her dining room and had stopped by to see her!

Charlie walked on, his thoughts spinning out of control. What was he doing? What was he thinking? It was downright impossible! Not to mention obscene!

He didn't stop at Jerry's but just kept walking; going to bed alone was definitely not what he needed. He could picture himself, lying there in the dark, tossing and turning. No, he'd walk for a while; try to rid himself of the ridiculous thoughts running around in his mind – for that's what they were!

Charlie found himself at the corner of Hindley Street and King William Street. How had he managed to come this far without noticing it? He went to turn back and noticed a movement out the corner of his eye. He stopped and peered into the darkness. There... over by the fence... It was a woman and she was walking towards him.

'Hello, love. Out all alone tonight?' Her voice was low and a little raspy. Charlie knew right off what she was about, but he'd never paid for a woman's favours before in his life and he wasn't about to start now.

The woman came closer, into the light of the street lamps. She was a redhead. *Getting on in years too*, thought Charlie, or was it just that profession that made women appear older than they were? He didn't know. And what's more, he told himself, he didn't care.

His mind slipped back to Eleanor, her soft lips kissing him on the cheek, and he cursed himself.

The woman spoke again, only this time, she was only inches away. 'Are you after some company, love?'

Charlie peered down at her. 'What's your name, miss?'

She smiled at him, sidling closer still. 'Thelma.'

Charlie could smell her perfume; it was overpowering, not like...

Charlie tried to push the thoughts from his mind and

grabbed Thelma roughly. She responded by rubbing herself up against him.

'How much?' Charlie ground the words out, not liking what he was doing but knowing he was going to do it anyway. Perhaps she was just what he needed tonight…

'Sixpence… You got a place?' Charlie thought of Jerry's. *Not bloody likely.*

It was late and the street was empty save for one or two cars driving by. He knew he had to get off the corner. He felt too conspicuous standing here like this and so he steered her by the elbow down Hindley Street and into a side alley. He moved her over to the wall where it was darker.

Thelma held out her hand. 'Sorry, love; I've been stiffed before.'

The very idea of all the 'befores' made Charlie decide not to go through with it, but he found himself handing over the coins anyway. She immediately started rubbing up against him again, her hand stroking between his legs.

Charlie didn't budge. He could see her over-painted face in the moonlight and it repulsed him. He leant his head back against the wall, his mind instantly going back to another place earlier on in the night… and another face… a younger face, innocent and untouched by anything like this… How he wished…

Charlie swung her around so she was now up against the wall, his own hand rubbing up and down between her legs while he fumbled with his trousers. Seconds later, he had her dress up and her underthings down and he was plunging into her. That other face loomed in his mind and his movements took on an urgency… remembering, wishing, dreaming that it was her instead of… He drove into the woman… only now it wasn't some doxy he'd just met but *her!* He imagined burying himself in her… again and again… and again… He wrapped her legs around him… he imagined the auburn hair falling over him, and her face set in ecstasy… for *him*… He kept grinding, thrusting… more… and more… Charlie cried out his release, his thoughts screaming, *Eleanor!*

No sooner had he finished than he pushed the woman away from him. His strength suddenly left him and he stumbled slightly, his breathing ragged. He was disgusted with himself. How could he have done such a thing? How could he have even thought of Eleanor in such a way? He was more than twice her age – closer in age to her father… his best friend!

He leant on the wall a little away from the accommodating Thelma. Turning back to her, he tried to smile but failed. Thelma didn't seem to notice. She was busily putting her clothes to right. Probably to go back out and see what else she could pick up.

He felt suddenly ashamed. He knew what times were like; knew there were more women taking to the streets as a result of it… though Thelma looked a little more seasoned than most. This didn't make him feel any better though, and on impulse, he reached into his pocket and pulled out a pound note. Taking hold of her hand, he closed her fingers over the money.

'Go have yourself an early night.'

Charlie walked away, leaving an astonished Thelma staring into her hand and then back up at him.

Charlie didn't know if she would follow his advice, and he didn't care. He felt he'd done what he could, given the circumstances, and now he was tired. He would get back to Jerry's as fast as he could and in the morning, he would go back west.

CHAPTER SEVEN

It was Lizzie's wedding day. The last few months had been exhausting, to say the least, with an endless whirlwind of fittings, ceremonial and reception arrangements – who to invite, who not to invite and so on. After Lizzie's long infatuation with Benjamin Kerns, and having finally hooked him, she'd suddenly done a complete turnaround, breezing into the house one day and announcing to all that she was engaged to none other than Bobby Pinkle! On hearing the news, Eleanor had remembered Lizzie's long-ago declaration that she couldn't possibly marry Bobby because she wouldn't want to be known as Elizabeth Pinkle.

Eleanor hadn't been able to help teasing. 'So you're going to be Mrs Elizabeth Pinkle after all!'

But to her credit, Lizzie had just laughed. 'Yes! Indeed I am! Absolutely! Oh yes!'

The Depression was all but over. Its ending was not marked by a particular date or a declaration from some prominent political figure. Rather, its ending was measured by the gradual recovery of the economy as unemployment eased and wages began to creep up once more. Many had lost homes and jobs and even their life savings as they'd tried to keep their families afloat through some of the darkest years Australia had ever seen, with the exception of the Great War. And then gradually but steadily, employment increased as factories – some old, some new – opened wide their doors, and businesses began to grow and prosper once more. Those who had been trying to exist on sustenance were now seeing light at the end of a long bleak tunnel, and with it came the glimmer of hope… and the chance to start over again.

Eleanor studied her reflection in the full-length mirror of her bedroom. She was to be second bridesmaid, the responsibility of head bridesmaid falling to Kathy, Lizzie's lifelong best friend. Eleanor hadn't wished to be put on display at all, but as Lizzie's only sister, she was duty-bound.

Her mother had applied herself tirelessly to the never-ending details of her oldest daughter's wedding while Lizzie herself had sulked, whined and pouted, forever changing her mind about colours, flowers and styles to the point where one day her father had finally lost his temper and put his foot down. 'I refuse to spend one more penny on this outlandish affair, young lady! Not until you can display some semblance of rational thinking and a lot more common courtesy to others than what I have so far witnessed!

Her father's words had worked. Lizzie had settled, and for all those involved in the wedding preparations, most of all her mother, it had been a godsend.

And now Eleanor assessed her appearance. As a bridesmaid, she'd been decked out in an ensemble of baby pink chiffon over baby pink cotton, the bodice scattered with tiny white sequins. This sickly creation made her feel like she was to be served up as the main dessert at the reception, like a great lump of candy floss on a stick! On Kathy, the same pink creation matched well with her dark hair, one offsetting the other, but on Eleanor, with her auburn hair, it only served to make her appear mottled and blotchy.

Eleanor kept staring into the mirror. The moderately attractive and carefully composed features that stared back at her gave nothing away of the turmoil that simmered just beneath the surface. By all outside appearances, she was the calm and unpretentious young woman she'd always endeavoured to project. Underneath, though, she was burning for change… anything that would take her out of the protective shell that others had built around her and that she, if she was honest, had helped put there herself. She was now sick of words like propriety, decency and respectability. She wanted to be swept away on a raging sea of adventure, explore the unexplored regions of her soul… venture into the untouched territories of her own sensuality…

Eleanor smiled at herself. Perhaps her father was right – she read too many books…

She wondered why she wasn't content with anything around her, when she had no real reason to feel anything else. Hadn't life been relatively easier this time around? Both she and her family had fared remarkably well during the height of the Depression. Her father was back working full-time again, and without the previously enforced ten-per-cent cut to his hourly rate. Lizzie had held on to her job at John Martins with a steady increase of hours, and Ted had finally been put on the books with Mr Crowley; a position that had 21-year-old brother strutting about the house behind an impenetrable shield of self-deluded importance. As for Eleanor, she'd yet to gain a position anywhere, her high marks and much-heralded abilities as one of the top students of her school having done little to equip her in dealing with the realities of the outside world.

The fact that Eleanor remained unemployed had little

bearing on her discontentment though. She saw herself as living a normal life within a normal family and had normal friends. And if she looked ahead, she could see nothing but a normal future stretching out before her with its required number of ups and downs and tears and laughter – and it filled Eleanor with nothing more than a kind of lethargic curiosity. Given what she knew about her existence, she was unable to muster up much ambition, her sense of purpose remaining unclear.

Her eyes remained fixed on her own reflection. They glazed over in her reverie and in her distracted state, Eleanor became aware of a figure standing directly behind her... tall, with long black hair and eyes the colour of a midsummer sky. She stared, unmoving – she knew who it was, but never had she seen him in her conscious state... standing there so... tangible, so... *physical*.

She dared not move for fear of destroying the illusion, for that's what he surely must be.

She swallowed. The illusion moved. She swallowed again. He was dressed in... what *was* he dressed in? Some sort of crude leather material that surrounded his waist, and from there up he was naked, causing Eleanor to hold her breath. He continued to stare at her, his eyes growing dark in colour, velvety almost... *seductive*. The word popped into her mind. It was a word known to her only through the printed page, not from her own vocabulary.

She stood before him, her own fluffy pink image made all the more ridiculous by its contrast to his own raw masculinity. She saw his hand come up, felt it on her shoulder, roughened skin scraping the material of her dress. Her heartbeat quickened, she closed her eyes... and immediately the sensation was gone. Her eyes flew open and she spun round, but he was gone.

The illusion had fled.

'Parquin?' Eleanor could feel him still present, but she couldn't see him. Why had he left?

She frowned. More importantly… why had he appeared?

'Oh, Eleanor, you look sensational!' Marjorie's voice, gushy and breathless from the doorway. 'Truly, you do! Mark is going to be proud as punch when he sees you!'

Eleanor stood, eyes wide and searching, and only half listening to her friend's well-intended flattery. She quickly pulled herself together, managing a half-hearted smile.

'I look like a bloody great lollipop is what I look like!' She turned back to the mirror, her hands grasping the sides of the dress and fluffing it out in a show of exaggerated silliness, her mind still reeling from the sight of Parquin. Had he been real? Had he really been standing behind her?

'Eleanor! Tell me I didn't hear you swear just now!' Marjorie's eyes were as wide as saucers.

'I didn't swear!' Eleanor gave a half-smile and raised her eyebrows at her friend.

'Liar! I heard you!' Marjorie brought her hand to her mouth and started to giggle.

'Marjorie Cummings, you *asked* me to lie so it doesn't count!' Eleanor joined in with her friend's laughter. Her outburst had been brought on by her bewilderment in actually seeing Parquin behind her in the mirror. To vent one's confusion or frustration in a swear word was a remarkable offset to those emotions, and it was suddenly clear to Eleanor now why her father swore so frequently… much to the disappointment of her mother.

Marjorie stopped laughing, her face full of dreamy wonderment all over again. 'Another hour and you'll be walking down the aisle… aren't you excited?'

'In this? Hardly! I assure you, when I get married – *if* I

get married – I'll insist on a simple affair with one or two witnesses down at the registrar!' Eleanor's eyes now took on a dreamy look. 'Then again… imagine how romantic it would be to actually *elope!'*

Marjorie flounced down on the bed in a pretended huff, her own powder-blue dress with its nylon sleeves floating out around her. 'You mean to tell me you wouldn't have a splendid wedding with all the trimmings if it was yours for the asking? And what's more, you'd do me out of the chance to be bridesmaid?' Marjorie leant back on her elbow, waiting for Eleanor's answer.

'I suppose not, but… oh, Marjorie, don't you want to do anything else first? See what else life has to offer… and who else you might meet?'

Eleanor could see by the look on her friend's face that she was confusing her. Marjorie, for all her sometimes inane remarks about the opposite sex, remained loyal to that steadfast ilk of women who dreamt of meeting that one man, who, though as yet faceless and nameless, they would someday marry and live happily ever after with.

Eleanor thought back on her many lives and smiled to herself. She could tell Marjorie a thing or two about 'happily ever after'.

'What do you mean… *who else* you might meet? You have a perfectly fine man in Mark Worthington-Cooke! And here you are saying that you'd like to meet someone else?'

Oh yes, thought Eleanor. Strange how she quite often forgot about Mark.

He was handsome, athletic… a true gentleman by all accounts, and his parents had a flourishing business in the building trade, one that would most certainly be handed down to him – a sound prospect for any girl hell-bent on a life of security, comfort and a respectable position in the community. Whatever that meant.

Out loud, she said, 'No, I don't want to meet anyone else in that regard. Mark has all the qualities of a first-rate husband.' *But not for me*, she thought.

It was true, Mark had been all those things when she'd first met him – polite, friendly, and endearing himself to her and her family in all the right ways. But as time went on and they'd grown more accustomed to one another, Eleanor had expected something more from him, though she was uncertain quite what. He had remained simply polite and friendly and little else! Even in their most intimate moments.

His character held no fascination for her. She sometimes thought that his dashing rescue of her that horrid day might well have been out of character, for she'd seen no real display of that kind of emotion since. It was a good six weeks before he'd even kissed her goodnight, a kiss that left her with no driving needs, no dreamy anticipations. He was too staid, too… sedate!

To Eleanor it was a matter of course that they would finally have sex, and when they did, she'd wondered to herself what all the brouhaha was about. He'd been hesitant, mindful of what they were doing to the point of telling her all the way through that they shouldn't be doing it at all. She'd had to reassure *him*! She sighed. Surely that wasn't all there was? She wanted more: she wanted more warmth, more heat – she wanted to burn!

Eleanor wanted the fire!

'Does this mean we'll be attending another wedding in the near future?'

Eleanor swung round to see her father standing in the doorway, her face going instantly red at what she knew him to have heard. Marjorie stood up quickly and smoothed her dress down.

'Hello, Mr Grayson.'

'Hello, Marjorie.'

Marjorie also wondered how long Eleanor's father had been standing there and how much he may have heard of her side of the conversation. Mentally, she picked her way back through her words, trying to think if she'd said anything improper. Apparently not, for he stood there smiling with his eyes fixed on Eleanor.

'I don't think so, Dad. I'm... not ready.' Eleanor wasn't exactly lying. She most definitely wasn't ready for marriage, to anyone. What she didn't say was that she most probably wouldn't be ready for marriage to Mark... ever!

Harry shrugged it off. 'Plenty of time for that anyway. One wedding is enough to think about in anybody's family at one time. Your mother sent me in to hurry you along – we have to get going shortly.'

He went to walk out and then stopped and looked at her, a strange look upon his face.

'Dad?' Eleanor raised her eyebrows and stared back at him, as did Marjorie, but Harry wasn't listening. His mind was soaring back to a time long ago. In an instant he was there... guns in the distance... blood all around him, men on stretchers... and Charlie leaning over him, his pain a distant thing... numbness... that voice telling him... and a girl... a girl dressed in pink... no, with pink ribbons in her hair.

Harry's mind flew back to the present and he refocused on Eleanor. 'Are you wearing a ribbon in your hair at all?'

Eleanor blinked. 'A ribbon?' She giggled nervously. 'You don't think I look too much like an Easter egg as it is?'

Harry smiled and shook his head. He sought to cover up

his odd question. 'I thought your mother said something about it, that's all.'

Eleanor groaned – all this and a ribbon in her hair? 'No, Dad, no ribbon.'

Harry shrugged awkwardly and walked out. Eleanor looked at Marjorie. 'I think I'll be glad when this wedding is finally over.'

An hour later, they were all assembled at the back of the church. The guests were assembled at the front on each side, a long aisle between. *Too long*, thought Eleanor as she peered through the gap in the crushed velvet curtains at the back…

There were so many people! They were all there: people Lizzie had known since childhood, friends from school and Lizzie's job – apart from Benjamin Kerns, who was conspicuously absent. Her grandmother and Ted were down the front, the chair next to him empty, waiting for her mother, who was doing last-minute fussing around Lizzie's veil behind her. Somewhere out there were Marjorie and Mark, but Eleanor couldn't see them, and behind Ted sat Ruby and Lenny Jenson… Uncle Charlie too, looking most distinctly uncomfortable in his formal attire as well as his surroundings. And at the front stood Bobby, nervous and fidgeting, his best man – his brother Richard – close by.

'Eleanor! Get ready!' Nettie whispered loudly, waving frantically at her to get behind Kathy. Eleanor obliged. She glanced over at Lizzie standing nervously by her father. She really did look beautiful in her white satin and lace, and Eleanor felt a sudden stab of envy. She'd been told that every bride looked beautiful on her wedding day, but Eleanor felt sure she could never look quite so lovely as her sister did at this moment.

Nettie adjusted the small piece of lilac netting on her own hat and, after kissing Lizzie on the cheek, stepped through the curtain and hurried down to take her place next to Ted. She nodded at the organist. The wedding march began.

∼

Charlie was watching her glide down the aisle, her face looking neither right nor left and he smiled to himself. He knew she felt exposed; could see it in her eyes.

He'd braced himself for this first sight of her, hoping his ridiculous fixation of two years ago would be realized as just that, borne from imbibing one too many beers. He'd deliberately kept his distance from the Grayson household, placating Harry with trumped-up stories of not being able to get to Adelaide until the actual day of the wedding. He'd lied of course. He could have come over a week ago, but he'd told himself it was for the best – which in itself was an uncomfortable reminder that he wasn't over her at all, ridiculous fixation or not.

When the organist had commenced playing, Charlie, along with everyone else, had turned to stare up the aisle at the approaching bride. Lizzie looked resplendent in her dress, a vision any father would be proud to escort on his arm, and catching Harry's eye, he'd grinned in commiseration, knowing his friend was feeling like a trussed-up turkey dinner in his wedding finery.

Lenny's daughter had followed; a fetching young girl who Charlie presumed would grace an aisle herself before long. And then he'd seen *her*. And he'd held his breath for a full five seconds before willing himself to start breathing again. He told himself that it would be all right, that he would stay for the wedding and the reception afterward, and then he would make his excuses and leave. He told himself that he could conquer this, that he was foolhardy in his fantasies, that he would marry the first starry-eyed beagle to set her cap for him when he arrived back on Mell Pell…

Charlie watched her, and she suddenly turned her head and stared right at him. And then he thought, perhaps he would dance with her… Just once…

Eleanor was trembling; she could feel it all the way down her legs, and she prayed they would support her long enough to get her through this ceremony. How she hated it. How she hated the whole affair – the people sitting in their seats who felt it necessary to gawk at her. She even hated Bobby Pinkle for proposing to her sister!

She kept her eyes directly in front of her, concentrating on Kathy's dark hair, pulled back as it was into a perfectly rounded bun with a few tendrils strategically left loose around her hairline to set off against her pink dress.

How long was this aisle anyway? It hadn't seemed overly long when they'd visited a few weeks ago. Eleanor took one step after the other, trying to keep in time with the music, and then suddenly, for no reason she could think of, she turned her head and saw him. Uncle Charlie sat staring back at her, and suddenly she was transported back to her kitchen when last he'd visited, when she'd looked up into his eyes and he'd looked at her in exactly the same way he was now. And then he'd acted funny, they'd laughed at something and her stomach had done flip-flops… and then Mark had knocked on the door.

The wedding procession had come to the end of its walk and Eleanor now stood slightly to the side – and in this position she was staring directly at Uncle Charlie, no more than ten feet away. His eyes seemed to darken as he looked at her, though Eleanor couldn't be sure at this distance. If only she could get closer... much closer. Her face flamed at where her thoughts were leading her and she looked quickly away.

Charlie couldn't believe it. She was staring at him with such candour, he felt sure that just for a moment, she had been thinking the same as he... and then she'd turned away. Had he imagined it? Was his head so full of her that he now found himself pretending she returned his fantasies?

Charlie frowned and looked away too.

Nettie, Ted, Hillary and everyone else down the front had their eyes fixed on the bridal couple... everyone except Ruby.

Ruby had let her eyes stray to the bridesmaids. As a mother would, she took a particular delight in seeing her daughter looking so lovely. Their dresses were beautiful, even though she knew Eleanor had been less than keen on the colour.

And then she saw it... a look so obviously filled with... Dare she think it? Was that *desire* she saw in Eleanor's eyes! No! It couldn't be!

Ruby followed Eleanor's gaze and her heart skipped a beat. Charlie! Ruby could *definitely* see what was in his look! No mistaking anything there! She'd been given that look often enough by her own husband!

Oh bosh! What should she do? Should she tell Nettie?

Ruby fidgeted in her seat at the thought, causing Lenny to glance sideways at her. He placed a hand on her knee and gave it a soft pat, and she smiled at him and turned her eyes back to the ceremony, feigning an earlier interest she now had no hope in regaining.

She darted a look back at Eleanor, only to find her now looking on at the wedding proceedings. Had she imagined it? She looked over at Charlie, who now seemed just as heavily engrossed in the proceedings. Yes! She'd imagined it.

She took a deep breath and settled herself. Just the same, she thought, best to keep an eye on things.

The wedding reception was in full swing out the back of the Grayson house. Harry had been meticulously weeding, mowing and sweeping off the veranda for the past month. Nettie, with considerable help from Ruby – and Bobby's mother, Gladys – had been baking non-stop for the past three days, and Harry and Lenny had erected a huge trestle up along the back wall, its surface now covered with pastries, sweets and savouries spread over a snow-white linen tablecloth that hung to the veranda. A two-tiered wedding cake sat pride of place in the middle, compliments of Gladys.

Another smaller table was erected over in the corner, its surface piled high with presents for the happy couple. Nettie had commented to Harry that for all the effort involved, it might have been better to hire a hall or some such thing after all. But Harry, knowing his wife felt the arrangements to be a little inadequate, assured her that she'd done a marvellous job, and that Lizzie and Bobby didn't seem to be worried at all, and so why should she be?

Chairs were placed all around, the one thing that Harry and Nettie had hired, as they hadn't nearly enough to go around, though some people were still forced to stand. But all and all, everyone seemed to be having a wonderful time.

The old box piano had been dragged out to the lobby, with many offering their services to play – some of whom were accomplished... and some rather less so. As a respite from the mixed bag of tunes being banged out across the keys, Lizzie had also set up her prized gramophone in the kitchen, with strict instructions, should it be used, that only Eleanor, Kathy or Ted were allowed to change the records. Lizzie didn't want someone like the Holt boys changing records and accidentally doing damage to them... she'd witnessed them at other parties after they'd been drinking.

Jerry had come round earlier in the day and set up a keg a little further up the side path, and he'd been invited back for a drink after closing. There was lemonade, sarsaparilla and Coca-Cola for the ladies and non-drinkers, as well as sherry, claret and white wine for those who liked something stronger but didn't have a taste for beer.

Eleanor had discarded the pink dress as soon as she'd been able and now stood at Mark's side in a light green frock of gauzy material. Mark's arm was draped possessively around Eleanor's waist, a gesture that made her feel somehow constrained and also made her want to squirm. Yet for all outside appearances, they looked like a contented couple, with some whispering that, pretty soon, there would be another wedding to attend.

Hillary watched the entire proceedings like a hawk eying its prey, sniffing indignantly every now and then at the display of revelry by those of the younger set who were not so adept at holding their liquor. For once though, she didn't voice her complaints.

Harry, Lenny, Charlie, Richard and Bobby's father Douglas all took up residence by the keg halfway through the night, while Nettie, Ruby and Gladys saw to the food, the cups of tea for those who were ready for one, the cutting of the cake, the display of the gifts and making everyone generally feel welcome.

Lizzie and Bobby weaved their way through the crowd, graciously accepting well wishes and congratulations from all. They would make their departure in an hour or so. The parents of the happy couple had pooled their money and bought them a wedding night at the South Australian Hotel on North Terrace. After which they would take up residence with Bobby's parents until such time as they could afford rent on their own house.

Someone shouted out for dancing, and couples started making their way to the spare patch of lawn at the centre of the yard. One of the more accomplished piano players picked up the tune of a waltz and Mark turned to Eleanor.

'Come on – let's dance.'

Without waiting for her answer, he led her out to the clearing, and holding her at a respectable distance, he began to whirl her about on the lawn. The ground was a little uneven for a dance floor, causing many couples to bump into one another. This did not deter anyone from wanting to dance however, and so with much apology and laughter, the spare patch of lawn was filled in no time.

Lenny led Ruby out onto the grass, his big burly frame easily carving a path through the other couples. To bump into a dancing Lenny was almost perilous.

Harry tried dancing with Nettie, even though his leg was a bit of a hindrance, but they managed a couple of rounds on the outer circle. That left Charlie, Richard and Douglas over by the keg, though they didn't seem to mind being left to drink and talk. When Charlie and Douglas ended up deep in conversation about the latest farm machinery though, Richard stood eying Marjorie, who was being flung around the grass by Lance Holt. Finally, he went to her rescue, much to Marjorie's delight.

Kathy stood with two of the girls from Lizzie's work, all three engaging in an animated conversation about the skills of dressmaking, with Kathy running her fingers over the seams of the bridesmaid dress she still wore, holding it up in places and turning it this way and that to show how it had been stitched.

Ted, meanwhile, was chatting with a few young men about the performance of various makes of engines, an intermittent tap on the shoulder by Nettie warning him to take it easy on the beer.

Eleanor told Mark she could do with a bit of a breather, and Mark, as gentlemanly as ever, led her over and deposited her next to Hillary. Eleanor didn't mind sitting next to her grandmother; she hadn't had a chance to talk to her all evening, and she much preferred her company to that of other people nearer her age... even Mark, she realized.

But then Eleanor put that down to her discontented mood of late, plus the fact she hadn't been able to settle all night, though she knew the reason for that well enough. *He'd* come back. He hadn't spoken to her all day, and apart from that look he'd given her in the church, he hadn't glanced her way again. Perhaps she'd imagined it. Perhaps it was just her overblown romantic fantasies at work again and she should focus more on Mark instead of something that could never be... At least he was closer to her age and within her reach.

Her thoughts turned unexpectedly to Parquin and what he was making of all this. And then she remembered his sudden appearance in her room before the wedding... standing there looking as real as her own reflection, so real it had made her head spin. He'd teased her imagination, touched her shoulder – she was certain of it – and then he was gone. Were men always like that? Did they always breeze in close and then keep themselves frustratingly out of reach?

She thought of Mark. He didn't... Oh why did one not reach out and grasp what they knew they could have? Life would be easier, more peaceful... *and not much else!* Her own thoughts were at conflicting odds within her mind.

Eleanor became suddenly aware her grandmother was talking to her...

'... but of course, a girl like that is no more to blame for the way she is than her mother was, given the way her mother was raised. Like mother like daughter, I always say, and so it goes...'

Eleanor switched off. Her grandmother had obviously found some friend of Lizzie's to heap blame upon for today's wayward youth.

It was getting late and Eleanor searched the crowd for Mark. She finally spotted him over by her father, looking attentive and seemingly hanging off his every word, even though her father was obviously the worse for drink and was more than likely talking a load of rubbish by now. Eleanor grinned. Serve Mark right!

She realized her grandmother was talking again and she gave Hillary her full attention once more.

'I'd best be off, Eleanor. It's been a long day and I'm not exactly twenty anymore... I arranged for a taxicab to come at ten o'clock and I see it's past that now.' Hillary was peering at her watch.

Eleanor smiled. 'Want me to get Dad to see you out?'

'Heavens no! Haven't you noticed the state your father's in? I'd end up supporting *him* down to the gate!' Hillary sniffed and then flashed one of her rare smiles when Eleanor laughed.

Just then, Mark returned to her side.

'We'll see you out to the gate, won't we, Mark?' Eleanor said.

Mark nearly fell over himself to be of assistance to the Grayson family matriarch. 'Of course we will! I can't think of anything that would give me greater pleasure!'

The only thing left for Mark to do now was to get down on his knees and kiss the hem of Hillary's skirt! Eleanor was half surprised when he didn't.

By the look on her grandmother's face, Eleanor suspected that she'd thought something similar. 'Hmm,' was all she offered in response as she rose from her seat.

Hillary linked her hand through Mark's obliging arm, and with Eleanor walking behind, they made their way out through the side entrance of the house. As Hillary had predicted, a taxicab stood at the ready by the footpath.

After helping her grandmother into the back seat and kissing her on the cheek, both Eleanor and Mark stood waving as the cab took off slowly down the road.

The night air was still agreeably warm, and as Mark went to walk away, Eleanor stopped him. 'Can't we stay out here for a while?'

Mark simply stared at her. 'If you like, but I don't think we should stay out here too long – it wouldn't look right.'

Eleanor stared back at him. 'It wouldn't look right?'

'I mean, people might get the wrong impression.' Mark shoved his hands inside his pockets as he took another step back the way they'd come.

Eleanor couldn't help thinking he seemed almost too eager to get back to the party. She stood her ground. 'Let them!' Eleanor was feeling suddenly defiant.

'Don't be silly now, Eleanor. Come on – we have to get back.' He held out his hand to her, like a gesture of compromise. Eleanor didn't budge.

'Mark, we've been seeing each other for nearly two years now. Don't you think people expect us to take a few moments for ourselves? I hardly think they would get the wrong idea!' She sidled up to him. Mark looked uncomfortable.

She placed her hand on his arm and decided to throw caution to the wind. 'Kiss me!'

Mark hesitated, looking around for any signs that they might not be alone, then he bent over and kissed her quickly on the mouth. Eleanor wrapped her arms about him and tried deepening the kiss, but he stepped back out of her reach. 'Eleanor! What are you doing?'

He looked almost repulsed by her forwardness. Eleanor became angry.

'What am I doing? I'm trying to kiss you the way two people are supposed to kiss! The way two people should *want* to kiss after knowing each other as long as we have! It's not like we haven't done more before!'

Mark didn't answer. To Eleanor it was suddenly clear. She'd unwittingly stumbled across the truth in her own words. He *didn't* want to kiss her. This was no gentlemanly restraint on his part; Mark wasn't fighting to keep any deeper emotions in check at all. For the past two years, he'd been calling on her as regular as clockwork three times a week, being gracious to her family, polite to her friends and treating her with the utmost respect and courtesy.

It now suddenly dawned on her that he wasn't particularly interested – perhaps never had been – and she wondered why he'd been striving to make it appear otherwise. She thought of their most intimate moments together and it suddenly occurred to her that the reason those times had left her nothing more than lukewarm was because he felt no passion for her – just as she felt none for him. The pause in their conversation began to stretch out uncomfortably.

She frowned at him. 'Why do you bother?' Her voice, though quiet, pierced the still night air.

Mark chose not to answer, merely standing with his hand offered out to her instead. 'Let's go back in.'

Eleanor turned her back to him, her shoulders set stiffly in resentment. 'No thank you,' was all she could say. Tears formed in her eyes, and she felt foolish. She'd thrown herself open to him, paved the way for him to finally let down his defences, hoping to free some sort of tightly leashed baser instincts, only to find he had none… at least not where she was concerned. She felt betrayed.

'Would you like to be alone for a while?' he asked.

Eleanor didn't trust herself to answer. Tears now ran freely down her face and so she merely nodded in reply. She heard the sound of his footsteps on the gravel as he walked away and then she hung her head and cried.

Charlie had had enough chit-chat for one night. He and Douglas Pinkle had talked of farm machinery, shearing, both old and new methods, the effects of drought and the price of wool. When Douglas had brought up the subject of the war, Charlie had made his excuses, feigning the need to relieve himself, and ambled off through the crowd.

As he'd weaved through the couples on the grass, Harry had stumbled into him and then grabbed him, intent on waltzing him around, until Harry's leg had given way and he'd fallen, nearly taking Charlie with him. After righting his friend again, Charlie had led him to a seat where Nettie had intervened, berating her husband and telling him he'd better take himself off to bed. Charlie had left them then, chuckling to himself and, deciding to take a break from the festivities, had slipped out through the side entrance, hoping to have a cigarette in peace for a while.

But on reaching the front yard, he'd happened to spy Eleanor and Mark out by the road. He'd wondered if he should turn back round again, but instead he'd pulled a cigarette from his case and lit the end, leaning back on the side brush fence, partially hidden by bushes as he blew a thin stream of grey smoke into the air.

He'd watched the whole scene play out before him. He'd heard Eleanor's words, had seen how upset she was, even from where he stood, and had watched as Mark had walked back up the gravel path, right past him. If he'd known Charlie was there, he hadn't acknowledged it, and now Charlie watched as Eleanor gave way to tears.

He thought about talking to her but then hesitated and told himself to leave her to it. A young girl's tears were not his domain.

But he'd ground his cigarette into the grass and was already walking towards her. He would only stay long enough to offer his comfort, tell her about life being full of disappointments and that she'd get over it.

He hesitated. What was he doing? He spun on his heel to go back.

'Uncle Charlie?'

Her voice rang out on the night air, stopping him in his tracks. He turned slowly. Charlie didn't want to go any nearer to her than this, but it was as though his legs had other plans. He walked towards her, pretending a casualness he didn't feel.

'Isn't it about time you called me Charlie? I'm not really your uncle, you know.'

'I know that.' She stood there staring at him, all teary-eyed and embarrassed at having been caught so.

Eleanor had heard his footsteps on the gravel and had half expected it to be Mark returning. On seeing who it actually was, her heart had leapt into her throat.

She turned her face away from him to look at the road. 'You going so soon?'

'No, I came out to have a smoke – take a breather away from the crowd.' He'd stopped about two feet away from her.

Eleanor's eyes widened and she looked back at him. Had he witnessed her making a fool of herself? 'How long have you been out here?'

'Long enough.' His voice was quiet, pitying, and Eleanor became angry.

'I suppose you think I'm some sort of immature ninny! Some inexperienced adolescent who doesn't know anything!'

Charlie took a step towards her, bringing himself closer still. At this distance she appeared shorter… and younger.

'Immature, no… inexperienced, yes.'

His eyes had taken on a different light, and Eleanor noticed the change in them at the same time she smelt his aftershave. Her heart was thumping in her chest, her breathing irregular. Was it because she was excited or was it because she was afraid? Eleanor didn't know. What she did know was that she wanted… something – something more.

She swallowed, all traces of her anger gone now as she searched his face for an answer. He just kept looking at her in that way of his: eyes intense, face unreadable.

Eleanor let her gaze wander pointedly down to his mouth. She bit her lip.

'I only asked him for a kiss. Is that so wrong?'

Charlie drew a deep breath and averted his gaze. Now was the time to tell her about life's disappointments, tell her she'd get over it, tell her that in time she would meet someone else and that Mark would become nothing more than a dim memory. But the words wouldn't come.

He cursed inwardly. She should be talking to her mother about these things, not him… not when she stood so close, looking at him with those eyes of hers. She'd thrown him a line with that mention of the kiss, but he had no intention of taking the bait.

'Perhaps you haven't met the right one yet. Perhaps in time…'

Eleanor had stepped even closer, her breasts brushing lightly against his shirt, effectively cutting him off in mid-sentence. He took a step back.

'Don't… You don't know what you're doing.' Charlie looked down at her. He couldn't believe she was standing there in front of him, staring up at him, her eyes wide with wanting… Hadn't he dreamt of this very moment? Hadn't he lain awake some nights imagining what it would be like?

He went to move towards her again but pulled himself back at the last second, then, turning on his heel, he abruptly strode off. Eleanor ran after him and caught him halfway up the path, grabbing his arm, and he spun back round to face her, his expression now serious – almost angry.

Charlie looked down at her hand holding on to his arm. He pushed it away and grabbed her roughly by the shoulders, his voice low but urgent. 'Eleanor, I am forty years old! And you are eighteen! For Christ's sake, I was already off fighting in a bloody war the day you were born! Your father and mother are my best friends! Doesn't any of this mean anything to you?' Charlie was shaking, barely holding on to his self-control.

Eleanor stifled a sob as she continued looking up at him. She shook her head.

Charlie pulled her roughly over to the side behind the

bushes and shoved her up against the fence, bringing himself hard up against her in one fluid motion. He looked down at her, his expression anguished, his voice a whisper. 'What am I doing? Eleanor... tell me to stop.'

Eleanor's answer was to reach up and wrap her arms about his neck. Charlie groaned and threaded his fingers through her hair, balling it into a fist and pulling her head back as he brought his mouth to within an inch of hers, his eyes searching, his breath hot on her face.

Eleanor gazed up at him, her lips slightly parted, waiting... inviting him... offering them to him. He brushed her lips lightly, once, twice... and then he brought his mouth down hard, ravaging, exploring... plundering her mouth, almost brutal in his intensity, his arms crushing her to him as he pressed his full length up against her.

Eleanor reveled in the feel of him. This was no dutiful kiss on the lips, no polite pretense of affection. He wanted her as she wanted him! This was how it was supposed to be – real desire... real want! *This* was her fire!

No sooner had Eleanor formed these thoughts than Charlie wrenched her roughly away from him. Eleanor stumbled, her mind in a whirl, left suddenly bereft of his warmth, breathless and trembling. 'Charlie?'

But Charlie had turned his back on her. He couldn't look at her, couldn't let her see the torment in his eyes... nor the evidence of what she'd done to his body. Shame washed over him. He turned on her, anger and disgust now plainly visible on his face.

'Satisfied? Is that what you wanted?' His words cut through Eleanor like a hot blade and tears sprang instantly to her eyes. All she could do was stare back at him in confusion.

She didn't understand. What was the matter?

Charlie's eyes swept over her dishevelment in contempt,

his mouth now curled in a cruel sneer. 'See to yourself! And then' – Charlie spun away from her, the rest of his words flung over his shoulder – 'get out of my sight!'

Eleanor pressed her hand to her mouth as tears ran freely down her face, swallowing convulsively against the anguished sob that threatened to escape her throat.

There was a sudden noise at the side of the house – people cheering, cries of 'good luck' and 'best wishes' ringing out on the night air. Of course! Lizzie and Bobby! They were leaving!

Eleanor collected herself, her fear at being caught in the bushes alone with Charlie now taking precedence. She fled in the direction of the front door, her only chance of getting through to the backyard without being seen, and threw a quick glance over her shoulder before entering the house, just in time to see Charlie step forward into the crowd and shake Bobby's hand, as though he'd merely been out taking a stroll in the front yard.

Eleanor slipped into the hallway and immediately leant against the wall, her sides heaving as she sobbed, her slender shoulders bent over and shaking, her hands covering her face as she remembered the way Charlie had looked at her and his scornful words.

'Eleanor.'

Her reaction was instant. She held her breath. *'Parquin?'*

She could feel him, could sense his hesitation.

'Parquin… I'm here.' Eleanor's thoughts reached out to him once more as she wiped her eyes with the back of her hands.

'Yes, I can see that you are.'

Eleanor sensed his amusement and was slightly put out it. *'Don't mock me, Parquin… not now!'*

There was no answer. Eleanor nearly started crying again.

'Parquin! Don't do this… speak to me!' She called out to him loudly, her words ringing out in the empty house.

'Go to your sister… we will talk soon.'

Lizzie! Eleanor came to her senses and flew down the hallway and out through the kitchen. Quickly she ran outside and, taking a deep breath, darted into the crowd, weaving her way through to her sister. On reaching Lizzie, she threw her arms about her.

Lizzie saw her sister was upset but put it down to the fact she was now leaving their home for good and that Eleanor was going to miss her. She laughed and hugged her sister tight. 'Eleanor, you look a fright! Don't worry, I'm not leaving the state. We won't be more than a mile away!'

Eleanor gave a tremulous smile, and then turning to Bobby, reached up and kissed him on the cheek, a thought popping into her head that her mouth still carried the feel of Charlie's kiss. She spied him through the crowd a little way off, but he hadn't seen her. *Or wouldn't dare look at me, more like*, she thought.

The party had thinned out quickly after Lizzie and Bobby left, and Eleanor now lay in her bed, blankets up to her chin though it was a warm night, the green gauzy frock now pooled on the floor where she'd stepped out of it, listening to the last of the guests as they left. She'd wanted to get away from the party as quickly as she'd been able and had told her mother that she'd overdone things a bit and didn't feel well.

As for Mark, Eleanor had hardly been able to look him in the eye, and for once she'd been glad for his usual apathetic manner as he hadn't pressed her for any explanations. He'd merely bid her goodnight and kissed her on the cheek… on the cheek, for heaven's sake! Eleanor had already made up her mind that she would share her time with no man who could be satisfied with merely kissing her politely on the cheek!

As for Charlie, Eleanor had made her departure so quickly after Lizzie had left, she hadn't seen him again after that quick glimpse of him through the crowd… and at this moment, she didn't want to.

He'd shocked her with his outburst and hurt her deeply with his words. She'd done her fair share in instigating their tryst in the bushes, but she'd thought he'd wanted it too, that any attraction had been mutual, no matter how he'd tried to make her see reason in the beginning.

It was after one o'clock in the morning when Eleanor's turbulent thoughts finally exhausted her and she nodded off to sleep.

He watched her as she slept – fitful… troubled. He'd witnessed her sorrow, known her despair… and he'd taken it from her as best he could. Perhaps she needed to sleep, needed to let her mind wander within its own subconscious state… no matter how limited he knew that primitive state to be. But he could see her dreams, watch her unconscious thoughts playing out before him… disjointed… fragments in a swirling fog… Pictures of the man in the garden spun round in her mind, still more of the other known as Mark… both troubling her, giving her no peace.

There was nothing made clear to her. Nothing in them she could make use of.

Time for him now.

He slipped into her dreams, pushing his way through her pictures and forming himself before her.

She merely sensed him at first, the fog beginning to clear... then his presence blocked out all else as he drew her out towards him, enfolding her in his energy and binding her will to his side once again. It was time to show her more.

'Eleanor.'

'Parquin?' Eleanor was relaxed now; he could feel her inner peace. She sensed his approval and smiled.

'Where are we going, Parquin?' He didn't answer.

'I want to know.'

Parquin hesitated. 'I'm going to show you us...

'I've seen "us" before.' Eleanor smiled. 'Though I'm always ready to see us again.'

'I'm going to show you something more, something you may not remember, though you know it to be.'

With that, Eleanor felt herself being sucked back... spiraling through time... back through the past...

She watched in fascination as her own history began to whirl back before her... She saw herself younger, daydreaming out the window in her social-studies class as the teacher droned on at the front... now sitting opposite her doll with her tea set spread out before her on the bedroom floor...

Then she was Evie, sitting in a rocking chair on the porch, Jonah's letter slipping from her aged fingers as she dozed... now running towards Gans, home from the war, her young heart fairly bursting at the sight of him... and further back, running as a young girl over the springy grass on the hill towards the river, fleeing from Sugar Lil and laughing as she caught up with the mischievous Gans.

Now she was Eve, crying at her parents' bedside with the minister in attendance, mumbling his words of useless prayer... now kneeling in church as she and Molly made faces at each other across the aisle and stifled a giggle behind their hands.

Back further still... she was Estelle, readying herself for court, adjusting her décolletage before the mirror, the maid powdering her wig behind her... On... and on... back further...

Ellen, frightened and alone, a cruel, taunting crowd around her... then laughing and running through the trees with Jamie and Mary, shoes off, hair streaming in the breeze...

Eleanor now sensed a slowing down... she knew she'd been going back through the past, but now it was as though she was moving forward. She saw mountains, blue sky... She was drifting lower... land and trees... water... a house...

To Eleanor, it was as though she was hundreds of years away from her life, but she knew she still slept on soundly in her bed. Her mother and father were asleep in the next room... Ted in his...

Parquin watched her; she was unconsciously detaching herself, unknowingly placing herself back in her present. He immediately willed himself to filter through her, catching her mind, controlling it once more...

'Eleanor! Stay with me! Do not summon it – all is well.

Eleanor felt instantly lighter. She clung to him... smiling at him... trusting him.

'Look there.'

Eleanor looked down. She saw Parquin as he appeared to her now... as he'd been then – his black hair long, past his shoulders... a tunic of sorts around his waist, the familiar hunting knife at his hip... And there was Elexia, her hair longer than Parquin's – black hair, straight... dark eyes... beautiful. Eleanor gasped. Why had she not noticed how beautiful she'd been before?

'Parquin! Look at me! I was so pretty!'

Parquin smiled. 'Yes, you were... you are.' His words washed over her.

'Come, Eleanor. Come with me.'

Eleanor felt herself being pulled down.

'The day grows warm, Elexia... let us swim.'

Eleanor found herself looking up into vivid blue eyes. It took her a moment to adjust... then she was Elexia once more. She felt the grass at her feet, felt the still, warm air on her skin, caught the scent of the river nearby...

'Swim? So soon? The sun has not risen to its zenith and you talk of swimming? I think I have taken an idle and lazy man to husband.' She laughed and ducked out of his reach as he lunged for her.

'Idle? Lazy? I will show you lazy, my lovely wife!'

Elexia ran laughing around the side of their cabin, calling out to him... taunting him. 'Too slow by far, my precious!'

Parquin sped off after her, his black hair flying behind him. These were the times he liked best. He would catch the little minx and take her soundly where he found her... and then afterward, he would toss her in the river for her impudence. He grinned, his anticipation growing at the thought of how she would fight him... and how he would win.

Elexia darted behind the fowl pen, feinting to the left and then to the right as he crouched on the other side, waiting for her to make her move. She was breathing hard, knowing it was just a matter of time before he caught her, but oh what fun it was to bait him.

Rather than dart off either side, she backed away, turned and fled at the last moment as he leapt into the fowl pen, making it to the other side and over the wooden railings in two long strides, fowls squawking at the intrusion as they flapped their wings and stumbled over one another to get out of his way.

Elexia chanced a look backward only to see him come bounding over the railings and squealed with delight. She took refuge behind the water barrels at the back, crouched low and waiting for him to appear around the corner, but he didn't come. She waited a while longer. Where had he gone?

She stood up and took a tentative step out of her hiding place, craning her neck to see where he was.

'Ha!' Strong arms grabbed her from behind. 'Do not think you can best me, woman!'

Elexia gave a startled squeal and then laughed as he pulled her down to the soft grass at their feet.

'And now, dear one…' Parquin lay atop her, pinning her to the ground. She tried bucking him off but her actions proved useless other than to arouse him all the more, if what she could feel when he pressed his body against her was any indication.

He peered down at her, black hair falling forward, the blue-violet of his eyes darkening as he gazed upon her beauty. She looked up at him, her own dark eyes softening at his nearness. Was he not magnificent?

Parquin bent his head forward and kissed her… deep, almost leisurely. She could feel…

'Enough, Eleanor!'

Eleanor was lost in his kiss, floating on a sea of violet clouds… soft… warm…

'Heed me, Eleanor! Now!'

Parquin swirled around her, turning her, drawing her back…

Eleanor fought to remain 'there', with Parquin on the grass… the Parquin with Elexia…

Elexia! Not her, Eleanor, but Elexia! She was instantly aware once more.

'I cannot lose you, Eleanor. To leave you here in this time

would banish your present life and that I cannot do... dare not do. You have come so far... and I feel we are close.'

Eleanor felt suddenly deprived... desolate... as though she'd been robbed of all her reason for being.

'Why do you show me these things, Parquin? Why would you want to remind me of what I do not have... may never have again?'

Parquin swirled around her again, dispersing his likeness, reforming and dispersing once more. His intention was to make her follow him, concentrate on him, claim her mind wholly... He'd succeeded... she was his...

'Listen well and try to understand me. I am able to read your innermost thoughts. I can guide your dreams, awaken your hopes and quieten your fears, but you are of that time in your life where you may dwell on false loves, yearn for physical touch and may even covet that which can harm you. 'Tis nothing more than romantic folly, an impractical illusion conjured by the innocence of youth and the curious novice. If I were of your physical world... if I were flesh with a heart that beat within, I would willingly give you the illusion you seek, and you and I would once again walk the earth as husband and wife. But we exist in different realms you and I, and though at times I may appear before you as being of your physical world, I am of no more use to you than your impractical illusions – more it is I who has become the illusion.'

Parquin shifted, his energy flickering. He came up alongside her, willing her to look once more at the two lovers on the grass. Eleanor watched them, bodies entwined... She could feel their happiness... remember it in some strange way, though she was no longer part of it.

Parquin spoke again. 'I know what it is to feel and to touch in the flesh, and it is this, our time, that I thought to *show you so that you might know peace for a time, for I am unable to bring you this physical fulfilment… But in visiting here with me, you might remember that once… you knew what it was to be truly loved. As did I…'*

Eleanor listened, watching him shimmer and flicker before her, going in and out of focus as he spoke, like a kiddie's three-dimensional picture that threw off alternating scenes when it was tilted one way and then the other.

He truly was magnificent, just like Elexia had thought. She pondered now on what he'd told her and somehow it gave her peace… and sadness.

'We really did love each other once, didn't we?' She felt shy and silly.

He indulged her. 'Yes.'

She felt herself being pulled away.

'It's time to go back, Eleanor.'

Eleanor turned over in her bed, groaning, mumbling in her sleep. She felt hot… on fire – normal dream state now… almost. She lifted one leg and pushed the blankets down off her body with her foot. Her mind still clung to him, not wanting to let him go…

She called out in her sleep, unaware as yet that she was back in the physical world. 'Parquin… wait! I will love you again… I promise!'

As the remnants of sleep began to leave her mind, she thought she heard him reply, *'You do, Eleanor… more than you know.'*

'Serves you right! I have no sympathy for you! Not one bit!'
Nettie had been railing at her husband all morning as Harry,
his head pounding and a loathsome burning sensation in the
pit of his stomach, sat slouched over at the kitchen table,
feeling sorry for himself. His leg was aching like the devil
and his gout had flared up again.

Nettie poured him his fourth cup of tea of the morning,
tea being the only thing Harry felt he could keep down.

'I'm all right, Net, really I am… It's just my leg. Perhaps
I shouldn't have tried to dance… it's making me feel a bit
sick too, I think.'

Nettie was sitting opposite him at the small table and
nearly spat out her own tea at his words. She shook her head
and rolled her eyes. 'Oh of course, dear, it must be the
dancing, that's what it must be… Silly me thinking it must
have been the four or five gallons of beer you consumed last
night!'

Harry gave her a sheepish look. Then he smiled. 'Okay,
you've made your point, but I will say I'm not to blame for
all of it. That Doug Pinkle was pouring them as fast as I could
drink them.'

Nettie raised her eyebrows, her tone more than a little
sarcastic. 'What a considerate fellow Doug Pinkle must be…
very conscientious of your needs, I'd say.' Nettie couldn't
help the smile that followed. Harry's expression was dutifully
subdued and then he frowned, remembering Doug Pinkle had
been telling him something important…

Nettie rose to clear the cups away and changed the
subject.

'Better get Ted up, I suppose. I need him to stack those
chairs, get them ready to be picked up this afternoon.' She
smirked at Harry, about to say 'seeing as how his father

wouldn't be up to it' but changed her mind when she saw him frowning. 'What's wrong… leg playing up a bit too much?'

Harry was trying desperately to remember his conversation with Doug, but things were only coming back to him in snippets… just fragments… something about Mark Worthington-Cooke. He looked up at Nettie. 'How's Eleanor? Is she up yet?'

Nettie became instantly concerned and sat immediately back down again. 'No, she wasn't feeling too well last night. I thought I'd let her lie in… why?'

Harry was still frowning. He felt there was some vital piece of information sitting just on the fringes of his mind, but he couldn't grasp it. Nettie pressed him again.

'Harry, why? Did she and Mark have a tiff? She did seem a little upset last night, but I'd put it down to her not feeling well… Is it something else? For goodness' sake, Harry, tell me!'

Ted stumbled into the kitchen scratching his side then, his fair hair sticking out in every direction. He spotted the teapot. 'Oh yes! Is that still hot, Mum?'

Nettie pointed over her shoulder, not taking her eyes from Harry. 'Kettle's still on the stove.'

Ted stumbled over to the stove, darting a look at his parents and noticing something was amiss. 'What's going on?'

Harry looked up at Ted. 'Have you heard anything about Mark at all?'

Ted was standing with the kettle in his hand and looking like he had no idea what it was used for. He glanced down at his father, a frown on his face. 'Mark?'

'Oh here, give me that and sit down. You're as bad as your father!' Nettie took the kettle from his hand and placed it back on the stove. Then she reached for the teapot and set about making a fresh pot.

Harry was studying his son now. 'Yes… Mark. Did something happen last night that we should know about, Ted?'

Ted's eyes widened, as though something had suddenly dawned on him, then he instantly closed his expression off again as he shrugged and sat down. His eyes darted back and forth between his parents as they stared back at him, still waiting for him to answer, and Ted knew he would have to explain.

His words were quiet, almost casual. 'Richard Pinkle was talking to me about it… only rumour of course… Why?'

Nettie was at the end of her patience. 'For goodness' sake! Perhaps I should go and ask *Gladys* Pinkle! After all, the rest of the Pinkles seem to know what's going on! If you don't tell me, Ted, I'll be forced to pour this tea over your damned head!'

Both Harry and Ted looked at her in amazement, both thinking it must be the first time she'd used a swear word in her life. Harry cleared his throat and Ted quickly obliged with an answer. 'Well, it's only a rumour you understand, but Richard was saying that Lance Holt was saying that his brother Lionel – he's been working down at the swimming baths, you know, where Mark works?' Harry and Nettie nodded; Ted went on. 'Well, anyway, seems he was smitten with this girl, Maxine something-or-rather, and…'

'Yes! That's it! That's what I was told by Doug!' Harry's outburst hurt his head and he winced.

Nettie pulled a face at him. 'Oh so *now* you remember?' She looked back at her son and poured him a cup of tea. 'Go on, Ted.'

'Well, his father didn't take too kindly to his son getting

himself hooked up with her. Apparently, she's a bit of a…'
Ted stopped and looked at his mother, not sure whether to say
it or not.

'Oh go on! You mean she's a bit… loose! Is that it?'
Nettie was getting more impatient by the second. Harry rolled
his eyes and Ted stifled a grin.

'Yes, Mum, she's a bit… loose… if you want to put it like
that. Anyway, seems Mark's father insisted that he start
seeing someone like Eleanor – seems you made an
impression on him when you met him that time, Dad.'

Harry nodded in recollection.

'And his father told him that if he insisted on seeing this
Maxine girl that he would cut him off from all his allowance
– you know how well off those Worthington-Cookes are –
and with Mark not earning nearly enough from his part-time
job…'

Ted leant back and took a sip of his tea, while Nettie and
Harry looked at each other. Nettie frowned.

'But… he stopped seeing this Maxine and has been seeing
Eleanor for nearly two years now… Surely nobody, not even
his father, could make Mark see anyone he didn't feel
something for? Surely now he…'

'No, Mum, you don't understand – he's still seeing
Maxine! Or at least has been for the better part of a year or so
now.'

'What?' Both Nettie and Harry shouted the word in
unison. Nettie glared at Harry. 'You were told this last night
and you forgot?'

'Of course not! I didn't hear that part of it! I was told he'd
had a thing for some girl before he'd called on Eleanor. But
the most I thought was that his intentions hadn't started out
honourable, and that was bad enough, but I let it slide because
I thought that at least now he was as taken with Eleanor as

she was with him.' Harry's anger was flaring up now. Nettie looked from son to husband and back again, stunned by the news.

'But how is this possible? He's been seeing Eleanor on a regular basis... I mean, he wouldn't have had time for... Well, would he?'

'Believe me, Mum – these things are possible. Lionel Holt has been seeing two girls at the same time, and by all accounts, his brother Lance hasn't been particularly—'

'Oh the devil with the Holt boys! The only thing I'm interested in is my daughter!' Nettie was upset, her mind racing. She'd always seen Mark as a bit wishy-washy, but she'd always thought he'd been honourable in his intentions, and like Harry had said, Eleanor had seemed to like him well enough... She suddenly looked at Ted. 'And why didn't you say anything last night? Why didn't you simply have it out with Mark?'

Ted sighed. 'You'd have had me start a scene at Lizzie's wedding? Besides, I really didn't know if it was just hearsay... I thought I'd find out for myself and then sort out what to do about it.'

'Well, I know what *I'm* going to do about it!' Harry had sat up straight, his hangover momentarily forgotten, his bad leg the only thing stopping him from rising from his chair and pacing the room. He banged his finger down on the table as he stared at Nettie, his voice raised in anger. 'That simpering philanderer won't step foot in this house ever again! I won't have Eleanor going anywhere near him!'

At Harry's outburst, Nettie had instantly cooled, her own thoughts becoming rational the moment her husband's temper had risen, and she merely looked at him now, her face calm, her words quiet. 'No point in getting yourself in a fluster,

Harry. We have to think about Eleanor and what she's going to make of all this.'

Harry leant back in his chair, his face still reddened from his outburst, but his thoughts now centered on his daughter.

Ted sat by, quietly sipping his tea and not offering anything more.

There was a loud knock on the screen door then Hillary's voice called through the fly wire, 'Is someone going to answer this door? Or am I going to be left withering on the doorstep in this heat?'

Ted rose to let her in as both Harry and Nettie groaned. Hillary was the last person they needed to see right now.

Moments later, Hillary entered the kitchen in front of Ted, sniffing and complaining that she'd been knocking on the door for at least five minutes, and if they hadn't been so taken up with their own raucous chatter, perhaps one of them might have heard her! And if they *were* going to go on so, it wouldn't do for the neighbours to be privy to their conversation so they should have closed the main door! Hillary had merely heard her son's voice raised in anger, but not what he'd said, and she now stood expectantly, waiting for them to tell her what was going on.

Ted offered his grandmother the chair he'd just vacated, preferring to stand over by the stove and well out the way of what he presumed would be an uproar once Hillary was made aware of the situation.

Strangely, though, Hillary said nothing. She simply sat eying the teapot until Nettie, having temporarily forgotten her manners, asked her if she'd like a cup of tea.

'Yes, thank you, Henrietta. I'm positively parched, and I fear the day has not even begun to grow as hot as it will later.' She unpinned her wide-brimmed sun hat and placed it on the table at her side, fanning herself with her handkerchief and causing a few errant wisps of grey hair to float back and forth across her face. Nettie placed a cup of tea before her and Hillary brought it to her lips, gulping the hot liquid down greedily. The others looked on, momentarily taken aback by this uncharacteristic display.

Harry wasn't sure if his mother had even heard everything he'd told her. He went on in any case. 'And now Eleanor has to be told. I won't allow that… that…'

'Milksop!' Hillary finished for him. Harry stopped and stared at her, and she sighed. 'Harold, I may be old, and granted, my principles may also appear a little… well… "rigid" to the young people of today, but I still know a milksop when I meet one!'

She resumed fanning her handkerchief in front of her face and mumbled to herself. 'All that guff about "it would give me no greater pleasure, Mrs Grayson" and his honey-coated attentions to you and Henrietta! So considerate! So obliging and *oh* so respectful! I should have seen it from the start! I'm afraid those Worthington-Cookes are the sort of people who let their money go to their head!'

She sniffed. Ted widened his eyes behind her and glanced over at this mother, but Nettie frowned back at him, giving him an imperceptible shake of her head. Harry sat nonplussed.

'Who lets money go to their head, Grandma?'

Everyone turned as Eleanor entered the kitchen, her sudden appearance abruptly ending all conversation as they now sat staring at her. Eleanor felt suddenly self-conscious in her thin cotton overwrap, pulling it further around her while trying to push her hair back into some sort of order. Why were they all staring at her? What was wrong?

Nettie stood up and came over to her, her face maternally sympathetic. 'Eleanor, I have to tell you about Mark…'

Eleanor listened while her mother told her all that Ted had heard from Richard Pinkle the night before, with interjections from her father as to how he'd heard something along the same lines from Douglas.

What surprised Eleanor more than anything was that she *wasn't* surprised. Oh, she was mildly curious about this 'Maxine' and when and where Mark had been meeting her, and she was slightly amazed he had carried it off for so long, but everything was all now suddenly clear: Mark's lukewarm affections, his apathetic attentions to her, his unwillingness to let their relationship slip back into anything more than a chaste goodnight kiss – though on reflection, she didn't feel as though she'd missed out on anything.

Regardless of the facts that now faced her, Eleanor had already made up her mind, brought about by her own disconcerting experience the night before, that Mark Worthington-Cooke was definitely not what she was looking for… that in actual fact, on waking this morning, he had appeared to her like a fly in the ointment and this provided her the perfect excuse to flick him out of her life.

She now understood what Parquin had been telling her. He'd spoken of 'false loves' and coveting things that may harm her, though she realized the latter may well have been aimed at her near calamitous mistake with Charlie.

Parquin had shown her what it was like to *really* love, and to *be* loved by someone in return, wholly and without condition.

Eleanor had woken this morning with her emotions still tangled up in her dreams. She'd felt peaceful, contented, remembering a man with long dark hair leaning over her, his deep blue eyes turning violet – the same violet eyes that had come into her dreams night after night, year after year… time over time… And she was now determined she would settle for nothing less!

Her parents, her grandmother and her brother now stared at her, waiting for her reaction. She almost laughed out loud; instead she simply raised her eyebrows at them and shrugged. 'Well, I'm glad that's over then. Good riddance I say.'

And with that, Eleanor went to make herself a cup of tea. All her family could do was stare at her, flabbergasted.

An hour later, Ted was stacking the chairs in the backyard, Hillary had taken her leave after satisfying herself that Eleanor was indeed as unruffled as she appeared, and Harry, in an effort to clear his head, sat with his leg resting out in front of him, watching Ted from the back veranda. Nettie was also in the backyard, walking around the perimeter with Ruby and Eleanor, enjoying the morning air before it got too hot and discussing the events of the night before. Occasionally, one of them would stumble across some item overlooked by their disorderly guests, – a glass still half full of flat beer, another broken; various bottle corks and cigarette ends; and even a pipe, though no one present knew who it belonged to.

'I noticed Charlie's suit jacket is still inside on the drawing-room chair, Harry. Hadn't we better get it back to him? Isn't he leaving this morning?' Nettie shaded her eyes as she looked at her husband across the backyard.

Harry had been dozing. He merely shrugged and yawned, and Nettie threw her hands up in the air in exasperation. Ruby laughed, knowing exactly what Nettie was feeling – she'd had the same sort of reactions from her own husband this morning, Lenny refusing to move his large bulk from the sofa no matter how she ranted at him.

'I'll take it to him, Mum.' Eleanor wanted to have it out

with Charlie, and this provided the perfect opportunity. She didn't see Ruby look sharply over at her.

Harry roused himself. 'I wouldn't go to all that much trouble, Eleanor. It's not as though Charlie will be wanting to get dressed up in his suit again soon.' He chuckled to himself, remembering Charlie running a finger around the inside of his collar before the ceremony.

'It's no trouble, Dad. I'm going to see Marjorie in any case. Perhaps we'll take a walk afterward.'

Ruby felt she should say something. 'Charlie's staying at the pub, isn't he?' She knew Nettie and Harry wouldn't approve of Eleanor going inside a front bar.

Ted piped up instead. 'That's right, El – you can't go wandering in there alone to get him.'

Eleanor breezed past him. 'Don't worry, I won't go in – I'll send it inside to Jerry, and he can give it to him.' Eleanor had no intention of letting Charlie leave the state without seeing him. There were things left unsaid, and she had no idea when he'd be back in Adelaide again.

A few moments later, standing in the drawing room, Charlie's jacket over her arm, she wondered just how she was going to get to see him without entering Jerry's premises… then her face lit up as an idea came to her. She would place a note inside the hip pocket telling him to meet her somewhere. Surely he would come… but would he find the note? She would just have to take that chance.

A half hour later, Eleanor waited fretfully on the corner down from the pub where Charlie was staying. If the many people that passed by noticed the auburn-haired girl in the light grey dress and sun hat pacing in an agitated state, Eleanor didn't pay them any heed – her mind was on whether Charlie had found her note or, if he did find it, whether he would actually meet her.

She spotted him a few minutes later, dressed in dark trousers and a white shirt, his hat pulled down low over his eyes as he strode purposely towards her. Eleanor swallowed. She felt suddenly foolish. What was she going to say to him? What was he going to say to her?

As he approached, she started to smile, but Charlie grabbed her elbow, guiding her roughly across the street and into the park. On reaching a bench, he sat her down and then marched back and forth in front of her.

'What's going on, Eleanor? Do you know how foolish it was to do something like that?' Charlie knew there wasn't much danger in what she'd done, but after spending a night tossing and turning guiltily in his bed, sending himself to hell and back, only to be faced with the very same temptation the next day, he'd been livid when he'd read the note.

When he'd seen the words 'Meet me on the corner' written in a feminine hand, he'd thrown the jacket across his open suitcase on the bed, knowing full well whom it was from. For all of a few seconds, he'd told himself he wouldn't go… and then he'd yanked his hat off the rack and stormed out of the door.

'This has to end now! Do you understand, Eleanor?'

Eleanor had been watching him striding furiously backward and forward, his hands stuffed in his pockets.

'I agree with you.'

Charlie stopped in his tracks and looked at her. She looked so calm, sitting there on the bench, her auburn hair left unbound beneath her hat, the wide brim throwing her eyes into shadow, and he tilted his head to peer at her.

He stopped pacing and sat down beside of her, quieter now, calmer.

'You know if we're seen there will be the devil to pay. I don't know how I would explain why I'm sitting here on a bench next to the daughter of my best friend, a girl who's half my age… and me who's supposed to be getting on a train in an hour.'

'I know.' Eleanor peered over at him.

'What do you want?' Charlie's voice was quiet now.

Eleanor bit her lip. She had to know. 'I want to know if you only kissed me last night because I wanted you to, or if you… wanted… to… kiss me too.' Eleanor breathed the last few words out in a rush, suddenly embarrassed.

Charlie frowned at her. 'Of course I wanted to kiss you. Do you think I would've just made a grab for my best friend's daughter on her whim alone?'

Eleanor gazed out over the park. She didn't look at him. 'I wish you would stop referring to my father all the time as your best friend.'

'Well that's what he is… Why? Does it make you uncomfortable? Does it remind you of how old I am? Because I'm only a couple of years younger than him, and if you let yourself think about that as I have then you'll start feeling guilty too… and it's a different story when you let the guilt in, isn't it?'

Eleanor straightened herself on the bench, flicking an imaginary speck from her dress and still not looking at Charlie.

'Is this what the problem is? Age difference? Is that all?'

Charlie turned to her. 'Is that *all*? Look, let me explain something to you. If Harry were to learn about me taking up with some girl half my age in Western Australia, he'd probably be surprised, then laugh, even think I'd lost my senses and perhaps try to talk me out of it… but he would still be Harry – he'd still be my best friend. But if that girl was his own daughter? That's a different thing altogether. He would feel betrayed... he might even hate me for it, and perhaps even you too, and I wouldn't want to put him or Nettie through that – or me and you for that matter. This thing is impossible, Eleanor! It wouldn't work!'

'Is this what this is then? A thing?' Eleanor now turned to look at him; it was Charlie's turn to look away.

'No, but the idea has certainly occurred to me. And for that I'm sorry.' He turned back to her again. 'There's no denying that I felt – *feel* – an attraction to you, but that's all it is. It will pass, or I hope it will... No, it will, and I'm sorry I acted the way I did last night. I apologize for turning on you like that, but don't you see? I was angry at myself for taking advantage of the situation, and that's all my fault.'

Eleanor frowned at him. 'Why is it all your fault?'

'Because I'm the responsible adult. I'm the one who should be thinking clearly, and it was up to me to put a stop to things before they got out of hand.'

Charlie's words had unwittingly hurt Eleanor.

'So I'm not responsible for my actions, is that what you mean? I'm just this silly girl who throws herself at you with no thought to the consequences. I have no say in this? I have no ideas of my own?'

Eleanor stood up and faced him. 'Let me tell you a thing or two, *Uncle* Charlie. I know you're old enough to be my father! I know that kissing you last night was wrong, that it could well cause an unbridgeable gap between you and my father... and my mother! Did you think I would willingly dally with their best friend without knowing the consequences? I wasn't some silly schoolgirl hell-bent on discovering what it would be like to have her first real kiss. Did you think that I simply picked you because you were available? Well... I didn't! I liked you! I still do! And I know this *thing* is impossible – I know it can never be – but I had to know if you'd felt the same way and—'

Eleanor broke off, her voice shaking as she swung away from him. She felt tears stinging her eyes.

Charlie had been watching her intently all through her outburst. Now he rose and came round behind her. He placed his hands on her shoulders, feeling the tension in them, and turned her gently to face him. His voice was quiet, soothing.

'What I said last night about you not being immature, I meant it… I don't think you're some foolish, immature girl at all, Eleanor… but I have to confess, I did think you were inexperienced in these things, and in my usual, insensitive way, I suppose I thought it was up to me to think for the both of us… that *I* was the experienced one, that *I* knew how things really work in this world… and you didn't.'

Charlie sighed and held her close, the gesture doing nothing for his resolve to distance himself from what she was able to do to him. 'I'm sorry, Eleanor; I truly am. And as to your question about whether I felt the same… I did, and what's more… I still do.'

Eleanor was looking up at him now, her eyes watery, her face wet from her tears. He pulled his handkerchief out of his pocket and wiped her cheeks. Then he smiled at her and she smiled tearfully back at him, a little embarrassed.

'So now what?' Eleanor was so close she could hear his heart pounding.

'Now? Now I have a train to catch.' Charlie dropped his hands from her shoulders and stepped back, still looking at her. He took a deep breath as he stuffed his handkerchief back in his pocket.

Eleanor stared at him and took a deep breath also. After a time, she nodded in understanding. 'You going to our house to say goodbye to Mum and Dad?'

Charlie shook his head. 'No, I said my goodbyes last night.'

Eleanor nodded again. 'Well then... I'll see you next time you visit.'

Charlie sighed, his expression wistful. 'Yes... you most certainly will, Eleanor.' And with that, he turned quickly and walked away.

Eleanor watched him go. She watched him as he crossed the street and wove his way through the people on the opposite pavement, and she watched him as he turned the corner, now out of sight, now gone... from her.

She turned and looked out over the park, her face tilting up to breathe in the fresh air. The day was growing hotter, she suddenly realized. She could hear the hum of bees nearby, and she watched the gulls flying low to the ground a little way off, swooping for titbits of bread or whatever from somebody's leftover picnic lunch, some landing on the ground to pick at things in the grass. Eleanor found it hard to believe that in just twenty-four hours, her life had done a complete turnaround. Both Mark and Charlie would no longer figure in it, at least not in the way they had.

She found it ironic that the very day she'd become aware of her deeper feelings for Charlie, Mark had also come calling at her door, and now two years later, both, though for different reasons, had exited her life within the space of a day. How little she knew of life's twists and turns.

She looked up to the sky, an immense stretch of blue that seemed to go on forever, not a cloud in sight. Eleanor felt suddenly peaceful... as though everything was going to be all right. She turned and walked in the direction of the street, her thoughts now centering on only one person.

Eleanor could feel him, those violet eyes seemingly

watching her from all around, looking at her… studying her in that non-judgemental way he had.

'And now what, Parquin?'

There was no answer of course, just a slight feeling of approval emanating out towards her… and that slightly mocking and oh-so-infuriating amusement of his.

With a slight shake of her head, Eleanor smiled to herself.

CHAPTER EIGHT

By 1939, Australia was on the brink of another war. It was a war not anticipated by many Australians, even though newsreels spoke of Italy, Germany and Japan already on the march in Europe and visiting celebrities from abroad had labelled Adolph Hitler as a 'certifiable lunatic' and Mussolini not much better – a dictator with his own agenda. Many Australians took little notice of these things, unwilling to become involved in aggressions they saw as being so far away as to have little effect on Australia, and the remarks about Hitler and Mussolini were not appreciated by those who had been made contented, almost complacent by the peacetime of Australia's past several years. In short, many Australians simply did not want to know.

But as letters began to arrive from England to relatives in Australia outlining the very real threat that existed on their doorstep and newspapers wrote about women and children being evacuated from the streets of London, Australians started to take notice.

When Germany invaded Poland in September of that year, the relatively new prime minister, Robert Gordon Menzies, issued a statement by radio to the nation: 'It is my melancholy duty to inform you officially that, in consequence of the persistence of Germany in her invasion of Poland, Great Britain has declared war upon her and that, as a result, Australia is also at war.'

The statement was met by none of the zeal and enthusiasm of 1914, but rather with a grim but unfaltering acceptance of the inevitable.

Those who had been lucky enough to welcome home husbands, sons, uncles and brothers from the Great War of twenty years or so earlier now turned fretful eyes on their younger generation. Men who had fought in one war could not believe they might have to watch as their sons went off to fight another.

Harry was one of them.

'He's not going, Net! I won't allow it! I managed to come home by the skin of my teeth, and by God, I won't let any son of mine go through what I had to go through!'

Harry was pacing the kitchen, his bad leg swinging out in front of him, his arms waving wildly. Nettie tried calming him down. 'He's only joined the home defence, Harry! He won't have to go anywhere near the fighting. Do you think I'd be sitting here so calm if I thought he was going off to actually fight? They've made it compulsory now to do military training, but he has to actually volunteer to go overseas!'

Harry stopped pacing and slumped into the chair, his leg bumping the table in the process. He shook his head, his voice quiet, his tone defeated. 'I don't know whether I could stand it… I don't think I could cope… I mean, the waiting, the worrying… the hoping that—' Harry broke off and shook his head again.

Nettie knew only too well what it was like to contend

with a loved one being away at war, but she said nothing. Harry went on.

'I was so young, so stupid, thinking it would be some great adventure... Believe me, Ted's just as young and idealistic as I was, and if he's not itching to get into this war now, he soon will be – mark my words. But he has no idea of the very real horror of it all, Net... any more than I did.'

Ted's head was indeed full of the war in Europe, just as his father had feared. A lot of his mates had joined up, with some already determined to volunteer their services overseas. He knew of his parents' views on him going over, so he'd told himself that he would hold back as long as he could for their sake. But Ted, his mind already made up, knew that if and when the time came... he would fight.

Over the past three years or so, Ted had become a reliable asset to Crowley's Garage. At twenty-four years old, and before he'd been signed up for military training, the easy-going and likeable Ted had been much sought after by the unattached girls around town, but while he'd liked to ogle them well enough, and had even dated one or two here and there, he'd felt much more at ease in his grease-covered overalls, with his trusty rag hanging out of his back pocket and his head bent in concentration over some engine.

In the last few years, he'd constantly nagged his father to let him get his Model T back on the road, but Harry hadn't been interested. Due to the Depression years, when petrol had been too expensive and the added burden of a worsening leg as well as gout making it now nearly impossible for him to drive, Harry had seen no reason to keep the car maintained, and due to lack of use and the weather, it now sat close to a ruin in the backyard. Besides, Harry had told Ted that with the compulsory driving test he would now have to do, he would most probably fail due to his bad leg in any case.

When Ted had been about to leave for his military training, he'd grinned at his father, and told him, 'Don't get rid of the Ford, Dad. I still want to fix it up when I come back.' They'd all stood in the kitchen, Harry with his arm around a proud but teary-eyed Nettie. Lizzie and Eleanor had stood close by, Lizzie pensive while Eleanor stared at her brother, memorizing every detail of him so as not to forget what he looked like, even though she knew he was only going off for training.

Harry had shaken hands with his son. 'I'll take that as a promise, Ted, and I'll hold you to it.'

Lizzie and Bobby were now the proud parents of a two-year-old boy, Daniel, and had finally taken up residence in their own house the year before, their plan to be out on their own taking another full year, due to Lizzie having to give up work at John Martins in her fifth month of pregnancy. Sixth months after Danny was born, Lizzie got her old job back, though only part-time, while Gladys and Nettie took turns minding their only grandson. Lizzie had settled so much that Ted remarked to her one day that she was becoming a bore! Lizzie's answer to that had been to clip her lovable but impertinent brother across the ear, her action emphasizing to all present that she indeed still harboured some of her old flighty impulsiveness and that her temper was still quick to come to the fore. Ted had merely grinned back at her, saying, 'Now that's the Lizzie we all know and love!'

Hillary was finally starting to slow down, though her wit was as sharp as it ever was. At nearly eighty years old, she still managed to get under Nettie's skin occasionally, but she was mellowing. Rosie had succumbed to cancer approximately six months after Lizzie's wedding. Hillary had employed a full-time nurse for her long-trusted companion, and in the wee hours of an unusually warm August morning, Hillary had maintained a bedside vigil and watched on as her dear Rosie had quietly slipped away. She'd immediately set about disengaging the nurse, arranging Rosie's service and burial, and on the day, after attending Rosie's funeral, Hillary had come home and taken to her bed for a full month.

On rising after that time, she'd cleared out Rosie's room, giving her clothes to charity and storing her more personal items, like jewelry – though Rosie had not liked to wear much of it – and all of Rosie's letters from a sister in England, and then had Rosie's room cleaned from top to bottom. Hillary had then employed a 'daily' who came at eight o'clock in the mornings, left at midday and came back to prepare the evening meal at five o'clock. Hillary attended her ladies' auxiliary meetings, went to church on Sundays and, apart from visiting her family, was still visited by Eleanor once, sometimes twice a week.

Lenny had suffered a mild stroke at the relatively young age of forty-nine, and though he recovered quite well, he was ordered to change his eating habits and cut down on his tobacco and his beer. Ruby did her utmost to make her husband follow these instructions to the letter, constantly trying to enforce them on a grumbling Lenny, and railing at him every time she saw him light his pipe or have more than one glass of beer. Ruby had also cut Lenny's meals by half, but with Lenny's notoriously large appetite being deprived, he would slip next door to Harry and his good mate would scrounge a piece of cake or pie from the food cabinet when Nettie wasn't watching. Ruby and Nettie still visited each other practically on a daily basis, their newest subject matter the war and whose sons they knew that were joining up.

Kathy had obtained a position with Lizzie at John Martins, both of them still good friends, with Kathy visiting Lizzie on a regular basis. Kathy was not married, a status she so desperately craved, though to disguise this desperation, she emphatically denied that she had any interest whatsoever in the 'bonds' of marriage, stating she didn't wish to let herself be tied down. As a result, she went through one failed relationship after another, attracting the wrong sort of man who, on hearing her views on marriage, made the mistake of thinking she must be nothing short of a good-time girl. Unfortunately, the more decent and respectable men now saw Kathy in this carefree light as well, and thus she was a constant source of worry to Ruby and Lenny.

Eleanor did not see Mark Worthington-Cooke for months following the day of Lizzie's wedding. True to Harry's word, when Mark had knocked on the front door the next time he'd come calling, Harry had ordered him off his doorstep, informing him in a not so courteous manner that he was aware of Mark's *other* interests and that he was not welcome to court his daughter any longer.

When Mark's father had learnt of his son being turned away and the reason for it, he'd promptly cut off Mark's allowance. After a heated argument between father and son over Mark's affair with Maxine of the dubious reputation, his father had ended it by telling him that no money of his was going to be used on a girl like that, and as Mark had stormed out of their front door, his father's loud and parting remark had followed after him: 'But there's no need to worry – she could probably earn enough for both of you by walking down Hindley Street!'

As it had happened, Maxine, though not being the unsavoury sort suggested by Mark's father, turned her attentions to someone else within a few months, and Mark suddenly found himself a single man, a status that made him feel surprisingly unsure of himself. On a chance meeting with Eleanor down the street soon after, he'd been gracious, flattering of her appearance and reminiscent of their time together. Eleanor had been polite, laughed coyly at his flattery, smiled sweetly at his recollections… but had been totally uninterested. She'd bid him a quick goodbye.

Nothing much more was heard about Mark in the following months. He had reconciled with his father… he had been seen with a dark-haired girl, then a blonde, then with the blonde again someplace else. Then in 1940, Ted had written that he'd heard Mark was among those bound for Sydney, to be part of the first contingent to set sail for Europe.

Charlie had made several visits over the last few years. On one of those occasions, he'd had an offer for his Aunt Aggie's house, which of course was now his, though it hadn't been for sale. It had been merely closed up since his aunt's death and the idea of selling it had never occurred to him before. He'd realized he'd always lived on a kind of crossroad, one of those people who were reluctant to choose one way or the other for fear of it turning out to be the wrong direction, never completely committing to his life in Western Australia, nor to his roots in North Adelaide. When he'd been told of someone's interest in the house, it had forced Charlie to make a decision, and he'd decided it was high time he tied up loose ends and put both feet down firmly in one place. And so, for personal reasons, those being mostly about Eleanor… Charlie had chosen Mell Pell.

He still made regular visits to Harry and Nettie, staying at Jerry's pub when he came to town but eating his meals at Harry and Nettie's table. On his visits to their house, Eleanor had been quiet and self-conscious with Charlie while chattering constantly to others in his presence; Charlie had been polite and respectful to Eleanor while keeping his distance. Gradually, and as time went on, things became a little more comfortable for them both. To Eleanor, it was as though Charlie now paid her no more regard than he did Lizzie, while to Charlie, it was as though Eleanor looked on him now as her father's best friend and nothing more.

But each time Charlie rode the train homeward and before he could stop himself, his thoughts would turn not so inexplicably to the girl with auburn hair and intelligent eyes that he'd left behind… and he would curse himself for a fool.

Eleanor was working three days a week in Littleton's Book Store, a small but reasonably popular shop located off King William Street. Its walls were lined from top to bottom with books of all types, from the latest literature – be it fiction or non-fiction – displayed in the front window, to older editions of all genres along the back wall, some written by authors whom Eleanor had never even heard of. Mrs Littleton was of a stature that corresponded well with her name and sat on a high stool behind the sales desk, a woolen shawl forever draped across her thin shoulders, no matter the weather outside. Her face was so wrinkled in appearance that Eleanor, on first meeting her, would not have been surprised to hear that she had witnessed the first publication of some of the older books lining her shelves, though in fact, Mrs Littleton was a mere seventy-two years old.

Eleanor was comfortable enough with her life, though she found it a little uncolourful and at times longed for more excitement. Her worries were few other than her brother's well-being, and while she hoped he would not go overseas, she suspected it was simply a matter of time. She still went about with Marjorie, though Marjorie was now semi-attached to Richard Pinkle, and the tall black-haired beauty considered his brother and Lizzie the perfect couple and longed to be happily ensconced in what she thought would be her own domestic paradise.

Eleanor was doubtful that Richard saw his brother's marriage in the same light as Marjorie, suspecting that Richard in fact saw it as an endless lot of bills and responsibilities that he was as yet reluctant to take on, no matter his feelings for Marjorie. Eleanor, Marjorie, sometimes Richard and another girl they'd become friendly with named Hazel, who worked with Marjorie in her father's hardware store, would frequent the movies, go dancing at least twice a week and spend their Sunday afternoons walking along the Torrens, visiting the gardens along North Terrace or simply taking a stroll down the main streets to peer at the window displays.

Eleanor felt different to her friends in that she couldn't envision herself married at all. Like all unattached young women of her age, she loved to fantasize about romantic interludes with the likes of Clark Gable, Robert Taylor and William Powell. These daydreams were safe enough, for even the most steadfast of Gable fans didn't see themselves actually married to the man, of course, unless it meant they could dress in the gowns that Vivien Leigh wore in *Gone With the Wind* and be swept off their feet and carried upstairs as in the now-famous staircase scene by the dashing and unscrupulous Rhett Butler. Any red-blooded girl would then have given her eyeteeth to be married to the man.

But for the most part, Eleanor looked on movies for what they were – just a movie – and longed for her own romance, one that would be obtainable and within her grasp, but only love without the commitment… if there was such a thing. Eleanor also knew that the situation surrounding her long-standing fascination of Charlie remained unfinished, though how she would be able to make that come to fruition, she was unsure, because even if Charlie did still feel something for her, she knew he would refuse to enter into any dalliance with her. Eleanor wasn't even sure what it was she wanted from Charlie. All she knew was that he was the only man in this life that had ever come close to making her feel something other than obliging affection. She remembered how he'd set her emotions on fire that night in the garden… and oh how she longed to feel that fire again.

Eleanor wished she could be more like Marjorie and Hazel, both of her friends having a normal outlook on love and relationships, though Eleanor would remind herself that her life as well as her outlook was anything but normal. Parquin had seen to that, and at times she would even resent him for it. But then she would think of what it would be like not to know of all her past lives and what she'd done and whom she'd been as well as never having known about the life that she'd been privileged to share with Parquin himself so long ago. He was the only person who knew her completely, though he was still something of an enigma, a wandering soul that waited for her in her dreams and followed her about while never quite letting his defenses down completely. She despaired that she would never get to know him again as she once had, that they would go on forever in their parallel state, life after tedious life, existing side by side but never on the same plane.

In September of 1940, Nettie and Harry stood on the platform awaiting the arrival of Frank and Susan. Nettie was agitated and impatient, her hands constantly fidgeting with her wide-brimmed hat, smoothing down her dark blue skirt or pulling at the matching jacket.

Harry stood next to her, his hat tipped back slightly with his hands in his pockets and wondered if Susan would mind her husband coming down the pub after lunch, so soon after arriving. He spied his wife's fidgeting.

'For Christ's sake, Net! He's your brother! He doesn't care what you look like; he'll just be happy to see you!'

Nettie's face creased in worry. 'I know that… it's just that it's been so long! It's been nearly six years!'

Frank and Susan, along with Nettie's parents, had not visited since before the peak of the Depression. None of her immediate family had even been able to attend Lizzie's wedding – finances being what they were at the time, the expense of travelling had been out of the question. With her father's death two years ago, Nettie had longed to visit her mother, but it hadn't been possible, and she'd had to content herself with the fact that at least Frank was up in Queensland to comfort her. And now Ted too, being stationed in Queensland, visited her mother as often as he could, which gave Nettie some measure of comfort in return.

'I just hope Susan doesn't make a song and dance about Frank coming down for a beer. Some of the blokes want to see him again and Charlie is coming in tomorrow as well. You know Charlie – he'll want to have a beer for sure.'

Nettie rolled her eyes and was just about to tell him off for his usual twisted sense of priorities when the train rattled suddenly into view.

'Here it is!' Nettie turned to Harry. 'Quickly, do I look all right? Really?'

Harry smiled down at her. 'Don't worry, love… you look good enough to eat.'

'Harry!' Nettie feigned indignation at his words but was secretly pleased. She linked her arm through his and waited.

Frank stepped off the train amid the comings and goings

of the other passengers, many of whom were young men decked out in their uniforms, all with mixed feelings as they jumped aboard, families and friends – reluctant to see them go – jumping up with them to give them one last clinging hug as mothers stood dabbing handkerchiefs to their eyes on the platform below. Harry's mind was momentarily taken up with Ted, mentally thanking God his son was still stationed in Queensland but knowing it would just be a matter of time…

Harry's thoughts were cut off as Frank yelled out to them.

'Hey, Nettie! Harry!' Frank waved and shouted to them, and then turned to help Susan down off the train behind him. Nettie ran through the crowd and threw herself at Frank as he laughed and swung her round. And then, collecting herself, Nettie hugged Susan as well, though a little less boisterously.

The usually quiet and sensitive brunette grinned broadly at her sister-in-law. 'It's so good to see you again, Nettie!' Susan hugged Nettie once again. Harry wasn't far behind Nettie and shook Frank's hand warmly, then, leaning down, kissed Susan on the cheek.

'Hey, Nettie, you look a picture!' Frank eyed his sister up and down as Harry caught his wife's eye with an *I told you so* look.

Nettie laughed. 'You do too!' Frank had taken his hat off and she now ruffled his hair. 'Though I think those red locks have faded a tad over the past few years, haven't they?' Nettie teased him.

'Don't knock it – that's the only thing good about getting old. You know how I hated having carrot-red hair!'

They all laughed as Nettie now linked arms with Susan and they moved off ahead of the men, with Frank motioning to Harry behind them that he could do with a beer. Harry winked back at him and nodded.

Frank and Susan were to stay in Lizzie's old bedroom

while they were visiting. Nettie had cleared it out for them, having turned it into a bit of a storeroom after Lizzie was married, and although Ted's room was vacant at present, Lizzie's bedroom was considerably larger.

Frank and Susan had never had any children. After Susan had suffered three heartbreaking miscarriages, the couple had resigned themselves to the fact that they were not to be blessed with a family, a subject that the disappointed couple were not inclined to discuss a great deal, though Nettie had learnt from her mother that Frank would have liked to have presented their father with a grandson before he died – show him some proof that there would be someone to carry on the O'Donnell name.

Harry, Nettie, Frank and Susan sat around the dining-room table; their voices raised in excited chatter as they made their way through one subject after another. A long-neck bottle of Coopers stout sat two-thirds empty on the table in front of Harry and Frank, a glass each in front of them, while Nettie and Susan preferred to relax with a pot of tea.

Into this jovial scene walked Eleanor, home from the bookstore, and a half hour later, in came Lizzie with Bobby, carrying a bright-eyed Danny on his hip. After much hugging and still more cooing over little Danny, all sat down to chatter some more, the conversation having changed now to more domestic subjects, those of Lizzie and Bobby's home and what he was doing in the back garden and whether they would have any more children just yet and then on to Eleanor and when was she going to get married?

Nettie mentioned something about getting the tea on and, as she rose, in walked Ted…

And Harry's face fell.

Nettie's first reaction on seeing her son was that of ecstatic joy, then as she looked over at her husband's expression and noticed the quiet, withdrawn faces of those crowding her table, she was suddenly filled with a dawning apprehension. She swung back to look at Ted, her eyes suddenly bright with unshed tears.

'You're going?'

Ted gave a slight nod. 'Yes, Mum. I'm sorry… but I have to.'

Nettie swallowed. 'When are you leaving?'

'They've given us a fortnight's leave… I'll be leaving next Saturday.'

'So soon?'

'It's the travelling – takes time to get down from Queensland and back.'

Nettie didn't say anything for a time. All she could do was look at her only son, her eyes drinking in the sight of him: his brown eyes, his generous mouth that always made him look as though he was smiling even when he wasn't, his mop of blonde-brown hair that was now cropped so short… Nettie reached up and smoothed it back.

'They're making you leave? I thought it wasn't compulsory for you to go.'

Ted averted his eyes, avoiding his mother's searching look. He thought he'd prepared himself for this, but he now found it was harder than he thought. 'No, we don't have to, Mum, but… I'm going. There are blokes going over all the time and I can't stay back any longer… I feel so useless.'

Nettie could do nothing but stare at him.

There was a sound behind them as Harry pushed his chair back. Without looking at anyone, he rose and made his way quietly outside. The atmosphere was tense in the dining room save for the antics of Danny, who now busied himself with crawling under the table and reaching up for the tablecloth.

Lizzie stood close to Bobby, her arm linked through his.

Eleanor had taken up a position by the window and now stood peering out at the peach and apricot trees, noting idly that the fruit was nearly all gone now that the season was drawing to a close.

Ted was going to war… her Ted. Eleanor blinked back tears. It wouldn't do for him to see her so upset. In desperation to find out if he would come home unharmed, her thoughts reached out for Parquin, but there was no answer.

'Damn you, Parquin! How come you're not around when I need you most?'

But no sooner had she cursed him than Eleanor felt a peaceful calm descend upon her, all her worries and anxieties being washed away, and she sighed. And even though Parquin had said nothing, she had the distinct feeling that he was reprimanding her, reminding her that he was always around her and that she shouldn't allow herself to think otherwise.

Frank cleared his throat in the surrounding silence. 'Want a beer, Ted?'

Ted nodded at his uncle and smiled. 'Yes, sir! I could certainly do with one!' He tried to sound light as he placed his arm around his mother and led her back over to the table. Conversation was hesitant at first, but after a few moments, it began to get a little easier once more. Any talk of the war and its progression was carefully avoided, and no one mentioned the fact that Harry was still absent from the room.

A little while later, Ted excused himself and went in search of his father. He found him out in the back garden weaving his way through the tomato patch in the far corner behind the shed. Harry looked up as Ted approached and then looked quickly back at the tomato plants. He didn't smile. 'Should have planted more of these; they're really taking off this year. Lenny always has trouble with them, but…' He stopped and looked at Ted, who hadn't said a word. 'Why are you going, Ted? Why would you do this to your mother? Have you any idea what she went through when I went away?'

Ted's voice was quiet. 'But you went anyway, Dad.' He frowned. It wasn't what he'd wanted to say.

Harry straightened to his full height and stared at his son, his voice now raised. 'Yeah, and do you know how lucky I was to come home? And how lucky I was just to be walking around with this?' Harry brought his hand down on his bad leg. 'It could have been worse, you know… a lot bloody worse.'

Ted sighed. 'Dad, it's not like it was when you went over. There's not the kind of fighting you did… in the trenches I mean.'

'For Christ's sake, Ted! What bloody difference does it make what kind of fighting it is! War is war! You live or you die! And if you're lucky enough to come home alive, don't kid yourself that it ends there either, that everything will be hunky-dory again! Believe me, it isn't! Not by a long shot!'

Harry's outburst was followed by silence between the two men. Ted stood looking out over the garden as Harry began wandering aimlessly through the tomato patch once more. Both felt uncomfortable. Ted broke the silence.

'I *will* come home, Dad… I will.'

Harry stopped and took a deep breath. This wasn't the way to send his son off to war. Ted needed the support of his family, and it wouldn't do for him to go away remembering any ill feelings or words of disapproval from his father. It wouldn't do at all.

Harry sighed and nodded, his voice holding an uncharacteristic tremor as he spoke 'I certainly hope so, son.' Harry smiled then and approached Ted, placing a hand on his shoulder and giving it a couple of pats. 'Keep your head low and promise me you won't volunteer for anything! All right? And remember… we'll all be here waiting for you when you get back.'

Ted swallowed back the sudden rise of emotion that welled up within him. He nodded.

'Sure thing, Dad.'

The following day, Charlie arrived. He was met with the pleasant surprise of seeing Frank and Susan again as well as the disheartening news that Ted was going away to war. He could tell instantly that Harry and Nettie were steeling themselves against their son's departure, but he also realized it was not a subject open for discussion with Harry – at least not yet. So Charlie conducted himself the way he always did. He spoke about the latest goings-on at Mell Pell, enquired as to the people they knew and what they were up to, entered into a long conversation with Frank and Susan about their life in Queensland while spending a lot of his time at the bar swilling back a few beers with Harry, Frank, Lenny or Ted, sometimes with all of them, sometimes not.

The time for Ted's departure came all too soon. Frank and Susan had decided to leave with him, accompanying him up to Queensland. They all stood on the platform to see the small group off: Harry, Nettie, Lizzie and Bobby along with little Danny, Eleanor, Lenny, Ruby, Kathy, Charlie and Hillary. Ted hugged each in turn and then hugged his mother a second time, an action that merely served to crumble her pretence of self-control and she wept openly into his arms. Harry stood nearby, his jaw clenched, his eyes unblinking, while Lizzie sought the comfort of her husband and son as Hillary sniffed repeatedly, leaning heavily on her now-familiar walking stick alongside the silent Jenson family. Eleanor stood trembling while trying her utmost to remain calm.

Charlie came to her aid. He placed his arm around her

shoulders and she immediately leant against him, her face turning into the crook of his shoulder. Charlie stroked her hair and drew her closer, while thinking that of all the times he'd thought wistfully of having his own brood of children, this was one time he was thankful for not being a father. He could only imagine what it must be like for Harry and Nettie to see their only son go off to war, and given what he knew war to be, his heart went out to his long-time friends.

Nettie managed to collect herself long enough to wave at her son as he hung out of the train, waving madly alongside Frank and Susan.

As the train pulled out, and his family and friends began to grow smaller with the increasing distance, Ted still waved frantically, until the train moved around the bend and he finally lost sight of them.

He turned to Frank and Susan then, his face a little fretful.

Frank smiled. 'Best we find our seats then… shall we?'

Ted looked out through the window again then turned back to Frank. He simply nodded.

All was quiet among the small group left back on the platform as they made their way homeward. Charlie thought he could do with a beer and darted a look at Harry, but Harry was walking with his arm around Nettie and he realized now was not the time.

Not wanting to be part of the gloomy atmosphere Charlie felt would surely be waiting for them all once they'd reached the Grayson house, he opted to go for a walk instead.

'I'll call by later, Harry. I'm going to take myself off for a while… all right?'

Harry, his arm still curled across Nettie's shoulders, barely acknowledged Charlie's words but for a slight nod.

Eleanor, wanting to be anywhere else, suddenly thought walking with Charlie seemed like the perfect escape. Lest the moment pass her by, she blurted out, 'I'll come with you, Uncle Charlie… if that's all right.'

Charlie was taken aback by her suggestion but finally he shrugged.

Nettie attempted a bit of light-hearted teasing. 'Mind you don't have my daughter sitting at some bar, Charlie Bradford!'

They all laughed, even Hillary.

'Now would I do that, Net?' Charlie grinned at her.

She smiled and nodded. 'See you both for tea then.'

With that, Charlie and Eleanor walked off in the opposite direction, a thoughtful Ruby looking on after them.

Charlie and Eleanor walked for a while before Charlie finally spoke. 'So where would you like to go, Miss Grayson?'

'How about Mell Pell?' Eleanor was just as amazed at her answer as Charlie was. Had she even thought of going there before? Eleanor realized that the idea had only just come to her. She blinked and looked at Charlie for his reaction. Charlie hid his surprise well.

'That's a nice idea, but I don't think we'll make it home in time for tea, do you?'

'Charlie, I'm serious!' Eleanor had stopped walking and now stood looking at him. 'What do you think?'

Charlie, after first pondering on the fact that she'd immediately dropped the 'uncle' when out of range of her family, now raised his eyebrows and stared down at her. 'You know that's impossible.'

'But why? Why is that impossible? I think it's very possible, and even though I don't need the permission of my parents anymore, I'm sure they would go along with it.'

Charlie sighed. 'Look, let's just walk a while down by the Torrens and take in the sights, all right?' He moved off again.

Eleanor smiled to herself and moved alongside, linking an arm through his. He immediately disengaged it. 'Don't you think that looks a bit odd?' But Eleanor noticed he was smiling.

'You win,' Eleanor sighed but her expression was sly.

Charlie raised an eyebrow in her direction but didn't look at her. He pointed to a crowd gathered along the banks. 'Let's see what this is all about, shall we?'

They walked down the embankment towards the milling crowd. As they approached, the raised voice of a man could be heard above the thickening horde. They weaved their way to the front and stood looking up at the man on his makeshift podium, who was doing a lot of arm-waving as he expressed his views on the futilities of war. The crowd before him stood mostly silent but some nodded in agreement.

'… the blood of the young men and women of our country … this government had taken enough from us, many of you already paying the price the first time with the loss of sons, brothers and fathers. And I ask you now, good people, why should we enter into a war that has been dictated to us by a country so far away that…'

Charlie spoke quietly to himself. 'A bit bloody late now, isn't it, mate?'

Eleanor pulled on Charlie's arm. She didn't like crowds like this – they seemed to conjure up other crowds of long ago, in another time where she was the centre of attention, her hands tied behind her… shouts ringing out from the crowd as she'd stood rigidly before them. Once it was the guillotine; once it was the noose around her neck… and another time it was the dry tinder at her feet. Crowds like this had always meant death.

Eleanor was suddenly finding it hard to breathe. 'Charlie,

come on. Let's get out of here, I don't like it.' She pulled harder on his arm.

He looked at her and shrugged. 'All right, come on – I'll buy you an ice cream.' Charlie pointed in the direction of the small kiosk down near the boats.

Eleanor swallowed and nodded. 'Yes, an ice cream. I'd love one.'

Charlie chuckled and shook his head. 'Anything for the lovely Miss Eleanor!'

A little while later they walked back up the slope to the main road, an ice cream each clutched in their hands. Charlie was congratulating himself on his performance. He'd been careful not to overstep the boundaries of propriety, keeping himself in check at every turn in the conversation.

They wandered on past shops, stopping and browsing here and there at the items for sale in the window. Charlie laughed at what he saw as the latest atrocities in fashion and laughed even more at Eleanor's obvious delight in them, though it reminded him again of their age difference. Eleanor feigned a yawn at Charlie's interest in the latest farming equipment, and he returned the gesture when she gaped admiringly at the poster of Clark Gable and Vivien Leigh clutched in a romantic embrace inside the open foyer of the cinema.

All too soon, they were nearing the house again, and Charlie was suddenly seized by the ridiculous thought that he was returning her home after a date like they were a pair of silly kids. He shook the feeling off by way of mentally distancing himself from her.

Eleanor noticed the change in him but asked no questions. It had been a lovely afternoon, one she would not forget, but now it was over and he was to be suddenly Uncle Charlie again. There would be no changing it, she thought depressingly, unless…

They were still a few houses away from home and now Eleanor stopped and looked up at him. 'I *will* visit you one day, you know. I meant what I said before… about going to Mell Pell. One day, I will travel to Western Australia to see you. I realize now is not the time, but one day…'

Charlie gazed down at her, his eyes searching her face, and sighed. 'You know that can't happen, Eleanor. I…'

'But I really want to go… really I do!' Eleanor held up her hand before he could protest. 'Just hear me out, please. Charlie. If… well… nothing had happened between us the night of Lizzie's wedding and I had wanted to come and visit with you, what would you have said then?'

Charlie was silent for a few seconds. 'But something did happen, didn't it?' he said quietly. Why was his heart suddenly thumping in his chest?

'So this thing that happened at Lizzie's wedding reception is going to be there between us the rest of our lives? Is that what you're saying?' Eleanor was frowning at him, waiting for an answer.

Charlie sought to make light of the whole thing. 'It sounds to me that you're doing everything in your power to keep it there.' His tone was dry as he tried to smile.

Eleanor placed a hand on his arm. 'And if I was?'

Charlie's answer was to pull her along towards her gate. 'Best we get you home. Don't want the neighbours gossiping about us standing here, do we?'

'I thought he was in the 6th Division! And what is he doing in England?' Hillary was perplexed, her brow wrinkling in confusion.

'He was, Mum, he's still in the 18th Brigade, which was part of the 6th, then his brigade went to the 9th and now he's become part of the 7th Division. As far as what he's doing in England, I'm not sure. And for all we know, he's probably somewhere else now.'

Hillary, no more the wiser, shook her head as Harry turned the envelope over in his hands and peered at the date stamped on the front.

'For goodness' sake, Harry, put your glasses on!' Nettie held them out to him but he waved them away. Harry had already seen the date; it was marked January, three months ago. He placed the envelope on the table, his mind deep in thought.

Where was he? Where was his son? Was he now fighting for his life in some godforsaken place? Had he been wounded? Perhaps even stretched out in some army medic tent at this very moment and cursing himself for leaving the home shore? Harry's thoughts had taken him to hell and back on too many occasions, but he knew it didn't do any good to dwell on things.

He looked up to find Nettie staring intently at him. Harry had never been able to hide anything from her; he knew she could see straight through him. He tried to smile.

'He'll be all right, Net… you'll see.'

Nettie didn't answer but chose to busy herself at the kitchen bench. Harry thought, not for the first time, that his wife showed more grit than he ever had, and he found himself wishing that he were more like her. He became angry at his own lack of confidence.

He stalked out of the kitchen and snatched his hat from

the stand. 'I'm going down the pub for a beer.' As an afterthought, he turned to his mother. 'I'll see you on the weekend, Mum.' And to his wife, his tone a little softer now: 'I won't be long, love. I'll be home before Eleanor gets back from the store.'

Nettie merely looked at him and nodded, and he left through the front door.

'I suppose I'd best be on my way too, Henrietta. Could you tell Eleanor I'll see her when she comes to visit?'

Nettie looked over at her mother-in-law and nodded. 'I will.'

Hillary rose from the chair with some effort and made to leave but stopped and turned back, leaning heavily on her walking stick as she faced her daughter-in-law.

'You realize, Henrietta, that men don't handle these things as well as us, don't you? To play the waiting game is not in their nature, and so, unfortunately, they cannot be counted on to remain successful at it for too long. Unfair as it may sometimes seem, it quite often falls to the women of the family to do what the men cannot. It has always been so, and I am afraid to say that it will always be the same.'

Nettie said nothing. Hillary sniffed and went on. 'Harold is like his father. If George had been alive to see his son go to war, he would have tolerated it no better than Harold is doing for Edward.'

Nettie bit her lip at the mention of her son's name. She didn't want this pep talk from Hillary... if in fact that was what the woman was trying to do. But then she realized that Hillary, in her own oblique fashion, was trying to do just that. Nettie also realized that Hillary's words, while criticizing what she saw to be her son's weakness, were also absolving him from any accountability, supposedly owing solely to his gender. If Nettie hadn't felt in such a bleak mood, she might have actually laughed. Instead, her response was non-committal. 'He tries, Hillary; he really does.'

Hillary nodded. 'Yes… he tries.'

Nettie smiled. 'A good deal of the time, he can be quite good really.'

'Yes, I'm certain he can be.' Hillary sniffed and left through the front door.

Less than an hour later, Eleanor entered the kitchen to find her mother sitting at the table and weeping into her hands.

Eleanor came to an abrupt halt, thinking her worst fears surrounding her brother had been realized. But just as those thoughts had formed in her mind, they were quickly extinguished by the presence of Parquin as he reached out to her, instilling in her an awareness that Ted was all right. She mentally thanked him for it, then moved quickly to her mother and placed an arm around her shoulders.

'Don't cry, Mum. Ted's all right – I'm sure he is.'

Nettie started to laugh though her tears still ran freely. 'Why is it that everyone tells me he's all right when they have no idea themselves? We've just received a letter from Ted dated three months ago, but your father tells me he'll be all right! How in God's name would he know that? We're not even sure where he is! And just now, your grandmother had to make sure her precious son was exonerated from any blame for his lack of support, telling me some rubbish about it not being a man's domain to play the waiting game!' The last few words were exaggerated with a sweep of her arm as Nettie rose from the chair.

Eleanor screwed up her face in puzzlement, not entirely sure what her mother was talking about, although if her grandmother was involved, she could understand her mother's frustration. Those two women had been at cross-purposes for years.

Nettie went on as she now paced the floor, her emotions, so carefully kept in check over the last few months, now giving way to anger. 'I don't care what she says! Whether your father wants to wait or not, whether he's able to wait or not, has got absolutely nothing to do with it! He *has* to wait, just like me, for any news of our son! What's more, if he chooses to go down the pub and put on the pretense that everything is all right, then so be it! He does it his way and I'll do it mine!'

Nettie dissolved instantly into a fresh bout of tears. 'I'm sorry, Eleanor. I'm raving. I know I am. Nothing I'm saying is making sense.'

It was at this point they heard the front door open and close, and Nettie turned her back from the kitchen doorway, knowing it was Harry and not wanting him to see her in such a state. But Harry knew as soon as he came in, his eyes darting from Nettie to Eleanor, and just like Eleanor only moments before, he expected the worst. Eleanor shook her head, silently telling him that it wasn't from any news about Ted, and Harry sighed with relief, then went quickly to his wife. She turned and lurched into his arms as he wrapped them around her, and they stood there, clinging to each other as Eleanor looked on.

She watched them for a while and then decided it would be better if she left, and so, not wanting to disturb the tender scene, Eleanor slipped quietly from the room.

In August of 1941, Prime Minister Menzies resigned his office and Arthur Fadden stepped in to take his place. But a mere two months later, his government fell to the Australian Labor Party and John Curtin became Prime Minister.

In the early hours of 8 December of that year, Curtin was awakened by his secretary, informing him that Japan had attacked Pearl Harbor. Soon after, news came that Thailand, Malaya, Guam and Wake Island had been invaded and Manila, Shanghai, Singapore and Hong Kong had been attacked by air. Curtin addressed the nation saying, 'Australia is facing the gravest hour in her history.'

Australia braced itself against the very real possibility of a Japanese invasion. Emergency services manned with 300,000 volunteers, both men and women, were trained in first aid, firefighting and aircraft spotting. Air-raid shelters sprung up around the cities, equipped with respirators against possible gas attacks, and buildings were protected with sandbags while many householders dug trenches in their backyards. Schools, offices and factories held air-raid drills, and modified blackouts called 'brownouts' were enforced, while important signposts and landmarks were taken down or dismantled as a way of confusing any Japanese invaders. Beaches were fortified with tank traps and barbed wire and there was even a 'denial squad' set up to destroy important industrial plants and machinery should a Japanese invasion take place.

Darwin, on the other hand, though it was an important naval, air force and supply base, was quite unprepared for the large force of Japanese invaders that made two raids on 19 February 1942.

A few months later, Harry sat listening to the radio. The news over that time had been filled with reports of merchant ships and warships being sunk, as well as aircraft being destroyed in the air as well as on the ground. Harry shook his head. 'Didn't they learn *anything* from Pearl Harbor?' He had pulled his armchair up close to the radio, his frown deepening as he strained to listen, the signal going in and out and causing him to thump the side of the radio.

'Dad, that won't do it any good... let me.' Eleanor had been lounging back in the armchair and watching her father for the past few minutes, his face set in frowning concentration, his head tilted upward as he peered through the bottom of his bifocals and fiddled non-stop with the radio's tuning dial. He now looked at his daughter, his frown deepening.

'Don't try telling him anything, Eleanor. Yesterday I had to put up with him fiddling with the silly thing all the way through my serial... wouldn't let me... He finally got it right by the time his news came on!'

Nettie had been reclining also. She sat reading; her book turned to the fading light of the drawing-room window in her effort to make out the words.

Considering the war and its upheaval to everyday life, there was an uncharacteristic peace within the Grayson household. Over the past year, letters had come home from Ted, though a little erratic in their delivery, with some coming months apart and the last mail – two weeks ago – bringing three letters all at once. Ted had written letters from Tobruk, then Turkey, with his last letter informing his parents he was being sent home, though for how long or what was expected of him at home, he was unsure as yet. Both Harry and Nettie had breathed a great sigh of relief.

Harry looked at his wife with the same frown on his face. 'Net, either turn the lamp on or put your glasses on. You'll ruin your eyes like that.'

Nettie gave no reply and continued squinting. Eleanor sighed. She rose and then squatted down at the radio, turning the knob this way and that until she had a reasonable though somewhat scratchy reception. Then she rose again and walked over to the bureau along the far wall to retrieve her mother's reading glasses. She handed them to Nettie just as a knock sounded on the door.

Eleanor opened the door to an excited Hazel.

'Come on, Eleanor! Get your dancing shoes on! We're going out!' Hazel twirled around on the doorstep, her mop of bright red head bouncing around as she did so, and Eleanor started laughing.

'Out? What do you mean? Out where?' But Eleanor had immediately shut the door behind her friend and was already making a beeline for the bedroom, her thoughts skimming the contents of her wardrobe, already putting dress, shoes and accessories together in her mind's eye as Hazel did a little skip and caught up with her. Hazel leant close, her voice a loud whisper.

'The hall is going to be bouncing tonight! Full of Americans, Eleanor! What do you think?'

Eleanor faltered in her steps and turned to her friend. 'Americans?'

Hazel's eyes danced as she nodded. 'Uh-huh... they're out on leave from the barracks! Who knows, I might snare myself one of those tall, good-looking Yanks!'

Eleanor looked a little dubious. 'Just be careful, Haze... half of them are probably already married! Or at least spoken for back home.'

Hazel clucked her tongue in annoyance. 'Oh come on! Don't do this to me now! Marjorie has already turned me down – don't you do it too!'

'Marjorie didn't want to go?' Eleanor's eyes widened in surprise. Marjorie was always up for a dance.

Hazel pulled a dry face. 'Well, according to Richard, any truly patriotic Australian girl has no business exposing herself to such company.' Hazel let out a deep sigh. 'And so' – Hazel shrugged – 'Marjorie says she's not going.'

Eleanor was now busy rifling through her wardrobe, her words flung over her shoulder. 'I might agree with him on the company, though not for any reasons of patriotism… more that you and I had better watch our step with our American visitors. I've heard stories about girls who let themselves be talked into things that—'

'Oh, Eleanor, you and I are not that silly… are we?' Hazel cut her off, exasperated.

Eleanor held up a light green dress in front of herself before the mirror and smiled at Hazel's reflection. 'I don't know… are we?'

'Going out, Eleanor?' Nettie stood in the doorway. She knew instantly where her daughter was going. Ruby had voiced her concerns to Nettie that very afternoon about Kathy going to the dance at the Community Hall and about the American soldiers that would be in attendance.

Eleanor nodded. 'Thought we might have a bit of a look in at the hall tonight… there's a dance on.'

'Hello, Mrs Grayson,' was all Hazel could muster before she blushed. Nettie wondered for the umpteenth time how an intelligent girl like her Eleanor could keep company with such a whimsical and irresponsible girl like Hazel.

'Hello, Hazel.' Nettie then reprimanded herself for her uncharitable thoughts, telling herself that perhaps Hillary's stuffy attitudes and opinions were finally beginning to wear off on her. Nettie decided to smile indulgently at Hazel then. 'You look lovely, Hazel. That shade of brown agrees with your colouring.'

Hazel immediately preened. 'I think it does too, Mrs Grayson. It has a gold fleck through it, see?' Hazel swished her frock back and forth, which brought another indulgent smile from Nettie before she turned to Eleanor.

'What are you wearing, dear?'

'The green I think.' Eleanor was already undressing.

Nettie nodded. 'Well, have a good time, you two… and don't stay out too late, will you, Eleanor?'

Eleanor didn't miss the look in her mother's eyes and she nodded. 'Don't worry, Mum.'

The dance was already in full swing when Eleanor and Hazel arrived at the open double doors of the Community Hall. Hazel practically danced her way through the entrance, her feet marking time to the band playing a homespun version of Glenn Miller's 'In the Mood', her hips swinging outrageously as Eleanor held back and eyed her friend, suddenly having second thoughts about whether she should have come or not. Instantly, two American soldiers, decked out resplendently in their uniforms with hats tucked under their arms, approached Hazel, one holding out his hand to lead her over to the refreshment table. Hazel nodded and smiled graciously at the two men, but before letting herself be led away, she called out, 'Eleanor! Come on!' loudly in Eleanor's direction.

Eleanor swallowed, a little unsure of herself. She was used to the men in her neighbourhood, men she'd known since her youth. With them she felt at home, surer of herself. They'd quite often bored her senseless, but all the same, she'd always known what they were about. Looking over at the crowd of uniformed Americans standing around the refreshment table with a gleefully gushing Hazel in their midst, Eleanor felt suddenly like a lamb being led to slaughter.

'This is my good friend Eleanor!' Hazel announced.

Eleanor nodded at all in turn as they introduced themselves, beaming back at her. There were five of them in all. All had hair slicked back, their chins shiny from being recently shaved, their uniforms spotless with not a wrinkle to be seen and all oozing confidence. Eleanor swallowed again.

'Roland Jackson, please to meet you, miss. My friends call me Rollie!'

'Pete Sherman!' Pete nodded his greeting.

'I'm John Lockwood, at your service, ma'am, and this here is Mitch Denby. Say hello to the lady, Mitch!' John nudged the shy Mitch forward as the rest laughed out loud.

'Please to meet you, miss.'

Eleanor smiled while secretly wondering when she would be able to extricate herself. *Not without Hazel*, she thought determinedly.

She suddenly eyed the soldier at the back who hadn't rushed to introduce himself the way the others had. He caught her looking at him and she blushed.

He stepped forward. 'Eleanor isn't it? I'm Michael Ross.'

Eleanor noticed that he was the only one to make a point of remembering her name. She smiled back at him. 'Yes, Eleanor Grayson. Pleased to meet you.'

And she was.

Another Glenn Miller tune split the air and Rollie whirled Hazel out in front of him, spinning her through the couples already pairing off on the dance floor. John and Pete moved off to a group of girls standing nearby and asked two of them to dance as Eleanor stood between the shy Mitch and the quiet Michael, now at a loss as to what to say next.

'Would you like something to drink, Eleanor?' Michael stared across at her as Mitch merely smiled behind him.

'Yes, I would, thank you.' She swallowed. She was acting as though she'd never been to a dance before and told herself that if she didn't say something intelligent soon, they would write her off as some inexperienced, tongue-tied nincompoop.

Michael poured a ladle of the pinkish concoction from the nearby punch bowl into a glass and handed it to her. She accepted the drink with a smile and then all three of them turned back to watch the dancing for a while. Eleanor racked her brains as to what she could say while constantly sipping on the fruity drink, which gave her more time to think. She darted a look at the two tall Americans by her side and instantly received a smile from both. *Come on, Eleanor, think!* Suddenly her eyes brightened and she turned to them.

'Are you both stationed at the Port Woodside camp?' Eleanor turned enquiring eyes towards them, but as she spoke the music stopped and everyone cheered the ending of the song on the dance floor, which drowned out her question.

Mitch didn't even hear her, but Michael frowned and bent his head down towards her. 'I'm sorry, what did you say?'

Eleanor shook her head, indicating that it wasn't important as Hazel and Rollie breezed back into their midst. Hazel was flushed and excited. 'They're playing a lot of Glenn Miller songs tonight – must be for all you boys, I think!'

The men laughed. Eleanor too. *Now why didn't I think of saying something like that?*

Hazel waved a hand in front of her face. 'Goodness, I'm thirsty! What is that you're drinking, Eleanor? I might try some!'

Rollie obliged immediately. John and Pete suddenly swept back into their group, each now sporting a girl on their arms and Eleanor moved back, feeling suddenly awkward. Looking across the dance floor, she noticed Kathy engaged in close conversation with another American, the dark-haired girl's hand straying to his arm as she spoke, the man giving her his undivided attention.

Suddenly the man leaned over and whispered something in her ear and Kathy laughed. Eleanor couldn't help thinking that she must be the only one here tonight who didn't seem part of the proceedings.

Her gaze continued around the hall, and over by the far wall she suddenly spotted Richard Pinkle sitting close to a pretty blonde, and Eleanor's mouth dropped open. She immediately darted a look at Hazel, but Hazel was engrossed in frivolous banter with Rollie and Mitch.

She didn't have any more time to think on Richard and his partner, as just then, the band started up again, this time with a slower-paced song, and a voice whispered in her ear, 'Would you like to dance?'

Eleanor blinked and looked up to see Michael staring down at her enquiringly. She smiled and nodded, and he led her out onto the dance floor. His hand was warm on her back as he guided her around the floor, and Eleanor's awkwardness began to vanish a little as she started to relax into the dance. He was a good dancer, she decided, so why not simply enjoy it?

As they made their way around the floor, Eleanor noticed they were heading in Richard's direction, and she purposefully didn't look at him. When they whirled that way again, Eleanor noticed he was gone, the chair alongside his now empty as well, and she wondered if it was just coincidence or if Richard had seen her and had suddenly left through the side door.

'What are you thinking about?' Michael's voice was warm and deep, his accent making her smile.

'Nothing much. I thought I just saw someone I knew, but I was probably mistaken.'

He smiled back and held her a little closer. Eleanor frowned, thinking that he might be getting the wrong idea.

'You and your friends from Camp Woodside?'

He nodded. 'Yep, we've got leave for the next three days. Heading out for Brisbane next week.' He pronounced Brisbane with more emphasis on the 'bane'.

Eleanor looked up at him, the war suddenly entering her mind all over again and the reason why they were all here. He was staring at her, dark brown eyes boring into hers.

'You got someone overseas, Eleanor?'

Eleanor nodded. 'Yes, my brother, but Ted's on his way home, for how long we don't know.' She gave a slight shrug as the music stopped and the awkwardness came back all over again. Then the band started up again and Michael drew her back into his arms, a little closer this time, and once more Eleanor relaxed.

'Which part of America are you from?'

'Louisiana… mostly.'

'Mostly? Part of you from somewhere else?' Eleanor's eyes sparkled for the first time tonight.

He laughed. 'I mean, I was born in Louisiana but lived most of my life on the coast… San Francisco in fact, but my family still lives in Louisiana. I had a chance to spend some time with them before we came to Australia – we were stationed there in Camp Beauregard for a few months.'

'Louisiana.' Eleanor's eyes took on a faraway look. He tried to fathom it.

'You know someone there maybe?' His face showed a mild surprise.

Eleanor snapped back to what he was saying. 'Oh no… well, no, not really.' She changed the subject. 'They must miss you as we miss Ted.'

He didn't answer; instead it was his turn to change the subject.

'So what is there to do around your fair city of Adelaide?'

'I suppose that depends on where your interests lie.' As soon as Eleanor said it, she knew she shouldn't have – it sounded as though she were open for invitation and it caused her to falter in her step. He appeared not to take it that way though, and she was relieved.

'Oh I like most anything really. Back home I liked to fish in my spare time.'

'Fish? You like fishing?' Eleanor's mouth spread into a wide grin as she peered up at him.

'Yes, surely they fish in Australia!' He had his eyebrows raised in mock affront.

Eleanor laughed. 'I'm sorry, it's just that the sight of you standing here in your uniform, I mean… well, somehow, fishing is the last thing that would have entered my mind!' Oh what was she saying? She realized she'd just opened herself up again! But again he appeared not to notice.

'Well, I do like to go fishing. You've never been?'

Eleanor shook her head. 'I'm afraid water activities aren't really my thing.'

'Now that's strange! We're led to believe that you Australians do all sorts of things in the water!'

Eleanor raised her eyebrows. 'Why?'

He shrugged. 'I don't know. Perhaps because you're surrounded by water, your population is spread mainly along the coastline and any postcards I send home all have a picture of some beach or the ocean on the front.'

Eleanor giggled. 'I see what you mean. But I'm actually scared of the water.'

'Really?'

'Really.'

'So what do you think of when you think of the States?'

'Um… tall buildings, New York, that sort of thing… Oh, and cowboys and Indians.'

Michael threw back his head and laughed.

They whirled on through the dance, talking about various things – his interests, her interests, where she worked, what she did – and when the music stopped, Michael led her back towards the refreshment table.

'Another drink?'

'Thank you, Michael – I could do with one.'

'Call me Mike. Only my mother calls me Michael these days.'

Eleanor smiled. 'All right… Mike.'

She accepted the drink with a smile and suddenly felt lighter in her surroundings, her earlier thoughts of not feeling part of things beginning to disappear as she relaxed alongside the tall handsome gentleman called Michael Ross.

The night wore on. Eleanor danced with Mike twice more, then once with the shy Mitch, who was more intent on getting his steps right, and then a rousing fling around the polished floor with Rollie, leaving her mind spinning and trying to catch her breath as Hazel laughed and gripped her arm in an attempt to steady her trembling legs while whispering in her ear. 'Not bad, is he?'

Rollie twirled Hazel out onto the floor once more as Eleanor found her bearings. She was suddenly aware that the crowd had started to thin out as she looked around at the empty chairs and scattered remnants of revelry strewn atop the tables around the hall.

A voice made her jump. 'Can I see you tomorrow, Eleanor?' Mike smiled down at her before his face became serious. 'I would like to see you again – perhaps take in a bit of your Adelaide before we go away.'

Eleanor hesitated. Her first instinct was to say no, but then she thought why shouldn't she? She was a sensible-enough girl wasn't she? And Mike had been the perfect gentleman all night, not saying or even hinting at anything remotely disrespectful or improper. Eleanor thought he might well put most of the men of her acquaintance to shame.

'I have to work tomorrow, but I get off at two.'

Mike grinned broadly, his teeth white and even, dazzling her and causing her to smile widely back at him. 'Two o'clock it is then!'

The next morning, Eleanor dressed with care. She turned this way and that in front of the mirror, assessing her appearance critically while telling herself that she was being ridiculous. She smoothed down the beige linen dress around her hips, her face tilting to the side as she tried to view herself objectively. Eleanor found herself wondering what the women in America wore for an afternoon walk… did she look inadequate next to them?

She instantly scolded herself once more. What did it matter what she looked like? After all, she had to go to work and her beige dress was a perfect choice! Sedate enough to be working behind a bookstore counter as well as good enough for an afternoon out afterward! Just the same, she thought perhaps she should have worn her hair differently. She didn't look sophisticated enough with it down, but putting it up didn't really suit her.

'Oh stuff and nonsense!' Eleanor grabbed her wide-brimmed matching hat and her purse and stalked out of her bedroom. She shouted out her goodbyes to her parents, telling them she might be late home, and by the time she'd gone through the front door, she'd convinced herself that Michael

Ross must be a snob of the highest order if he thought she was going to kowtow to his ideas of what a woman should look like on his arm!

Though on the way to work, she began to smile as she remembered the events of the night before. She and Hazel had walked home with their arms linked, going over every juicy detail, though the smile left Eleanor's face as she remembered seeing Richard Pinkle with another girl. Perhaps there was nothing in it. Perhaps Marjorie already knew and it was just some girl that they were both acquainted with and therefore perfectly innocent. But if that was the case, then why had he been so set against Marjorie going there last night? Eleanor frowned. She decided she would keep it to herself… at least for the moment.

She stepped through the door of the bookstore, the top bell clanging as the door opened, and greeted Mrs Littleton, who greeted her in return while giving her young charge more than her usual cursory glance, given the way she looked this morning. Eleanor didn't notice and went straight through to the back, placing her hat and purse on the side bench in the small kitchen then making her way out to the front again. Mrs Littleton looked her up and down again and then quickly collected herself.

'I've left a stack of books on the corner table that need covering, dear… if you could see to them for me?'

Eleanor nodded. 'Yes, of course.'

She walked off humming to herself and Mrs Littleton smiled.

In the time that Eleanor had been working for her, Edwina Littleton had come to regard her as nothing but friendly and polite, though Edwina wasn't so old that she didn't notice the girl's attributes. The first thing that had struck her were the girl's eyes: intelligent eyes with a mystery all of their own that seemed to hold volumes of hidden secrets. If Eleanor had been much older, Edwina would have assumed her to have a *past*, a wealth of experiences that usually precedes that certain worldly look. But of course, Eleanor was too young to have experienced enough of life and its upsets and heartaches. Why the girl didn't even have a beau! Though Edwina now wondered if that was about to change.

She'd heard talk of the Worthington-Cooke boy and had been glad that she no longer went about with him, instantly dismissing him as not being right for her Eleanor, though she wondered about any intimacies they may have shared. Looking at Eleanor now, with her trim figure and that auburn hair, if her young charge hadn't dabbled in the more physical activities, or at least been looked at in that way, she would have been most surprised. Of course, Hillary Grayson's affection for her youngest granddaughter had been a well-thrashed-out topic on occasion amongst those of her clientele who were familiar with Eleanor's family, and by all accounts, Edwina had been led to believe that Hillary would prove to be a worthy adversary to any young man whom the old harpy deemed to be the wrong sort.

Eleanor, still humming a tune, re-covered the books as Mrs Littleton asked, which took most of the morning. She helped serve at the front counter, unpacked the newer arrivals and dusted off the higher shelves, a job that required her to climb the ladder – something Mrs Littleton was no longer able to do – and a little before two o'clock in the afternoon, Eleanor spied Michael Ross waiting outside the shop, his hands stuffed in his pockets under his uniform jacket, his cap pulled down low over his face and some sort of leather bag over his shoulder. Eleanor's stomach flipped at the sight of him and she glanced at the clock.

'Is there anything else, Mrs Littleton?'

Edwina had seen the tall American as well and now darted a look at Eleanor. By the way her young employee was suddenly fidgeting with her hair and smoothing down her dress, Edwina now understood the reason behind Eleanor's high spirits.

'Yes, dear, I think I can manage things here easily enough.' She nodded in the American's direction. 'Besides, I think your friend out there may well wear a hole in the pavement if you don't get out there and see him.'

Eleanor blushed. 'Thank you, Mrs Littleton. I'll see you tomorrow then?'

Edwina smiled broadly, her wrinkled jowls stretching upward, transforming her face to one of almost girlish delight. She nodded. 'Tomorrow, dear.'

The bell clanged as Eleanor went to leave.

'Oh, and Eleanor?'

Eleanor looked back. Edwina was still smiling.

'Have a lovely time.'

Eleanor blushed again and walked outside to meet Michael Ross as Edwina rested her chin on her hands and watched, sighing.

'Hello! You're early!' Eleanor thought he looked even better in the light of day than he had the night before and wished suddenly that she'd been able to freshen up a bit better.

He took off his hat in greeting and gave her that dazzling smile. 'Well, there's nothing for me to do really, not knowing the city very well. And I had a devil of a time finding the place. I didn't realize it was off the main street; finally, I had to ask someone. Just as well I started off early, otherwise I would have been late.'

He looked her up and down. Eleanor pretended not to notice as she put her hat on.

'You look nice today, even better than I remember… Hope you don't mind me saying that.' He offered her his arm.

Eleanor didn't. She smiled and threaded her arm through his.

'So what would you like to do first?' she asked.

'Have you eaten? I brought along some sandwiches from the inn I'm staying at. I noticed some nice parklands here about.'

That explained the satchel over his shoulder. 'There's plenty of seats down by the river if you want to go there.' She frowned. 'Inn?'

They headed off in the direction of the Torrens. 'Shrimpton's Bed and Breakfast. I'm staying there until tomorrow.'

Eleanor nodded. 'Oh yes, I know the one… So what was your bed and breakfast like? Are they taking good care of you?' Eleanor felt somehow as though it was her responsibility that he be comfortable while he was in town.

'Yep, comfy corner room overlooking the main street, huge breakfast… All I was missing was some good company for the day, and now I reckon I've got that too!'

His comment brought a radiant smile from Eleanor as they walked on down the street.

Their conversation was light, airy and about nothing in particular, but as they neared the banks of the Torrens, Eleanor suddenly felt the familiar presence of Parquin prickling up her spine. The smile froze on her face, and instantly her guard went up.

'Parquin?' No answer.

'Is anything the matter? Eleanor?'

Eleanor tried to shake off the feeling. Strange, she thought. She didn't feel as though anything was wrong exactly, just something… coming…

She frowned.

'Eleanor?' Mike touched her shoulder.

She looked down at his hand, his long, tapered fingers splayed out against the paleness of her dress, and suddenly she became aware that Mike was staring at her. She took a deep breath and managed a smile, pointing to the grass down below.

'There's a nice-enough place. What do you think?'

Mike looked a little nonplussed by her change in demeanor but then as he looked down at the captivating brown eyes staring up at him, waiting for an answer, he let it slide.

'Sure, seems like a good place to eat… a few swans nearby too.'

As they settled themselves upon the grass, Mike pulled his satchel around in front of him and unfastened the buckle on the leather flap. 'Hope you like corned beef – it was all Mrs Shrimpton had left over from last night's dinner.'

Eleanor nodded and adjusted her hat against the sun.

'I haven't brought anything to drink though. If you don't mind, I'll leave you here and go and get us some lemonade from that little shop over there… You like lemonade?'

'Yes, I do, very much.' Eleanor was still busy arranging her dress over her legs on the grass.

'Won't be a sec…' Mike got to his feet and strode off.

'I'll get the sandwiches out,' she called out to him.

Eleanor dragged the satchel over in front of her and reached in. She pulled out two neat brown paper bags screwed over at the top, obviously the sandwiches, then peered into the satchel. Satisfied there was nothing else in there, she pulled the flap down and placed it over to the side… and that's when she saw it.

Eleanor drew her breath in sharply, the cold prickly

feeling instantly shooting up her back as Parquin seemed to flood the air about her.

On the front of the satchel, there was a square piece of leather bordered by stitching, a different colour to the leather surrounding it, and on it was a picture, an etching of some kind...

'Parquin?' She felt stifled. Her mind was starting to spin. She felt giddy, disoriented, as though the very ground she sat on was tilting wildly to one side. Eleanor became scared. Never before had she felt like this, out of control like this...

'Do not be frightened, Eleanor.'

Eleanor realized she was holding her breath and let it out. She tried to swallow.

Tentatively, she reached for the satchel, her hand brushing up against it slowly as though it might reach out and bite her. She felt Parquin's amusement and became instantly irritated. *'I am not amused, Parquin!'*

'Nor are you frightened any longer.'

She pursed her lips at his impudence, but grudgingly she realized what Parquin said was true. She was no longer scared but simply curious. She pulled the satchel towards her almost defiantly and peered down at it.

She'd seen this picture before, long ago, a very long time ago... The words surged unbidden through her brain: a *lifetime* ago.

Eleanor ran her fingers over the picture and noticed it was very old, now realizing the reason why it was a different colour to the rest of the satchel. Her fingers traced over the etched lines... A lone figure by a... lake? Or a river perhaps? She turned it towards the sunlight, trying to make it out... so familiar... but where had she seen it? The answer seemed to sit just out of reach.

'Not hungry? Hey, I see you've been eying up my

picture.' Mike eased himself down upon the grass, two paper cups of lemonade balanced in one hand. He offered one to her. She took it, nodding her thanks... and felt Parquin back away immediately.

'Your picture?'

He reached for one of the brown paper bags and opened it. 'Yeah. I've had it ever since I was a little kid. It used to be a tobacco pouch or some such thing... I liked it so much, my dad gave it to me. Of course the pouch fell apart years ago, but I managed to save the picture, had it sewn into another bag...' Mike looked a little embarrassed. 'It's a little bit of home I like to cart around with me... Corny, huh?'

He bit into his sandwich and looked out over the river.

Eleanor's heart was suddenly pounding but she forced a smile at him. 'No, I don't think it's corny one bit. Where did your father get it from?'

Mike had swallowed and was just about to take another bite of his sandwich but stopped. He raised his eyebrows, his face set in reflection. 'Got it from a friend of his, or rather it was given to him when his friend died.' Mike took another bite of his sandwich.

Eleanor's mind was racing. She felt on the verge of something... Damn it! Where had she seen it?

It came to her in a rush. *Evie! Gans! Gans' tobacco pouch... sitting on the floor of their cabin, some coins spilling into her lap... her excitement... the picture... Oh my goodness!*

Eleanor fiddled nervously with the brown paper bag in front of her. 'What was the name of your father's friend?' It was an odd question, she knew – after all, he would probably wonder what possible difference it would make what the man's name was. He looked at her a little strangely, but then shrugged. 'Can't remember, it was so long ago… like I said, I was just a kid.'

Oh great! *Now he thinks I'm a complete idiot!* She tried to rectify the situation. 'I suppose that sounds silly. I like old stories about things, that's all. I get lost in them and want to know all sorts of silly details. You probably think I'm a bit mad.' She attempted to laugh it off.

Mike laughed along with her. 'No, that's okay. I don't mind; I like old stories myself.'

Eleanor smiled shyly at him, knowing he was simply being chivalrous. She thought she'd better drop the subject and tried putting a lid on her excitement. If it was something she was supposed to know, then in time, she would find out…

But her mind wouldn't put it aside, at least not completely… Somehow, Eleanor felt it was too important and her mind reached out for Parquin. But all she got for her trouble was a distinct feeling that she would indeed find out in time. *'Damn it!'* Patience was not Eleanor's strong suit.

She took a sip of her lemonade and then bit into her sandwich.

They sat eating their lunch for a time. The conversation was easy, amiable and Eleanor began to relax into his company. She decided that she liked him, while at the same time feeling a little dismayed that once he went away, she would never see him again. He spoke a lot about his family. There was a sister called Marion, a finicky old aunt that got under his skin but whom he had all the time in the world for, various cousins and of course his parents. Eleanor guessed by the way Mike spoke about them that they would dearly love him to come back to live in Louisiana. He hadn't mentioned a girl, and Eleanor wondered if he had one, though she would never dare ask.

She told him of her own family, her uncle Frank and aunt

Susan who lived in Queensland along with her grandmother on her mother's side, whom she rarely saw, her friends and her 'other' uncle, named Charlie, who was not really an uncle though they all looked on him as such. Of course, she omitted any of the deeper feelings she had for him. She told him of her fear of water, her penchant for history, which reinforced her reasons for questioning him so intensely before, and her relief for her brother, who would be returning home soon. They spoke about other things… movies they've seen, the Depression and who among their relatives had taken part in the first war.

It occurred to Eleanor that neither of them spoke of things to come, no plans, and no hopes for the future – nothing at all about what would happen after the present war. It was as though they had simply borrowed a precious day or two, taken time out from their vastly different lives to spend a few stolen hours in each other's company.

The shadows had long since lengthened by the time they rose to leave.

As they made their way back along the street in the direction they'd come, it was already beginning to get dark, and with the descent of the sun, Eleanor felt the chill and rubbed her arms. Mike took off his jacket and placed it around her shoulders.

'I'm sorry, I didn't realize the time. I shouldn't have kept you out so long. Will your parents be worrying?'

Eleanor pulled the sides of his jacket around her. 'Not worried exactly… perhaps a little curious. I've usually put in an appearance by now.'

They'd stopped and were now facing each other. Mike looked down at her and, on impulse, pulled her close and kissed her. Eleanor was taken by surprise. It wasn't a long kiss. She'd no sooner felt the softness of his lips and the brush of his chin and then he was pulling away again.

She stepped back and looked about her, suddenly embarrassed. People were drawing their curtains against the approaching dark, pulling their blinds down on the outside night. She saw a mother ruffling her son's hair as he sat at the table, a man bending over to turn on his radio, another carrying a plate to the table. She heard the cries of a baby, the laughter of a child, a door slamming somewhere. She looked up and down the street and felt as though they were the only two people left out in the increasingly cold night air and suddenly she didn't want to leave him alone. More importantly, she didn't want to go home and be alone herself. The privacy of her bedroom suddenly didn't feel comforting to her anymore. She looked up at him.

Mike was staring at her, the fading light making it hard to define the expression on his face. He sighed and ran a hand along his jaw and up the side of his face.

'Look, I'm sorry, Eleanor... I guess I just got carried away. It's been a good day... and...'

'No, no, that's fine... I mean, don't be sorry. I was just...' She shrugged. 'I just wasn't prepared... didn't expect it...'

Mike kissed her again, cutting off her words, this time longer, deeper, and Eleanor felt her head spin slightly. His arms tightened around her. He finished with a light kiss on her forehead and looked down at her. 'Will you meet me tonight?' He was frowning now, almost as if he thought his question was one he shouldn't ask.

'Meet you? Where? Where do you want to go?'

He saw that she was smiling and he quickly looked away. This was wrong; he knew it, but he liked her. She was open, no pretence of anything other than what she was, no falseness of character – what you see was what you got, and he liked that. She was everything Samantha wasn't… but he refused to think about that. She stood before him, so unaware of what she did to him, and by the look of her face, which was turned up to him, those eyes shining innocent against the streetlight, she was also unaware what he was asking. He suddenly decided he couldn't insult her with such a suggestion… he wouldn't do it.

'I'm sorry, Eleanor. I'm going to be perfectly honest with you because I like you and I respect you. Just now when I asked you if you would meet me tonight, I had something else completely different in mind and for that I truly do apologize.'

Eleanor blinked, her expression changing to one of stunned bewilderment. 'You were asking me to… to…'

'No – well, yes, I guess I was… but you don't understand. I go away tomorrow and I… I don't know what's going to happen, and I know guys say this sort of stuff all the time, but I really do like you. I mean, this isn't just some line…' He swallowed and shook his head. 'Then again, I guess that's exactly what it sounds like, doesn't it?' He placed his hand under her elbow and steered her on towards home.

Once there, Eleanor paced the floor of her bedroom, going over what Mike had said to her. He'd been courteous, polite, almost as though he'd said nothing inappropriate at all when he'd bid her goodnight at her gate. He'd made her reflect on her own meagre experience with men. She hadn't known men on an intimate nature apart from Mark, and she'd found him wanting. And then there was Charlie, a man whom she thought could bring her happiness, at least on some level. She'd found him wanting as well, though not for the same reasons. And then of course there was Parquin, always Parquin, a residual apparition of her past existence, who by reminding her of what she'd once had also reminded her of what she'd been unable to have since. And now Mike… who if she'd met under any other circumstances, might have become something more to her… but then if it wasn't for this war, Eleanor knew she would never have met him, and so all she was left with were these circumstances.

Eleanor stopped pacing and stared at herself in the mirror. She suddenly knew what she was going to do, had known all along, and that it was the real reason for her pacing… she would go to him.

Less than an hour later she stood beside a huge gum tree outside Shrimpton's Bed and Breakfast and scanned the windows upstairs. What room was his? she wondered. He'd said something about a corner room, hadn't he? She peered along the windows and noticed a light on in the far corner. Just then, a matronly woman appeared at the side of the building carrying a bucket. Eleanor stepped back out of sight behind the tree and watched as the woman emptied the bucket into one of the tin rubbish bins along the side fence.

When she disappeared back into the building again, Eleanor made her move.

She darted across from the tree through to the side of the building, keeping close to the red brick wall as she went, and was instantly taken back to when, as a child, she and Lucy Phipps had done much the same thing through the backyard of Lucy's house. She remembered the danger that had awaited them once they'd finally got inside and the feel of Parquin all around… warning her perhaps? Or preparing her? Eleanor had no such feeling now and briefly wondered why.

She peeked through the back door into a kitchen and a staircase beyond, then took a deep breath and slipped through, running as quickly and as quietly as she could up the carpeted staircase. At the top she came to a halt and tried to get her bearings. *Sweet Jesus, what am I doing?*

She heard voices down the bottom of the stairs and made a dash to the end of the hall and stopped outside the last door. Was this his room?

She went to knock and stopped herself. And if it was? What would she say to him? What would *he* say?

She hesitated a few seconds more and then tapped lightly on the door. She felt suddenly foolish... she should have gone through the front and simply asked for him. She should have sent him a note perhaps. She should have—

The door swung open.

Eleanor froze.

CHAPTER NINE

He stood there, a towel draped over one shoulder, his skin dark against the white singlet he wore, army identification tags resting against his broad chest. He still wore his uniform trousers though his belt was undone, his bare feet sticking out below the cuffs. His shortly cropped brown hair was damp and swept sideways as though he'd just finished rubbing it… presumably with the towel. He stared at her, his face set somewhere between astonishment and disbelief.

'Eleanor!' He did a quick run through his hair with his fingers.

'Hello,' was all she could manage in return.

Mike frowned and stuck his head out the door to look in the direction of the stairs. He looked back at her.

'No one knows I'm here.' It sounded dumb. But then she *felt* dumb. And for all she knew, she probably *looked* dumb!

He stared at her, his expression contemplative. He opened the door wide and moved aside, bidding her to enter.

Eleanor stepped through the door, and as she heard the soft click of it closing behind her, she was suddenly swamped with a feeling that she'd crossed the point of no return. Nervously, she peered around the room.

She saw an open overnight bag on the floor, its contents spilling out through the opening, toiletries next to a lamp upon a nightstand beside a washbasin, a mirror on the wall above it. A small wardrobe stood on the same wall as the door she'd come through, its door slightly ajar revealing two crisply starched uniform shirts on wooden coat hangers inside. A rather uncomfortable-looking armchair sat in the corner and she noticed Mike's uniform jacket draped over the side, his satchel perched on the seat in front, reminders of the day they'd had together. The sight of them did little to reinforce her purpose.

Eleanor wouldn't look at him… couldn't look at him. She felt she would be exposing too much of herself, leaving her feelings too unguarded for him to trample if he so wished, or laugh at… and that was one thing she couldn't bear.

Eleanor was suddenly self-conscious of her outfit; it was the same beige dress she'd had on all day. *Why couldn't I have at least changed?*

She felt his hands on her shoulders, gently turning her round to face him. He ran his fingers through her hair, pushing it back off her face. 'Anyone ever tell you that you have beautiful hair?' He spoke softly to her, his voice low.

She finally looked directly into his eyes and she smiled. 'Anyone ever told you how green your eyes are?'

He grinned down at her, his voice still low. 'My eyes are green? How about that!'

She giggled, instantly feeling some of the tension leave her.

His smile faded as he searched her face and then, tucking a finger under her chin, he bent forward and kissed her lightly on the mouth. Eleanor leant forward into the kiss and his arms came about her, pulling her close.

Bravely, she ran her hands over his chest and up to curl around the back of his neck, and he gave a slight moan as his own hands began moving down her back to circle briefly over her hips before pulling them up in line with his own. Eleanor could feel his arousal, and after a moment of uncertainty, she pushed herself against him.

He let out a strangled groan and stepped quickly away from her, leaving her feeling suddenly deprived of his closeness and wondering if she'd done something wrong. He turned and walked over to the window, his back to her now, seemingly turning his attentions to the view through the curtains. Eleanor blinked and rubbed her arms, suddenly feeling nervous all over again.

Mike pulled the blind and turned to stare at her. She stood there, her mouth slightly open, her face set in confusion; he sighed and closed his eyes to shut out the sight of her. When he opened them again, he looked over at her, muttered an oath and crossed the room towards her in three long strides. Reaching for her, he pulled her into his arms, his kiss no longer gentle as he ground his mouth down on hers. Eleanor felt her body instantly respond as a delicious heat surged down into her belly, her legs suddenly feeling too weak to support her weight as she leant against him.

Who cared if she wasn't supposed to be here? Who cared what anyone said about Americans? He was going away, back to the barracks, and then to war, and if what she was doing was wrong, then she would think about it tomorrow. At this moment, it felt good. It felt right! And she wasn't going to miss her chance to feel wanted! All the Marks, the Charlies and even Parquin were firmly pushed to the back of her mind.

Tonight she would take the fire that was offered… and let it burn her!

Mike swept her up into his arms and carried her over to the bed. Eleanor's heart was pounding as he lay down beside her. He unbuttoned the front of her dress and slipped it back off her shoulders, bending over to run his lips down her neck and to the top of her breasts.

Eleanor closed her eyes as he slipped her dress down further, pulling at her petticoat underneath. He lifted his head and kissed her once more on the mouth, his hand sliding down under her hips, pulling her onto her side to face him. Instinctively, she slid a leg across and over his hips and he gripped her thighs as he rubbed up against her.

Eleanor's senses were spinning, her breathing rapid, as though struggling to keep pace with her heart, her body having taken on a mind of its own. She couldn't seem to get enough of him, couldn't seem to get close enough to him. She slid her hands up his arms, over his chest and down the side of his body, and then, slipping in between their bodies, she worked her hand down over his hardness, making him groan. Quickly he undid his trousers and pulled them open to accommodate her. She obliged.

He gasped, instantly grabbing her hand and putting a halt to her actions. 'My God but you're beautiful!'

Urged on by his words, she pushed herself into him. Suddenly, he sat up and lifted her dress together with her petticoat up over her head and cast them aside. Swiftly, he discarded the rest of her underwear and she lay there naked, her legs slightly open as his eyes devoured the sight of her. He stood briefly to rid himself of his trousers and undershorts. Reaching up, he drew his singlet over his head and tossed it away. Eleanor caught a glimpse of hardened muscles, a tight, flat stomach and solid thighs. On seeing his erection, she drew in her breath sharply. And then just as quickly he was back down on the bed beside her and then he was atop her, nudging her legs apart. Lifting himself up onto his elbows, he looked down into her face, his eyes questioning, silently asking if she was sure, if she was ready. She looked into his eyes and swallowed and lifted her hips to meet him, showing him she was indeed ready, and so, reaching down, he guided himself into her.

Eleanor was no longer a virgin, hadn't been since her experiences with Mark, experiences she now looked on as nothing more than a series of clumsy half-hearted fumblings. In no way could they possibly compare with tonight!

Mike didn't want to hurt her and moved slowly at first. She was so tight, and as he made to enter her, he paused and looked down into her eyes. 'Too fast? Tell me if you want me to go slower.'

Her only reply was to smile up at him. He slid all the way in. Eleanor held her breath, her eyes widening. He stopped abruptly and withdrew, thinking it may have been too much for her, or too fast, but she smiled again and lifted her hips towards him. He relaxed and moved again, sliding into her once more, and she wrapped her legs around his hips. He tried holding himself in check, tried keeping himself under control, but she was urging him on… he let himself go… she moaned… and moaned again. His mind spun, perspiration breaking out on his forehead.

Eleanor gripped his shoulders and closed her eyes, giving herself up completely to the glorious sensations pervading her body. He plunged deeper, faster, more urgently. She met him with every thrust – harder, faster. She felt herself being swept away on a torrent of emotions; unaware she was moaning aloud. He ground into her, thrusting faster, harder still. Suddenly, she cried out, her body racked by wave after wave of rapturous sensations. He felt her close around him, felt her pulsating deep inside and he quickly followed, groaning loudly, calling her name over and over.

He collapsed on top of her, and they lay there for a time, both exhausted, their bodies damp with perspiration, hearts still pounding. Gradually, their breathing slowed. He kissed her softly, on the mouth, on the nose, her forehead, and then back on her mouth again, then he rolled off her, cradling her head in the crook of his arm.

Eleanor felt wonderfully relaxed, utterly depleted and thoroughly at peace.

She twisted her face up to look at him and he smiled down at her. She started to giggle. He joined her, chuckling low, squeezing her against him closer still. Then he stopped and moved his head on the pillow to look at her once again.

He searched her face. 'Why?'

Eleanor shrugged. 'I'm not sure.' She didn't want to examine it too closely, not now, not this minute... perhaps tomorrow.

Mike accepted her answer. After all, he didn't want to examine things too closely either. He was going to war. He may never come back, and if he did? What then? They were worlds apart, would never have even met if it hadn't been for this war... And then of course there was Samantha. He thought about telling Eleanor, and then instantly dismissed it. She would think him a philanderer, a phony, a womanizer of the worst sort. And he liked Eleanor; he liked her a lot. He'd been honest on that score, but if she found out? No, there was no point in her knowing. Let her think on this for what it was, a stolen day between two people who would never meet again: one precious night to store in his memory, to be taken out and remembered with fondness in the years to come –

God willing there would be years to come. But then if there was a way…

His thoughts were interrupted as she rose from the bed.

'I'd better get going.' She looked embarrassed.

'So soon? Why don't you stay awhile? I'm sure Mrs Shrimpton wouldn't mind sending something up.'

Eleanor looked horror-struck at his suggestion.

He laughed. 'She doesn't have to know you're here. She won't enter the room… Or better still, why don't we go out for a walk, perhaps grab something to eat?'

Eleanor spied her clothes lying in a crumpled heap on the floor, her expression dubious.

He stared down at them also and grinned. 'Mrs Shrimpton it is then.'

An hour later, Eleanor sat on the bed with Mike eating with their fingers off the one plate of cold meat and salad that Mrs Shrimpton had been so kind as to send up, a tray and utensils on the floor by the bed. Eleanor sat with one of his shirts around her shoulders, unaware how she looked to Mike, who raked his eyes across her appearance time and again while she talked. She'd draped her dress across the armchair in an attempt to let some of the wrinkles drop out.

Eleanor had never felt so relaxed, so free. She was sitting on a bed nearly naked with a man she had only just met, his shirt the only thing she had on and sharing a salad for goodness' sake!

'I think my shirt looks good on you.' Mike was teasing, the look in his eyes obvious as to what he was really looking at and she blushed.

Pulling the shirt tighter around her, she noticed an insignia of a red arrow on his shirtsleeve and pointed to it. 'What does this mean?'

Mike looked a little self-conscious and pulled a face. 'The

emblem of a barred arrow, chosen for the Red Arrow Division, who supposedly broke through every German line it came up against in World War One… or so the story goes.'

'You don't believe the story?'

'No, I believe it to be fact. The insignia was chosen by a Major General Bill Haan.'

Eleanor was impressed. 'Something to be proud of then?'

'Yeah, I guess, it's just that I don't think I've done anything to deserve it… yet.'

Eleanor felt a shiver at his words, the war suddenly pushing its way into their idyllic setting. She felt the magic of their private world suddenly beginning to lose its edge and her mood began to change. She spied his satchel on the chair and quickly changed the subject.

'I do like that satchel.'

He leant towards her, his hand slipping through under the shirt. 'Then perhaps one day I'll send it to you.' He ran his hand over her breasts and around her back and pulled her towards him. Eleanor's legs became tangled in the bedspread and she lost her balance, toppling over him, the dinner plate with its remnants of lettuce, cucumber and tomato being scattered to the floor at the foot of the bed.

She laughed. 'You'll ruin your shirt!'

He gave no reply other than to kiss her long and deep.

They took their time, savouring, lingering over one another. It was to be the last time they would ever be like this and they both knew it. They were saying their final goodbyes.

A little over two hours later, Mike stood at Eleanor's gate. Getting out of Shrimpton's Bed and Breakfast undetected wasn't as bad as Eleanor had thought. Mike had simply led her down the stairs and out through the front door as soon as the coast was clear.

They stood now, gazing at one another. Mike frowned and

opened his mouth to speak, but Eleanor placed a finger to his lips and shook her head.

He sighed and closed his arms about her, holding her tight. Bending his head, he brought his lips down on hers, kissing her softly one more time. He finished it with an even tighter embrace, and then, adjusting his hat, he turned and strode away. Eleanor watched him leave. She felt the familiar tingling up her spine of Parquin close by... and then she knew.

She would never see Michael Ross again.

It was after eleven when Eleanor finally crawled into bed. She felt a little forlorn, lost almost, a kind of numbness starting to take hold. She wondered if tomorrow, she would feel guilty at what she'd done, that in the space of a mere few hours, she'd gone against everything she'd been taught, against everything expected of her by those who trusted her to do the right thing. She even smiled briefly. But she would think about that tomorrow. At this moment she was tired, too tired to think straight, and so, turning onto her side, she drifted off to sleep.

Parquin swept into her dreams like a whirlwind, a swirling maze of golden mist that shifted and blurred through her mind. He seemed purposeful, almost pleased, and slightly... impatient?

'Come, Eleanor.' He stood before her now – long black hair, piercing eyes that shimmered from deep blue to violet and then back again.

'Parquin?'

He was impatient! She felt the pull of him almost immediately, sucking her back through time. She moaned in her sleep, her head turning on the pillow.

'It is time for me to show you, Eleanor.' She was being pulled, almost dragged along, the force of it almost overwhelming her mortal senses.

As though suddenly aware of her more fragile capabilities, he slowed his pace, and, wrapping himself about her in that strange way he had, he now guided her.

Eleanor always felt peace when he was close like this; he merged himself with her until they became one unit. His force fused with hers, lending her strength and enabling her to see what he saw, feel what he felt... and the experience went beyond anything she'd ever known before. He rarely blended so closely with her in this way, and she wondered why he did so now.

She realized they'd stopped.

'I must leave you here for a time. 'Tis only a short while. You will see me, but not as you do now. You need only believe, trust me... and all will become clear.'

Parquin broke away from her, his likeness instantly dissolving before her. Eleanor didn't understand.

'Parquin? What are you doing? Where are you going?' She felt strange. *'What's happening to me?'*

Eleanor felt herself being pulled once more, and she was suddenly thrust towards an enormous expanse of light, blinding, so bright it filled her senses, merged them, until they seemed to burst within her, shattering out and away until all she was now was the light, her whole being now existing as part of an immensely powerful and compelling energy. She was all-seeing, all-controlling, knowledgeable in all things, and above all else... at peace. She felt there was more, a crackling force beyond her comprehension, waiting just out of reach, and she knew immediately that if she were to go there, there would be no coming back. She knew instantly that that *place was forbidden, that it would remain out of bounds to her.*

Suddenly, she became aware of something... another energy nearby, an energy she was being drawn to, lured to, like an invisible magnet. She felt herself being sucked towards it, a sensation of being pulled... she was being moulded, formed, taking shape though she remained insubstantial... and then there he was!

She could hear his thoughts, see his mind, feel his emotions, almost as though he were part of her. He was all that was tangible, living, breathing; she could feel the beat of his heart. He was mortal and she was... Elexia!

Elexia sifted through the space around him as he sat with his back against the tree, flames from the small fire in front of him flickering their reflection on his knee-high boots, his legs stretched out in front of him and crossed at the ankles, all his thoughts centered on the leather pouch he held in his hands. His time was upon him, though he was as yet unaware. Elexia knew of the approaching men as they sneaked through the bushes; she watched them... unable to stop them. It was out of her control. She would simply wait and when his time came, she would be there... ready...

His bayonet rifle rested at the back of the tree; his horse, Calibre, was tethered off to the side, still saddled, its slender neck bending low to nibble at the soft grass nearby. The animal sensed her, she knew. Calibre bobbed his head, whickering softly at her presence and turned soft, trusting eyes towards his owner, but the animal's sounds went unheeded.

Martin ran his hands almost tenderly over the deep lines etched into the hardened leather and turned it towards the firelight to see it more clearly. He drew his eyebrows together and wondered for perhaps the hundredth time what the picture meant. It was something he'd been compelled to draw, and though he knew instinctively that it was her, and that she stood by water, the true meaning of the scene still managed to elude him. He'd not seen her for a time, nigh on a fortnight, but he'd come to know she was there all the same, and he let his head fall back against the tree, a smile playing on his lips as he summoned her image to mind… an angel that came to him in his dreams, a beautiful vision who shared his innermost thoughts.

He frowned then, noticing the night chill was increasing, and he pulled the red uniform coat up around his neck and over his shoulder-length brown hair while squashing his tricorn down to cover his ears. He couldn't dally long. His orders from Smith had been to deliver a message for more reinforcements to Boston; he would make it back in plenty of time to his regiment, who were now regrouping near Concord. He'd made good time and he'd done as he was ordered and now he was tired… so very tired. What difference would a couple of hours make?

The cool breeze picked up and he thought he heard a whisper through the trees. *'I'm here, Martin…'*

He sat suddenly erect and sent his thoughts out into the night. 'Elexia?'

Suddenly, Calibre reared his head in warning, but it came too late. A half dozen or so men burst from the bushes, their rifles raised to him as a shout rang out, 'Stand and be counted, sir!'

Martin was up on his feet instantly and running for his horse. He felt a ball whiz past him, then another as he leapt across ground, once, twice, then onto the back of his horse while cursing his own foolishness at leaving his rifle so far out of reach. He caught a glimpse of the bayonet resting against the tree, its metal blade glinting in the moonlight as though mocking him for his stupidity. He didn't have time to ponder it more as he thumped Calibre's sides with his heels, and then he was off and riding through the brush. Calibre sensed his rider's urgency, his hooves stretching wide over bush and stump, galloping almost blind in the night, his powerful muscles rippling with every stride, his long black mane flowing free and whipping Martin's face as he bent down low over the horse's back.

Elexia watched on… waiting… knowing…

Martin heard the fading off of his pursuers and went to rein in his horse, but a ditch seemed to appear out of nowhere and in a split second, Calibre faltered and went down. Martin felt himself leave the saddle, nothing but darkness all about him as he was catapulted through mid-air over Calibre's head, coming down to land hard on the other side of the ditch. The last thing he'd been aware of was a dull crunch as he hit the ground… and then nothing…

He didn't understand, didn't know what was happening. He'd fallen, hadn't he? He felt no pain… why? Where was he? Where was Calibre? He felt lost, alone… and then… he sensed her presence. 'Elexia?'

'Martin… I am here. Come with me now…'

No sooner had she uttered those words than she felt the energy pulling away, the light closing in on her, forcing her out, back to where she'd come from. She didn't want to leave. She wanted to stay with the peace; he was there and she wanted to be with him. She tried holding back, and then suddenly, she was wrenched out…

Eleanor once more.

Parquin whirled around her now, calming her, instilling a sense of normality back into her. Eleanor felt instantly lighter… and amazed at where she'd just been.

'That was you! Martin was you!'

'Yes.'

Eleanor thought on where she'd been. 'I didn't want to leave. I wanted to stay as Elexia... stay with you.'

'Yes, Eleanor, I know.'

She was slightly put out. 'Is that all you can say? That you know?'

He was amused, no sign of the impatience he seemed to be carrying with him earlier. 'I can say a lot more.'

'But you won't – you never do.' Eleanor sulked.

'Look... look there...'

Parquin took her with him, though she merely seemed to drift alongside him, controlled by him more than led.

She looked on the scene below. The men who had come upon Martin by the campfire were now rifling through his things. One of the men picked up the leather courier pouch lying by the fire and peered inside. 'Nothing in there. Think whatever it was, has already been delivered? What do you say, Frenchy?'

Another stepped forward, his face showing his distaste for the other man's address of him. 'I try not to think about your war, monsieur. I would very much like to be back on my plantation instead of here with you in this uncivilized place.'

The other man snickered. 'Well, whether you like it or not, you're here, and what's more, it was your own frog-eatin' friends that asked that you be put here in this uncivilized place with me.'

The Frenchman sniffed and looked away.

Another voice sounded from the side of the circle. 'That will be enough of that, Corporal! We are to be extremely grateful that the French have offered to join our fight.' He walked over to the outspoken corporal and snatched the pouch from his hand.

Just then, another man came into the firelight, leading a

badly limping Calibre. 'British soldier stretched out by the creek, sir – got his neck broke. This be his horse, running blind in the dark I'd say.'

The man who seemed to be in charge nodded. 'Right, take a couple of men and bury the body. Nothing too deep; we haven't got time. Just get him out of the way. Corporal? Put this fire out and grab that weapon.'

He looked at the pouch, noticing for the first time the picture that had been etched into the side. He passed it to the Frenchman. 'Here, La Salle. You like this kind of fancy work, don't ya? Something to tell your grandchildren about.'

Vincent La Salle studied the pouch, admiring the craftsmanship.

'Come, Eleanor.' Parquin pulled her back.

Eleanor was reluctant to leave. She understood now. The pouch, handed to Vincent Le Salle, Master Jonathon's grandfather, somehow ending up in Stella's hands… and Stella? She'd known. Perhaps not all, but she'd known to pass it on to Evie, and that day Evie had sat by the fireplace in the cabin, that day so long ago when Evie, when she, had felt an odd feeling come over her… déjà vu the French called it. She'd felt the same thing when she'd seen the picture on Mike's satchel… she'd known it almost instantly, and now she knew where it had come from. Martin had made it, had painstakingly burnt the picture into a piece of leather, a picture given to his mind's eye by Elexia… by her! And Martin – Parquin – had etched it out.

Eleanor's revelations left her feeling weak, her energy starting to ebb away.

Parquin instantly surged through her, reinforcing her, lending her strength… her force clung to his.

'You must take caution, Eleanor… 'tis too much at this time.'

Eleanor reassembled her jumbled thoughts. She looked at him, saw him studying her, those violet eyes so intense. She still felt a little bewildered by it all and slightly baffled. She turned to him now.

'Parquin, how did Mike come to have the picture?

Parquin was silent for a time. 'Some things are better left unknown... 'tis not important that you know all, only that you've seen what you needed to see.'

'Tell me... please! I was meant to see it, wasn't' I? All this – this business with Mike was meant to happen, wasn't it? How silly I must be to you! The silly girl with her silly earthly ideas... thinking I'd surged ahead and done something completely unconventional... and all the time, I was meant to do it, controlled, led through it all like some puppet on a string. '

Parquin whirled round her, his likeness blurring with the speed, a mist of shimmering gold whipping past her, circling her, sweeping through her. He formed himself in front of her, his eyes drawing her in... making her listen, making her understand.

'Yes, you were meant to meet him, meant to see the picture, meant to remember... and 'tis good that you did... but all that you ventured into after that moment was your own doing, based on your own needs, your own wants... 'twas of your own making.' He gave her a rare smile. 'Now come, Eleanor – 'tis time to go back.'

Eleanor held back... but only slightly. 'But how did the picture come to be in Mike's possession?'

Parquin turned away from her. 'It was given to his father by the doctor's wife.'

. . .

Eleanor sat bolt upright in bed, her body bathed in sweat, her heart pounding… then fell back on the pillow feeling weak, so weak. Her body ached, her skin burning as chills racked her body. She rose feebly out of bed and stumbled out to the kitchen. She needed a drink of water; her throat was parched. Her dreams spun wildly through her mind… *The doctor's wife?*

Eleanor poured herself a tall glass of cool water and gulped it down. Placing the empty glass on the sink, she made her way towards the bathroom, feeling her way along the darkened passageway. She pulled a towel from the hook, her only light coming from the moon through the window, dampened it under the tap and wiped her forehead and the back of her neck. She caught her reflection in the mirror in the dim light and frowned. *He did say a doctor, didn't he? The doctor's wife?*

Eleanor slumped over the basin, feeling suddenly dizzy. She heard a click behind her and the bathroom suddenly flooded with light.

'Eleanor? What are you doing up?'

Eleanor turned to see her mother standing in the doorway. She held the familiar mauve dressing gown firmly around her with one hand, the other resting on the door frame, her auburn hair, flecked here and there with grey, dishevelled and pillow flattened. Eleanor smiled weakly at her. Nettie stepped forward and placed a hand to her daughter's forehead.

'Goodness, you're burning up! Get yourself back to bed this instant!'

Nettie took the towel from her daughter and led her back to bed, mumbling to herself about 'late nights' and 'coming home at all hours'. Eleanor let herself be led, too weak to argue.

Eleanor was back in bed now, her mother sitting to the side, wiping the dampened towel across her brow. Eleanor smiled up at her through half-closed eyes. 'What time is it?'

'A little after three... What time did you get in? Where did you go last night?'

Oh God, thought Eleanor, *tomorrow is already here.* 'Just out with the girls. Didn't realize I was home so late.'

'Well, you'd best not go to the store in the morning. Don't think you'll be up to it... I'll send word round to Mrs Littleton.'

Eleanor nodded, the action hurting her head. She turned over and was asleep before her mother had left the room.

She was ill, the journey of her mind having weakened her body... He would help her and she would recover. He'd known from the outset of her time here that she would have an open mind... known that when the time was right, she would allow it in...

There was more for her to know, but he'd deliberately held it back... it was up to her to discover and forbidden for him to show her. In time she would know it all, and he'd already stretched his boundaries, already told her more than he should...

He looked at her now, sleeping fitfully, her body fevered, her pain... It would be so easy to push her illness the other way, let it take her now, but he knew this wasn't the way, knew that if she joined him now, she would only be sent again, even he was not given all the answers, and so, reluctantly...

He filled her space, enveloping her in his strength, his

healing. There was weakness in her chest. He went deeper. Her lungs were beginning to labour... he went there, absorbed the weakness. He felt her breathing ease immediately, felt the airflow clear. Time to leave now.

He would take part of her fever with him, lessen her time of recovery and hasten her restoration...

He went to leave her but couldn't help himself... he whispered to that part of her that was susceptible only to him. 'Soon, Eleanor...'

He saw her smile in her sleep and he was satisfied... for now.

Eleanor sat up in bed. The day outside was warm and bright, a slight breeze blowing through the open window, and she cursed the sickness that had come over her so quickly. Her mother had called the doctor in. 'A mild case of influenza,' he'd said, 'but at least we can be thankful that there appears to be no infection in her chest, Mrs Grayson.' That had been four days ago and still, she was not permitted to get up. Eleanor thought she would go crazy from her idleness.

Her time in bed had at least allowed her time to think about all that had happened with Parquin. The bag, Martin, Elexia, Vincent La Salle, Stella – it all spun round in her head, but somehow, it all made perfect sense, though she had yet to determine the meaning behind the picture. And Mike had brought about her opportunity to see it again.

Eleanor sighed. She decided she would not think about him. She would put him out of her head. But then a mental picture of warm hands and wanton feelings came unbidden to her mind and her face flamed at the memory. She stifled a giggle.

There was a light tapping on the door and Eleanor looked

over to see her grandmother stick her head around it. 'Well, you're certainly looking a lot brighter than you were the other day! Why is this window open?'

Eleanor ignored Hillary's question. 'You were here? When?'

Hillary, aided by her walking stick, made her way slowly across the floral-patterned rug and perched herself gingerly on the end of the bed. Eleanor moved her feet over.

'I came the first day – quite the ailing patient then.' Hillary sniffed as she searched her handbag for her handkerchief. She pulled it out and dabbed at her mouth.

'I don't know how I picked it up, Grandma. I was fine at work, and then… well, then I wasn't.'

Hillary patted her granddaughter's knee and nodded knowingly. 'Well I do, Eleanor! It's that bookstore, I'm sure! All sorts of different people coming and going and Lord only knows what they bring with them! I've already told your mother that if it were up to me, I wouldn't allow you to work there at all!' Hillary finished with a flourishing dab of her mouth and nose.

Eleanor smiled to herself. *And I'm sure Mum sat still for that piece of advice!*

'But I've been working there for over a year, Grandma, and this is the first time I've ever been sick like this.'

Hillary sniffed. 'Yes, well, there *is* always the first time. But then…' Hillary gave a *can't tell the younger generation anything* shrug. 'If you must keep on working there, then it's up to you, isn't it?'

Eleanor changed the subject. 'How have you been anyway, Grandma? I missed our visit this weekend.'

'Oh, can't complain really. I attended the fifteenth anniversary of the opening of our ladies' auxiliary club on Wednesday. Of course, Gertrude Forster had to show her face, didn't she? Never comes but once or twice a year, then decides to grace us with her presence at the anniversary! And then proceeds to go blowing off about her pumpkin scones… Of course I brought my drop scones the way I always do – I've told you before how everyone likes them, didn't I? Anyway, I told Mable Brown – you know the one whose husband they call Moses, although I'm sure his real name can't be *Moses!* And if it was, I'm sure I don't know why he would admit to it! Anyway, I said to Mable…'

Eleanor put on the attentive face she always did when talking with her grandmother and let the older woman ramble on, interjecting here and there in the appropriate places with a 'Really?' and a 'Hmm'. It became a drone to Eleanor's ears.

Her gaze shifted to the open window. How she longed to be out in the sunshine and breathe in some fresh air. To walk down the street and perhaps visit Hazel – after all, she hadn't spoken to her since the night of the dance. It might be fun to listen to a bit of gossip, discuss the events of…

'… and I said, well, that couldn't have been Eleanor! Not with an American! How dare she say…'

Eleanor's stomach lurched. What was her grandmother saying? She cut her off. 'Who said this, Grandma? What was that about an American?'

Hillary sniffed, looking slightly put out. 'Haven't you heard a word I've been saying? I'm talking about that Ruby Jenson! Her daughter said you were dancing with an American at some dance the other night – both you and that flibbertigibbet, Hannah…'

'Hazel, Grandma – her name is Hazel… and I *was* dancing with an American. He was… nice.' Eleanor dropped her eyes, suddenly no longer able to look at her grandmother.

'An American? But you know what they say about them, don't you?'

Eleanor shrugged, her face beginning to blush. 'It wasn't like that – really it wasn't.'

Hillary stared at her intently. 'Are you… seeing him again?'

Eleanor tried to laugh it off. 'Hardly! I believe the Americans were called back to their base… and as you know, I've been sick the last few days.' She shrugged.

Hillary stared hard at her granddaughter a while longer, her keen eyes not missing the barely concealed agitation or the sudden fidgeting of the smooth youthful hands. She decided if there was anything to hide, then it was better off hidden, and if there wasn't, then she had no cause to worry in any case.

Hillary leant forward and patted Eleanor's knee. 'Well, I suppose if he'd been planning anything… well… unseemly, then I'm sure your own common sense would have prevailed. After all, you are a level-headed girl – everyone knows that!' She sniffed and gave Eleanor one of her rare smiles. 'You just get yourself better.'

And as she rose and went to go, she turned back. 'Besides, I dare say anyone, even an American, would be better than that Worthington-Cooke fellow!' Hillary sniffed, her face taking on a pained look. 'And now I suppose I will have to swallow my pride and apologize to that Ruby Jenson!'

With that, Hillary left the room and Eleanor groaned as she let herself flop backward on the bed.

Two weeks later, Eleanor was feeling much better and was back at work. Mrs Littleton was glad to have her back, telling Eleanor that she was sure her clientele had dropped off since she'd been away. Eleanor didn't think so, but it was nice of

Mrs Littleton to say. She offered no information about the day she met Mike out the front of the store, nor did Mrs Littleton press her. For that, she was thankful. She would rather it be forgotten… at least by those who had seen her with him.

Ted was home. He stood upon the platform, the cold wind whipping up around him and making his long coat flap about his legs. He looked every inch the returned soldier, his expression one of relief to be home mixed with a certain world-weariness of one who had experienced more than he cared to remember. He was nearly twenty-seven years old, yet he felt much older, as though a lifetime of experience had crammed itself into the year or so he'd been away. And he wasn't finished. How on earth was he to tell his mother that he would be going away again in a few days?

He spotted them at the same time they saw him.

Nettie ran up and threw her arms about him and wept nearly as much as when she'd stood on the platform waving him goodbye the year before. Even Harry came close to tears and had to keep blinking and looking away. Lizzie was there with little Danny, the swell of her stomach indicating there was another on the way, though she tried to keep it hidden beneath her coat. Ted let the feel of his family wash over him. He hugged his older sister to him and grinned down at his nephew.

'Boy has he *grown*, Lizzie! What have you been feeding him?' He gave a pointed look down at her stomach. 'Come to think of it, what on earth have *you* been eating?'

Both Nettie and Lizzie opened their mouths in shock, with Nettie slapping her son on the arm while Harry covered his mouth with his hand to hide his smirk.

Nettie started to smile. 'Really, Ted!' And then they all laughed, even little Danny, though he had no idea what was so funny.

'It's a good thing your grandmother isn't here to hear you say such things!'

Ted rolled his eyes at the thought. 'Where's El? She working?'

'No, actually she's visiting with Hillary, but she should have been here by now. I don't know what's keeping her... Oh, here she is now!'

Eleanor, her hand clasped on top of her head to keep her beret in place, her coat flapping out behind her, came running up to her brother, and, laughing, she threw her arms about him. He swung her around. 'I tried to get here earlier! I missed the bloody tram and had to wait for the next!'

Ted laughed and hugged her again.

'Eleanor!' Nettie was taken aback by her daughter's language. 'I swear I don't know what's happening to this family! I really don't!'

Eleanor looked suitably apologetic. 'I'm sorry, Mum, it just slipped out in my excitement.' But Eleanor couldn't take the smile off her face.

Nettie waved it away. 'Well, come on everyone! Let's get home for a cup of tea and get out of this weather before it starts raining.'

It had been a wonderful afternoon. Nettie couldn't have been more thrilled to have her whole family sitting around her table once more. There had been much conversation and laughter as Nettie, Eleanor and Lizzie kept the pots of tea coming. Half-eaten cake and leftover pasty slice littered the plates across the table. Danny had long gotten tired with all the gossiping back and forth between the adults around him and had sauntered off to lie on the sofa. He was now fast asleep.

Ruby and Lenny dropped in around mid-afternoon, a perfect opportunity for Harry to open a beer, and he, Lenny and Ted absconded to the kitchen to stretch out and relax into the kind of conversation that they deemed not fit for the women. Besides, Lenny could smoke his pipe out of sight from Ruby in the kitchen. Bobby came over after work to check on his growing family and immediately pulled up a chair to sit with the men.

Kathy called round after work also, and after hugging Ted and speaking with him for a few minutes, she settled down in a chair next to Lizzie, who now held an irritable Danny on her lap. It was getting dark when Nettie interrupted the men, telling them to take their beer and smoking out into the drawing room so she could heat up the cottage pies she'd made earlier in the day. Lenny, Ruby and Kathy were invited to stay for tea, and after the meal was finished, and the dishes had been washed and put away, the conversation began to take on a more serious tone.

They'd been talking of the mail they'd received from Ted and its irregularity, and he'd told them of how sometimes he would write a letter and then by the time the first was sent out, the other would go with it. 'And then someone said that the mail sometimes gets held up and that the ones we've been writing catch up with it. That's probably why you sometimes had a few arrive at once, Dad.'

Harry nodded his understanding.

'See anyone we know over there, Ted?' Lizzie had handed Danny to her husband and now sat holding a cup of tea, her expression enquiring.

Ted went a bit quiet. He shrugged. 'No, not really.'

Harry and Lenny exchanged a knowing look. It was too

soon for Ted to go talking about people he knew and their outcome, both men reflecting on their own experiences.

Lizzie went on oblivious. 'The Holt boys went over there. Lance was injured and sent home. He got shot in the eye but he can see all right now.'

Eleanor screwed up her face. 'He wasn't shot in the eye, Lizzie. How can anyone get shot in the eye and now be able to see again?'

There were a few smirks around the table, and then Ted broke out into a grin, effectively breaking the mood.

'Oh well, you know what I mean. His eye was, well… you know…'

'Yeah, we get the picture, Lizzie.' Ted was still grinning at her. There were a few giggles at Lizzie's expense. "Actually, there are that many men from all over, and not just Australians. Sometimes, I think I catch a glimpse of someone I know from home, but well… in the thick of things, I'm never sure." Ted sobered a bit. "Apart from Ben Kerns, and I suppose you've heard about him."

The giggles stopped.

"Benjamin?" Lizzie placed her cup on the table and now sat stock-still. "What about Ben?"

Ted didn't know what to say; he'd felt sure they would have heard. He cursed himself for his blunder and looked beseechingly over at his father for some kind of help. Harry obliged with as much as he could tell him. "His parents took the family for a trip to Melbourne. That was… oh, about four months ago I think. They haven't been back since. We just assumed old man Kerns had got work over there, or… something… I'm ashamed to say I didn't think about it much."

The question concerning Benjamin Kerns' fate still hung in the air.

Ted didn't look at anyone, especially Lizzie. He spoke quietly, haltingly. "Well, he was… carried in on a stretcher and…" Ted darted a look at his mother and sighed, shaking his head. The atrocities of the battlefront were not something he wanted to bring home to his mother's drawing room.

"Did he say anything to you?" Lizzie's voice was trembling.

Ted looked over at her, his eyes unblinking. A picture flashed through his mind of poor Ben lying in a bloodied mess, his arm having been blown from his body at the shoulder, and his stomach… Ted swallowed. He shook his head again. "Lizzie, he… he didn't even know who I was."

The small group had gone quiet. Lizzie reached for her son and held him to her. Danny seemed to sense his mother's distress and let himself be hugged as Bobby slid an arm around both of them. Nettie looked over at her son, thinking it could have so easily been her Teddy instead of that poor Kerns boy and she silently thanked God for his safe return.

Eleanor's stomach was churning; her thoughts centered on much the same thing as her mother as she too looked at her brother. Ruby had threaded her arm through Lenny's while thanking the stars in heaven that she'd not had a son to worry about like Nettie and Harry. Kathy sat quietly by, her thoughts skimming back over the times that she, along with Lizzie, Lance and Lionel Holt and Benjamin Kerns had gone about together.

Harry glanced around at the serious faces and thought, '*This is no good*' He took a deep breath and held up his beer. "Well, here's to Ted, home safe and sound!"

"Here, here!" Ruby grabbed Lenny's glass and downed the contents in one swallow, her husband's hand grabbing mid-air where his glass had sat only seconds before.

Harry threw back his head and laughed while slapping the

table. "Looks like you're gonna have to be quicker than that around Ruby, Len!" He let out another loud guffaw as others joined in. Ruby couldn't hold it all in however, and beer dribbled down her chin to slop on the front of her dress. She quickly tried to wipe it off.

"Oh bosh! Now I've done it!"

Nettie burst out laughing and fell into Harry. Ted laughed also as Eleanor giggled behind her hand, her eyes wide as they darted to Ruby's dress and back to Lenny's bewilderment at how his beer had disappeared. Kathy sat mortified, a hand over her eyes and shaking her head, thinking that she couldn't take her parents anywhere without one of them embarrassing her, but on looking over at Lizzie and Bobby, who now laughed along with everyone else, she too joined in.

Ted raised himself slightly from the chair, his amusement evident. "Thanks, Dad... and thank *you*, Ruby! Dad, I think Lenny's glass needs another refill... but you'd better keep it well out of Ruby's reach!"

Ruby's impulsive toast set the scene for the remainder of the evening, and by nine o'clock, it was a happy group that filed out through Nettie and Harry's front door.

The next few days were bliss for Nettie. Even the day-to-day news of the war couldn't dampen her spirits. She had her son home, safe and sound. Her family was complete again and she felt truly blessed. Harry, on the other hand, was not so relaxed. He knew there was a war still going on and Ted had not been to see about getting his old job back with Crowley's Garage; nor had he been particularly enthusiastic when Nettie had spoken to him of his bedroom and how she would fix it up now that he was home. Harry had noticed that Ted hadn't been particularly enthusiastic about *anything* that suggested a long-term arrangement.

He sat now, across from Ted in the bar. Lenny had gone home and those who knew Ted had said their congratulations and wished him well and had also gone on their way. Now it was just him and Ted. He took a deep breath and decided to come straight out and say it. 'Okay, Ted, what's up? You going back?'

Ted couldn't look at his father. Placing his beer back on the counter, he merely nodded.

Harry's stomach lurched but he kept his voice even. 'Where? When?'

'Brisbane and then on to New Guinea. When? Not sure. Expecting a telegram any day.'

Harry felt the adrenalin rise up in his stomach as Ted's words sank in. 'Why didn't you say? Why didn't you tell us? Your mother…' Harry shook his head. God, what was Nettie going to be like?

Ted sighed. "I wanted to tell you, both of you, but there never seemed to be the right moment, and then Mum was… so…" Ted threw his hands up. Harry let out a deep breath and nodded.

"She'll be beside herself." Harry wanted to rail at him, hit something, he felt so helpless, but he kept his emotions at bay.

"I gotta see this thing through, Dad. Look, I hate this war just as much as you do, hate what it is doing to men. Normal men, men who would never even think of pointing a weapon at anyone in any other circumstances, men with families sitting home just like you and Mum, men with wives, kids… and then there's men like Benjamin Kerns. Don't you see? I *have* to see this thing through." Ted stared at his father. 'It's not finished, Dad… and I have to finish it.'

Harry closed his eyes slowly and let out a deep breath. "I suppose short of binding you hand and foot till this bloody war's over, I don't have a choice, do I?"

Ted attempted a smile. "Neither do I"

Harry thought of Nettie and his heart sank. "Better let me tell your mother."

Later that night in the privacy of their bedroom, Nettie lay beside her husband and wept into his shoulder. Harry held her close, letting her cry it all out as he lay staring, unseeing, into the darkness. He fought to keep his own anxiety down, suppressing his anger, holding his own fears at bay for Nettie's sake. Harry was not a praying man, but at this moment he was willing to do whatever it took.

'Just once more, I'm begging you – watch over him one more time… bring him home safe…'

Harry listened to the heartbreaking sobs of Nettie and he blinked, striving to hold back his own anguish. *'You hear me, you bastard? Bring my son home alive!'*

No longer able to hold his own emotions in check, Harry squeezed his wife closer and, turning his face into her hair, wept silently along with her.

CHAPTER TEN

E leanor was pregnant. With the events surrounding Ted going away and her mother's sadness at him going, Eleanor had not taken much notice of the signs that now, when she looked back, seemed to have been staring her in the face. The nausea, the mild dizzy spells, her sudden abhorrence at tea and the smell of burning wood, her puzzling fetish for milk and of course the absence of her monthly flow all pointed to the inevitable. She was going to have a baby.

She was two and half months along, of that she was sure, for the father could only have been Michael Ross, and after counting back on the calendar, she was able to pinpoint the exact time he'd been staying at Shrimpton's Bed and Breakfast.

What on earth was she to do? She thought of her parents, her grandmother, the people who knew her. Her little secret concerning the night with Mike would, in a month or two, be evident to one and all, and she wouldn't be able to do a thing about it! Eleanor decided there was nothing for it – she would have to tell her mother first and foremost.

She walked home slowly from work, her thoughts going

over how she would broach the subject, dismissing one idea after the other, and by the time she'd turned the corner towards home, she was a mass of jumbled nerves. It wasn't so much that her mother would be angry at her, or even berate her for being so silly as to let herself be caught. It was more that she'd felt she'd let her parents down, that they'd expected more of her. She felt ashamed and hated the thought that they'd be disappointed in her.

Eleanor approached her front door with trepidation but stopped as she heard the voices from inside.

'If you put your glasses on, Harry, then you'd *see* it wasn't straight! You're always telling me to put my glasses on but you won't be told the same thing back, will you?'

Eleanor frowned. What on earth were they going on about?

She heard her father's voice in reply. 'Give me the bloody hammer. I'll take it out and then *you* can put it in if you don't trust me!'

Eleanor opened the door and walked down the hall and into the drawing room to see her father up a ladder, her mother standing close by with a picture frame under her arm.

'No need to swear at me!'

Harry looked around at his wife, his face twisted in frustration and then he saw Eleanor. His face brightened. 'Good, you're home! Look at this, Eleanor. I think that—'

'*He* thinks that the picture should be hung higher, Nettie cut in, 'but it won't hang straight from way up there – the nail has to come lower!'

Harry rolled his eyes and climbed down the ladder, his bad leg hindering his descent as he hopped with his good one down the last two rungs. He handed the hammer to Nettie with a great deal of ceremony. 'Here you go, my dear... it's all *yours!*'

Nettie pursed her lips and glared at him. Eleanor leant against the doorway looking at her parents and shaking her head, a smirk upon her face. Harry caught his daughter's look and turned to his wife. 'Eleanor's got two good legs – she'll get up there and do it for you, won't you, Eleanor? I'm off to the pub!'

'Me? Up on that ladder? I can't climb a ladder!' Eleanor was grinning at him. He winked at her as he strode past to grab his hat from the stand in the hallway.

Nettie stormed from the room with a loud 'Oh!'. Seconds later, they heard the kettle being clanged loudly on the stove in anger. Eleanor turned raised eyebrows to her father; Harry sighed and said quietly, 'When your mother calms down, tell her I said she looks beautiful when she's angry.' He winked again and plonked his hat down on his head. 'Won't be long.' With that he left quietly through the front door.

Eleanor smiled to herself and went through to talk to her mother.

'I suppose you think I'm being silly!' Nettie stood ramrod straight at the stove, her words flung over her shoulder as she watched the kettle.

'I don't think it's going to boil any faster, Mum. Come and sit down – I want to talk to you.'

Nettie didn't seem to hear her. 'Every time he gets fed up, where does he go? The pub!'

'Mum, sit down. He'll be home soon.'

'All I asked him to do was hang a stupid picture on the wall, and do you think he could do that? Oh no! He'd rather go down to the pub, rather spend time with his cronies than…'

'Mum! Sit down! Please!'

'I bet if *Jerry* asked him to hang a picture in the bar, he'd jump up there, bad leg and all! I bet—'

'Mum, I'm pregnant.'

Nettie swung round, her eyes opening wide. She took one step to the table and flopped down in the chair, her anger at Harry all but forgotten, a multitude of things going through her mind all at once – how, when, who? 'Pregnant?'

'Yes… nearly three months.'

Nettie's look was incredulous. 'Oh, Eleanor! Are you sure?'

Eleanor nodded. All Nettie could do was stare at her. 'But are you sure? *Really* sure?'

Eleanor nodded to both questions. 'I haven't been to a doctor, but all the signs are there. It can't be anything else.'

Eleanor went on to tell her mother of all her symptoms and Nettie slumped further into her chair. She'd been pregnant often enough herself to know that what Eleanor was saying was true. Everything pointed to it.

'Mum, I'm sorry.' Eleanor's eyes misted over.

Nettie sat upright immediately. 'Now you listen to me! There's no reason for you to be sorry at all! These things happen, and they happen to the best of us! We're just going to have to sort out what we're going to do, that's all.' She looked over at Eleanor then. 'Who's the father? Have I or your father met him?'

Eleanor swallowed. It was the most logical question for her mother to ask. *Here we go.*

'His name is Michael Ross… he's an American soldier.'

Nettie closed her eyes and leant back in her chair. 'Oh no! Eleanor! An American?' Then Nettie opened her eyes, her face suddenly thoughtful. 'The night of the dance, wasn't it? The night you got sick, that's when it started… and all this time? How could I have been so blind!'

Eleanor shook her head. 'Mum, nothing started! It was just… once. I met him the night of the dance and then again the next day – that was the night I got sick – and that's all there was.'

Nettie's lips formed a circle, mouthing a silent 'Oh'.

There were so many things Eleanor hadn't imagined her mother might think, like her relationship with Mike being an ongoing affair. She wished it was, somehow – that didn't seem so bad as only the one night!

The kettle began to boil. Nettie stood and moved it from the heat then sat back down again. 'He didn't… well, he didn't force you or anything, did he? I mean, you just seem too sensible to do anything *willingly* – I mean without any thought to the consequences.' Nettie frowned. 'It's that Hazel, isn't it? I knew she was a bad influence, always flouncing around here and…'

'It's got nothing to do with Hazel, Mum. After all, Hazel will still have her reputation intact. It's me who's pregnant and I don't let myself get influenced unless… I want to be.'

Nettie's thoughts suddenly changed tack. *Reputation! I hadn't even thought of that!* She straightened in her chair as though bracing herself. 'Want to tell me about it?'

Eleanor shrugged. 'There's nothing much to tell really. It was just one of those things. He was going away; I'd met him at the dance the night before as you know, and then I met him the next day after work and…'

Nettie studied her daughter, noting the auburn hair, the large brown eyes with eyebrows that swept evenly up and out, naturally arched and in need of no help from cosmetics. Nettie's own features were more petite, more like Lizzie's. Eleanor favoured Harry in her looks, with his generous mouth. She was an attractive girl, not one that would turn a young man's head right away, but she had a certain depth to her that one would discover on longer acquaintance. All things considered, Nettie was surprised her daughter hadn't married long before now, or at least had some man courting her, someone besides that Mark, who in all probability wasted too much of Eleanor's young life when she could have been...

'Mum, stop looking at me like that! Mike was nice, very nice. And yes, I wasn't thinking of the consequences at the time, apart from people finding out. I really didn't think about *this* happening; it never entered my mind.'

Nettie was startled from her thoughts. 'I'm sorry. I was just wondering why you've never married when you have so much going for you.'

Eleanor sighed. 'I don't want to get married. I don't think I ever did. Is that so wrong? Is that so bad to not want to do what every other girl is hell-bent on doing? I mean, am I abnormal? Marjorie and Hazel talk about marriage all the time, but the thought of it leaves me a bit cold and I don't know why. Is there something wrong with me?'

Nettie leant forward and covered her daughter's hands on the table. 'Of course not! Perhaps you haven't met the right man yet, that's all. What about this Michael?'

But Eleanor was already shaking her head. 'No, I told you – it wasn't that sort of thing.'

'Not that sort of thing? So it wouldn't bother you if he had a girlfriend back home... or even a wife? Tell me, Eleanor, what sort of *thing* was it?'

Eleanor shook her head. 'It makes no difference now, Mum; I'll never see him again.'

Nettie was silent. No point in getting all upset about it now. What's done is done. *No point in shutting the stable door after the horse has bolted,* her mother used to say. Nettie thought of Harry and what he'd say... oh Lord, and then there was Hillary!

'I'll have to talk to your father when he comes home and see what he says. Perhaps he'll think of something…'

'Dad?' The enormity of it was just now dawning on her. 'I suppose he'll have to know, won't he?' Eleanor covered her face with her hands. Oh God! Her father!

'You didn't think you could get away without your father knowing, did you? Oh don't worry, Eleanor, he'll naturally be upset and a little hurt, but he was once young as well. *I'll* remind him of that!' Nettie shook her head and sighed. 'Just the same, I think you'd better brace yourself. In fact, I think we'd both be better off expecting the worst.'

Harry ranted, he raved, he swore, he cursed the Americans, the war, and every man in the vicinity who was between sixteen and sixty. He blamed Eleanor; he blamed Nettie, then Marjorie, Hazel and all the youth of the day, especially the ones that had passed through his front door over the years, while Eleanor sat closed off in her room in heart-wrenching tears upon her bed.

Nettie sat serenely on the armchair in the drawing room while he paced from one side of the room to the other, her hands clasped in front of her and saying nothing the whole time he railed on. She was in her element, doing what she did best, and that was remaining calm while all hell broke loose about her. She was the guiding light in a raging storm and she knew that sooner or later, her husband would start to settle and set his course for her.

He did, and sooner than she thought. 'What on earth is she going to do, Net?' His anger had finally burnt out and with his leg paining him from all the pacing, he dropped into the chair alongside hers. Nettie saw he was now upset, which meant it was her turn.

'She simply lost her head for one night. You and I have done the same on many an occasion. Just because we've had the sanctity of marriage to protect us doesn't mean it won't happen outside the marital state. She *is* twenty-four now.'

Harry sighed, now thoroughly worn out. 'Well, it would've been better if she'd been married,' he said unnecessarily.

'Of course it would have been, but she's not and now we have to think of *her*. And the first thing you should do is go in and talk to her.' Nettie nodded in the direction of Eleanor's bedroom. 'She's upset because you're upset. She's feeling ashamed of herself, and believe it or not, she's hurting a good deal more than you are right now.'

Harry sighed, his voice low. 'But why *isn't* she married? You said it; she's twenty-four years old now – why hasn't there been anyone for her? She's not unpleasant to the eye, she's intelligent, rounded off in all the right places...'

'And her teeth are sound? Harry! She's your daughter, not some prime piece of horseflesh at an auction!'

'I didn't mean it that way – you know I didn't. Eleanor's special to me, always has been. I just don't understand why no one else has seen her the way I do, that's all!'

Harry leant closer to Nettie, his voice not much more than a loud whisper. 'You don't think that Worthington-Cooke lad spoilt her for anyone, do you? She doesn't still pine for him, does she?'

Nettie tossed her head impatiently. 'Of course not! You remember how she was when they went their separate ways – she couldn't have cared less!'

Nettie nudged her husband and nodded towards Eleanor's door once more. 'Go on, Harry – you'll both feel better once you do.'

Eleanor sat on the bed, her eyes swollen, her face

reddened by her recent crying session. She toyed with a handkerchief in her hands, bringing it up now and then to dab at her face. Her father hated her, of that she was sure. She'd heard him as he'd raged in the drawing room, the terrible things he'd said and the way he'd yelled and carried on so – it was now obvious to her that he thought her to be some silly, thoughtless and shameful girl who paid no mind to anyone but herself. Eleanor felt fresh tears forming in her eyes and went to fall down across the bed, but a light knock on her door stopped her and she straightened her posture instead.

'Yes?' Her voice wavered, sounding thick from her tears.

Her father stuck his head around the door. Eleanor blinked back the tears, her vision blurring. He stepped into the room and stuffed his hands in his pockets, looking awkward as he peered over at her, his eyebrows raised in silent question, as though assessing the surrounding mood to see if he would be welcome or not.

Harry saw straight away that she'd been going hard at it by the puffiness around her eyes, and he could see still more tears threatening to fall. He felt suddenly ashamed of himself, knowing he'd been the cause of them. He sighed and stepped towards her, holding out his arms. 'Eleanor, I'm so sorry.'

Eleanor flung herself from the bed and into his waiting arms. He hugged her close as she clung to him, her hands going up around his neck as she sobbed into his shirt. 'Oh, Dad, I didn't mean for you and Mum to go through all this mess... what with Ted being away and...'

'Shh, don't worry, we'll sort something out. Now stop your crying. It'll be all right, you'll see... Shh, Eleanor. Come on, your mother has gone to put the kettle on, so why don't you go and wash your face and we'll all sit down in the kitchen and talk about this, okay?' Harry rocked her slightly, waiting for her tears to cease.

Outside the open doorway, Nettie was listening and smiled to herself before tiptoeing silently back to the kitchen.

A little while later the small group sat huddled around the kitchen table.

'What about Queensland? She could go and stay with your mother, Net… What do you say, Eleanor? Or Frank and Susan perhaps?' Harry leant back in the chair; to him it was the logical idea.

'But then how would they explain me to their friends? I'd feel like I was burdening them with my problems.' Eleanor sat with her hands wrapped around her cup, her elbows resting on the table.

Nettie had been saying very little throughout the conversation, her thoughts seemingly on something else. She now spoke up. 'Eleanor, have you given much thought to when the baby comes along?'

Harry piped up. 'But that's what we've been trying to work out for the last half hour.'

'No, we've been talking about hiding Eleanor's condition. But there's going to be a baby at the end of all this and we've been talking about Eleanor's reputation, and I think we should be looking ahead to what's going to happen when the baby actually gets here. I think a lot of what she plans on doing now depends on that, don't you?'

Both Harry and Nettie looked at Eleanor.

Eleanor *had* thought about the baby, but the main thing on her mind had been breaking the news to her parents before sorting anything else out. It didn't surprise her now that they would naturally think ahead to the actual outcome of her present dilemma.

'Do you plan on raising the baby yourself?' Nettie looked at her daughter and waited for an answer. Harry broke in, his voice a little hesitant.

'Eleanor, if you decide to keep the baby, then we will be behind you all the way. After all, a baby born to one of my kids will still be treated like any other grandchild in this house, born out of wedlock or not! But if you decide not to raise him yourself, then I guess… well, we'll stand by you on that as well…'

Nettie turned misty eyes towards her husband. She could have leant across the table and kissed him for what he'd just said!

Eleanor shrugged, not sure what she should do. A baby! Another person to whom she'd be responsible… the rest of her life! It was all too daunting… but wouldn't it be wonderful? She didn't know; she had to have time to think on it some more. Right now, she wasn't sure of anything… perhaps as her pregnancy moved along she would be able to make a decision. But she needed time. 'I don't know. I really don't know what to do… I think yes… then I think no…' Eleanor finished with a shake of her head.

Nettie spoke up once more. 'Well, if you are going to raise the baby yourself, then there would be no point in you going anywhere! People will know right away that the baby is yours. To go away and then come back with a baby in tow would probably cause more gossip than if you'd simply stayed here from the first!'

Nettie became angry. 'I don't know why a woman has to account for her actions in this way, I really don't! I say to the devil with all of them! After all, this is 1941 for goodness' sake! We don't live in the dark ages anymore… do we, Harry?'

Harry leant forward and patted her hand. 'No, we don't, but why feed the gossips if we don't have to? Why put Eleanor through that if it isn't needed.'

Eleanor shrugged again. 'Then we're back to square one.'

She nodded, her mind made up. 'I'll go away, and if the baby comes back with me, then I'll just weather the storm until something else comes along for people to talk about. It happens all the time. Besides, I think I'm grown-up enough to be able to take it on the chin… after all, if I decide to keep my baby, then I defy anyone to make me feel ashamed of it!'

'Good girl!' Nettie smacked her hands together while Harry looked skeptical. 'So do I write to my mother or Frank?'

Harry's face was still doubtful. 'I've got a better idea. What about Charlie?'

Eleanor felt as though her heart had suddenly sunk to the pit of her stomach.

'Uncle Charlie?' she said in a small voice.

'Why Charlie?' Nettie frowned.

'Because Charlie is the only person I trust in the world *outside* my own family. Look, Net, I know I suggested your family in Queensland, but now I'm thinking that bringing your mother or Frank and Susan into this would only complicate matters. Oh, I'm sure they'd welcome Eleanor with open arms, but I feel the fewer people that know about this, the better. Whatever Eleanor decides to do, I think she'd be better off doing without any influence from relatives. Frank and Susan have always wanted a baby and I don't think they would understand if she decided not to keep it. Your mother might try and swing her the other way, thinking solely of her reputation and…'

Nettie got huffy. 'My mother happens to be very broad-minded, thank you very much.'

Harry held up his palms towards her. 'Yes, well, she probably is, more so than *mine,* and by the way, that's another person who definitely shouldn't know, not until Eleanor decides what she wants to do.'

Nettie shuddered. 'Oh Lord!'

Harry went on. 'The least amount of people in the family that know about it at the present time, the better, and I won't have my daughter being judged by my own family! Charlie wouldn't do that. And Eleanor has always thought the world of Charlie, and he of her, even from when she was little girl.'

Eleanor swallowed, her eyes widening slightly. She hadn't realized she'd been so transparent… and so stupid. *But Charlie knew… he'd always known… tried to warn me. Lord, I am stupid!*

'But on a station? She'll have no one but men about her for company!'

'There are women there too, you know! And Charlie's got himself a pretty comfortable spread over there by all accounts. Eleanor would probably be better off staying out in the fresh air of a station than she ever would here… and it may be a little isolated, true, but it will give her space to think.'

Harry leant towards Eleanor, his eyes searching. 'Whatever you decide to do, remember, it will be you that will have to live with it from then on.'

Nettie let out a deep breath. 'So what do you think, Eleanor? It's up to you? Where's it to be? Queensland or Western Australia?'

Eleanor had always wanted to visit Mell Pell, but this wasn't exactly the way she'd envisioned it. And what would Charlie think? Her father trusted him, probably knew more about him than anyone else, but he didn't know anything of what had happened between her and Charlie in the past. Would Charlie welcome her or would he despise her?'

'You think Charlie wouldn't mind? Really?'

Harry chuckled to himself. 'Of course not! Knowing

Charlie, he'd be as proud as punch to be able to show you around the place!'

Eleanor looked over at her mother. 'What do you think, Mum?'

Nettie smiled, which then turned into a smirk. 'Well, one thing Charlie is for sure and that's broad-minded! He's never given a penny's worth of consideration for the conventions of society at any time in his life... and he doesn't have a judgmental bone in his body!' Nettie nodded. Charlie might well be the best person after all.

Eleanor swallowed. 'All right, I'll go to Mell Pell.'

Eleanor rested her head against the glass as the train pulled out of Cook. She felt ill. The rattling sway of the train did little to help her swallow down the bile threatening to rise up her throat. If she made it to Kalgoorlie without throwing up, it would be a miracle.

Her journey was thankfully two-thirds the way through, the conductor informing her that they would arrive in Kalgoorlie tomorrow. She'd eaten little and had slept even less on the trip over, preferring to sit rather than lie down in her berth. Crossing the Nullarbor had done little to occupy her time, having looked out on nothing but saltbush as far as the eye could see. Eleanor thought now that she should have been more prepared for such a long and tedious journey. As she looked about her at the other occupants of the car, she noticed that a few had brought a book with them, and they sat heavily engrossed in their reading. Another woman sat busily knitting – had been so for most of the journey. Eleanor had watched on as the item the woman was working on grew steadily bigger throughout the hours.

They'd pulled in to Cook to replenish their wood and

Eleanor wished she'd got off for a stretch of the legs like everyone else… now she felt exhausted and stifled, and more than a little apprehensive of her meeting with Charlie. Would he be irritated that she had been dumped on him? Her father had said little when he'd arrived back from the Post Office. He'd gone there to ring Charlie; said he'd sooner talk to him personally than try putting it in a letter. Though her father had *seemed* happy enough on his return, hadn't he? That was two weeks ago and now here she was, on a train going to Western Australia to live on a station for the rest of her confinement. In a matter of weeks her life had taken a direct turn, one that had more to do with necessity than it did with choice.

It was ten thirty in the morning when the train pulled into the station amid a crowd of people who moved back as steam gushed out from the side, and as Eleanor alighted from the train, the first thing she noticed was the heat. She pulled absently on the collar of the dark brown linen suit she was wearing. It had been suitable enough when she'd left Adelaide, but not for here. Western Australian weather was not unlike Adelaide weather, though the temperature must have climbed a little since she'd left home. At least it was fresh air. Now, without the motion of the train and her legs on solid ground again, she felt a little strange, her equilibrium having been altered a little, and she felt a little off balance. She wasn't sure if it was due to her condition or the train journey, as both were new experiences.

Eleanor took stock of her surroundings. There were people bustling by her, some welcoming others who stepped down from the train, and Eleanor saw the knitting lady being hugged by a group of children, all ranging in size, then watched them move off down the platform. She inadvertently stepped into the path of a baggage man, who struggled to bring his load to a halt when, at the last minute, he saw her standing in his way. With a hasty apology, she stepped out of his way and searched the crowd for Charlie. She was just wondering if she should go and ask someone when there was a tap on her shoulder, making her jump.

'Miss? You be Eleanor?'

Eleanor looked into the face of an Aboriginal man. She'd seen a few in her time, but not many, and never had she spoken to any. She collected herself and nodded. Then, holding out her hand, she said, 'Yes, I be... um... I mean I *am* Eleanor – Eleanor Grayson. Pleased to meet you.'

He grinned broadly and took her hand, pumping it once, his teeth showing pearly white against his skin. 'Name's Billy... Boss said come and get ya, so here I am. Please...' He waved at her to follow him and so she did.

'Your boss Charlie Bradford?' Eleanor had to quicken her step to almost a run to keep up.

'Yes, miss. He's out in the far paddock chasing up the strays. Went out at sunrise, sent me back to get you. Said he'd see you later.'

Billy was moving so fast Eleanor had to lean forward to hear everything he was saying.

'Strays? Oh, sheep you mean?'

'Yes, miss. Some get themselves lost, can't find their way back to the rest.'

Billy stopped so sudden that Eleanor nearly bumped into him. He opened the door of a jeep and motioned for her to get in. She did.

'Be back in a minute, miss – get your bags.' With that he was off, leaving Eleanor to rest her head against the back of the seat and try to catch her breath.

The ride out to Mell Pell was bumpier than the train ride,

with dips and bends in a road that was little more than a track. By the time the station came into view, Eleanor was more intent on getting out and away somewhere fast so she could throw up than the lush panoramic scene that awaited her with its collection of sheds, outbuildings and fenced-off enclosures around the main house.

The jeep came to an abrupt halt at what she realized must be the front of the house, and not waiting for Billy to open the door for her, she stumbled out and ran directly to the side of the house, and with one hand leaning on the stone wall, Eleanor bent nearly double as she retched and heaved until nothing more would come up.

She slid down the side wall, not caring that her skirt caught on the rough stonework and was being hitched up around the top of her legs, and slowly, her mind cleared and her breathing returned to normal as she took great gulps of precious, fresh clean air.

'You must be Eleanor!' The voice was light and cheery, and… feminine.

Eleanor looked up to see a woman of indeterminate age looking down on her. Her hair had flecks of grey through it, her face exceedingly tanned, her brown eyes friendly, though at this moment, a little sympathetic, and her smile wide. She was dressed in a pale-yellow house frock, and Eleanor couldn't help thinking that the dress looked infinitely more comfortable than her linen suit.

'My name is Lillian Cotterswold, but everyone calls me Lily.'

Eleanor blinked at the last name and Lily laughed.

'I know, dreadful isn't it? And to think I already knew Brian's name when he asked me to marry him and was still willing to take it on!' She laughed again, a high musical tinkle, and Eleanor smiled for the first time today.

Lily reached out a hand for Eleanor and pulled her to her feet.

'Thank you,. I'm sorry about… all this… The train ride and the coming here…'

'Don't give it another thought. In your condition I would have been the same. Matter of fact, I have been… twice.'

They'd started to make their way around the side of the house and Eleanor now froze in her tracks. Lily looked at her. 'Oh dear, Charlie didn't tell you… but then of course not – he hasn't seen you yet, has he? Now don't you worry about a thing, love, and please don't blame Charlie for telling me. He thought it best that I know – after all, it's going to become evident soon enough, and with me and Brian living so close, it would have hardly gone unnoticed now, would it?'

Lily put her arm around Eleanor's shoulders. 'Come into the house. The fans are on, it will be a lot cooler in there and I'll get you something to drink.'

Eleanor walked dutifully beside the friendly Lily, her mind striving to take it all in. They climbed the two steps onto the veranda that lead to the front door and on entering the house, Eleanor stopped. 'It's lovely!'

Lily smiled. 'Yes, it is. It's no wonder your uncle Charlie has been sought after by everything in a skirt this side of Kalgoorlie!'

Eleanor felt something akin to jealousy rear up in her chest but instantly ignored it. And the fact that Lily had called him her 'uncle Charlie' had been duly noted as well, but she reminded herself not to say too much until she'd had a chance to talk with him.

She looked about the room and marveled at its homeliness, its warmth. She was standing in the middle of what she assumed to be a kind of drawing room or front room. There was deep polished mahogany furniture set up about the room: a side dresser, a desk, a sofa and three plush armchairs in front of the biggest fireplace Eleanor had ever seen. There were scattered tables, a telephone on the wall and a huge wall-to-wall bookcase that went from ceiling to floor, its shelves crammed with all different kinds of books.

She noticed a radiogram in the corner, probably the only piece of furniture that stood out for its lighter colouring. On the floor where she stood was an oval rug, its rose design reminding her of the one her parents had on their drawing-room floor, and for a brief moment, she experienced a pang of homesickness. Another smaller rug was laid out in front of the chairs at the fireplace, simpler in design with small flowers around its outer edge.

Lily stood off to the side, a smile on her face as she watched the younger girl take in her surroundings.

Eleanor turned to her. 'This is Ch— Uncle Charlie's house?'

Lily nodded. 'Yep. Brian and I live across the creek. After the war, Charlie came to work here, and then with the Depression, he went in with us. Couldn't have made it through if he hadn't. Anyway, he took up living here. This is the old homestead – well, I say "old" but I'm certain that now it outshines the newer house where we live.'

Lily laughed again. 'These older houses don't have as many rooms as you're probably used to. There's just the main one here, a kitchen, though it's a good size, a kind of lobby come laundry off the back, the bathroom, with copper or chip heater, which Charlie made an entrance to from the end of the hallway – a person used to have go outside to enter it – and two bedrooms. Oh, and a smaller room through there, but I think that used to be for storing wood and the like. There's no window in it... come and have a look.'

Eleanor followed Lily through to the kitchen and was astonished at the size of it.

'He wanted the double wood stove to remain where it was, and as you can see, this is where he eats his meals but it's plenty big enough.'

Eleanor nodded. It was bigger than the one they had back home. She looked around at the cabinets and counters, noticing a plate of scones on a tray set out on the table. Lily saw her look at them.

'I didn't know whether you'd want something when you arrived, so I whipped something up. Charlie is pretty good with a steak or a lamb stew, but he has no idea what to do when it comes to cakes and sweet things.'

Lily pointed to the scones, her way of offering, but Eleanor declined, her stomach still not quite right yet.

Lily didn't seem to mind. 'That's all right, love. Once you settle in, you'll start feeling a little hungry I'm sure.'

Lily went to the refrigerator and took out a jug of water. Pouring a glass, she handed it to Eleanor who gratefully drank most of it down in one swallow.

'Wait till you get a look at your bedroom! When Charlie found out you were coming to stay, he immediately set about getting the room ready. He had me looking at bedspreads, sheets, drapes and whatnot, and I don't know why he dragged me into town at all – he ended up picking out the colours himself in any case. All I had to do was match the drape material and then sew them up for him.' Lily rolled her eyes. 'Believe me, sewing is not my strong point!'

Eleanor followed Lily down the small hallway to what would be her bedroom for the next six months or more, her glass still in her hand. She caught a glimpse of what she assumed was Charlie's bedroom, but all she could make out was a four-poster bed… unmade as yet.

As she went through the door of her own room, she stopped and gaped.

'Oh dear. You don't like it?' The look of dismay on Lily's face made Eleanor laugh.

'No, I think it's beautiful! And you did all this?'

Lily was chuffed. 'Well, only the drapes really. Made the bed up, that sort of thing. The furniture was already here – just needed a polish, a couple of doilies.'

Eleanor surveyed the contents of the room. It was relatively small, though perhaps appearing smaller due to the huge bed that sat squarely in the centre of the back wall. There was a tall chest of drawers, a wardrobe, a nightstand and a dressing table; they all blended well though none exactly matched. On the bed was a pale lime eiderdown dotted with tiny blue roses, the effect of which was rather eye-catching. The drapes had been made from the same pale green though minus the roses and backed with heavy cotton to keep out the sun.

'Uncle Charlie picked out this material?'

'He did... I think it suits you quite well with your colouring too, if you don't mind me saying.'

Eleanor didn't mind and smiled engagingly at her. She felt a tingle of pleasure at the thought of Charlie shopping around for a colour that would suit her.

Lily went over and closed the drapes. 'Would you like to lie down for a while? Charlie won't be back for ages I should imagine...' There was tap on the door frame and both Lily and Eleanor turned to see Billy standing there with Eleanor's bags.

'Oh, Billy, thank you. If you could just put them down there, just inside the door, Eleanor will probably get to them later.'

Billy did as he was bid and looked up at Eleanor.

'You all right now, miss?'

Eleanor felt embarrassed, remembering the way she'd made a dash from the jeep. 'Yes, thank you. Long trip, but I'm all right now I think.' She smiled at him and received that same broad smile in return. Tipping his hat, he walked away.

'Is there anyone else that lives here? I mean, at this house?'

'Ah, well, let me see… there's Billy, whom of course you've met; Jim, who at present is out with Charlie, Roger and Robert – now *that* gets confusing – they're probably out scouting the fences; and Dave. It's a wonder you didn't see him when you came in. They all live out in the station hand's house. But don't worry, I'm only a couple of miles away across the creek if you want some female company – a couple of miles are considered very close out here.

'I have two daughters, Linda and Sarah, both married, but they visit quite often and we'll make sure to invite you out. There's Laura who comes in once a week to dust and clean, but she doesn't stay – has a bit of a thing for Jim we think… though neither of them is saying. And then there's Dimitri, who comes by to check on the livestock, any ailments to the horses, that sort of thing. And of course, the shearers will be coming through in a couple of months. But you'll meet lots more from the district when we have our barbeques. Believe me, if anyone so much as has a tooth pulled out here, it's an excuse for a barbeque and a beer! I would have thought Charlie would have got lonely out here, what with him coming from the city, but he's taken to it quite well over the years. There's always plenty of work, I suppose, to keep him busy. And of course, he loves his visits to Adelaide to see your family too!'

Eleanor gave her a weak smile, wondering if Lily was ever going to stop talking.

'Anyway, love, if you want to lie down awhile, or relax and read a book or something, it's up to you… like I said, Charlie won't be back for hours so you may as well get some rest.'

'Thank you, I will, and thank you for being so kind, Lily.'

'Not at all, love. I'd best get back home now myself. Cheerio then.'

With a swish of her yellow frock she was gone, and Eleanor let out a deep breath. She wandered over to the window and looked out at the lush green, an idle thought occurring to her that stations were supposed to be barren sort of places, weren't they? All dust and flies and not much else? But then what would she know? She'd never been out of Adelaide until now.

Eleanor kicked off her shoes and stripped off her suit jacket. She eyed her bags and thought, *Later.* Right now she was tired, and so she stretched out on the green eiderdown, worming her body down into the softness of the bed and marveled once more that Charlie had actually picked out the colours for *her*.

It was just on dusk when Charlie walked through the front door, his boots clumping loudly across the floor as he went. He instantly noticed there were no lights on, no evidence of anyone in the house, and wondered where she was. He hadn't been able to get her out of his thoughts all day. When Harry had telephoned him about what he had in mind, Charlie had found himself suddenly being carried along on a river of emotions. He'd been jealous, angry, upset and even wary, pretty much in that order, all of which had been eclipsed by a certain kind of happiness and silly excitement.

He sat on one of the chairs and pulled off his boots and

then walked up to the spare room – *her* room – and peeked inside. He found her softly snoring on the bed, and he stood there for a long moment looking down at her. Then he walked quietly over to the bed and sat down next to her. She woke instantly, turning over to look at him... then immediately sat up and threw her arms about him.

'Oh, Charlie, I'm sorry... I didn't mean for this to happen. Please don't think badly of me. I don't know what I'd do if you thought I was—'

'Shh, I don't think that of you – nothing of the sort.' Charlie was frowning though she couldn't see him. He hadn't expected her to react like this and it took him by surprise. All he could do was hold her, the nearness of her clouding his senses – the smell of her hair, the softness of her body. He knew he should keep his distance, put down some ground rules immediately, let her know right from the outset that while she was here, they would be nothing more than companionable in their relationship, but instead he held her close, rocking her.

Just this once, he told himself...

∾

[For the third and final installment of the Thursday's Child Trilogy, see 'Thursday's Child – Eleanor – Part Two]

ABOUT THE AUTHOR

Shana J Carr

Shana resides near the city of Adelaide in South Australia, working in a busy office as an administrative officer with the state health department. In her free time, she is constantly writing. Thursday's Child was originally released as one book but thought to be too large for a single tome, and so re-released as a trilogy.

Author's Note:

I hope you have enjoyed the second installment of Thursday's Child and I hope you will stay around to read the final book - 'Thursday's Child – Part Three -Eleanor.' I loved writing about early to mid-20th Century Australia. A lot of it was reminiscent of stories told to me of those times by my Mum and Dad. The family into which Eleanor was born held a kind of nostalgia for me…even though I wasn't born in that era. In certain ways it reminded me of the family I was privileged to grow up in.

Thank you for reading.

ALSO BY SHANA J CARR

Further books from the 'Thursday's Child' Trilogy

- Thursday's Child - Evie

- Thursday's Child – Eleanor (Part Two)

Own them now as e-book or hard copy.

Lightning Source UK Ltd.
Milton Keynes UK
UKHW020634260421
382641UK00010B/801